WITHDRAWN

CRI. LLC 04/11

Tel 01738 444949 | www.culturepk.org.uk

2 3 JUL 2019 2 2 OCT 2019		

Please return/renew this item by the last date shown.
Items may also be renewed by phone or online.

D1345213

PERTH & KINF

05656275

The Echo Man

ALSO BY | RICHARD MONTANARI

Deviant Way

The Violet Hour

Kiss of Evil

The Rosary Girls

The Skin Gods

Broken Angels

Play Dead

The Devil's Garden

Richard Montanari
The Echo Man

WILLIAM HEINEMANN: LONDON

Published by William Heinemann 2011

2 4 6 8 10 9 7 5 3 1

Copyright © Richard Montanari 2011

Richard Montanari has asserted his right under the Copyright, Designs
and Patents Act 1988 to be identified as the author of this work.

This book is a work of fiction. Names and characters are the product of the
author's imagination and any resemblance to actual persons, living or dead, is
entirely coincidental.

This book is sold subject to the condition that it shall not, by way of trade or
otherwise, be lent, resold, hired out, or otherwise circulated without the
publisher's prior consent in any form of binding or cover other than that in
which it is published and without a similar condition,
including this condition, being imposed on the subsequent purchaser.

First published in Great Britain in 2011 by
William Heinemann
Random House, 20 Vauxhall Bridge Road,
London SW1V 2SA

www.rbooks.co.uk

Addresses for companies within The Random House Group Limited can be
found at: www.randomhouse.co.uk/offices.htm

The Random House Group Limited Reg. No. 954009

A CIP catalogue record for this book
is available from the British Library

HB ISBN 9780434018918
TPB ISBN 9780434018925

The Random House Group Limited supports The Forest Stewardship
Council (FSC), the leading international forest certification organisation.
All our titles that are printed on Greenpeace approved FSC certified paper
carry the FSC logo. Our paper procurement policy can be found at
www.rbooks.co.uk/environment

Mixed Sources
Product group from well-managed
forests and other controlled sources
www.fsc.org Cert no. TT-COC-2139
© 1996 Forest Stewardship Council

Typeset in Janson Text by Palimpsest Book Production Limited,
Falkirk, Stirlingshire
Printed and bound in Great Britain by
Clays Ltd, St Ives plc

MAN

All seems evil until I
Sleepless would lie down and die.

ECHO

Lie down and die.

– William Butler Yeats
Man and the Echo

PERTH & KINROSS COUNCIL	
05656275	
Bertrams	30/03/2011
MON	£9.99
CA	

FOR EVERY LIGHT THERE IS SHADOW. FOR EVERY SOUND, SILENCE.

From the moment he got the call Detective Kevin Francis Byrne had a premonition this night would forever change his life, that he was headed to a place marked by a profound evil, leaving only darkness in its wake.

'You ready?'

Byrne glanced at Jimmy. Detective Jimmy Purify, sitting in the passenger seat of the bashed and battered department-issue Ford, was just a few years older than Byrne, but something in the man's eyes held deep wisdom, a hard-won experience that transcended time spent on the job and spoke instead of time earned. They'd known each other a long time, but this was their first full tour as partners.

'I'm ready,' Byrne said.

He wasn't.

They got out of the car and walked to the front entrance of the sprawling, well-tended Chestnut Hill mansion. Here, in this exclusive section of the northwest part of the city, there was history at every turn, a neighborhood designed at a time when Philadelphia was second only to London as the largest English-speaking city in the world.

The first officer on the scene, a rookie named Timothy Meehan, stood inside the foyer, cloistered by coats and hats and scarves perfumed with age, just beyond the reach of the cold autumn wind cutting across the grounds.

Byrne had been in Officer Meehan's shoes a handful of years earlier and remembered well how he'd felt when detectives arrived, the tangle of envy and relief and admiration. Chances were slight that Meehan would one day do the job Byrne was about to do. It took a certain breed to stay in the trenches, especially in a city like Philly, and most uniformed cops, at least the smart ones, moved on.

Byrne signed the crime-scene log and stepped into the warmth of the atrium, taking in the sights, the sounds, the smells. He would never again enter this scene for the first time, never again breathe an air so red with violence. Looking into the kitchen, he saw a blood-splattered killing room, scarlet murals on pebbled white tile, the torn flesh of the victim jigsawed on the floor.

While Jimmy called for the medical examiner and crime-scene unit, Byrne walked to the end of the entrance hall. The officer standing there was a veteran patrolman, a man of fifty, a man content to live without ambition. At that moment Byrne envied him. The cop nodded toward the room on the other side of the corridor.

And that was when Kevin Byrne heard the music.

SHE SAT IN A chair on the opposite side of the room. The walls were covered with a forest-green silk; the floor with an exquisite burgundy Persian. The furniture was sturdy, in the Queen Anne style. The air smelled of jasmine and leather.

Byrne knew the room had been cleared, but he scanned every inch of it anyway. In one corner stood an antique curio case with beveled glass doors, its shelves arrayed with small porcelain figurines. In another corner leaned a beautiful cello. Candlelight shimmered on its golden surface.

The woman was slender and elegant, in her late twenties. She had burnished russet hair down to her shoulders, eyes the color of soft copper. She wore a long black gown, sling-back heels, pearls. Her make-up was a bit garish – theatrical, some might say – but it flattered her delicate features, her lucent skin.

When Byrne stepped fully into the room the woman looked his

way, as if she had been expecting him, as if he might be a guest for Thanksgiving dinner, some discomfited cousin just in from Allentown or Ashtabula. But he was neither. He was there to arrest her.

'Can you hear it?' the woman asked. Her voice was almost adolescent in its pitch and resonance.

Byrne glanced at the crystal CD case resting on a small wooden easel atop the expensive stereo component. *Chopin: Nocturne in G Major.* Then he looked more closely at the cello. There was fresh blood on the strings and fingerboard, as well as on the bow lying on the floor. Afterwards, she had played.

The woman closed her eyes. 'Listen,' she said. 'The blue notes.'

Byrne listened. He has never forgotten the melody, the way it both lifted and shattered his heart.

Moments later the music stopped. Byrne waited for the last note to feather into silence. 'I'm going to need you to stand up now, ma'am,' he said.

When the woman opened her eyes Byrne felt something flicker in his chest. In his time on the streets of Philadelphia he had met all types of people, from soulless drug dealers, to oily con men, to smash-and-grab artists, to hopped-up joyriding kids. But never before had he encountered anyone so detached from the crime they had just committed. In her light brown eyes Byrne saw demons caper from shadow to shadow.

The woman rose, turned to the side, put her hands behind her back. Byrne took out his handcuffs, slipped them over her slender white wrists, and clicked them shut.

She turned to face him. They stood in silence now, just a few inches apart, strangers not only to each other, but to this grim pageant and all that was to come.

'I'm scared,' she said.

Byrne wanted to tell her that he understood. He wanted to say that we all have moments of rage, moments when the walls of sanity tremble and crack. He wanted to tell her that she would pay for her crime, probably for the rest of her life – perhaps even *with* her life – but that while she was in his care she would be treated with dignity and respect.

He did not say these things.

'My name is Detective Kevin Byrne,' he said. 'It's going to be all right.'

It was November 1, 1990.

Nothing has been right since.

ONE

ALLEGRO

SUNDAY, OCTOBER 24

CAN YOU HEAR IT?

Listen closely. There, beneath the clatter of the lane, beneath the ceaseless hum of man and machine, you will hear the sound of the slaughter, the screaming of peasants in the moment before death, the plea of an emperor with a sword at his throat.

Can you hear it?

Step onto hallowed ground, where madness has made the soil luxuriant with blood, and you will hear it: Nanjing, Thessaloniki, Warsaw.

If you listen closely you will realize it is always there, never fully silenced, not by prayer, by law, by time. The history of the world, and its annals of crime, is the slow, sepulchral music of the dead.

There.

Can you hear it?

I hear it. I am the one who walks in shadow, ears tuned to the night. I am the one who hides in rooms where murder is done, rooms that will never again be quieted, each corner now and forever sheltering a whispering ghost. I hear fingernails scratching granite walls, the drip of blood onto scarred tile, the hiss of air drawn into a mortal chest wound. Sometimes it all becomes too much, too loud, and I must let it out.

I am the Echo Man.

I hear it all.

ON SUNDAY MORNING *I rise early, shower, take my breakfast at home. I step onto the street. It is a glorious fall day. The sky is clear and crystalline blue, the air holds the faint smell of decaying leaves.*

As I walk down Pine Street I feel the weight of the three killing instruments at the small of my back. I study the eyes of passersby, or at least those who will meet my gaze. Every so often I pause, eavesdrop, gathering the sounds of the past. In Philadelphia Death has lingered in so many places. I collect its spectral sounds the way some men collect fine art, or war souvenirs, or lovers.

Like many who have toiled in the arts over the centuries my work has gone largely unnoticed. That is about to change. This will be my magnum opus, that by which all such works are judged forever. It has already begun.

I turn up my collar and continue down the lane.

Zig, zig, zig.

I rattle through the crowded streets like a white skeleton.

AT JUST AFTER EIGHT A.M. *I enter Fitler Square, finding the expected gathering – bikers, joggers, the homeless who have dragged themselves here from a nearby passageway. Some of these homeless creatures will not live through the winter. Soon I will hear their last breaths.*

I stand near the ram sculpture at the eastern end of the square, watching, waiting. Within minutes I see them, mother and daughter.

They are just what I need.

I WALK ACROSS THE *square, sit on a bench, take out my newspaper, halve and quarter it. The killing instruments are uncomfortable at my back. I shift my weight as the sounds amass: the flap and squawk of pigeons congregating around a man eating a bagel, a taxi's rude horn, the hard thump of a bass speaker. Looking at my watch, I see that time is short. Soon my mind will be full of screams and I will be unable to do what is necessary.*

*I glance at the young mother and her baby, catch the woman's eye, smile.
'Good morning,' I say.*

The woman smiles back. 'Hi.'

*The baby is in an expensive jogging stroller, the kind with a rainproof
hood and mesh shopping basket beneath. I rise, cross the path, glance inside
the pram. It's a girl, dressed in a pink flannel one-piece and matching hat,
swaddled in a snow-white blanket. Bright plastic stars dangle overhead.*

'And who is this *little movie star?' I ask.*

The woman beams. 'This is Ashley.'

'Ashley. She is beautiful.'

'Thank you.'

I am careful not to get too close. Not yet. 'How old is she?'

'She's four months.'

*'Four months is a great age,' I reply with a wink. 'I may have peaked
around four months.'*

The woman laughs.

I'm in.

*I glance at the stroller. The baby smiles at me. In her angelic face I
see so much. But sight does not drive me. The world is crammed full of
beautiful images, breathtaking vistas, all mostly forgotten by the time the
next vista presents itself. I have stood before the Taj Mahal, Westminster
Abbey, the Grand Canyon. I once spent an afternoon in front of Picasso's
Guernica. All these glorious images faded into the dim corners of memory
within a relatively short period of time. Yet I recall with exquisite clarity
the first time I heard someone scream in anguish, the yelp of a dog struck
by a car, the dying breath of a young police officer bleeding out on a hot
sidewalk.*

'Is she sleeping through the night yet?'

'Not quite,' the woman says.

*'My daughter slept through the night at two months. Never had a
problem with her at all.'*

'Lucky.'

*I reach slowly into my right coat pocket, palm what I need, draw it out.
The mother stands just a few feet away, on my left. She does not see what
I have in my hand.*

The baby kicks her feet, bunching her blanket. I wait. I am nothing if not patient. I need the little one to be tranquil and still. Soon she calms, her bright blue eyes scanning the sky.

With my right hand I reach out, slowly, not wanting to alarm the mother. I place a finger into the center of the baby's left palm. She closes her tiny fist around my finger and gurgles. Then, as I had hoped, she begins to coo.

All other sounds cease. In that moment it is just the baby, and this sacred respite from the dissonance that fills my waking hours.

I touch the Record button, keeping the microphone near the little girl's mouth for a few seconds, gathering the sounds, collecting a moment which would otherwise be gone in an instant.

Time slows, lengthens, like a lingering coda.

I withdraw my hand. I do not want to stay too long, nor alert the mother to any danger. I have a full day ahead of me, and cannot be deterred.

'She has your eyes,' I say.

The little girl does not, and it is obvious. But no mother ever refuses such a compliment.

'Thank you.'

I glance at the sky, at the buildings that surround Fitler Square. It is time. 'Well, it was lovely talking to you.'

'You, too,' replies the woman. 'Enjoy your day.'

'Thank you,' I say. 'I'm sure I will.'

I reach out, take one of the baby's tiny hands in mine, give it a little shake. 'It was nice meeting you, little Ashley.'

Mother and daughter giggle.

I am safe.

A few moments later, as I walk up Twenty-third Street, toward Delancey, I pull out the digital recorder, insert the mini-plug for the earbuds, play back the recording. Good quality, a minimum of background noise. The baby's voice is precious and clear.

As I slip into the van and head to South Philadelphia I think about this morning, how everything is falling into place.

Harmony and melody live inside me, side by side, violent storms on a sun-blessed shore.

I have captured the beginning of life.

Now I will record its end.

TWO

'**M**Y NAME IS PAULETTE, AND I'M AN ALCOHOLIC.'

'Hi, Paulette.'

She looked out over the group. The meeting was larger than it had been the previous week, nearly doubled in size from the first time she attended the Second Verse group at the Trinity United Methodist Church nearly a month earlier. Before that she had been to three meetings at three different places – North Philly, West Philly, South Philly – but, as she soon learned, most people who attend AA meetings regularly find a group, and a vibe, with which they are comfortable, and stay with it.

There were twenty or so people sitting in a loose circle, equally divided between men and women, young and old, nervous and calm. The youngest person was a woman around twenty; the oldest, a man in his seventies, sitting in a wheelchair. It was also a diverse group – black, white, Hispanic, Asian. Addiction, of course, had no prejudice, no gender or age issues. The size of the group indicated that the holidays were rapidly approaching, and if anything pressed the glowing red buttons of inadequacy, resentment, and rage, it was the holidays.

The coffee, as always, was crap.

'Some of you have probably seen me here before,' she began, trying to affect a tone of lightness and cheer. 'Ah, who the hell am I kidding? Maybe I'm wrong about that. Maybe it's ego, right? Maybe I think I'm the shit, and no one else does. Maybe that's the *problem.*

Anyway, today is the first time I've really had the balls to speak. So, here I am, and you have me. At least for a little while. Lucky you.'

As she told her story, she scanned the faces. There was a kid in his mid-twenties on the right – killer blue eyes, ripped jeans, a multi-color Ed Hardy T-shirt, biceps of note. More than once she looked over at him and saw him scanning her body. He may have been an alcoholic but he was still most definitely on the make. Next to him was a woman in her fifties, a few decades of heavy use mapped in the broken veins on her face and neck. She rolled a sweaty cellphone over and over in her hands, tapped one foot to some long-silenced beat. A few chairs down from her was a petite blonde in a green Temple University sweatshirt, athletic and toned, the weight of the world just a snowflake on her shoulder. Next to her sat Nestor, the group leader. Nestor had opened the meeting with his own short and sad tale, then asked if there was anyone else who wanted to talk.

My name is Paulette.

When she finished her story everyone clapped politely. After that other people rose, talked, cried. More applause.

When all their stories were exhausted, every emotion wrung, Nestor reached out his hands to either side. 'Let's give thanks and praise.'

They joined hands, said a short prayer, and the meeting was over.

'IT'S NOT AS EASY as it looks, is it?'

She turned around. It was Killer Blue Eyes. At just after noon they stood outside the main church doors, between a pair of emaci-ated brown evergreens, already struggling through the season.

'I don't know,' she replied. 'It looked pretty hard to begin with.'

Killer Blue Eyes laughed. He had put on a short cognac leather jacket. A pair of amber Serengeti sunglasses were clipped to the neck of his T-shirt. He wore thick-soled black boots.

'Yeah. I guess you're right,' he said. He clasped his hands in front of him, rocked back slightly on his heels. His good-guy, not-to-worry pose. 'It's been a while since I've done it for the first time.' He held out his hand. 'Your name is Paulette, right?'

'And I'm an alcoholic.'

Killer Blue Eyes laughed again. 'I'm Danny. Me too.'

'Nice to meet you, Danny.' They shook hands.

'I *can* tell you this, though,' he continued, unasked. 'It gets easier.'

'The sobriety part?'

'I wish I could say that. What I meant was the *talking* part. Once you get comfortable with the group it gets a little easier to tell your stories.'

'Stories?' she asked. 'Plural? I thought I was done.'

'You're not done,' he said. 'It's a process. It goes on for a long time.'

'Okay. Like, how long?'

'Did you see that guy in the red flannel shirt?'

Danny was talking about the older man, the guy in his seventies, the guy in the wheelchair. 'What about him?'

'He's been coming to meetings for thirty-six years.'

'*Jesus*. He hasn't had a drink in thirty-six years?'

'That's what he says.'

'And he still wants one?'

'So he says.'

Danny looked at his watch, an oversized Fossil chronograph. The move looked just slightly less calculated and rehearsed than it probably was. 'You know, I don't have to be at work for a couple of hours. Can I buy you a cup of coffee?'

She looked appropriately suspicious. 'I don't know.'

Danny put up both hands. 'No strings. Just coffee.'

She smiled. 'Irish?'

'Bad Paulette. Bad, *bad* Paulette.'

She laughed. 'Let's go.'

THEY PICKED A PLACE on Germantown Avenue, sat at a table near the window, small-talked – movies, fashion, the economy. She had a fruit salad. He had coffee and a cheeseburger. Neither would rate Zagat's.

After fifteen minutes or so she held up her iPhone, tapped the touch screen. She did not dial a number, did not send a text or an email, did not make an entry onto her contact list or schedule something in iCal. Instead, she took a picture of Killer Blue Eyes, having earlier in the day deselected the option that attached the sound of a clicking camera to the operation. When she was done she looked at the cellphone's screen in mock frustration, as if something was wrong. Nothing was wrong. The photograph, which the young man could not see, was perfect.

'Problem?' he asked.

She shook her head. 'No. It's just that I can never get much of a signal around here.'

'Maybe you can get a signal outside,' Danny said. He stood up, slipped on his jacket. 'Want to give it a shot?'

She hit one more button, waited until the progress bar made its way fully to the right, and said: 'Sure.'

'Come on,' Danny said. 'I'll get the check.'

THEY WALKED SLOWLY DOWN the street, wordlessly window browsing.

'Don't you have to make that call?' Danny asked.

She shook her head. 'Not really. It's just my mother. She's just going to give me shit about what a loser I am. I can wait.'

'We might be related,' Danny said. 'Like *closely* related. I think we have the same mother.'

'I thought you looked familiar.'

Danny looked around. 'So, where are you parked?'

'Just up this way.'

'Would you like me to walk you to your car?'

She stopped. 'Oh *no*.'

'What?'

'You're not a gentleman, are you?' she accused him flirtatiously.

Danny raised a hand, three fingers up, Boy Scout style. 'I swear to God I'm not.'

She laughed. 'Sure.'

They turned the corner into a dim alleyway, heading toward the parking lot. Before they took three steps she saw the glint of the revolver.

With a strong forearm Danny slammed her against the bricks and brought his face very close to hers.

'You see that red Sebring over there?' he whispered, nodding toward the Chrysler parked near the end of the alley. 'Here's what we're going to do. We're going to walk over there and you're going to get in that car. If you give me any trouble, make a single sound, so help me God I will shoot you in the fucking face. Do you hear me?'

'Yes.'

'Do you doubt what I say?'

She shook her head.

'I want you to say it out loud. I want you to say "I understand, Danny."'

'I understand, Danny.'

'Good. Good,' he said. '*Paulette.*' He kept a hand on her, leaned away. 'You know, you've got great tits. You wear this loose shit to hide them, but I can tell. *And* you're a goddamn drunk. Do you know what a plus that is?'

She just stared.

'Me? I've never had a drink in my life. I just have this weakness for weak women. Always have.'

He ran his left hand slowly over her right hip, his other hand remaining on the butt of the gun. He smiled.

'I think we're going to do it right here. What do you think of that?'

'You won't hurt me?'

'No,' he said. 'But admit it, *Paulette*. There *is* something exciting about doing it in public. Especially with a total stranger.' He pulled down his zipper. 'But that's why you drink, isn't it? Because you hate yourself? Because you're a whore?'

She didn't know if it was really a question. She remained silent. He continued.

'Of course it is. And you know what? I bet you've gotten plenty loaded over the years, and fucked plenty of guys in alleys. Right?'

This was definitely a question. When she didn't answer he took the revolver from his waistband and stuck it between her legs. Hard.

'Answer . . . the fucking . . . *question.*'

'Yes.'

He ran the barrel of the gun up and down, applying even more pressure. 'Say it.'

'I've fucked a lot of guys in alleys.'

'And you loved it.'

'And I loved it.'

'Because you're a fucking whore.'

'Because I'm a fucking whore.'

'I thought so.' He slipped the gun back into his waistband. 'You know that other girl? She gave me a hard time. She didn't have to die.'

'The other girl?'

'The redhead. The fat one. *Marcy* something, the papers said. Smelled like a cheap slut. Which she was, of course.'

He leaned in, sniffed her hair.

'You don't smell cheap,' he said. 'You smell good.'

A shadow crawled slowly across the ground, pooling at their feet. Danny noticed, spun around.

Behind him, a few paces away, stood the petite blonde from the AA meeting, the one wearing the green Temple University hooded sweatshirt. In her hand was a Glock 17, pointed at the center of Danny's chest.

'My name is Nicci,' the blonde said. 'And I'm a police officer.'

'Hi, Nicci!' Detective Jessica Balzano responded.

During the previous three weeks, on her undercover assignment to catch the AA Killer, Jessica had been Paulette. No last name. Just Paulette. She discovered early on in the assignment that no one had a last name at AA.

Behind Detective Nicolette Malone stood two other detectives, as well as a veteran patrolman named Stan Keegan. At either end of the alley were a pair of sector cars.

Danny looked at Jessica, his hands trembling now. 'You're a *cop*?'

Jessica stepped back, drew her own weapon from a holster at the small of her back, leveled it. 'Put your hands behind your head and interlace your fingers.'

Danny hesitated, his eyes shifting from side to side.

'Do it *now.*'

Danny froze.

'Suit yourself,' Jessica said. 'But if you don't do what I tell you to do, you will die where you stand. In an Ed Hardy T-shirt, no less. *With* your zipper down. Your call.'

The suspect, whose real name was Lucas Anthony Thompson, seemed to realize his two choices. He was leaving this alley either in handcuffs or on a gurney. In an instant his will was broken. His shoulders sagged. He put his hands on top of his head, fingers interlaced.

Jessica had seen it a hundred times. And it never failed to warm her heart.

Gotcha.

Nicci Malone stepped forward, pulled the weapon from the suspect's waistband, handed it to Officer Keegan, who put it in an evidence bag. Nicci then swept the suspect's legs from beneath him. He hit the ground hard, face down. An instant later Nicci dropped a knee into the center of Thompson's back, cuffed him.

'It's almost impossible you're this fucking stupid,' Nicci said.

Jessica holstered her gun, stepped forward. Each grabbing an arm, the two detectives pulled the suspect roughly to his feet.

'You are under arrest for the murder of Marcia Jane Kimmelman,' Jessica said. She read him his Miranda rights. 'Do you understand these rights?'

Thompson nodded, still dazed.

'You have to answer out loud,' she said. 'You have to say "yes."'

'Yes.'

'Actually, I want you to say, "Yes, I understand, Detective Goddess Balzano."'

Thompson didn't say it. He was still a bit stunned.

Ah, well, Jessica thought. *Worth a shot.* She reached into her pocket, pulled out the small digital recorder. She rewound the recording, clicked Play.

You know that other girl? She gave me a hard time. She didn't have to die.

Jessica clicked off the recorder. Thompson hung his head.

They had plenty with which to charge him. An eyewitness, a good sampling of DNA, ballistics. The recording was just icing on the cake. The DA's office loved recordings. Sometimes a recording made all the difference in the world.

As uniformed officers led Thompson away, Officer Stan Keegan leaned against the brick wall, crossed his arms over his kettle-drum chest, a Cheshire-cat grin on his face.

'What's so funny?' Jessica asked.

'You two,' he said, nodding at her and Nicci. 'I'm just trying to figure out which one of you is Batman and which one is Robin.'

'Batman? Dream *on*, mortal,' Jessica said. 'I'm Wonder Woman.'

'And I'm She Hulk,' Nicci added.

The two women bumped fists.

THERE WAS A YOUNG man standing next to the sector car, talking to one of the uniformed officers. He was tall, dark-haired, lanky, and had about him a nervous energy. He carried an expensive-looking digital video camera. Jessica soon realized who he was, and what he was doing there.

She had gotten the memo the week before, and had forgotten all about it. Somebody from Penn State was making a documentary about the homicide unit – a day-in-the-life sort of thing – and the directive from high on high was to cooperate. The memo said the filmmaker would be there for a week.

As Jessica approached, the young man noticed her. He smoothed his hair with his free hand, stood a little taller.

'Hi,' he said. 'I'm David Albrecht.'

'Jessica Balzano.'

They shook hands. David Albrecht wore a gold crucifix around his neck, along with a Nittany Lions long-sleeved T-shirt. He was cleanshaven, save for a sparse bleached-white soul patch beneath his lower lip. It was the only thing keeping his face from being feminine.

'I'd know you anywhere,' he said. He pumped her arm with a little too much enthusiasm.

'Really? And why is that?' Jessica asked, retrieving her limb before it was shaken off.

Albrecht smiled. 'I do my research. You were in that *Philadelphia*

Magazine feature a few years ago, the one about the "new breed" of female detective. Remember that?'

Jessica remembered the article well. She had fought against it but had lost the battle. She was not crazy about having details of her personal life made public. Police officers, especially detectives, were big enough targets for crazies as it was.

'I remember,' Jessica said.

'And I followed the Rosary Killer case pretty closely.'

'I see.'

'Of course, I was in high school then,' Albrecht said. 'I went to a Catholic school. We were all pretty mesmerized by the story.'

High school, Jessica thought. *This kid was in* high school *then*. It seemed like yesterday to her.

'By the way, that was a great photo of you on the cover of the mag,' he added. 'Real Lara Croft. You were kind of a pinup for a lot of the guys at my school for a while.'

'So, you're making a movie?' Jessica asked, hoping to get off the subject of the article.

'Gonna try. Making a feature is a lot different from making a short. I've done mainly webisodes so far.'

Jessica wasn't really sure what a webisode was.

'You should stop by my site and check some of them out,' Albrecht said. 'I think you'll like them.'

He handed her a card bearing his name and a website address.

Jessica did the polite thing, scanning the card before putting it into her pocket. 'Well,' she said. 'It was great meeting you, David. Anything you need.' She didn't mean it, of course. She pointed at the just-arrived police transport van. 'I've got to get this started.'

Albrecht held up a hand. 'No sweat. Just wanted to introduce myself.' He smoothed his hair again. 'I'll be around, but you won't even notice me. I promise not to get in your way. I'm a mouse.'

A mouse, Jessica thought. *We'll see about that*.

TWO HOURS LATER, WITH paperwork completed, reports filed, and suspect delivered to the police administration building at Eighth and Race Streets – commonly known as the Roundhouse – the team met at a restaurant called the Hot Potato Café on Girard Avenue.

In addition to Jessica and Nicci Malone there was veteran detective Nick Palladino, as well as a relatively new detective in the unit, Dennis Stansfield. Stansfield was in his early forties and was God's gift to women, at least in his own mind. His clearance-rack suits never quite fit, he wore too much cologne and, among his many annoying habits, he seemed to be in constant motion, as if he always had somewhere else to be, something else to do that was far more important than talking to you.

He had only been with the unit for a few months and had yet to make a friend. No one wanted to work with him. His abrasive personality was only one of the reasons. His sloppy work habits, and his uncanny ability to get a witness to clam up immediately, were two others.

Jessica and Nicci held down one side of the table, while Stansfield and Nick Palladino sat on the other.

Nick Palladino – whom everyone called Dino – was a lifer, a South Philly boy with a knack for sniffing out con men and thieves, two categories of criminal of which the city of Philadelphia had no shortage.

They were all on duty for a few more hours, so it was coffee and Cokes for now. They lifted a glass to their day.

Lucas Anthony Thompson, 26, late of Port Richmond, currently a guest of Hotel Homicide, stood accused in the aggravated murder and sexual assault of a young woman named Marcia Jane Kimmelman. According to witnesses, the two had met at an AA meeting in West Philly but, because last names were never used, no one knew who Thompson was. They had a general description, but that was about it.

Marcia's body had been found in a vacant lot on Baltimore Avenue near 47th Street. She had been sexually assaulted, shot once in the head with a .38 at close range. Three months later Thompson met and attacked a young woman after a meeting in Kingessing, but the woman, a secretary for Comcast named Bonnie Silvera, survived. DNA found in semen left behind by her attacker matched that of Marcia Kimmelman's killer. Bonnie Silvera gave police a highly detailed description of Thompson, and there began an undercover operation that ultimately involved a dozen detectives and brought them to more than six districts.

'So how'd you ID him?' Dino asked.

Nicci deferred to Jessica. 'Talk to the mastermind.'

'Well, we had a little help from the Audio Visual Unit on this one,' Jessica said. 'But when Thompson and I were sitting in that coffee shop I took his picture with my cellphone. Then I sent the photo via SMS to Nicci's phone. Nicci and two uniforms were out in the van, about half a block away, with Bonnie Silvera. A few seconds later Nicci got the photo, opened it, showed it to Bonnie. The witness made the positive ID, Nicci sent me a text, letting me know we were on, and we knew we had him.'

'That was *your* play?' Dino asked.

Jessica blew on her nails, buffed them dramatically on her blouse.

'My God, you are a dangerous woman,' Dino said.

'Tell the world.'

'I should tell your husband.'

'Like he doesn't know,' Jessica said. 'Right now he's painting the fence behind our house. I'm going to let him draw me a bubble bath later.'

Detective Dennis Stansfield, perhaps feeling left out, piped in. 'You know, I read in a recent survey that, in her lifetime, the average American woman receives 26.5 miles of cock.'

If there was one thing Jessica hated, it was a cop who found a way to make a sex joke after hearing about a rape. Even worse, a rape/murder. Rape had nothing to do with sex. Rape was about violence and power.

Stansfield glanced over at Jessica. It seemed that she had gotten the assignment to be the flustered, blushing female officer in his presence, the one ill at ease in the wake of his shabby jokes. Was he kidding? Jessica had been born and raised in South Philly, and had grown up around cops. She was swearing like a longshoreman by the time she was five. She had even gotten to like the taste of soap.

'Twenty-six miles, huh?' Jessica asked.

'Twenty-six point *five*,' Stansfield replied.

Jessica looked at Nicci, at Dino, back at Stansfield. Dino looked at the table. He didn't know exactly what was coming, but he knew *something*.

'So, let me get this straight,' Jessica said, squaring off.

'Sure.'

'Is that 26.5 miles counting each insertion, or all the cocks added up individually?'

Stansfield, all of a sudden, started to redden a bit himself. 'Well, I'm not sure. I don't think the survey said.'

Nothing killed a dirty joke like discussion and analysis. 'Not very scientific, then, is it?'

'Well, it was—'

'Now, if we're counting per insertion,' Jessica continued, unbowed, 'that might be just one hell of a weekend.' She leaned back in her chair, crossed her arms. 'If we're counting each dick just once . . . let's see.' She looked at Nicci, while gesturing to Stansfield. 'How many times does four inches go into twenty-six miles?'

'Twenty-six-five,' Nicci added.

'Right,' Jessica said. 'Twenty-six-five.'

Stansfield was now as red as a Roma tomato. 'Four inches? Uh, I don't think so, darlin'.'

Jessica looked behind her, at the woman setting up the next table. 'Hey, Kathy, is there a ruler in the office?' Kathy was one of the owners of the Hot Potato Café.

'Oh yeah,' Kathy said with a wink. A Philly girl herself, she had heard the whole exchange and was probably dying to leap into the fray.

'All right, all right,' Stansfield said.

'Come on, Dennis,' Jessica said. 'Drop that big hot spud on the table.'

Suddenly Stansfield had somewhere else to be. He glanced at his watch, downed his coffee, mumbled his goodbyes, made his exit.

Jessica could ignore the Cro-Magnons of the world on a day like this. A killer was in custody, they had a pile of evidence against him, no civilian or police officer had been injured in the arrest, and a gun was off the street. It didn't get any better than that.

*

TWENTY MINUTES LATER THEY split up. Jessica walked to her car alone. She knew that she had to keep up a front with her fellow detectives, a shield of hubris and bravado. But the cold truth was that she'd had a gun pointed at her. She knew that everything could have been taken away in the time it took to pull that trigger.

She stepped into a doorway and, making sure she was not observed, closed her eyes, a tidal wave of fear rushing over her. In her mind she saw her husband Vincent, her daughter Sophie, her father Peter. Both Peter Giovanni and Vincent Balzano were cops – her father long retired – and knew the risks, but Jessica envisioned them both standing over her casket at St. Paul's. In her mind she heard the bagpipes.

Jess, she thought. *Don't go there. If you go there, you might never come back.*

On the other hand, after all was said and done, she was tough, wasn't she? She was PPD. She was her father's daughter.

Fuck it all, she was *dangerous*.

By the time she reached her car her legs were steady. Before she could open the door she noticed someone across the street. It was David Albrecht. He had the camera on his shoulder. He was filming her.

Here we go, Jessica thought. It's going to be a long week.

She got in her car, started it. Her cellphone rang. She answered, and learned something she'd always suspected.

She wasn't the only dangerous female in her family.

THREE

I HEAR A TRUCK PULL INTO THE DRIVEWAY. A FEW MOMENTS LATER, A knock at the door. I open it. In front of me stands a man of forty, just begin- ning to paunch. He is wearing a red windbreaker, paint-splattered jeans, a pair of soiled running shoes with frayed laces. In his hand is a clipboard.

'Mr. Marcato?' the man asks.

Marcato. The name makes me smile.

'Yes.' I extend my hand. The man's skin is rough, calloused, stained. He reeks of cigarettes and turpentine.

'I'm Kenny Beckman,' he says. 'We spoke on the phone.'

'Of course. Please come in.'

Except for a few plastic trash barrels and dusty glass display cases, the space is empty.

'Man, what's that smell?' Beckman asks.

'It's coming from next door. There used to be a sausage shop there and I think they left some meat to rot. I intend to speak to them about it.'

'You better. You're not gonna do any business in here if it smells like this.'

'I understand.' I gesture at the room. 'As you can see, we're going to need quite a bit of work here.'

'You can say that again.'

Beckman walks around the room, touching the moldering drywall, fingering the dust-caked sills, shining a flashlight along the baseboards. He produces a measuring tape, takes a few dimensions, jots them on the clip-board. I watch him carefully, calculating his speed and agility.

A minute or so later: 'You've got a pretty good sag in the floor joists.' He bounces a few times, driving home his point. The parched joists creak beneath his weight. 'The first thing we're going to need to do is shore that up. You really can't do too much else with the floor out of level.'

'Whatever is necessary to bring this up to code.'

Beckman looks around the room again, perhaps in preparation for his closing. 'Well, you've got a ways to go, but I think we can handle it.'

'Good. I'd like to get started right away.'

'Sounds like a plan.'

'And by the way, you've come highly recommended.'

'Oh yeah? Who recommended me? If you don't mind me asking.'

'I'm not sure I recall. It was a while ago.'

'How long?'

'March 21, 2002.'

At the mention of the date Kenneth Beckman tenses. He takes a step backward, glances at the door. 'I'm sorry? 2002? Is that what you said?'

'Yes.'

'March of 2002?'

'Yes.'

Another glance at the door. 'That's not possible.'

'And why is that?'

'Well, for one thing, I wasn't even in business then.'

'I can explain,' I say. 'Let me show you something.' I gesture to the dark hallway leading to the back room of the first floor. Beckman takes a moment, perhaps sensing that something is slightly off kilter, like a radio that cannot quite find a signal. But he clearly needs the work, even if it is for a weird man who speaks in riddles.

We head down the hallway. When we reach the door I push it open. The smell is a lot stronger here.

'Fuck!' Beckman exclaims, recoiling. He reaches into his back pocket, takes out a soiled handkerchief, brings it to his mouth. 'What the hell is that?'

The small square room is spotless. There are two steel tables at the center, both bolted to the floor. The night-black walls have been expensively soundproofed; the drop ceiling is made of acoustic tile purchased by mail order from a Swiss company specializing in outfitting the finest recording studios in the world. Above the tables is a microphone. The floor is a high-gloss enamel, painted red in the name of practicality. Beneath the tables is a drain hole.

On one of the tables rests a figure, supine beneath a white plastic sheet pulled up to the neck.

When Beckman sees the corpse, and recognizes it for what it is, his knees trick.

I turn to the wall, unpin a photograph, a clipping from a newspaper. It is the only adornment in the room. 'She was pretty,' I say. 'Not beautiful, not in the Grace Kelly sense, but pretty beneath the coarseness of all this paint.' I hold up the picture. 'Don't you think?'

In the pitiless fluorescent light Beckman's face contorts with fear.

'Tell me what happened,' I say. 'Don't you think it's time?'

Beckman retreats, waving a forefinger in the air. 'You're fucking nuts, man. Fucking psycho. I'm outta here.' He turns and tries the knob on the door. Locked. He pulls and pushes, pulls and pushes. It is a mounting frenzy, with no success. 'Open the goddamn door!'

Instead of unlocking the door, I step forward, remove the sheet from the figure on the table. The body underneath has begun to decompose, its eyes now descended into their sockets, its skin fallen sallow, the color of overripe corn. The form is still recognizable as human, albeit emaciated and on the precipice of putrefaction. The hands are gray and shriveled, fingers stiff in supplication. I do not gag at the sick-sweet smell. In fact, I have begun to anticipate it with some measure of desire.

I pry back the index finger on the corpse's left hand. There is a small tattoo of a swan. I look at Kenneth Beckman, and say, in my best broken Italian:

'Benvenuto al carnevale!'

Welcome to the carnival.

Beckman staggers against the wall, horrified by the sight, the fresh surge of decay in the air. He tries to speak, but the words bottleneck in his throat.

I lift the Taser and place it to the side of Beckman's chest. Blue lightning strikes. The man folds to the floor.

For a moment the room is silent.

As silent as a womb.

I TAKE THE THREE *killing instruments out of their sheaths, lay them on the table, next to the salon-quality hair trimmer. I open the hidden cabinet concealed behind a door that has a touch latch, revealing the recording equipment. The sight of the matte-black finish on the six components, free of dust and static, fills me with an almost sexual sensation. The warmth coming off the components – I always warm everything up at least an hour before a session – coats me in a thin layer of perspiration. Or maybe that is just anticipation.*

Beckman is shackled to the table with tape over his mouth. His head is held in place by a neurosurgical clamp, a precision device used to fix a patient's head to a table during stereotactic procedures for the placement of electrodes, an operation requiring rigid immobilization. A year ago I ordered the apparatus from a German firm, paying by international money order, receiving the product through a series of remailers.

I slip on a surgical gown, stand next to the table, open the straight razor. With the index finger of my left hand I probe the soft skin on the man's forehead. Beckman howls into his gag, but the sound is muffled.

That is about to change.

With a steady hand I make the first cut across the forehead, just beneath the hairline, taking my time. I watch the skin bisect slowly, revealing the glossy pink tissue beneath. The surgical clamp does its job well. The man cannot move his head at all. With a foot pedal I press Record, then remove the gag.

The man gulps air, pink foam leaking from the corners of his mouth. He has severed the tip of his tongue.

He begins to scream.

I monitor the sound levels, make a few adjustments. Beckman continues to shriek, blood running down both sides of his face now, onto the polished stainless steel of the table, onto the dry enamel of the floor.

A few minutes later I blot the blood on Beckman's forehead, clean it with an alcohol pad. I go to work on the man's right ear. When I am finished I take out a measuring tape, measure down from the cut on the forehead, mark the spot with a red felt-tip pen, then take the second killing instrument in hand, hold it to the light. The carbon tip is a dark, lustrous blue.

One final check of the sound levels and I set about my penultimate task. Slowly, deliberately – largo, *one might say – I proceed, knowing that just a few feet away, on the other side of the outside wall, the city of Philadelphia is passing by, oblivious to the symphony being composed inside this common looking building.*

Then again, has not the greatest art in history come from humble surroundings?

Zig, zig, zag.

I am Death in cadence.

When the power drill reaches its full RPM, and the razor-sharp bit nears the skin covering the frontal bone, in an area just above the right eye, Kenneth Arnold Beckman's screams reach a majestic volume, a second octave. The voice is off key, but that can be fixed later. For now, there is no need to hurry. No need at all.

In fact, we have all day.

FOUR

SOPHIE BALZANO SAT AT ONE END OF THE LONG COUCH, LOOKING EVEN smaller than usual.

Jessica stepped into the outer office, talked to the secretary, then entered the main office, where she chatted with one of Sophie's Sunday-school teachers. Jessica soon returned, sat next to her daughter. Sophie did not take her stare off her own shoes.

'Want to tell me what happened?' Jessica asked.

Sophie shrugged, looked out the window. Her hair was long, pulled back into a cat's-eye barrette. At seven, she was a little smaller than her friends, but she was fast and smart. Jessica was five-eight in her stocking feet, and had grown to that height somewhere during the summer between sixth and seventh grade. She wondered if the same would happen for her daughter.

'Honey? You have to tell Mommy what happened. We'll make it better, but I have to know what happened. Your teacher said you were in a fight. Is that true?'

Sophie nodded.

'Are you okay?'

Sophie nodded again, although this time a little more slowly. 'I'm all right.'

'We'll talk in the car?'

'Okay.'

As they walked out of the school, Jessica saw some of the other kids whispering to each other. Even in this day and age, it seemed, a playground fight still generated gossip.

They left the school grounds, headed down Academy Road. When they made the turn onto Grant Avenue and the traffic halted for some construction works, Jessica asked, 'Can you tell me what the fight was about?'

'It was about Brendan.'

'Brendan Hurley?'

'Yes.'

Brendan Hurley was a boy in Sophie's class. Thin and quiet and bespectacled, Brendan was bully-bait if Jessica had ever seen it. Beyond that, Jessica didn't know a lot about him. Except that on the previous Valentine's Day Brendan had given Sophie a card. A big *glittery* card.

'What about Brendan?' Jessica asked.

'I don't know,' she said. 'I think he might be . . .'

Traffic began to move. They pulled off the boulevard, onto Torresdale Avenue.

'What, sweetie? You think Brendan might be what?'

Sophie looked out the window, then at her mother. 'I think he might be G-A-E.'

Oh boy, Jessica thought. She had been prepared for a lot of things. The talk about sharing, the talk about race and class, the talk about money, even the talk about religion. Jessica was woefully unprepared for the talk about gender identity. The fact that Sophie spelled the word out instead of saying it – indicating that, to Sophie, and her classmates, the word belonged in that special classification of profanities not to be uttered – spoke volumes. 'I see,' was all that Jessica could come up with at that moment. She decided not to correct her daughter's spelling at this time. 'What makes you say that?'

Sophie straightened her skirt. This was clearly difficult for her. 'He kind of runs like a girl,' she said. 'And throws like a girl.'

'Okay.'

'But so do I, right?'

'Yes, you do.'

'So it's not a bad thing.'

'No, it's not a bad thing at all.'

They pulled into their driveway, cut the engine. Jessica soon realized that she had no idea how much Sophie knew about sexual orientation. Even thinking about the words 'sexual orientation' in connection with her little girl freaked her completely out.

'So, what happened?' Jessica asked.

'Well, this girl was saying mean things about Brendan.'

'Who is this girl?'

'Monica,' Sophie said. 'Monica Quagliata.'

'Is she in your grade?'

'No,' Sophie said. 'She's in third. She's pretty big.' Consciously or subconsciously, Sophie balled her fists.

'What did you say to her?'

'I told her to stop saying those things. Then she pushed me and called me a skank.'

That *bitch*, Jessica thought. She secretly hoped that Sophie had cleaned the little shit's clock. 'What did you do then?'

'I pushed her back. She fell down. Everyone laughed.'

'Did Brendan laugh?'

'No,' Sophie said. 'Brendan is afraid of Monica Quagliata. *Everyone's* afraid of Monica Quagliata.'

'But not you.'

Sophie glanced out the window. It had begun to rain. She traced her finger on the misting glass, then looked back at her mother. 'No,' she said. 'Not me.'

Yes, Jessica thought. *My tough little girl.* 'I want you to listen, okay, honey?'

Sophie sat up straight. 'Is this going to be one of our talks?'

Jessica almost laughed. She checked herself at the last second. 'Yes. I guess it is.'

'Okay.'

'I want you to remember that fighting is always the last resort, okay? If you have to defend yourself, it's all right. Every single time. But sometimes we need to take care of people who can't take care of themselves. Do you understand what I mean?'

Sophie nodded, but looked confused. 'What about you, Mom? You used to fight all the time.'

Ah, *crap*, Jessica thought. *Logic from a seven-year-old.*

After Sophie was born, Jessica had discovered boxing as an exercise and weight-loss regimen. For some reason she took to it, even going so far as to take a few amateur bouts before letting her great uncle Vittorio talk her into turning pro. Although those days were probably behind her – unless there was a Senior Tour for female boxers closing in on thirty-five – she had begun to visit Joe Hand's Gym in anticipation of a series of exhibition bouts planned to raise money for the Police Athletic League.

None of that training helped her at this moment, however, a moment when she was faced with explaining the difference between fighting and boxing.

Then Jessica saw a shadow in her side mirror.

Vincent was walking up the drive, carrying a pizza from Santucci's. With his caramel eyes, long lashes and muscular physique, he still made Jessica's heart flutter, at least on those days when she didn't want to kill him. Sometimes he dressed in suits and ties, cleanshaven, his dark hair swept back. Other days he was scruffy. Today was a scruffy day. Jessica was, and always had been, a pushover for scruff. She had to admit it. Detective Vincent Balzano looked pretty damned good for a married man.

'Sweetie?' Jessica asked.

'Yeah, mom?'

'That thing we were talking about? About fighting versus boxing?'

'What about it?'

Jessica reached over, patted her daughter's hand. 'Ask your father.'

THEY HAD LIVED IN the Lexington Park section of Northeast Philadelphia for more than five years, just a few blocks from Roosevelt Boulevard. On a good day it would take Jessica forty-five minutes to get to the Roundhouse. On a bad day – most days – even longer. But all that was about to change.

She and Vincent had just closed on a vacant trinity in South Philly, a three-story row house belonging to old friends, which was how many houses in the neighborhood changed hands. Rare was the property that made it to the classifieds.

They would be living in the shadow of their new church, Sacred Heart of Jesus, where Sophie would be starting school. New friends, new teachers. Jessica wondered what the effect on her little girl was going to be.

Jessica's father, Peter Giovanni, one of the most decorated cops in PPD history, still lived in the South Philadelphia house in which Jessica had grown up – at Sixth and Catharine. He was still vibrant and active, very much involved in the community, but he was getting on in years, and the trip for him to see his only granddaughter would eventually become a burden. For this, and for so many other reasons, they were moving back to South Philly.

With her daughter fast asleep, and her husband ensconced in the basement with his brothers, Jessica stood at the top of the narrow stairs to the attic.

It seemed as if her entire life was in these boxes, these cramped and angled rooms. Photographs, keepsakes, awards, birth and death certificates, diplomas.

She picked up one of the boxes, a white Strawbridge's gift box with a piece of green yarn around it. It was the yarn with which her mother used to tie her hair in autumn, after the summer sun had made her brunette hair turn auburn.

Jessica slid off the yarn, opened the box: a faux-pearl mirror compact, a small leather change purse, a stack of Polaroids. Jessica felt the familiar pangs of pain and grief and loss, even though it had been more than twenty-five years since her mother had died. She slipped the yarn back around the box, put it by the stairs, gave the room one last survey.

She had been a cop for a long time, had seen just about everything. There wasn't too much that unnerved her.

This did.

They were moving back to the city.

FIVE

'FUCKIN' CITY,' THE MAN SAID. 'FIRST MY CAR GETS BOOTED, THEN they tow it, then I hadda go down to PPA and spend two hours standing around with a bunch of smelly lowlifes. Then I hadda go down to Ninth and Filbert. *Then* they tell me I owe three-hunna-ninety dollars in tickets. Three-hunna-ninety *dollars*.'

The man slammed back his drink, washed it down with a mouthful of beer.

'Fuckin' city. Fuckin' PPA. Buncha Nazis is what they are. Fuckin' racket.'

Detective Kevin Byrne glanced at his watch. It was 11:45 p.m. His city was coming alive. The guy next to him had come alive after his third Jim Beam. The man migrated from tales of woe that began with his wife (fat and loud and lazy) to his two sons (ditto on the lazy, no data on body type) to his car (a Prism not really worth getting out of hock) and his ongoing war with the Philadelphia Parking Authority. The PPA had few fans in the city. Without them, though, the city would be chaos.

They were sitting at the bar in a corner tavern in Kensington, a hole in the wall called The Well. The place was half-full. Kool and the Gang were on the juke; an ESPN wrap-up of the day's sports was on the television over the bar.

Byrne slipped in the earbuds, blotting out the *Parking Wars* victim, looked at the screen on his iPod, dialed down to his classic blues playlist. The jukebox in the bar was now playing something by the Commodores, but here, inside Byrne's head, it was 1957, and Muddy Waters was going down to Louisiana, saying something about a mojo hand.

Byrne nodded to the bartender, the bartender nodded back. Byrne had never been to this tavern before, but the barkeep was a pro at what he did, as was Byrne.

Byrne had grown up in Philadelphia, was a Two-Streeter for life, had seen the city's best days and its worst. Well, maybe not its best. It was, after all, the place where the Declaration of Independence had been signed, the place where the Founding Fathers had gathered and hammered out the rules by which Americans, at least to some small degree, still lived.

On the other hand, the Phillies had won the World Series in 2008, and for a Phillies fan that trumped some faded old document any day.

In his time on the job Byrne had investigated thousands of crimes, worked hundreds of homicides, had spent nearly half his life among the dead, the broken, the forgotten.

What was the Thomas de Quincy quote?

If once a man indulges himself in murder, very soon he comes to think little of robbing; and from robbing he comes next to drinking and Sabbath-breaking, and from that to incivility and procrastination.

Byrne had his own word for it.

Slippage.

To Kevin Byrne, slippage was about accepting levels of behavior that previous generations would have considered unthinkable, standards that had slowly become the norm, new lows from which the cycle could begin again, inching ever downward.

Lately he found himself thinking obsessively about all the innocent, the unavenged. He thought about the short, inconsequential life of Kitty Jo Morris, aged three, scalded to death by her mother's boyfriend, a man angered over the little girl's habit of taking the remote from the living room; of Bonita Alvarez, not quite eleven, who was pushed from the roof of a three-story building in North Philly for hiding one of her older sister's Rice Krispie treats in the broom closet;

of Max Pearlman, aged eighteen months, left in a car overnight in January while his father smoked crack underneath the Platt Bridge.

No headlines here. No NBC White Paper specials on the state of the American family. Just a little less space in the graveyards. Just a little slip.

Now, in Byrne's head, it was 1970. Blues legend Willie Dixon was proclaiming that he ain't superstitious. Neither was Kevin Byrne. He had seen too much to believe in anything but good and evil.

And evil is in the house, Byrne thought as he considered the man sitting across the bar from him at that moment, a man who had the blood of at least two people on his hands, a murderer named Eduardo Robles.

ON A HOT SUMMER afternoon in 2007, Eduardo Robles and his girl-friend were walking down a street in Fishtown. According to Robles, at around 1:30 p.m. a car cruised slowly by, the deep bass of a rap song rattling the windows of nearby buildings. Someone in that car pointed a gun out the window and fired. Robles's girlfriend, a seventeen-year-old named Lina Laskaris, was struck three times.

Robles called 911, and when he arrived at the police station, after having his statement taken by a patrol officer on the street, a divisional detective assumed that the young man was a suspect, not a witness. The detective cuffed Robles and stuck him in a holding cell.

Byrne got the call at eleven p.m. When Robles arrived at the Roundhouse – nearly ten hours after the incident – Byrne removed the cuffs, sat Robles down in one of the interrogation rooms. Robles said he was hungry and thirsty. Byrne sent out for hoagies and Mountain Dew, then began to question Robles.

They danced.

At three o'clock the next morning Robles rolled, and admitted it had been he who'd shot Lina Laskaris. Byrne arrested Robles for murder at 3:06 a.m., read him his Miranda warnings.

The problem with the case was that, according to the law, the police had six hours to determine someone's status as a witness or a suspect.

Three days later the grand jury came back with a no-bill because they believed, rightly so, that the arrest had begun the moment Robles was mistakenly put in cuffs at the station house. In that moment Robles went from witness to suspect, and the clock began to tick.

Five days after killing his girlfriend in cold blood, Eduardo Robles was a free man, courtesy of the astonishingly incompetent work of a divisional detective who, incredibly, due to some unfathomable political connection, had recently been rewarded for his incompetence with a job in the Homicide Unit, at an increase in pay.

That man's name was Detective Dennis Stansfield.

Robles went back to the life and within months was involved in the murder of a man named Samuel Reese, a night clerk at a bodega in Chinatown. Police believed that Robles shot Reese twice, took the surveillance disk from the recorder in the back room, and walked out with sixty-six dollars and a can of brake fluid.

It was all circumstantial – no ballistics, no physical evidence, shaky witness accounts – nothing that would stand up in court. In terms of the reality of the law, bullshit.

Byrne had spent the past two days building a case against Robles, but it was not going well. Although they had not found the murder weapon, Byrne interviewed four people who could put Robles in that bodega at that time. None of them were willing to talk to police, at least not on the record. Byrne had seen the fear in their eyes. But he also knew that talking to a cop on the street corner, or in your living room, or even at your place of business was one thing. Talking to a district attorney in front of a grand jury, under oath, was something else. Everyone called to testify would understand that committing perjury in front of a grand jury carried a prison term of five months, twenty-nine days. And that was for each lie.

In the morning Byrne would meet with Michael Drummond, the assistant district attorney assigned to the Robles case. If they could get four people to implicate Robles, they might be able to get a search warrant for Robles's car and apartment, perhaps finding something that would create a daisy chain, and the evidence would roll in.

Or maybe it wouldn't get that far. Maybe something would happen to Robles.

You never knew about such things in a city like Philadelphia.

Were the police partially responsible for the death of Samuel Reese? In this case they were. Robles should never have gotten back on the street.

Slippage.

On the day Robles was arrested, Byrne visited Lina Laskaris's grandmother. Anna Laskaris was a Greek immigrant in her early seventies. She had raised Lina alone. Byrne told the woman that the man responsible for Lina's death was being brought to justice. He remembered the woman's tears, how she held him, how her hair smelled of cinnamon. She was making *pantespani*.

What Byrne remembered most was that Anna Laskaris had trusted him, and he had let her down.

Byrne now caught a glimpse of himself in the filmy mirror behind the bar. He wore a ball cap, and the glasses he had been forced to start wearing lately. If Robles had not been drinking he might have recognized Byrne. But Byrne was probably just a blur in the near distance to Robles, as well as to everyone else in the bar. This was no upscale Center City watering hole. This place was for hard drinkers, for hard men.

At 12:30 Robles stumbled out of the bar. He got into his car and drove down Frankford Avenue. When Robles reached York Street he turned east, drove a few blocks, parked.

Byrne sat in his car across the street, and watched. Robles got out of his car, stopped twice to talk to people. He was looking to score. Within minutes a man approached.

Robles and the other man walked, a little unsteadily, down the alley. A moment later Byrne saw light flare against the dirty brick wall of the alley. Robles was hitting the rock.

Byrne got out of his car, looked both ways up the street. Deserted. They were alone. Philadelphia was once again sliding into slumber, except for those who moved silently through the harbor of night.

Byrne stepped into shadow. From somewhere, perhaps deep inside him, a long-forgotten melody began to play.

It sounded like a requiem.

SIX

MONDAY, OCTOBER 25

T HE EARLY MORNING RUN THROUGH PENNYPACK PARK HAD BECOME a
 sacrament, one that Jessica was not quite ready to relinquish. The
people she saw every morning were not just part of the landscape but
part of her life.

There was the older woman, always meticulously turned out in
1960s pillbox chic, who walked her four Jack Russell terriers every
morning, the dogs in possession of a wardrobe more extensive and
seasonal than Jessica's. There was the *tai chi* group who, rain or shine,
performed their morning rituals on the baseball diamond near Holme
Avenue. Then there were her buddies, the two Russians, half-brothers,
both named Ivan. They were well into their sixties, but incredibly fit,
as well as shockingly hirsute, given to jogging in their matching lime-
green Speedos in summer. For half-brothers they looked almost
identically alike. At times Jessica could not tell them apart, but it didn't
really matter. When she saw one of them she simply said, 'Good
morning, Ivan.' She always got a smile.

When she and Vincent and Sophie moved to South Philly there
would still be a few places for her to jog, but it would be a long time
before Jessica could run again without caution, like she could here.

Here, where her route and path were well worn, she could sort things out. It was this she would miss most of all.

She rounded the bend, ran up the incline, thought about Marcia Kimmelman, and what had been done to her. She thought about Lucas Anthony Thompson, and the startled look in his eyes when he'd realized it was over, the moment the cuffs clicked shut on his wrists and he was yanked to his feet, dirt and gravel on his face, his clothing. Jessica had to admit she liked the dirt-and-gravel part, always had. Mud, weather permitting, was even better.

With this comforting image in mind she turned the corner, onto her street, and saw someone standing at the end of her driveway. A man in a dark suit. It was Dennis Stansfield.

Jessica let her feelings morph from apprehension to annoyance. What the hell was this jackass doing at her house?

She slowed to a walk for the last one hundred feet, catching her breath. She approached the man, who seemed to realize he was out of place.

'Detective,' Jessica said, suddenly conscious of her appearance. She wore loose sweatpants and a tight tank top, a sports bra beneath. She had worked up a sweat and taken off her fleece hoodie, tied it around her waist. She saw Stansfield's stare do a quick inventory of her body, then find her eyes. Jessica took a moment, caught the rest of her breath, drilling the look right back. Stansfield flinched first, looking away.

'Good morning,' he said.

Jessica had the option of putting her hoodie back on, zipping it up, but that would be telling Stansfield that she had a problem. She had no problems. Not one. She put her hands on her hips. 'What's up?'

Stansfield turned back to her, clearly doing his best to look at her face. 'The boss said Detective Burns might not be back today, and that if it was okay with you—'

'Byrne,' Jessica said. 'His name is Kevin Byrne.' Jessica wondered if Stansfield was intentionally busting her chops or was really that clueless. Right now it was a toss-up. It wasn't that Kevin was Superman, but he did have a reputation within the unit, if not the entire department. Jessica and Byrne had worked some high-profile cases over the past few years, and unless you were a rookie you had to know who he was. Plus, Byrne was off cleaning up Stansfield's mess, and this could not possibly have been lost on the man.

'Byrne,' Stansfield said, correcting himself. 'Sorry. The boss said that he might not be done with the grand jury today, and that we should partner up for the duration. At least until Detective Byrne gets back.' He shuffled his feet. 'If that's all right with you.'

Jessica didn't remember anyone asking what her thoughts were on the subject. 'You have the notification sheet?'

Stansfield reached into his suit-coat pocket, retrieved the form, held it up.

As he did this, Jessica glanced at the house. She saw a shadow near the window in the front bedroom, saw the curtains part a few inches. It was Vincent. Jessica might have been a police officer, and even when she jogged these days she was armed – at that moment she had the sweetest little Browning .25 at the small of her back – but when Vincent saw her talking to someone in front of the house, someone he didn't know, his antennae went up. The number of police officers killed had risen sharply over the past few years, and neither Jessica nor Vincent ever let down their guards.

Jessica nodded, almost imperceptibly, and, a few seconds later, the curtain closed. She turned back to Stansfield.

'All in a day, detective,' Jessica said. 'Let's partner up.'

The twisted, phony smile on Stansfield's face all but shouted his disappointment at her tepid response. 'That's good news,' he said. 'Because we have a job.'

We, Jessica thought. What a true delight this was going to be. She knew she was up on the wheel. The wheel was the roster of detectives on the Line Squad. When you caught a new case you went to the end of the line, worked the case, slowly making your way back to the top. When you reached the number one position, regardless how many cases you had on your plate, you were up again. Rare was the day in the unit where you cleared your cases when a new body fell.

'All right,' she said. 'Let me a grab a shower. I'll be out in ten minutes.'

Two things immediately registered on Stansfield's face. One, the idea of her taking a shower. Two, the fact that he hadn't been invited in.

THE CRIME SCENE WAS at the northern end of the Pennsport section of South Philadelphia. Pennsport was a working-class neighborhood, bounded by Passyunk Square to the west, the Delaware River to the east, Queen Village to the north, Whitman to the south.

One of the oldest sections of the city, Pennsport had been slow in the development of new projects, with some of the homes dating back to 1815. It was quite possible to have a new block of row houses bookended by structures that had been built when James Madison was president of the United States.

When Jessica and Stansfield pulled up to the crime scene – a boarded-up storefront near the corner of Fifth and Federal Streets – a sector car was parked diagonally across the street. Both Federal and Fifth were one-way streets and at either end of the block stood a pair of uniformed officers, diverting traffic. The Crime Scene Unit had not yet arrived, so there was no tape ringing the perimeter yet. Budget cuts had forced the city to curtail new hires, to postpone updating equipment, and these days there could be a two-hour or longer lag in the arrival of key crime scene personnel.

But while CSU was not yet there, David Albrecht was, camera in hand.

'Morning!' he shouted from across the street.

Great, Jessica thought. *Another morning person.* Her husband and Sophie were morning people. Everyone around her was a morning person. Except Byrne. It was one of the reasons they worked so well together. On most days they grunted at each other until noon.

Jessica waved at David Albrecht, who promptly put up his camera and filmed the gesture. Then Jessica glanced at Dennis Stansfield. Stansfield, seeing he was on camera, buttoned his coat, sucked in his gut, and tried to look official.

*

THEY SIGNED ONTO THE log. The uniformed officer pointed down the alley.

'Inside or outside?' Jessica asked.

'Inside,' he said. 'But just.'

The scene was the rear entrance to a closed-up independent shoe store called All Soles. In the back were steps leading down to the basement, a door through which the various retail establishments that had been located there over the years received their shipments. The small area behind the store was littered with fast-food trash, discarded tires, the sort of urban detritus that people found too time-consuming to put in the Dumpster that was located just a few feet away.

Jessica and Stansfield stopped at the top of the steps. There was an iron handrail leading down. Just as Jessica made a mental note to ask CSU to dust the railing, Stansfield put his hand on it, striking a macho pose, lording his gold badge over the gathering personnel.

'Um, detective?' Jessica said.

Stansfield looked over. Jessica pointed at his hand. Stansfield realized that he was possibly contaminating the site, and withdrew his hand as if he were grabbing a red-hot poker.

Jessica turned her attention to the entrance to the crime scene.

There were four steps. She scanned the immediate area, saw no blood trail. The door was open just a few inches. She walked down the stairs, edged open the door, Stansfield a little too close behind her. His cologne was nauseating. It would soon become welcome.

'Holy shit,' said Stansfield.

The victim was a white male of undeterminable age – undeterminable partly because they could not see all of his face. He was lying in the middle of the small dusty storage room, amid cardboard boxes, plastic buckets, wooden forklift pallets. Jessica immediately saw the deep purple bruises on his wrists and ankles. The victim, it appeared, had been shackled. There was no blood, no sign of struggle in this room.

But two things gave her pause. First, the victim's forehead and eyes were wrapped in a band of white paper. The paper was about five inches wide and completely encircled the man's head. Across the top of the band was a streak of brown, a straight line drawn in what could have been dried blood. Beneath it was another spot, this one a nearly perfect oval about an inch wide. The paper overlapped at the left side of the man's head. It appeared to be sealed with red sealing wax. The right side had another smear of blood, which looked to be in the shape of a figure eight.

But that wasn't the worst of it.

The victim's body was completely nude. It appeared to have been shaved clean, head to toe. Pubic hair, chest hair, arm hair, leg hair – gone. The body's scraped and abraded skin indicated that it had been shaved roughly, violently, perhaps in the past day or so. There appeared to be no new growth.

The sight was so grotesque that it took Jessica a moment to take it all in. She had seen quite a bit. Never anything like this. The indignities of homicide were legion, but there was something about the final degradation of being left naked that made it all worse, a communiqué from the killer to the rest of the world that the humiliation of violent death was not the last word. For the most part, you didn't just die in this life. You were *found* dead.

Jessica took the lead, more out of instinct than from any sense of duty. Hers was a boys' world and the sooner you peed in the corners, the better. She had long since turned the word *bitch* from an epithet to a badge, an emblem as golden as her shield.

Stansfield cleared his throat. 'I'll, uh, get started on a canvass,' he said, and quickly took his leave.

There were some homicide detectives who liked the *idea* of being a homicide detective – the prestige, the pay, the cachet of being one of the chosen – but couldn't stand being at a crime scene. Apparently, Stansfield was just such a detective. *Just as well*, Jessica thought.

She crouched next to the victim, placed two fingers on his neck, checking for a pulse. She found none. She examined the front of the body, looking for some sort of entrance or exit wound. No holes, no blood.

She heard voices outside. She looked up to see Tom Weyrich coming down the steps, his gear in his hand, his photographer in tow. Weyrich was an investigator for the medical examiner's office with almost twenty years on the job.

'Top of the morning, Tom.'

Weyrich was in his early fifties, with a dry wit and a reputation as a thorough and exacting investigator. When Jessica had met him five years earlier he had been a meticulous and classically attired man. Now his mustache was irregularly trimmed, his eyes red and tired. Jessica knew that Weyrich's wife had recently died after a long fight with cancer. Tom Weyrich had taken it hard. Today he appeared to be running on fumes. His slacks were pressed, but Jessica noted that his shirt had probably been slept in.

'Had that double up in Torresdale,' Weyrich said, running his hands over his face, trying to wring out the exhaustion. 'Got out of there about two hours ago.'

'No rest for the righteous.'

'I wouldn't know.'

Weyrich stepped fully inside, saw the body. 'Good God.' Somewhere beneath the trash and shredded cardboard an animal scurried. 'Give me a good old execution-style two taps to the back of the head any day,' he added. 'I never thought I'd miss the crack wars.'

'Yeah,' Jessica said. 'Good times.'

Weyrich tucked his tie into his shirt, buttoned his suit coat, snapped on a pair of gloves. He went about his business. Jessica watched him, wondering how many times he had done this, how many times he had placed his hands on the cold flesh of the dead. She wondered what it was like for him, sleeping alone these days, and how he, more than anyone, needed to sense the warm flesh of the living. When Jessica and Vincent had been temporarily separated a few years earlier, it had been the thing she'd missed the most, the daily intimate contact with the warmth of another human being.

Jessica stepped outside, waited. She saw David Albrecht across the street, getting exterior shots of the building. Behind him, Jessica saw his sparkling new van, which had his website address painted on the side. It also had what Jessica figured was the title of his movie.

Coming soon: AREA 5292

Clever, Jessica thought. It was obviously a play on Area 51, the area in southern Nevada central to UFO conspiracy theories. The number 5292 was PPD parlance for a dead body.

Fifteen minutes later Tom Weyrich emerged.

'Bringing all my training to bear,' he began, 'I would conclude that this is a deceased person.'

'I knew I should have gone to a better school,' Jessica said. 'COD?'

'Can't even give you a presumptive cause of death until we unwrap his head.'

'Ready?' Jessica asked.

'As ever.'

They stepped back inside the storage room. Jessica snapped on latex gloves. Of late they were bright purple. They knelt down on either side of the body.

The band of paper was fastened with a small wad of sealing wax. The wax was a glossy crimson. Jessica knew this would be a delicate operation, if she wanted to preserve the sample.

She took out her knife – a four-inch serrated Gerber that she always carried in a sheath around her ankle, at least when she was wearing jeans – and slipped it under the circle of hard wax. She pried it gently. At first it looked as if it might split in two, but then she got lucky. The specimen fell off in one piece. She placed it into an evidence bag. With Weyrich holding the opposite side of the paper band, they unveiled the victim's face.

It was a horror mask.

Jessica estimated the victim to be about thirty-five to forty, although most of the lividity was gone and the skin had begun to sag.

Across the upper portion of the victim's forehead was a single laceration, running laterally, perhaps four or five inches in length. The cut did not appear to be very deep, splitting just the skin in a deep violet streak, not deep enough to reach bone. It appeared to have been made with either a razor blade or a very sharp knife.

Just above the right eye was a small puncture wound, the diameter of an ice pick or a knitting needle. This too seemed shallow. Neither wound appeared to be fatal. The victim's right ear looked to be mutilated, with cuts along the top and side, all the way down to the lobe, which was missing.

Around the neck was a deep welt. Death appeared to be a result of strangulation.

'You think that's the COD?' Jessica asked, even though she knew that the cause of death could not be conclusively determined until an autopsy had been performed.

'Hard to tell,' Weyrich said. 'But there is petechiae in the sclera of his eyes. It's a pretty good bet.'

'Let's see, he was stabbed, slashed and strangled,' Jessica said. 'Real hat trick.'

'And that's just the stuff we know about. He might have been poisoned.'

Jessica poked around the small room, carefully overturning boxes and shipping pallets. She found no clothing, no ID, nothing to indicate who this victim might be.

When she stepped outside a few minutes later she saw Detective Joshua Bontrager walking across Federal Street, clipping his badge to his jacket pocket.

Josh Bontrager had only been in the unit a few years but he had developed into a good investigator. Josh was unique in a number of ways, not the least of which was the fact that he had grown up Amish in rural Pennsylvania before making his way to Philadelphia and the police force, where he spent a few years in various units before being called into the homicide unit for a special investigation. Josh was in his mid-thirties, country-boy blond, deceptively fit and agile. He did not bring a lot of street smarts to the job – most of the streets on which he'd grown up had been barely paved – or any sort of scientific logic, but rather an innate kindness, an affability that completely disarmed all but the most hardened criminal.

There were some in the unit who felt that Josh Bontrager was a country bumpkin who had no business in one of the most respected elite urban homicide divisions in the country. But Jessica knew that you underestimated him at your own peril, especially if you had something to hide.

Bontrager crossed the alley to Jessica's side, lowered his voice. 'So, how do you like working with Stansfield?'

'Well, aside from the racism, sexism, homophobia and completely exaggerated sense of self-worth, it's a blast.'

Bontrager laughed. 'That bad?'

'Nah. Those are the highlights.'

'How come no one seems to like him?'

Jessica explained the Eduardo Robles case, including Stansfield's monumental fuck-up – a fuck-up that to all intents and purposes had led to the death of Samuel Reese.

'You'd think he would have known better,' Bontrager said.

'You'd think.'

'And we definitely like this Robles guy for that second body?'

'Yeah,' Jessica said. 'Kevin's at the grand jury today.'

Bontrager nodded. 'So, for messing up royally Stansfield gets a promotion *and* a kick in pay?'

'The brass works in mysterious ways.'

Bontrager put his hands in his pockets, rocked on his heels. 'Well, until Kevin is back, if you want another partner next time you're up on the wheel, let me know.'

'Thanks, Josh. I will.' She held up a folder. 'Write me up?'

'Sure.'

He took the folder from her, extracted a body chart, clipped it to a clipboard. The body chart was a standard police-department form that had four outlines of the human body drawn on it, front and back, left and right side, as well as space for the rudimentary details of the crime scene. It was the first and most referred-to form in the binder that would be dedicated to the case.

The two detectives stepped inside. Jessica spoke while Josh Bontrager wrote.

'We have a Caucasian male, aged thirty to forty-five years. There is a single laceration across the forehead, what appears to be a puncture wound above the right eye. The victim's right ear is mutilated. A portion of the ear lobe is missing. There is a ligature mark across the base of the neck.'

Bontrager went over the form, marking these areas on the figure.

'The victim is nude. The body looks to have been recently shaved from head to toe. He is barefoot. There are bruises on the wrists and ankles, which indicate the victim may have been restrained.'

Jessica continued to describe the scene, her path now forever crossed with that of this dead man, a dead man with no name.

*

TWENTY MINUTES LATER, WITH Josh Bontrager back at the Roundhouse, and Dennis Stansfield still on canvass, Jessica paused at the top of the stairs. She turned 360 degrees, scanning the landscape. Directly behind the store was a double vacant lot, a parcel where a pair of buildings had recently been razed. There were still piles of concrete, bricks, lumber. There was no fence. To the right was a block of row houses. To the left was the rear of some sort of commercial building, with no windows overlooking the alley. If someone were to have seen anyone entering the rear of the crime scene, they would have had to have been in a back room of one of the row houses, or in the vacant lot. The view from across the street was partially obscured by the large piles of debris.

Jessica approached the responding officer, who stood at the mouth of the alley with the crime-scene log. One of his duties was to sign everyone in and out.

'Who found the body?' Jessica asked him.

'It was an anonymous tip,' the officer said. 'Came into 911 around six o'clock this morning.'

Anonymous, Jessica thought. A million and a half people in her city, and they were all anonymous. Until it was one of their own.

SEVEN

HE AWOKE, DREAMBOUND, STILL IN THE HYPNOTIC THRALL OF troubled sleep. This morning, in his final reverie, as the light of day filtered through the blinds, Kevin Byrne stood in the defendant's well of a cavernous courtroom that was lit by a sea of votive candles. He could not see the members of the jury but he knew who they were. They were the silent victims. And there were more than twelve. There were thousands, each holding one light.

Byrne got out of bed, staggered to the kitchen, splashed cold water on his face. He'd gotten four hours of sleep; three the night before. Over the past few months his insomnia had become acute, a routine part of his life so ingrained that he could not imagine living any other way. Nevertheless, he had an appointment – doctor's orders and against his will – with a neurologist at the University of Pennsylvania Sleep Clinic.

He took a long hot shower, rinsing off the previous night. He toweled, dressed, pulling a fresh shirt out of the dry-cleaning bag. He put on a new suit, his favorite tie, then sat at his small dinette table, sipped his coffee. He glanced at the Sleep Clinic questionnaire. All one hundred sixty probing questions.

Question 87: Do you snore?

If I could get someone to sleep with me, I might be able to answer that, he thought.

Then Byrne remembered his little experiment. The night before, at around two a.m., when he'd found that he couldn't drift off, he'd dug out his small Sony digital recorder.

He got back in bed, took two Ambien, turned on the recorder, flipped off the light, and closed his eyes. Four hours later he awoke.

And now he had the results of his experiment. He poured more coffee, played the recording from the beginning. At first he heard some rustling, the settling of the unit on the nightstand. Then he heard himself turn off the lamp, a little more rustling, then a bump of the table, which was so loud that it made him jump. He turned down the volume. Then, for the next five minutes or so, he heard nothing but white noise, the occasional car passing by his apartment.

Byrne listened to this rhythmic breathing awhile, which seemed to get slower and slower. Then he heard the first snort. It sounded like a backfire. Or maybe a pissed-off Rottweiler.

Great, he thought. So he *did* snore. Not constantly, but about fifteen minutes into the recording he began to snore again, loudly for a few minutes, then not at all, then loudly again. He stared at the recorder, thinking:

What the fuck am I doing?

The answer? Sitting in his small dining room, barely awake, listening to a recording of himself sleeping. Did it get dumber than this?

Man, he had to get a life.

He pressed the fast-forward button, and every time he came across a sound he stopped, rewound for a few seconds, played it back.

Byrne was just about to give up on the experiment when he heard something that sounded different. He hit Stop, then Play.

'*You know*,' came his voice from the recorder.

What?

Rewind.

'*You know.*'

He let it run. Soon there was another noise, the sound of the lamp clicking on, and his voice saying, clear as a bell:

'*2:52.*'

Then there was the snap of the lamp being turned off, more rustling, then silence for the rest of the recording. Although he had no memory of it, he must have awakened, turned on the light, looked at the clock, spoken the time aloud, and gone back to sleep.

Except there was no clock in his bedroom. And his watch and cellphone were always on the dresser.

So how did he know what time it was?

Byrne played it all back, one last time, just to be certain that he was not imagining all of it. He was not.

2:52.

You know.

As BYRNE WAITED IN the park, he thought about another moment in this place, a time when his heart had been intact. His daughter Colleen had been four years old, and was trying desperately to get a kite in the air. She ran in circles, back and forth, her blonde hair trailing, arms raised high, repeatedly getting tangled in the string. She stamped her feet, shook a fist at the sky, untangled herself, tried again and again. But she never asked him for help. Not once.

It seemed as if it were just a few weeks ago. But it was not. It was a long time ago. Somehow, Colleen, who had been deaf since birth, the result of a condition called *Mondini Dysplasia*, was going to Gallaudet University, the country's first and most preeminent college for deaf and hard-of-hearing undergraduate students.

Today she was off on an overnighter to the Gallaudet campus in Washington D.C. with her friend Lauren, ostensibly to scope out the campus and the possibilities for living quarters, but quite possibly to scope out the nightlife and the young men. Byrne knew the tuition fees were steep, but he had been saving and investing for a long time, and Colleen had a partial scholarship.

Byrne had wanted Colleen to stay nearer to Philadelphia, but it had been ages since he had been able to talk her out of anything once she set her mind to it.

He had never met Lauren, but Colleen had good taste in friends. He hoped Lauren was sensible too, and that he wouldn't be getting a phone call from the D.C. police telling him that the two of them had been picked up at some out-of-control frat kegger.

Byrne sensed someone approaching on his right. He looked around to see his daughter walking across the square, dressed in a navy blue suit. She didn't look like a college student, she looked like a businesswoman. Had he missed something? Had he been asleep for four years?

She looked heart-stoppingly beautiful, but something was wrong. She was holding hands with a guy who had to be at least thirty. And they weren't just holding hands, they were doing that wrap-around-at-the-wrist thing, and brushing up against each other as they walked.

When they got closer Byrne saw that the kid was younger than he had first thought, perhaps around twenty-two, which was still far too old and worldly for his taste.

Unfortunately, in matters such as these Kevin Byrne's taste didn't matter in the least.

Colleen let go of the guy and kissed Byrne on the cheek. She was wearing perfume. This was getting worse by the second.

'Dad, I'd like you to meet my friend Laurent,' Colleen signed.

Of course, Byrne thought. It wasn't Lauren. It wasn't even a girl. It was *Laurent*. His daughter was going on an overnighter with a *man*.

'How are you?' Byrne asked, not meaning it or caring, extending his hand. The kid shook his hand. Good grip, not too firm. Byrne thought about taking the kid to the ground and cuffing him, arresting him for daring to touch Colleen Byrne right in front of him, for daring to think of his only daughter as a woman. He put the impulse on hold for the moment.

'I'm quite well, sir. It's a pleasure to meet you.'

Not only was Laurent a guy, he had an accent.

'You're French?' Byrne asked.

'French Canadian,' Laurent said.

Close enough, Byrne thought. His daughter was being romanced by a *foreigner*.

They chatted about nothing at all for a while, the sorts of things young men talk about while on the one hand trying to impress a girl's father and on the other trying not to embarrass the girl. As

Byrne recalled, it was always a delicate balancing act. The kid was doing all right, Byrne thought, seeing as the routine was complicated by his having to speak out loud to Byrne, and sign everything to Colleen.

When the small talk was exhausted, Laurent said: 'Well, I know you two have things to talk about. I'll leave you to it.'

Laurent wandered a few feet off. Byrne could see the young man's shoulders relax, heard a loud sigh of relief.

Byrne understood. Maybe the kid was okay.

Colleen looked at her father, both eyebrows raised. *What do you think?*

Byrne butterflied a hand, smiled. *Eh.*

Colleen gave him a pretty good shot on the upper arm.

Byrne reached into his pocket, handed Colleen the check that was discreetly contained in a small envelope. Colleen spirited it away in her purse.

'Thanks, Dad. A couple of weeks, tops.'

Byrne waved another hand. 'How many times have I told you that you don't have to pay me back?'

'And yet I will.'

Byrne glanced at Laurent, then back. 'Can I ask you something?' he signed. He had learned to sign when Colleen was about seven and had taken to it surprisingly well, considering what a lousy student he had been in school. As Colleen got older and a lot of their communication became nonverbal, relying on body language and expression, he stopped studying. He could hold his own, but found himself completely lost around two or more deaf people blazing away.

'Sure,' Colleen signed. 'What is it?'

'Are you in love with this guy?'

Colleen gave him the look. Her mother's look. The one that said *you just encountered a wall, and if you have any thoughts or dreams or hopes of getting over it you better have a ladder, a rope, and rappeling hooks.*

She touched his cheek, and the battle was over. 'I'm in love with *you*,' she signed.

How did she manage to do this? Her mother had done the same

thing to him two decades earlier. In his time on the job he had been shot on two different occasions. The impact of those two incidents was nothing compared to a single look from his ex-wife or daughter.

'Why don't you just ask me the question you're dying to ask?' she signed.

Byrne did his best to look confused. 'I don't know what you're talking about.'

Colleen rolled her eyes. 'I'll just go ahead and answer the question anyway. The one you were not going to ask me.'

Byrne shrugged. *Whatever.*

'No, we're not staying in the same room, Dad. Okay? Laurent's aunt has a big house in Stanton Park, and there are a million extra bedrooms. That's where I'll be sleeping. Locks on the door, guard dogs around the bed, honor and virtue intact.'

Byrne smiled.

Suddenly, the world was once again a wonderful place.

Byrne stopped at the Starbuck's on Walnut Street. As he was paying, his cellphone vibrated in his pocket. He took it out, checked the screen. It was a text message from Michael Drummond, the assistant district attorney handling the Eduardo Robles grand jury investigation.

Where are you?

Byrne texted Drummond his location. A few seconds later he received a reply.

Meet me at Marathon.

Ten minutes later Byrne stood in front of the restaurant at 18th and Walnut. He looked up the street, saw Drummond approaching, talking on his cellphone. Michael Drummond was in his mid-thirties, trim and athletic, well-dressed. He looked like the archetypal Philadelphia defense attorney, yet he had somehow stayed in the prosecutor's office for almost ten years. That was about to change. After being courted for years by every high-powered defense firm in the city, he was finally moving on. There was a going-away party scheduled for him at Finnigan's Wake in a few days, a soiree at which Drummond would announce which white-shoe firm he had chosen.

'Counselor,' Byrne said. They shook hands.

'Good morning, detective.'

'How does it look today?'

Drummond smiled. 'Do you remember the tiger scene in *Gladiator*?'

'Sure.'

'Something along those lines.'

'I'm just a flatfoot,' Byrne said. 'You might have to explain that one to me.'

Drummond looked over Byrne's shoulder, then over his own. He turned back. 'Eddie Robles is missing.'

Byrne just stared at Drummond, trying to keep all expression from his face. 'Is that a fact?'

'Facts are my life,' Drummomd said. 'I called over there this morning, and Robles's mother said Robles didn't come home last night. She said his bed is still made.'

'This guy has two bodies on him and he lives with his mother?'

'That does have a little bit of a Norman Bates vibe to it, now that you mention it.'

'We don't really need him to indict him, do we?' The question was rhetorical. The DA, as the saying went, could indict a ham sandwich. The sandwich did not need to be present.

'No,' Drummond said. 'But the jury is hearing another case today. That triple at the Fontana.'

The Fontana was a recently opened luxury condominium in Northern Liberties, a 100-million-dollar renovation project that had taken more than four years to complete. Three people had been shot, gangland style, in one of the units. It turned out that one of the victims was a former debutante who'd had a secret life that involved exotic dancing, drug dealing, and trysts with local sports celebrities. It was about as lurid as it got, which meant the story went viral within hours.

As of that morning, police had seven suspects in custody. The singing at the Roundhouse would commence shortly. Which meant that players for the Sixers, Eagles, Phillies, and Flyers were all sweating big time.

'I've got some serious time on this,' Byrne said. He knew that he had to play the game, and he was as good as anybody at it. Probably better.

'I know, Kevin. And I apologize. The Fontana case is high priority, and you know how things go. People forget, people run, people mysteriously disappear. Especially with a drug-homicide case.'

Byrne understood. The passions on a shocking and bloody case such as the Fontana ran high.

'What are we looking at?' he asked.

Drummond checked his BlackBerry. 'The jury will be back on Robles in three days when they meet again. I promise.'

It might not matter. Byrne knew that Philadelphia had a way of solving its own problems.

'Thanks for meeting with me, Michael.'

'Not a problem. Are you coming to my party?'

'Wouldn't miss it.'

They shook hands again. 'Don't worry about a thing, Kevin. Not a thing. Eddie Robles is history.'

Byrne just stared, impassive. 'Keep me posted.'

BYRNE THOUGHT ABOUT HEADING to the Roundhouse, but he wasn't expected for a while. He had to think. He drove to York Street, parked across from the alley down which Eduardo Robles had walked.

Eddie Robles is missing.

Byrne got out of the car, looked up and down the street. A half-block away he found what he was looking for, something that he had not noticed before.

There, high above the sidewalk, glancing indifferently down at the street, was a police camera.

EIGHT

THE HOMICIDE UNIT AT THE ROUNDHOUSE WAS A STUDY IN CONTROLLED bedlam. There were ninety detectives in the unit, working three shifts, seven days a week. The first floor was a winding labyrinthine warren of half-round rooms which made it a real challenge to place desks, file cabinets, computer tables – in other words, everything that might be needed in an office. Not that anyone went out of their way to give even a simple nod to the concept of decor in this place.

But there was a system, and that system worked. Philly Homicide had one of the highest solve rates of any homicide division in the country.

At noon, with most of the detectives at lunch or on the street, Jessica looked up to see Dana Westbrook crossing the room.

Sergeant Dana Westbrook was the new day-work supervisor, taking over for the retired Ike Buchanan. In her late forties, Westbrook was the daughter of a retired police inspector, and had been raised in Kensington. She was a Marine veteran of Desert Storm.

At first glance she was not the most intimidating figure. With her bobbed cut, just turning gray, and measuring in at just over five-four, she towered over no one. But she was in great physical shape, still adhered to the Marine circuit-workout four days a week, and could outrun and outperform women on the force half her age, as well as many of the men.

Being a woman in what was still and would probably always be a boys' club, her military training came in handy.

As in all police departments, indeed any paramilitary organization, there was a chain of command. From the commissioner to deputy commissioner, from chief inspector to staff inspector to captain, all the way to lieutenant and sergeant, then detective, officer, and recruit, it was a highly regimented institution. And shit, as they say in the military, doesn't flow uphill.

From day one, Dana Westbrook took a lot of shit.

When a call came in during day work – the eight a.m. to four p.m. shift – the desk detective took the information and brought it to the supervisor on duty. It was then the supervisor's job to initiate and coordinate the first crucial hours of the investigation. A lot of this involved telling men – some of whom had been in homicide for more than twenty years, all of whom had their own way of doing things, certainly their own pace and rhythms – where to go, who to talk to, when to come back. It involved judging their fieldwork, sometimes calling them on the carpet.

For male homicide detectives, who felt as if they were the Chosen, having someone tell them what to do was not an easy pill to swallow. To be told by a woman? This made the medicine bitter indeed.

Westbrook sat next to Jessica, opened a new file, clicked her pen. Jessica gave her the basic details, starting with the anonymous 911 call. Westbrook made her notes.

'Any sign of forced entry to the building?' Westbrook asked.

'Not sure. The place has probably been broken into many times, but there was no new splintering on the jamb.'

'What about vehicles parked near the scene?'

Jessica noticed for the first time that, besides her modest earrings, Dana Westbrook had four empty piercings in her right ear. 'We're running plates in a two-block radius, along with the vehicles parked in the school parking lot, cross-referencing the owners with wants and warrants. Nothing so far.'

Westbrook nodded, made a note of it.

'And we could also take a look at some of the footage our budding

Oscar winner took. I saw Albrecht getting some shots of the crowd across the street.'

'Good idea,' Westbrook said.

Sometimes a criminal, especially one guilty of murder, returned to the scene. Police were always aware that a crowd at a crime scene, or one gathered at a funeral, might contain the person they sought.

'And speaking of Albrecht, how much access does this kid get?' Jessica asked.

'Within reason,' Westbrook replied. 'He doesn't get inside the ME's office, of course. Or a hospital.'

'And why are we doing this, again?'

'He's the deputy commissioner's wife's cousin's son. Or something like that. He's plugged in, let's just put it that way. The deputy commissioner is a Penn State grad, you know.'

'Is Albrecht allowed to film a crime scene?'

'Well, word is, the brass is going to see a rough cut of this film and has final approval over it all. If anything compromises an ongoing investigation or is blatantly disrespectful to a victim or a victim's family it won't see the light of day. You can count on that.'

'So, we have the right to chuck him off a scene?'

'Absolutely,' Westbrook said. 'Just make sure Kevin doesn't do it when you're going seventy on I-95.'

Jessica smiled. It hadn't taken long for Sergeant Dana Westbrook to get up to speed. 'I'll make a note.'

Westbrook stood. 'Keep me in the loop.'

'You got it, boss.'

Until they got an ID on the victim there wasn't too much they could do. The faster you got an ID, the faster you could get information such as where the victim lived, worked, went to school, played, and the faster you could begin to collect witness statements. Once identification was made, a person was also run through the various databases, specifically the National Crime Information Center and its local version, the Philadelphia Crime Information Center.

The victim was fingerprinted as soon as the body got to the morgue, but all you could do before identification was canvass the area around the crime scene, process any forensic material, and hope for the best. If they couldn't ID the victim, the best hope was that by the next day someone would have heard the news about the body and would start making calls about their husband, brother, son.

After finishing her initial report, Jessica would head back to the scene. People working early shifts would be getting home soon and just might have something to tell her.

She made a note to ask Kevin to reach out to a friend of his, a detective who worked out of South Detectives. The more eyes and ears on a homicide, especially at this stage, the better. Divisional detectives knew their turf and their criminals better than anyone.

Before she could do that she sensed someone nearby. She turned. Dennis Stansfield stood behind her. He was like a virus that she couldn't seem to shake.

'Can I help you with something, detective?' Jessica asked.

Stansfield pointed to the notepad on the desk. 'I didn't mean to look over your shoulder.'

'And yet?'

'Well, lately I've heard some things about him.'

'Him?'

'Yeah. Detective Byrne.'

Jessica closed the folder on her desk, closed her notebook. She spun her chair around, stood up. She was not going to talk to this guy while she was sitting down. 'Like what sort of things?'

Stansfield glanced around the duty room, looked back, lowered his voice. 'Well, like maybe his heart's not in it anymore.'

'Really?'

'Yeah, and like maybe he's looking for the door. Like maybe he's not quite the cop he used to be.'

Jessica nodded. 'Interesting.'

'I'm just saying, you know? This is what I've heard. And from more than one person.'

'Well, *Dennis*,' Jessica said. 'Maybe you're right.'

Stansfield looked surprised. 'I am?'

'Yeah. Can I tell him you said this? I'm sure he'd like to hear it, seeing as it's going around.'

'Well, I'd really prefer you didn't,' Stansfield said. 'See, I was just saying that—'

'Then again, why don't you tell him yourself?'

'What do you mean?'

'He's right behind you.'

Stansfield spun around to find Kevin Byrne, who loomed over him by about five inches, standing there. It looked for a moment as though Stansfield was going to extend his hand in greeting. It looked for a moment as though Byrne was going to throw Stansfield out a window. Both men then thought better of it.

'Detective,' was all that Stansfield managed.

Byrne stared at him until Stansfield got really interested in the time of day. He glanced at his watch, then back at Jessica.

'I'm going to follow up on the owner of the building,' Stansfield said. 'I'm mobile if you need me.'

'Yeah,' Jessica said when Stansfield was out of earshot. 'That'll happen.' She turned to Byrne. 'Done with the grand jury already?'

Byrne shook his head. 'Postponed. They're hearing the Fontana case today.'

'Did Drummond tell you when you're back on?'

'Maybe next week.'

'Sucks.' The longer it went on, the more likely that people were going to catch amnesia.

Byrne pointed across the room, at the departing Stansfield. 'When did he go on day work?'

'Today,' Jessica said. 'The boss put him with me this morning. I caught a case.'

Jessica filled Byrne in on what they had found. They did not have crime-scene photographs yet, but Jessica had taken a few still pictures on her cellphone. She made it a practice never to print off any crime-scene photographs that she took with her own camera, even though there were no rules against it. It just made it a little too likely that personal photographs would get mixed in with official photographs, and things like that were what defense attorneys lived for. PhotoShop had changed everything.

Byrne stared at the images for a full minute, scrolling through them one by one.

'No ID yet?' he asked.

'Not yet,' Jessica said. 'Body's still on scene.'

Byrne handed back the phone. 'Any witnesses?'

'Nothing. I'm heading back there in a few minutes.'

Byrne looked across the room. David Albrecht sat at one of the desks, playing back footage on his camera's viewfinder.

'Who's the kid with the camera?'

Jessica explained David Albrecht's presence.

'Great,' Byrne said. 'Just what we need.'

Byrne checked the body chart, taking in the general details of the wounds to the victim, the placement of the body. 'Want some company?'

'I'll drive,' Jessica said.

'Let me get my stuff out of my car.'

In the rear parking lot they stopped at Byrne's car. It was a Kia Sedona minivan. Jessica had never seen it before.

'When did you get this?'

'It's a loaner from my cousin Patrick. Colleen is going to be moving soon and we're trying to keep the costs down. I'm bringing some of her stuff to a storage locker this week.'

'Do you like it?'

'Oh yeah,' Byrne said. 'Kias are true babe magnets. Had a few college cheerleaders flash me the other day.'

Byrne unlocked the passenger door, reached in, grabbed some things from the back seat. When he closed the door and turned around, Jessica did a double take.

Kevin Byrne had a stylish leather messenger bag over his shoulder.

'Oh my God,' Jessica said.

'What?'

'Hang on.' Jessica took out her cellphone, opened it, pantomimed dialing a long phone number. A *really* long phone number. She held up a finger. 'Hi, is this Hell?'

Byrne shook his head.

'Yes,' Jessica continued. 'I was calling to get the current temperature. What's that you say? Five below? Snow squalls expected?'

'Funny stuff,' Byrne said. 'Let me get a table so I can catch the whole act.'

Jessica smiled, closed her phone. She leaned against the car, crossed her arms. 'I can't believe it. Kevin Byrne carrying a purse. I am *so* blogging about this.'

'It's a man bag.'

'Ah.'

'And it's a Tumi. Tumi makes good stuff.'

'There's no question about that,' Jessica said. 'I have a Tumi purse myself.'

'This isn't a purse, okay? It's a—'

'Man bag,' Jessica said.

'And, just for the record, I never want to hear the words *metro* and *sexual* in the same sentence. Okay?'

'Promise,' Jessica said. Her fingers were secretly crossed behind her back. 'So, what made you decide to do this?'

Byrne leaned closer. 'It's just getting harder and harder to leave the house, you know? You have to have your keys, your cellphone, your pager, your sunglasses, your regular glasses, your iPod—'

'Wait. You have an iPod?'

'Yes, I have an iPod. What's so odd about that?'

'Well, for one thing, you still buy vinyl records. I just figured in a few years you'd make the giant leap to audiocassettes. Maybe even CDs one day.'

'I buy vinyl because it's collectible. Especially the old blues.'

'Okay.'

'Remember your uniform days when everything went on your belt? And what didn't go on your belt fitted in your shirt pocket?'

'I remember. But keep in mind there's even less room up there for female cops.'

'I'm a detective,' Byrne said. 'I've noticed that.'

He took a few steps back, gestured to the cut of his new suit, which Jessica had to admit looked pretty good on him. It was a charcoal gray two-button.

'Think about it,' he said. 'If I put all that stuff in my pockets it would ruin the line.'

'The line?' Jessica put her hand on the butt of her weapon. 'Okay, who are you and what have you done with my partner?'

Byrne laughed.

'Well, now that you carry a bag,' Jessica continued, 'you should keep in mind one of the first things they taught us at the academy.'

'I may be older than slate, but I seem to recall going to that academy myself. Over on State Road, right?'

'That's the one,' Jessica said. 'But what I meant by "us" was, well, *women*.'

Byrne braced himself, said nothing.

'They taught us to never, ever, carry your weapon in a purse.'

There was that word again. Byrne looked at the sky, back at Jessica. 'This is going to go on for a while, isn't it?'

'Oh yeah.'

THE CSU TEAM was still processing the scene on Federal Street, which now had crime-scene tape crossing both ends of the alley. As always, a crowd had gathered to watch the proceedings. It always amazed Jessica how no one ever saw anything, heard anything, witnessed anything, but as soon as the investigation got underway, as soon as there was some sort of urban circus to attend, everyone was suddenly available to gawk and rubberneck, conveniently off work and out of school.

When Jessica and Byrne came around the corner there was a meeting of supervisors. Among them was ADA Michael Drummond.

'Counselor,' Byrne said.

'Twice in one day,' Drummond replied. 'People will talk.' He turned to Jessica. 'Nice to see you, Jess.'

'Always a pleasure,' Jessica said. 'But what brings you out here?'

'I've got court in about an hour, but these were orders from Valhalla. New DA, new initiatives. Anything that happens this close to a school gets priority. My boss wants to watch this one from the beginning. He barks, I fetch.'

'Gotcha.'

'Copy me in on everything?' Drummond asked.

'Not a problem,' Jessica said.

Jessica and Byrne watched as Drummond crossed the street, positioning himself far from the crime scene. Jessica knew why. If an ADA was close to the action, he might witness something, and therefore be called as a witness on his own case, which was grounds for dismissal. It was a game they all knew how to play.

Jessica watched as Byrne walked up to the mouth of the alley, spoke to the uniformed officer. The uniform pointed to the two buildings behind the crime scene, nodded his head. Byrne took out his notebook, began to jot down details.

Jessica had seen it before.

Murder had been done here, and Kevin Byrne was in his element.

NINE

B YRNE WALKED DOWN THE ALLEY, HIS SENSES ON HIGH ALERT, HIS adrenalin surging. It was odd, to say the least. No matter how fatigued he was – today, on a 1 to 10, he would clock in at a bone-weary 7 – it all seemed to melt away when he got to a crime scene. Crime scenes were crack for investigators. Addictive, euphoric, replenishing, ultimately depleting. There was no other feeling like it. The best meal, the finest wine, even soul-shaking sex did not come close.

Okay, Byrne thought. *Maybe sex*.

He took in the approach to the area where the body had been found. The air was suffused with the stench of rotting fruit coming from the Dumpster a few yards away, and the unmistakable aroma of death coming from the shoe store.

He walked down the stairs, opened the door. Although the smell was almost overpowering in here, it was not the first thing he sensed. Instead, that was a feeling, an impression that he had just stepped across the boundary of a killer's mind, had just become an interloper in a realm of madness.

There is a pairing, a balance, a partnership.

Byrne stopped, waiting for more. Nothing. Not yet.

In addition to his upcoming appointment with the sleep-study clinic, he had his annual MRI screening. He'd had yearly MRIs for the past five years, ever since he had been nearly fatally injured in a shooting. He knew everyone in the hospital radiology department, and the mood was always light-hearted when he went there, but they all knew what it was about. There was, and always would be, a possibility of a brain tumor. He'd read all the books on symptoms and signs – blackouts, voices in your head, sometimes unexplained smells.

In a separate incident, many years earlier, he had confronted a suspect in a bar beneath the Walt Whitman Bridge. During the course of the arrest Byrne had plunged into the frigid Delaware River, locked in combat with the suspect. When he was pulled out of the water Byrne was declared dead. One full minute later he came to.

Not long after that the visions had started. They were never full-blown apparitions. He did not show up at a scene, close his eyes, and see any sort of recreation of the crime in Technicolor and THX audio. Instead, it was more of a feeling. Sometimes it crossed over into the dominion of sense and sensation, but mostly he got a feel for the victim, the perpetrator. A thought, a dream, a desire, a habit.

Byrne had been to group-therapy sessions of every kind, even going to a regression-therapy group that tried to take him back to that moment when he'd plunged into the river, an attempt to bring him back to the person he had been before the incident. Byrne now knew that was impossible.

The visions had diminished over the ensuing years as had the accompanying migraines. These days they were few and far between.

He had not had anything close to a full-blown migraine lately, but he knew something was happening inside him. More than once, in the last few months, he had experienced something . . . not pain, more of a presence, a thickness in his head, along with a slight blurring of vision. And with these feelings came the clearest inner visions he'd ever had, now accompanied by sounds. Then, sometimes, a blackout.

He was still undecided on whether or not to mention these things to his doctor. Telling a doctor something like this only led to more tests.

HE STEPPED INTO THE room where a dead man lay on the floor. Byrne's heart picked up a beat, quickening with the knowledge that a killer had stood in this spot no more than twenty-four hours earlier, breathing the same air.

Just when he was about to begin his routine, a warm sensation filled his head. He held onto the door jamb for a second, attempting to ride it out. With the warmth came the knowledge of . . .

. . . *something that has burned for many years, a feeling of loss and desire, a dark passion that will forever be unfulfilled, a love story unwritten, unwritable, the hunger to create a legacy* . . .

Byrne knelt down, snapped on a latex glove, then instantly thought better of it. He removed the glove. He needed the feel of the flesh. A dialogue happened between the skin of the dead and his senses. A superior officer, or a representative of the medical examiner's office would surely object. That didn't matter at the moment. He was alone with the dead, alone with what had happened in this room, alone with the rage that drove someone to brutally take a life.

Alone with himself.

Kevin Byrne reached out and touched a finger to the dead man's lips. He closed his eyes, listened, and the dead man spoke.

TEN

JESSICA AND BYRNE SPENT THE NEXT HOUR SEPARATELY CANVASSING the neighborhood for a second time. They learned a great deal about cheating spouses, lazy landlords, illegal parking, possible international drug cartels, alien invasions, more illegal parking, and – a fan favorite – government conspiracies. In other words, nothing.

At three o'clock Jessica met Byrne back at the corner of Fifth and Federal to compare notes.

'Jess,' Byrne said, pointing down the street.

Jessica turned and saw two figures sitting in a vacant lot, sandwiched between a pair of old row houses. The detectives were being observed.

Jessica and Byrne walked a half-block up Federal. David Albrecht, who had just returned from getting some high-angle shots from nearby rooftops, followed, but kept his distance.

Two older men sat on lawn chairs across the street from the ball field. They had racing forms on their laps, along with the sports sections of that morning's *Inquirer*. They were in their late seventies and had their chairs positioned in such a way that each could see what was approaching but still be close enough to converse. Jessica had the distinct feeling they didn't miss much.

One of the guys wore at least three cardigans, each a slightly different shade of maroon. The other wore a fishing hat with a button saying *Kiss Me I'm Italian* on it, a button so old that most of the letters were rubbed off. Now, from a few feet away, it looked like *Kiss It*. Jessica wondered if that wasn't on purpose. She showed her badge, introducing herself and Kevin Byrne.

When the men saw they were police officers they sat a little straighter.

Jessica asked: 'You fellows out here every day?'

'Every morning, every afternoon,' Cardigans said. 'Rain or shine. 'Cept when it rains, then we sit over there.' He pointed to an old storefront with a metal awning.

'In winter we meet at Mulroney's,' added Fishing Hat.

Mulroney's was a tavern on the other side of the playground, a fixture that had been around since sometime during the Truman administration.

Jessica asked the men what, if anything, they had seen the previous day. After a brief rundown of the day's events – a *Philadelphia Inquirer* delivery truck got a flat tire, some idiot on a cellphone was yelling at his wife or girlfriend and almost walked into the traffic on Federal, a dog came up and snatched one of their lunch bags right from under the chair – they got around to what they had seen at or near the crime-scene building.

Nothing.

'You didn't see anybody doing anything suspicious, anybody you haven't seen in the neighborhood before?' Byrne asked.

'Nah,' Cardigans said. 'We're the only suspicious characters around here.'

Jessica jotted down the meager information.

'You guys got here pretty quick earlier this morning,' Cardigans said.

'We were on a donut run around the corner,' Jessica said. 'It was on the way.'

Cardigans smiled. He liked her.

'Not like the last time,' Fishing Hat interjected.

Jessica glanced over at Byrne, back. 'I'm sorry?' she said. 'The last time?'

'Yeah. That other one?'

'The other one.'

'The other *dead* one they found in there.' Fishing Hat pointed to the crime-scene building, saying all this like it was common knowledge, worldwide.

'There was another victim found in that building?' Jessica asked.

'Oh, yeah,' he said. 'Place is a slaughterhouse. A regular abbytwar.'

Jessica figured he meant *abattoir*. She stole another glance at Byrne. This was getting better by the minute. Or worse. 'When was this again?'

'2002,' Fishing Hat said. 'Spring of 2002.'

'Nah,' Cardigans said. 'It was '04.'

Fishing Hat looked over, as if the other man had just told him the pope was a woman. '2004? What are you, drunk? It was 2002. March 21st. Mickey Quindlen's grandson broke his arm on the playground. My wife's brother came in from Cinnaminson, rammed his fucking car into the house.' He looked at Jessica. 'Excuse my German.'

'I speak German,' Jessica said.

'Uniforms came around noon. Suits didn't show up until midnight. I believe I can say all this without fear of contraception.'

Cardigans nodded, acquiescing.

'Uniforms? Suits?' Jessica asked. 'Did you used to be a cop?'

'Cop? Nah. I worked the docks, forty-one years. I just like that *Law and Order* show. The guy with the big teeth says that kind of stuff all the time.'

'He's dead now,' Cardigans said.

Fishing Hat looked at his friend. 'He is? Since when?'

'Long time now.'

'He ain't dead on the show.'

'No. Not on the show he ain't. Just in real life.'

'Damn.'

'Yeah.'

A respectful silence fell over the group for a moment.

'He was a longshoreman, too,' Fishing Hat said then, crooking a thumb at his buddy. 'Back in the day, we were all over. *All* over. Oregon Avenue, up to South Street, Front Street, Third Street. Not like now. Now I got a lawyer living next door to me. A *lawyer*. There goes the neighborhood.'

Jessica made a few more notes as Cardigans looked closely at Byrne. 'You look familiar,' Cardigans said. 'You ever work the docks?'

'My father did,' Byrne said. 'Thirty-five years.'

Cardigans snapped his fingers. 'Paddy Byrne.'

Byrne nodded.

'You look just like him.' He turned to Fishing Hat. 'Did you know Paddy?'

Fishing Hat shook his head.

'This guy was a legend on Pier 96.' He turned back to Byrne. 'How is he these days?'

'He's good,' Byrne said. 'Thanks for asking.'

'So how come you didn't follow in his footsteps? Get an honest job?'

'The docks are too dangerous for me,' Byrne said. 'And I prefer a higher class of criminal.'

Cardigans laughed. 'Yeah. You're Paddy's boy.'

'So, what else can you tell me about this other victim?' Jessica asked, trying to bring the conversation back around.

Both men shrugged in tandem. 'Not much, 'cept that it was a woman,' Fishing Hat said. 'They locked the place up for years. Guy who owned it couldn't even go back in there. Said he was afraid of ghosts or something. He sold it to some guy from Pittsburgh, who sold it to someone else.'

Jessica looked around. 'What's the neighborhood, guys?'

'Some say Queen Village but they don't know shit.'

'What do *you* say?'

'We say Pennsport. Because it *is* Pennsport. We're south of *Washington*, for Chrissake.'

'Did a detective talk to you guys about that case back in '02?' Jessica asked.

'Just me,' Cardigans said.

'Do you remember their names? The detectives?'

Cardigans shook his head.

'He don't remember his kids' names,' Fishing Hat said. 'And he's only got four of 'em.'

'Did you know the victim?'

'No. I heard she was a real hot number, though. Damn shame.'

The information would be easy enough to find, but probably wasn't relevant. Jessica thanked the two men, got their contact information – names, addresses, phone numbers – and gave them both a business card, along with the standard request for them to call if they thought of anything else.

'You come back anytime,' Fishing Hat said. 'We always have time to talk to pretty young girls.'

Jessica smiled. *Pretty young girls.* She'd come back tomorrow.

JESSICA AND BYRNE RETURNED to the Roundhouse, collated their witness statements, putting them in the binder. While they waited for the coroner's preliminary reports, as well as any forensic findings, they turned their attention to other matters of importance.

They each had a case on which they were working. Both cases had stalled, and there was no worse feeling for a homicide detective than the sense that an investigation was slipping away from them. While Byrne made calls to the four witnesses he needed for the grand-jury probe of Eduardo Robles, just to keep the pot simmering, Jessica looked up some addresses, trying to align the witnesses in another case.

Two weeks earlier a gun had been left at the scene of a drug-related homicide. The weapon had been traced back to a woman named Patricia Lentz, a known drug addict and prostitute.

The Lentz apartment was on North 19th Street near Cecil B. Moore. When Jessica and Byrne arrived, they found the door open, TV blasting, something burning on the stove. The first floor was a haze of vile smoke, a landfill of soiled mattresses, broken furniture, spent crack vials and empty liquor bottles.

They found Patricia Lentz passed out beneath a pile of clothing in the basement. At first Jessica did not think she was going to find a pulse. But the woman had just passed out and, once she'd been revived by paramedics, was taken into custody without incident.

Whereas the suspect was in custody, her apartment had not yet been cleared. Jessica was quite familiar with the layout of these row houses and knew there were two more rooms upstairs. While Byrne turned the barely coherent woman over to the uniformed officers for transport to the Roundhouse, Jessica continued upstairs. She cleared the first small bedroom, and the bathroom. When she walked into the second bedroom she found there was a closet. She eased open the door.

Jessica froze. There, on the floor in front of her, partially hidden by a plastic garbage bag bursting at the seams with rotting trash, was a little boy. No more than two years old. A dark-haired little boy dressed in a ragged T-shirt and diaper. It appeared that he had crawled beneath the garbage for warmth.

Reaching down into the closet, she picked up the boy. He was shivering with fear, miserable in his soiled diaper. There were rashes on his arms and legs.

'It's okay, little man,' Jessica said. 'It's okay.'

On the way out of the house, Jessica found a pile of papers on a card table near the front door. They were mostly unpaid bills, flyers for pizza and Chinese takeout, shut-off notices. Also on the table was a photograph of an infant lying on a dirty bed sheet. Jessica could not mistake those eyes. It was the little boy she had in her arms. She flipped the picture over. It read *Carlos age three months*.

His name was Carlos.

Jessica brought the boy back to the Roundhouse to await a representative from the Department of Human Services. She had stopped along the way and bought diapers, wipes, lotion, powder. It had been a long time since she had done these things with Sophie, but it was like riding a bike: she hadn't forgotten.

Cleaned up, shiny and combed, Carlos sat at one of the desks, on top of a pile of phone books, secured to the chair with an empty ammunition belt. Someone found a Philadelphia Eagles child's sweatshirt. It was a little too big, so they rolled up the sleeves and Scotch-taped them gently around the boy's wrists.

The boy's mother, Patricia Lentz, was booked on first-degree murder charges, and the case was a lock. They had the murder weapon, ballistics matched, and Lentz would not be coming back for a long time. Carlos would have children of his own by the time she got out.

'What's going on with Carlos?' Byrne asked, bringing Jessica back to the present and the new case at hand.

Jessica had to take a second. The last thing you wanted to do in this room, even with your partner, who knew you better than anyone in your life, was display any emotion besides anger.

'Nothing,' Jessica said. 'They still haven't been able to find Patricia Lentz's sister. Word is that she's an even bigger crackhead.'

Jessica knew it was no secret, especially to Kevin Byrne, that she and Vincent had been trying for two years to have another child. Sophie was now seven, and the longer they waited, well, all the books said you really didn't want too much of an age gap between siblings. The very notion of undertaking the monumental task of adopting Carlos was, of course, a ridiculous idea. During daylight hours, anyway. But when Jessica lay awake in the middle of the night it all seemed possible. Then the sun would come up again and she realized it would never happen.

'How is he doing?' Byrne asked.

'Good, I guess,' Jessica said. She really didn't know if that was true or not, but it was the only answer she had.

'If you want, we can stop in at the Department of Human Services and check on him.'

The sooner Jessica let go, the better it would be. Still, she knew what she was going to say. 'Sure. That would be good.'

Before they could discuss it further, Nicci Malone poked her head into the duty room. 'Kevin, you have a call.'

Byrne crossed the room, hit a button, answered. A few moments later he pulled out his notebook, wrote something in it, punched a fist through the air. It was clearly good news. Jessica needed some good news.

Byrne hung up, grabbed his coat. 'That was the ID Unit.'

The ID Unit processed latent fingerprints.

'Are we on?' Jessica asked.

'We are,' Byrne said. 'Our cleanshaven dead man has a name. Kenneth Arnold Beckman.'

ELEVEN

THE BECKMAN HOUSE WAS A GAUNT AND PEELING POSTWAR ROW HOUSE
on West Tioga Street, in the Nicetown area of North Philadelphia.
Nicetown was a blue-collar section of the city that was slowly recov-
ering after three decades of slow decline, a slide culminating in the
Tastykake company moving out of the area in 2007. At one time it
was rumored that Trump Entertainment would be building a casino
on Hunting Park Avenue. It never happened. The only gambling being
done in Nicetown these days was among those residents and store
owners debating whether or not to hang onto their property.

Before leaving the Roundhouse, Jessica asked Josh Bontrager to
run a check on Kenneth Arnold Beckman. Bontrager would call if
there was anything to report.

WHEN JESSICA AND BYRNE pulled to a stop in front of the Beckman
house, near Schuyler Street, it began to rain. The wind picked up, and
when they stepped onto the porch wet leaves gathered at their feet.

Jessica rang the bell three times before noticing that there was a
wire hanging out from the bottom of the rusted panel. The bell didn't
work. A quick look at the crumbling porch, with its leaning support
pillars and brickwork desperately in need of tuck pointing, explained
why. She knocked on the door, gently at first. The second time she

knocked harder. Eventually they heard the deadbolts begin to turn. There were three of them.

The woman who answered the door was a hard forty. Her platinum hair was perm-fried, her make-up looked like it had been applied with a paper towel. She wore black Capri pants and battered pink running shoes. A lighted cigarette hung from the corner of her mouth.

Looking Byrne up and down, she tossed a sideways glance at Jessica.

'Are you Mrs. Beckman?' Byrne asked.

'Well, now,' she replied. 'That would depend on two things, wouldn't it?'

'And what would those two things be?'

'Who you are and what the fuck you want.'

Oh boy, Jessica thought. *We've got a real charmer here.*

Byrne took out his ID, badged the woman. She stared at it far too long. Jessica figured this was an attempt on the woman's part to establish some sort of power dynamic. What the woman didn't know was that Kevin Byrne could outlast a glacier. She looked at Jessica, raising a painted-on eyebrow. Jessica reached into her pocket, showed the woman *her* ID. The woman sniffed, turned back to Byrne.

'Well, that answers one of my questions,' she said.

'May we come in?' Byrne asked.

The woman blinked a few times, as if Byrne was speaking another language. 'Can you hear me?' she asked.

'Ma'am?'

'Can you hear my voice?'

'Yes,' Byrne said. 'I can hear your voice.'

'Good. I hear you too. We can talk right here.'

Jessica sensed Byrne's gloves coming off. He pulled out his notebook, flipped a few pages. 'What's your first name, ma'am?'

Pause. 'Sharon.'

'Is your husband Kenneth Arnold Beckman?'

The woman snorted. 'Husband? That's one way of putting it.'

'Are you married to him, ma'am?'

The woman took a long drag on her cigarette. Jessica noted that the nicotine stains on her fingers reached down to her knuckles. She blew out the smoke, and with it her answer. 'Barely.'

'When was the last time you saw him?'

'Why?'

'Right now I just need you to answer the question, ma'am. I'll explain why in a moment.'

Another drag. Jessica estimated that, if they were going to get through the basic questions at this pace, Sharon Beckman would go through a pack and a half. 'Yesterday afternoon.'

'About what time?'

Another sigh. 'About three o'clock.'

'And where was this?'

'It was at the MGM Grand in Vegas. I'm a dancer there.'

Byrne stared, the woman stared. She rolled her eyes.

'It was right about where you're standing,' she said. 'I think he said something like "Clean the kitchen, you lazy fucking bitch." Real Hallmark moment.'

The wind picked up again, blowing a thin cold rain across the porch. Byrne moved a few feet to his right, making sure that Sharon Beckman caught the rain directly in her face.

'Was he alone at the time?'

'Yeah,' Sharon Beckman said, stepping back a foot. 'For once.'

'And he did not come home last night?'

The woman snorted. 'Why break with tradition?'

Byrne pressed on. 'Does anyone else live here?'

'Just my son.'

My *son*, Jessica thought. *Not* our *son*.

'How old is he?'

The woman smiled. Her teeth were the same color as her tobacco-stained knuckles. 'Why, officer. That would be giving away my age.' When Byrne didn't respond, didn't budge, didn't seem to be weak-kneed by the woman's coquettish charms, she repositioned her scowl, hit her cigarette again, and said, 'He's nineteen. I had him when I was six.'

Byrne made the note. He then asked her what the kid's name was. She told him. Jason Crandall.

'Where does your husband work?'

'*Hey*. You writing a fucking book here? My autobiography, maybe?'

'Ma'am, we're just trying to—'

'No. What you need to do is tell me what this is about or we're done here. I know my rights.'

Jessica knew the notification was coming, so she watched the woman's face as she took in the news. You could tell a lot from the initial reaction to the news that a loved one has been killed. Or even one not so loved.

'Mrs. Beckman, your husband was murdered yesterday.'

The woman drew a sharp intake of breath, but other than that betrayed nothing. Except, perhaps, for a slight shake in her hands, which deposited a long cigarette ash on the floor. She stared out at the street for a moment, turned back. 'How did he get it?'

Get it, Jessica thought. Most people said 'What?' or 'Oh my God' or 'No!' or something like that. *How did he get it?* No, not too many people ask how the deceased became deceased. That usually came a bit later in the conversation.

'May we come in, ma'am?' Byrne said. 'It's getting a little nasty out here.'

The news had undone the woman's resolve, as well as her animosity. Without saying a word, she opened the door and stepped to the side.

They entered the house, a standard porchfront-style row house, large by Philly standards, probably measuring around 1500 square feet on three floors. It was quickly degenerating, already long past its sell-by date.

The living room was directly to the left, with a hallway leading to a kitchen and a stairway at the back of the house. The walls were painted a cheerless, faded baby blue. The furniture was worn, mismatched, spring-shocked. A half-eaten Weight Watchers dinner sat on a coffee table, next to an overflowing ashtray. Cat hair covered nearly every surface. The place smelled like microwave popcorn.

Sharon Beckman did not offer them a seat. Jessica would have passed on that offer anyway.

'Ma'am,' Byrne said. 'We're here because your husband was a victim of homicide. We're trying to find out who did this, and bring that person to justice.'

'Yeah? Well, look in the fucking mirror,' the woman spat.

'I understand your anger,' Byrne continued. 'But if there's anything you can think of that might help us, we would really appreciate it.'

The woman lit another Salem off the first cigarette, held them both for a few moments, one in each hand.

'Can you think of anyone who might have had a problem with your husband?' Byrne asked. 'Someone he owed money to? Someone with whom he had a business problem?'

The woman took a full five seconds to answer. Maybe she did have something to hide.

'Do I need a lawyer?' Sharon Beckman asked. She butted out the short cigarette.

'Have you done anything wrong, Mrs. Beckman?' Byrne asked. It was Cop Speak 101. Standard across the world when police arrive at the lawyer moment.

'Plenty,' she said.

Wrong answer, Jessica thought. The woman was trying to be cute, but she didn't realize that a picture was being painted, and every stroke mattered.

'Well, then, I can't answer your question,' Byrne said. 'If you feel the need for counsel at this time, by all means call your attorney. I *can* tell you that you are not suspected of anything. You are a witness, and a very important witness. All we need to do is ask you a few questions. The more you tell us, the likelier it will be that we can find the person who did this to your husband.'

Jessica made another quick perusal of the room. There were no photographs of the Beckmans on the mantel over the bricked-in fireplace, no soft-focus wedding day portraits in tacky gold-painted frames.

'If you'll just bear with us a little longer,' Byrne continued, 'we'll get the information we need, and we'll leave you to your thoughts and your arrangements.'

Sharon Beckman just stared. Byrne led her through the rest of the standard questions, giving her the standard assurances. He concluded by asking her if she had a photograph of her husband.

While Sharon Beckman was in the hallway, going through a legal-sized cardboard box, looking for the photograph, the front door opened.

The kid who entered looked younger than nineteen. Stringy blond hair, surfer cool, hooded, stoned eyes. When he saw Byrne he must have figured him for a cop, and he shoved his right hand deep into his baggy shorts. Dope pocket.

'How ya doin?' the kid mumbled.

'Good, thanks,' Byrne said. 'Are you Jason?'

The kid looked up, shocked, like there was no way that Byrne could have possibly gotten this information. 'Yeah.' Barely audible. The kid leaned back on his heels, as if that might increase the distance between them. Jessica could smell the marijuana on his clothes from ten feet away.

'Kenny's dead,' Sharon Beckman said, walking back into the room, a pair of old snapshots in her hand. She handed them to Jessica.

Jason stared at his mother, blinking. It was as if the words hadn't yet reached his brain. 'Dead?'

'Yeah. Like in not alive anymore?'

Jessica looked at the kid. No reaction.

Over the next few minutes Byrne asked Jason the basic questions, got the expected answers. Jason said he had not seen his stepfather in more than three days.

'Once again, we're sorry for your loss,' Byrne said to them both, putting away his notebook. He dropped a pair of business cards on the cluttered coffee table. 'If you think of anything that might help us, please call.'

THEY WALKED THE HALF-BLOCK to the car, adrift on their own thoughts, sizing up the subdued reactions of Beckman's widow and stepson. It was not the usual response they got from notification, to say the least.

The temperature had dropped a few degrees since they had entered the Beckman house. The rain continued, getting colder. For the first time that year, it felt as if it might snow.

IN THE PARKING LOT at the Roundhouse they saw Josh Bontrager getting into one of the detective cars. Spotting them, Bontrager closed the door and crossed the lot. Dennis Stansfield, already in the car, wisely stayed put.

'What's up, Josh?' Byrne asked.

'Have you made notification yet?'

'Just did. What do you have?'

'I ran Kenneth Beckman,' Bontrager said. 'A couple of things jumped out.'

'Such as?'

'Well, at one time he was a person of interest.'

Bontrager meant that the deceased had been looked at by the police for some sort of crime.

'What was the job?' Jessica asked.

'A homicide.'

Jessica felt her pulse kick up a notch. 'This guy was looked at for a murder? When was this?'

'2002.'

'How far did the investigation go?'

'They had him in, but I guess he didn't roll,' Bontrager said. 'The detective working the case kept an eye on the guy for a few years, made a few more notes, but then it went cold. Nothing in the file since '06.'

'Who was the victim?'

Bontrager pulled out his notebook. 'A nineteen-year-old girl named Antoinette Chan. Cause of death was multiple blunt-force trauma. Weapon was a claw hammer found at the scene. The weapon had been wiped clean of prints.'

'What was the date?' Jessica asked.

Bontrager flipped a few pages. 'March 21, 2002.'

A cold finger traced a path along Jessica's spine. It was the date that the old codgers had mentioned earlier. She shot a look at Byrne, who also seemed transfixed by the information.

'I'm going to take a ride over to Record Storage, get the whole story,' Bontrager said.

'We'll do it,' Byrne said. 'Check out the next of kin in the Chan family, see where they are, who they are. If they held Beckman responsible they may be worth looking at.'

'No problem.'

Josh Bontrager got into the car, drove away, a stone-faced Dennis Stansfield in the passenger seat.

'What do you think?' Jessica asked.

Byrne took a few moments to answer. He absently ran a finger over the small V-shaped scar located above his right eye, a keloid souvenir of the time he had been grazed by a bullet years ago. Jessica knew this meant the wheels were turning.

'I think we need to see that original file.' He looked at his watch. 'But first I want to have another word with the lovely and talented Mrs. Beckman.' He looked back at Jessica. 'Funny she didn't mention any of this.'

'Right. When I asked her if she knew who might have done this and she said "Look in the fucking mirror" I didn't really get it. Now I do. She blames the police.'

'What a rarity,' Byrne said. 'And she seemed so nice.'

'Real debutante,' Jessica said. 'I'll run checks on her and the stoned kid. See where they were and what they were doing in March '02.'

'I'll meet you at Record Storage,' Byrne said. 'Call me if she has any wants or warrants. I don't care if Sharon Beckman did just lose her husband. I'd love to toss her in a cage for a while.'

'Oh, please,' Jessica said. 'You just like putting women in handcuffs.'

I N THE FIRST TEN MINUTES AFTER THE POLICE LEFT HER HOUSE, SHARON Beckman found she couldn't move. She stood by the front door, paralyzed.

Jason went back out. God only knew what he did these days. What Jason had not told the cops was that the last time he had seen Kenny the two had gotten into a fist fight. The last thing Jason had said to his stepfather was 'If you ever touch me again I'm going to fucking kill you.'

That was not something you told the police. *She* knew Jason would never do anything like that, but *they* didn't.

The house was quiet.

Kenny was dead.

Sharon knew she was supposed to be feeling something, something akin to grief, something like heartache, but she didn't. All she felt was a faint cold fear. And the knowledge that she had to move. Fast.

From right when she'd first met Kenny, Sharon had known it was all going to fall apart one day. It wasn't like she didn't know who he was when they'd met, what kind of life she was getting into. She was no angel herself. But eight years ago, when Kenny had robbed all those houses and put himself on the police radar, she'd known a day like this would come.

When she had set fire to the house on Lenox Avenue, back in 2002, destroying all that evidence, she'd known she'd pay for it some day. Today. She had been a little sorry that the whole block had gone up in flames, but no one had got hurt. She didn't lose much sleep over it. There was no love lost between her and her neighbors on Lenox Avenue anyway. *Fucking lowlife crackheads.*

She turned around three times in the living room, trying to organize her thoughts, trying to think straight.

She should have left a long time ago. When cops followed up on things it was a clear sign that they had you in their sights. Cops always knew a lot more than they let on. It was like those jobs she used to go on with her father when she was small. Her dad would work on somebody's plumbing, and when he was all done he'd turn the water back on and slide a sheet of newspaper under the pipes. If one drop of water fell, blotting out on the paper, the job was shit. Her father would always tear it out and start over. If there was one solitary drop there was certain to be more.

Same thing with cops.

Drip, drip, drip.

Then they had you.

Kenny had put all the new stolen merchandise into a storage locker on Linden Avenue. He'd learned the first time not to keep anything in the house. They both had. She wasn't sure what he had in there these days and that was fine with her. The less she knew, the better.

Sharon also knew what Kenny had done to that girl in 2002, even as she tried hard to block it out of her mind. Of course, there wasn't a jury in the world that would give a shit. They had gotten away with it once, but now that Kenny was dead everything was going to fall on her like a load of bricks. There was no way she could deal with this on her own. She knew at least a dozen people who might have wanted to do Kenny in, a dozen people who'd had a beef with him, and once the police realized this they were going to see her as a link. It was only a matter of time until they revisited the Antoinette Chan case. She knew how hard cops worked on burglaries. They didn't give up until they had you in a jail cell.

Murder?

Forget it.

Sharon ran upstairs. She would load the car with what she could, go find Jason. She would get the keys to the Master lock that was on the door at the storage locker, throw them in the Delaware River, and she and her son would be long gone.

But where would they go? They couldn't go to her sister's in Toledo. That would be the first place they'd look. She had exactly eight hundred twenty-six dollars to her name. Plus whatever was in the coin jar, plus whatever was in the gas tank.

Sharon was only forty-four. Still young. Still had her looks, or whatever looks she'd had to begin with. She'd start a new life. Meet a man with a real job.

Kenny was dead.

Before she could get her things out of the drawers in the upstairs bedroom she heard a noise.

'Jason?' No answer.

She listened for a few more moments, heard nothing. Must have been the brats next door, she thought. One day they'd thrown a basket-ball against an adjoining wall for three straight hours. She wouldn't miss them.

She grabbed her two battered suitcases from the top shelf of the bedroom closet, began to stuff them with clothing. She soon realized she would need some big plastic garbage bags to take it all.

Sharon ran down the stairs, her mind racing in a hundred different directions. When she turned the corner toward the kitchen she saw the shadow on the wall. She stopped, spun around, her heart pounding.

'Jason, we—'

It wasn't Jason.

THIRTEEN

THE BUILDING AT 31ST AND MARKET STREETS WHERE OLD POLICE records were kept had once been the offices and publishing plant of the *Evening Bulletin*. The *Bulletin*, published from 1847 to 1982, was at one time the largest evening newspaper in the United States.

Now the massive and deceptively benign-looking building was fenced and sealed like Fort Knox, with concertina wire ringing the exposed public areas. The enormous brick wall that faced the parking lot rose more than four stories and boasted only five small windows near the roofline. A dozen or so parking-lot lights jutted from the wall like rusted bowsprits.

Jessica signed in at the gate, drove in, parked. She was about twenty minutes late, but had not spotted Byrne's van. She decided to wait in the car.

Before leaving the Roundhouse she had run Sharon Beckman and Jason Crandall through the databases. The kid had a misdemeanor possession charge from last year, a charge that was dropped when Jason did community service.

Sharon Beckman had no record.

Jessica thought about how the case was developing. The bizarre condition of Kenneth Beckman's corpse was still a mystery and indicated something that festered deep in the heart of the killer, something personal and twisted. She thought about the paper band wrapped around the victim's head, the way the cut traversed the forehead, the way the—

There was a loud sound, inches from her left ear, a cracking noise that made her jump. She spun in her seat, her hand automatically unsnapping her holster.

Byrne had tapped her window with his ring. Jessica slowly rolled down the window, making him wait in the drizzling rain.

'This is how people get shot, you know,' Jessica said.

'I could use the rest.'

She took her time getting out of the car, driving home her point. A minute later they entered the building, walked over to the elevators, shaking off the rain.

'Did you talk to Sharon Beckman again?' Jessica asked.

Byrne shook his head. 'She wasn't home,' Byrne said. 'Neither was Spicoli.'

Referencing the Sean Penn role in *Fast Times at Ridgemont High*, Byrne was, of course, referring to Jason Crandall. Jessica had no idea where Kevin Byrne's frame of cultural references began and ended.

IN THE EXTENSIVE BASEMENT were records for thousands of crimes, some going back two hundred years, the residue of a city's shame: names, dates, weapons, wounds, witnesses. What was absent was the evidence of loss. There was no record to be found here of a father's tears, a son's loneliness, or a grandmother's empty Sundays.

Instead, here were block after block of huge steel shelving racks, some reaching twenty feet high, each packed firm with thousands of cardboard boxes, each box tagged with a white label detailing name of the deceased, case number, and year.

They split up the Beckman files. Byrne read the witness statements and forensic reports, while Jessica went through the original police reports and the notes written by the lead detective.

Just inside the binder was a picture of Antoinette Chan. She'd been a pretty girl, with flawless skin and a beguiling smile. Jessica moved on to the police report on Beckman.

Kenneth Arnold Beckman, born in 1970, was originally from the

Brewerytown area of Philadelphia. At the time of Antoinette Chan's murder he had worked as a handyman for a pair of apartment complexes in Camden, and had lived in the Nicetown/Tioga area on Lenox Avenue.

By the age of twenty-nine he had been arrested five times for breaking and entering, twice convicted of possession of stolen merchandise.

In 2001 Beckman took his ten-year-old stepson Jason trick-or-treating on North 18th Street between Westmoreland and Venango. They went door to door, with Beckman accompanying the boy to each stoop. Some of the people in the neighborhood later remarked about how Beckman hovered a little too close to the door, how he seemed to be looking into the houses with a little too much interest as the little boy received his candy.

Over the next five months there were six burglaries in the neighborhood, all occurring during daylight hours when the residents were at work. Each time the same sort of items were stolen: cameras, jewelry, cash, MP3 players. Nothing too big to fit in a pillowcase.

A pair of astute divisional detectives noticed the pattern and created a photo lineup of people living in a one-mile radius of the break-ins who had a criminal history of burglaries. One of the people in that lineup was Kenneth Beckman.

After getting positive IDs of Beckman as someone who had come to neighborhood houses on Halloween, the detectives placed him under surveillance. Within a few days they followed him to a pawnshop in Chinatown, a known address for fencing stolen items. In forty-eight hours they set up a sting operation, with a detective posing as an employee of the shop. But Beckman, perhaps sensing a problem, never returned.

In mid-March 2002 they received a call from a young woman they had spoken to earlier, a woman named Antoinette Chan, the daughter of one of the burglary victims. She said she had gone down to her basement for the first time in a few weeks to do laundry and had seen a shoe print in the small lavatory off the furnace room. Whoever had broken into her house had come through the basement window. It appeared that the burglar had made a comfort stop. The original investigators had never looked in the lavatory.

The shoe print matched a size twelve Frye boot. Surveillance photos of Kenneth Beckman revealed him wearing the exact model.

Detectives visited Beckman's place of employment, only to discover that he had left.

When detectives arrived at the Beckman house on Lenox Avenue, search warrant in hand, they found a pair of PFD ladder trucks on the scene, and the block of row houses – four in all – ablaze. The old wooden structures burned to the ground in a matter of hours.

Across the street, sitting on a curb, smoking a cigarette, was Sharon Beckman. There was little doubt in anyone's mind about who had started the blaze, and no doubt at all why. Unfortunately for the investigators, there was no direct evidence. Sharon was not formally questioned or charged.

According to police, later that night Kenneth Beckman kidnapped Antoinette Chan, brought her to a location in South Philly and bludgeoned her to death. When Beckman was found in a motel in Allentown three days later and brought in for questioning, he dummied up and requested a lawyer.

Without any witnesses, and without any opportunity to search his house, all charges against Kenneth Arnold Beckman were dropped.

And now he was dead.

Jessica opened the folder with the crime-scene photos and felt her heart leap. 'Holy *shit*.'

'What?' Byrne asked.

Jessica put two of the Antoinette Chan crime-scene photos on the table, took out her iPhone, opened the photos folder, swiped over to her most recent photographs. She put the phone on the table, next to the printed pictures.

There was no mistake.

The man they had found dead that morning, Kenneth Arnold Beckman, the lead suspect in an eight-year-old murder case – that case being the bludgeoning to death of a young woman named Antoinette Chan – was posed inside a building on Federal, the same place where Antoinette Chan had been found.

Eight years before it became the Beckman crime scene it had been the Chan crime scene.

'The suspect in an unsolved homicide gets murdered himself and placed in the same location as his victim,' Jessica summed up.

'Yep,' Byrne said.

'As in *exactly* the same place. Posed in *exactly* the same position as the original victim.' She held up both the photograph and her cell-phone. 'Kevin, these are absolutely identical crime-scene photos, only the second murder, our murder, was eight years later.'

'Eight and change, but yeah,' Byrne said. 'These are the facts as we know them.'

The two detectives looked at each other, knowing that this case had just crossed the line. It was now more than a vendetta murder, more than some act committed in the fiery grip of passion.

Jessica glanced again at the photographs. Some inner bell began to peal. In Philadelphia's history, any large city's history, there were many unsolved murders, victims of insanity and fury who for years went unavenged, evil echoing across time.

There was just such a legacy in the City of Brotherly Love, shame and guilt and madness that ran beneath the cobblestone streets like a blood river. Staring at photographs taken eight years apart, at the ragged flesh of two victims connected in a way neither she nor her partner yet understood, Detective Jessica Balzano wondered how much of this history they were about to see.

FOURTEEN

I FLOAT IN DARKNESS. I HAVE ALWAYS BEEN NOCTURNAL, ELUDING SLEEP, embraced by waking dreams.

Here the screams are scuttled and still. It is a place of repose and reflection, a place of wintry silence. For many years I have felt at home here.

I place the body on the ground. It is the third note. There are eight in this measure. Harmony and melody. I prop the leg against the low headstone. The music swells as I leap into the air, bringing down my full weight. The bone snaps. The sound echoes across the wet granite, the moonlit grass. I take the recorder in my hand, play back the sound. The cracking of bone is bright percussion.

I move among the dead, listening. The departed speak softly to me, etudes of grace and humility. Soon my movements become fluid, an exaltation of this moment, a dance of death. Le danse macabre. *Around and around I twirl. I am free here.*

> Death at midnight plays a dance-tune,
> Zig, zig, zag, on his violin.

I spin among the deceased, thinking about the next days, days leading up to All Hallow's Eve, when all the world's departed will rejoice.

Soon we will dance, the detective and I. We will dance, and in our embrace we will find that we are of the same heart, the same mind, two damaged souls sipping from a tarnished cup of blood.

TWO

SCHERZO

FIFTEEN

TUESDAY, OCTOBER 26

L UCINDA DOUCETTE LOOKED AT THE BATHROOM FLOOR, THINKING:
I live in a world full of pigs.

Le Jardin, a modern 300-room hotel near Seventeenth and Sansom streets, in the heart of Center City, was a monolithic gray edifice with angular black wrought-iron railings around its seventy balconies, a model of European modernity at the corner of what was now being considered Philadelphia's new French Quarter. Managed by a Belgian multinational firm that also managed properties in Paris, Monaco and London, Le Jardin, which had been completely renovated in 2005, catered to the upscale business and leisure traveler, with its highly polished mahogany trim, its frosted French doors, its expensive French amenities.

In addition to the guest rooms there were six suites on the penultimate floor, all of them with views of the city, along with a presidential suite on the top floor that had breathtaking views of the Delaware River and beyond.

For Lucinda Doucette, along with everyone else who worked in hotel housekeeping, the views were less than scenic, although sometimes just as breathtaking in their own right.

Like all hotels, Le Jardin lived and died by its 'star' ratings – Orbitz, Hotels.com, Expedia, Hotwire, Priceline.

And while the management looked to online sites for input and feedback, there were only two accommodation ratings that really mattered: Mobil and AAA.

Mobil 'shopped' hotels every few years. The American Automobile Association, on the other hand, was far more exacting, some might say stingy, with their Diamond ratings, and thus were the most feared and respected of all the organizations on whose assessment of accommodations, dining, and travel the success of any hotel depended. Disappoint AAA, and the drop in business was palpable within months.

What it all boiled down to was comfort, staff, accommodation, and cleanliness.

Le Jardin was rightfully considered an upscale establishment, consistently rated at four stars, and this was something the management guarded fiercely.

Lucy Doucette had worked in housekeeping at Le Jardin for just over a year, starting a few days after her eighteenth birthday. When she first got on staff she found herself visiting the various travel websites with some regularity, checking the guest reviews, the user opinions, especially in the area of cleanliness. Granted, if she wasn't doing her job, she would certainly have heard about it from the director of housekeeping, a chilly, no-nonsense woman named Audrey Balcombe who, it was rumored, held a Master's Degree in communications from the *Université d'Avignon* and had apprenticed as a hotelier with Kurt Wachtveitl, the legendary former general manager of the Mandarin Oriental, Bangkok.

Still, Lucy took pride in what she did, and wanted to hear about it, good or bad, from the guests themselves. One review on tripadvisor.com had given Le Jardin a single star (there was no option for zero stars, or this guest reviewer certainly would have used it) in the area of cleanliness, going so far as to compare the hotel to a locker room at an inner-city YMCA. The reviewer complained specifically about entering the bathroom upon checking in, only to find the toilet unflushed. Lucy thought that the guy who'd written and uploaded the review, not the toilet, was the one full of shit – there was virtually no chance of this ever happening – but nonetheless, for the next two weeks, she worked doubly hard on her floor, the twelfth floor, checking and then rechecking the toilets before clearing the rooms for the arriving guests.

Most of the time her work ethic was its own reward – God knew the pay was not – but sometimes, not often, there were unexpected perks.

One guest, about five months earlier – an elderly, refined man – stayed for six days and when he checked out he left Lucy a one-hundred-dollar tip beneath the pillow, along with a note that said *To the girl with the haunted eyes: Good job.*

Haunted eyes, Lucy thought at the time. She wore sunglasses to and from work for weeks afterward.

Right now Lucy wanted to choke the man staying in 1212. In addition to the spilled coffee on the chair, the stained pillowcases, the broken beer bottles in the tub, the overturned breakfast tray, the hair-clogged sink, and the shampoo and conditioner bottles which had somehow ended up under the bed along with two pairs of stained and streaked underwear, every towel was soaking wet and had been piled on the floor. And although she was used to this, this time it was particularly gross. In one of the towels was a copious amount of what looked like vomit.

Jesus, what a pig.

Time to move. Lucy had four more rooms to clean before her lunch break and less than two hours to do it. Management knew exactly when she clocked into a room. If she took longer than forty minutes, they noticed.

In a given day, each room attendant had fourteen rooms to clean. If you were fast – and Lucy, at nineteen, had energy to burn – you could buy 'credits,' or other rooms to clean. Lucy often did. She was good at her job. She did not engage the guests in a lot of small talk in the hallways, she was always courteous and polite, and with a little make-up she was not that hard to look at. With her cornflower-blue eyes, her butterscotch hair and slender figure, she never had a problem fitting into her uniform and more than once had caught the male guests following her movement down the long hallways at the hotel.

Although the work was not particularly demanding, it was mentally taxing. The difference between a three-and-a-half-star and a four-star hotel was often in the attitude and the details.

Some things were out of the control of the employees – the quality of the linens and towels, for instance, or whether or not to include mouthwash in the bathroom, or services like an evening turn-down – while other things were clearly in the purview of the 'ladies' in housekeeping.

Today there was a convention checking into the hotel, booked for three days. Something called *Société Poursuite*, a group of people, as Lucy understood it, who looked into unsolved murders as some sort of strange hobby. They had purchased a third of all the rooms, including the entire twelfth floor.

Using her finely tuned sense of logic, Lucy deduced that the word *Société* meant Society. She just hoped the other word didn't stand for Pig.

As she finished Room 1210, Lucy thought about her lunchtime appointment that day.

She had seen so many so-called professionals in the past nine years, so many people who thought they knew what was wrong with her. She had even taken part in a pilot program on regression therapy at the University of Pennsylvania Hospital. Despite Lucy having no money to pay for the treatment, after three separate interviews they had agreed to take her. It hadn't gone well. For five straight days she'd sat in a group of eight people who'd pretty much talked about how, in previous lives, they were raped by Attila the Hun or played footsie with Marie Antoinette, or swapped spit with John the Baptist's severed head. *Yuck.* They had not really understood her problem. Lucy had yet to meet anyone who did.

She did meet some nice people there. The man who died and was brought back to life. The woman who was hit in the head and wandered around the city for three whole months, not knowing who she was.

Lucy had also been to a behavioral psychologist – exactly ten times. Her medical benefits at the hotel allowed her to see someone in the mental health field ten times in a calendar year, paying only her co-pay, which was twenty-five dollars. She could barely afford that.

Today, if she was lucky, all that was going to change. Today she was going to see the Dreamweaver.

She had found his card just sitting on her cart one day, probably tossed there by a passing guest. For some reason she had put it in her pocket and kept it. Just a week earlier she'd called the number out of the blue and had a brief conversation with the man, who had told her what he did.

He said he helped people explore their dreams. He claimed he could make her nightmares go away. She had made an appointment with him, an appointment for today at noon.

Lucy smoothed the top of the bedspread, scanned the room. Perfect. But while the room was finished, she was not.

She walked to the closet, stepped inside, and closed the door. She sat down, took the blindfold out of her pocket, wrapped it around her eyes, and tied it at the back of her head.

The darkness drew silently around her, and she welcomed it.

It had been this way for nine years, ever since the ground trembled beneath her feet, the devil had taken her hand, and three days of her life had been stolen.

WHILE LUCY DOUCETTE SAT in the closet, the ghosts of her past swirling around her, a man entered the hotel lobby, twelve floors below.

As with many who were on their way to Le Jardin this day, his interests ran to the morbid, the darker sides of human nature, the bleak and terrifying landscapes of the sociopathic mind. His specific interests were the kidnapping and murder of young girls, the mindset of the pedophile.

He would be renting Room 1208. The room had a history, a sinister fable with which the man was intimate.

Room 1208 was, of course, on the twelfth floor.

Lucinda Doucette's floor.

SIXTEEN

AT JUST AFTER TEN O'CLOCK JESSICA AND BYRNE GOT A CALL FROM THE Medical Examiner's office. The Kenneth Beckman autopsy had been scheduled for nine o'clock that morning, but Tom Weyrich's message said there was something he wanted the detectives to see before the doctor started the cut.

On the way to the ME's office Jessica made a call to the Department of Human Services. She was told that Carlos had slept through the night – for the first time in two weeks – and was up and playing. Jessica hung up, revisited by the feeling of paralysis, the feeling that, if she didn't make a move on this, Carlos would slip into the system. She had wanted to discuss adoption with Vincent but with the upcoming move on top of them and all the stress involved with that, she had not seen an opening.

Maybe she would bring it up tonight, she thought. Maybe she would soften Vincent up with a night of inebriated, lamp-smashing sex.

THE PHILADELPHIA MEDICAL EXAMINER'S OFFICE was located on University Avenue. The purview of the office, among other things, was to investigate and determine the cause in all sudden, violent deaths in Philadelphia County, including homicides, suicides, accidents, and drug-related deaths.

In recent years, the MEO had investigated an average of six thousand cases of death annually, of which almost fifty percent required a post-mortem examination. Other functions of the MEO included positive identification, preparation of autopsy reports, and expert testimony in court, as well as grief assistance for family members.

While Jessica and Byrne waited in the intake room next to the autopsy theaters, they were serenaded by the constant zap of insects, courtesy of the large rectangular blue bug light on the wall. The continuous drone of bugs, mostly blowflies, being flash-fried was maddening.

Jessica checked the schedule on the wall. It included the autopsies performed the previous week. Tom Weyrich approached them.

'I don't get it, Tom,' Jessica said. 'There're twelve autopsies and only eleven names.'

'You don't want to know,' Weyrich said.

'See, now I *have* to know,' Jessica said. 'It's my naturally curious nature.'

Weyrich ran his hand over his chin. Jessica noticed that he had cut himself no fewer than four times while shaving that morning. 'You sure?'

'Dish it.'

'Okay, last week we get a call from Penn. It seems someone threw an internal organ onto the front steps of Tanenbaum Hall.'

The Nicole E. Tanenbaum Hall was on the campus of the University of Pennsylvania and contained, among other things, the Biddle Law Library.

'Somebody threw body parts?'

Weyrich nodded. 'What a world, huh?'

'What a *city*.'

'We still had to treat it like normal John Doe remains. We ran all our standard pathology tests, did a standard cut.'

'I still don't understand why there's no name on the sheet. Is it because you haven't been able to make an ID on the remains?' Jessica asked.

'Yes and no.'

'Tom.'

'It was a cow stomach.'

Jessica looked at Byrne. Byrne smiled, shook his head.

'One question,' Jessica said.

'Sure.'

'Is it still a John Doe, or is it now an Elsie Doe?'

'Laugh it up,' Weyrich said. 'This job put both my kids through Villanova.'

Jessica lifted both hands in surrender.

'I have something to show you,' Weyrich said.

He wheeled a body into the center of the intake room.

THE BODY OF KENNETH ARNOLD BECKMAN rested on the gleaming stainless steel table, face up, covered to just below the chest with a sheet.

Weyrich directed the overhead light to the victim's right hand. He slipped on a glove, gently pried back the fingers.

'I wanted you to see this,' he said.

There, on the pad of the right index finger, was a small drawing, measuring approximately half an inch by one inch.

'What is that?' Jessica asked.

'It's a tattoo, believe it or not.'

'On his finger?'

'On his finger,' Weyrich said. 'When they cleaned him up to print him they found it.'

Jessica berated herself for not seeing it at the scene. She put on her glasses, looked closely. It looked like a highly stylized drawing of a lion. The colors were bright and primary, the outlines thick, the overall effect not unlike that of an illustration in a child's coloring book.

'I've read this guy's sheet,' Jessica said. 'He didn't strike me as the cartoon type.'

'It takes *all* types,' Weyrich said. 'I've taken a sample and sent it to the lab. They should be able to tell us the type of ink fairly soon.'

'You took a sample?' Jessica asked. 'A skin sample?'

'This is not a regular tattoo. It's a temporary tattoo.'

Jessica looked again. At this distance, and with skin art this size, she really couldn't tell the difference.

Weyrich handed her a large magnifying glass. Jessica looked again at the image of the lion. The ink, and its rich color, stood in bright contrast to the blood-leached pallor of the dead man's skin.

'It's not still wet, is it?'

'No,' Weyrich said. 'But it is new. I'd say it's been there less than seventy-two hours.'

When Jessica had been small, she used to go to a variety store in South Philly and buy little tattoos that she could apply simply by getting wet and pressing them on her skin. They usually washed off with one or two runs through the sprinkler, or a single dip in a pool.

'Does he have any other tattoos?'

'Surprisingly, no,' Weyrich said.

'Why do you think this is relevant?'

Weyrich directed Jessica to look with the magnifying glass at an area on the victim's left shoulder. Jessica repositioned the glass and saw a slight smudge there, a smear no more than a quarter-inch square or so in size. It was the same color as the yellow in the lion tattoo.

'I think this was done at the same time,' Weyrich said. 'I think the doer may have applied the tattoo, then made this smudge when he turned the body over.'

Jessica looked closely. There were no ridge marks. It was not a fingerprint, indicating that the killer might have worn gloves.

'Which brings us to the two other pieces of artwork on the body,' Weyrich said. He pulled down the sheet to reveal a section just above the rib cage on the right side. There were the two unmistakable marks left by a Taser, deep purple bruises looking like a vampire's bite.

'He was Tasered,' Jessica said.

Weyrich nodded. Jessica calculated the planning involved in this homicide. The cutting of the man's forehead, the measured puncture wound, the shaving of the entire body. It removed the crime from any heat of passion, certainly. This was cold, deliberate, calculated.

'What about the shaving?' Jessica asked.

'I think it was done pre-mortem, without benefit of any emollient or shaving cream.' Weyrich pointed to a few areas where the skin was deeply abraded. 'I believe it was done quickly with a hair trimmer, as opposed to a rotary-style shaver, which means he had to press a little harder. Still, he didn't get it all.'

Jessica made notes. Byrne just listened. This was their usual routine at the ME's office.

Weyrich then moved the glass to the victim's forehead. He pointed to the lateral laceration at the top. In the brutal light it looked like a mortal wound, as though the killer had been attempting to take off the top of Kenneth Beckman's head.

'This was done with a straight razor or a scalpel,' he said. 'Our guy took care not to cut too deeply. There is some level of skill here. The cut on the right ear was not nearly so clean.'

Jessica looked at the victim's ear. It had congealed into a scabrous brown mass. 'Can we tell if the cutter is right-handed or left-handed?' she asked.

'Not from this wound, I'm afraid. If he is right-handed, he would most likely start at the left side and draw right. That would be the most natural movement. But only if he was straddling the body.' Weyrich leaned over the cadaver and mimicked the motion of drawing a blade over the victim's forehead from left to right. 'Now, if he was up here . . .' Weyrich moved to the head of the table, putting the top of the victim's head near his waist. 'He could achieve the same result as a left-hander, drawing the blade right to left.'

'And this was done while the victim was still alive?' Byrne said.

'Yes.'

'How did he keep him still?'

'As well you might ask.' Weyrich pointed out four areas where there were small plum-colored bruises. On either side of the forehead, just above the temple, were contact marks in a circular shape, about a half-inch in diameter. There were also marks on either side of the lower jaw. 'His head was held in place at these four points.'

'With some kind of vice grip?' Byrne asked.

'A little more finesse than that, I believe. And a lot more expensive. I think it may have been a device similar to a surgical clamp. Whenever there is any cranial surgery performed, it is imperative, of course, that the patient be immobilized. Fortunately, we do not have that problem in *this* office. Our patients tend not to fidget much.'

'Do you think our boy has some medical training?'

'Could be.'

Jessica studied the bruises, thought about the horror of having one's head locked into a device. 'Where do you get an item like that?'

'It's pretty specialized. And expensive. I'll get you a list of medical suppliers.'

Jessica made a note to follow up.

'One other thing,' Weyrich said. He pointed at the puncture wound in the forehead. He handed back the magnifying glass to Jessica. She looked at the wound. 'What am I looking for?'

'See the area right around the puncture? The coloration?'

Under magnification the puncture did not look like such a clean wound, but rather twisted, shredded tissue, exploding outward like a tiny lava eruption. Jessica saw a small ring around the puncture that appeared to be red. An unnaturally *bright* shade of red. 'This is not dried blood, I take it.'

'No,' Weyrich said. 'That would be much darker. This was made with a Magic Marker of some sort. Maybe a felt-tip marker.'

Jessica looked up at Byrne, then back. 'A Magic Marker?'

Weyrich nodded.

'You're saying the killer marked the spot first?'

Weyrich nodded, politely smug in his findings. 'I've seen stranger things.'

'Why would he do something like that?'

Weyrich took the magnifying glass back, pulled the sheet over the body. 'That's above my pay grade, detective,' he said. 'You are the *chef de partie* here. I'm only the *commis*.'

WHEN THEY STEPPED OUT of the MEO, David Albrecht was waiting for them. For any number of reasons he had not been allowed inside the morgue.

'What did I miss?' Albrecht asked.

'Bunch of dead people,' Byrne said. 'I yelled "action," but nobody moved.'

David Albrecht soon dialed into the fact that he wasn't going to get anything out of Kevin Byrne on this matter. He turned to Jessica.

'Where to?' he asked.

'We're going to grab some coffee,' Jessica said. 'You're welcome to join us.'

'Thanks.'

'You can get some shots of us looking at a menu, putting cream in coffee, fighting over the check,' Byrne said.

Albrecht laughed. 'Okay, okay. I'll just ramp up the suspense in post.'

Byrne smiled, winked at Jessica. It wasn't a thaw, but it was a start. Jessica knew that Byrne was not particularly keen on being followed around with a camera. Neither was she.

Albrecht left his van at the ME's office and traveled with the detectives. They drove down University Avenue.

'So, are you getting what you want?' Jessica asked.

'Pretty much,' Albrecht said. 'I was at the district attorney's office earlier this morning. I'm running two story lines at the same time. I'm shooting two of the DAs at work as well. I don't think it's ever been done before.'

'You mean following both police detectives and district attorneys?' Byrne asked.

'Exactly.'

'You mean like every episode of *Law and Order*?'

Albrecht went quiet.

'I'm sure you'll put your own stamp on it,' Jessica said, shooting Byrne a look.

THEY STOPPED AT A coffee shop on Spruce Street. Albrecht, sitting two booths away, really did get footage of them looking at menus. On the second cup, he put down the camera and pulled up a chair to the booth.

'So we're not your only stars?' Byrne asked.

'No,' Albrecht said, smiling. 'I am painting a vast and varied canvas.'

'I've been meaning to ask you,' Byrne said. 'Did you shoot any footage of the crowd at the Federal Street scene?'

'Yeah,' Albrecht said. 'It came out good.'

'We'd like to take a look at it, if you don't mind. Maybe our bad guy showed up to gloat.'

'Right, right,' Albrecht said, nodding. 'I'll get that on a disk right away.'

'We'd appreciate it.'

The waitress came over with three cups of espresso. They weren't for the table. They were all for Albrecht. Jessica and Byrne exchanged a glance.

Albrecht saw the look, shrugged. 'Well, you know the old saying. *Sleep is a symptom of caffeine deprivation.*' He knocked back one of the small cups in a single gulp.

Byrne tapped the DV camera on the seat next to him. 'So tell me, how did you get into this?'

Albrecht stirred sugar into his second cup of espresso. 'Well, it was probably my dad. He used to take me to the movies a lot when I was a kid. He was big in the arts, you know. For some reason I gravitated to documentaries at a young age.'

'Do you remember the film you liked the most?'

'I think the movie that did it for me was called *In the Shadow of the Stars.*' He looked between Jessica and Byrne. 'Did either of you ever see it?'

Jessica had not. She told him so.

'That was the documentary on the choristers in the opera?' Byrne asked.

'Yes!' Albrecht said. He looked around. 'Sorry. That was loud, wasn't it?'

Byrne smiled. 'Not in this place.'

'Well, when I saw that – at the ripe old age of seven – I saw the possibilities of making movies about regular people. Nothing bores me more than celebrity. I never watch television.'

'That movie seems a little highbrow for a kid,' Byrne said.

Albrecht downed a second espresso, nodded. 'Like I said, my dad was big into the arts. I think we saw that film at a fundraiser. I was never the same afterwards. I was especially impressed with the music. The possibilities of sound editing in particular.'

Jessica suddenly made the connection. 'Wait a minute. Your father was Jonas Albrecht?'

'Yes.'

For more than twenty-five years Jonas Albrecht had been a force of nature in Philadelphia arts, business, and politics – one of the directors of the prestigious Pennsylvania Society. He was a wealthy man, having made his fortune in real estate. He founded a number of organizations, and was deeply involved with the Philadelphia Orchestra until he was tragically killed in a violent carjacking in 2003. Jessica had been on the force at the time, but it was before she had joined the homicide unit. She wasn't sure if the case had ever been closed.

'It was a terrible tragedy,' Byrne said. 'We're sorry for your loss.'

Albrecht nodded. 'Thank you.'

We are the sum of our experiences, Jessica thought. David Albrecht might not be doing what he was doing now if it had not been for the terrible tragedy that had befallen his father. It had taken Jessica a long time to realize that, if it were not for her own life's tragedies, among which was her brother Michael's death in Kuwait in 1991, her life might have taken another path. She had been headed to law school until that fateful day. It was Michael who had been going to follow in their father's footsteps and join the force. Life takes its turns.

While Byrne and David Albrecht talked documentary film – not one of Jessica's strong suits, she'd been halfway through *This is Spinal Tap* before she'd realized it was a spoof – she got on her iPhone, did a search for tattoo parlors in Philadelphia. She called a few of them and was told that they did not handle things like temporary tattoos. The last place she called, an emporium on South Street, mentioned a parlor that had recently opened on Chestnut, a place called Ephemera. The girl said they did temporary tattooing and had a good reputation.

EPHEMERA WAS ON THE second floor of a row house converted into retail space. The first floor was a retail shop selling Asian specialty foods.

While David Albrecht shot some exteriors of the building, Jessica and Byrne climbed the narrow stairwell, opened the frosted-glass door.

The front parlor was lit with dozens of candles. The walls were covered in tapestries of magenta and gold. There was no furniture, no stools, just pillows. It smelled of rich incense. There were no customers in the waiting area.

A few moments later a woman walked through the curtains and greeted them. She was Indian, elfin and delicate, about forty. She wore a turquoise silk *kurti* and black slacks. 'My name is Dalaja,' she said. 'How may I help you?'

Jessica took out her ID, showed it to the woman. She then introduced herself and Byrne.

'Is there something wrong?' Dalaja asked.

'No,' Jessica said. 'We just have a couple of questions, if you have a few moments.'

'Yes, of course.'

Dalaja gestured to the large pillows in front of the window overlooking Chestnut Street. Jessica and Byrne sat down. Well, *sat* was a loose term for Byrne's action. For a man his size, the best Byrne could do was aim himself at the pillow, then fall onto it.

'Would you like some tea?' the woman asked when they were settled.

'I'm fine, thanks,' Jessica said.

'Would a cup of Masala chai be too much trouble?' Byrne asked.

The woman smiled. 'Not at all. But it will take a few minutes.'

'No problem.'

Dalaja disappeared into the back room.

'Masala chai?' Jessica asked softly.

'What about it?'

'Do you have some sort of secret life I don't know about?'

'Well, if I told you it wouldn't be secret, would it?'

Jessica looked around the room. There were glass shelves on the far wall, each featuring a stack of brightly hued clothing. Another glass rack held carved artifacts and jewelry. The sound of modern Indian music floated softly from behind the curtain.

The woman soon emerged from the back room, sat on a large pillow opposite them. She was so light that she barely made an impression on the pillow. It was as if she floated above it. 'The tea will be ready shortly.'

'Thanks,' Byrne said.

'First, if you don't mind, can you tell me what you do here?' Jessica asked.

'This is a Mehndi parlor.'

'Could you spell that for me?' Jessica asked.

Dalaja did, giving her a few alternate spellings. Jessica wrote it all down. 'I'm not sure I know what that means.'

'Mehndi is a type of skin decoration practiced throughout South Asia, Southeast Asia, North Africa, the Horn of Africa.'

'These are temporary tattoos?'

'Technically no. Tattoos, by definition, are permanent, applied under the skin. Mehndi is temporary, and rests atop the skin.'

'What is it made out of?'

'Mehndi is applied with henna. It is mostly drawn on the palms of the hands and the feet, where the levels of keratin in the skin are highest.'

'And how long does it last?'

'Anywhere from a few days to a few months, depending on the henna paste and where the decoration is placed on the body.'

A young Indian woman came out of the back with a cup of tea on an ornate black lacquered tray. She was about nineteen, and wore traditional South Asian clothing. She was stunningly beautiful. Jessica went back to her notes, but, after a few seconds, noticed that the girl was still standing in front of them. Jesssica glanced at Byrne. He was looking at the girl with his mouth open, not moving, not speaking. She was that beautiful.

'Kevin.'

'Right,' he said finally, closing his mouth and taking the cup and saucer. 'Thank you.'

The girl smiled and, without a word, withdrew to the back room.

When she was gone, their hostess reached onto a nearby table and picked up a beautifully bound leather notebook. She handed the book to Jessica, who riffled the pages. The designs were intricate and skillfully drawn. Page after page of complex artwork in a rainbow of colors, drawn mostly on hands and feet.

'I'm afraid what we're inquiring about is a little different,' Jessica said. 'A little less . . . ornate.'

'I see.'

Jessica then caught the aroma of the tea – ginger and honey – and wished she had taken the woman up on her offer.

'May I show you a photograph?' Jessica asked.

'By all means.'

Jessica pulled out her iPhone, enlarged the photograph of the lion tattoo on Kenneth Beckman's finger.

'Oh, I see,' the woman said. 'This *is* different.'

'Do you know what it is?'

Dalaja nodded. 'This is very small, is it not?'

'Yes,' Jessica said. 'Maybe one inch long.'

'It appears to be a style of temporary body art called a transfer. Relatively inexpensive. And the quality, well . . .'

It was true. By comparison with the photographs in the leather-bound notebook the lion tattoo looked like it had been drawn with a crayon.

'I take it you do not offer this service or sell items like this,' Jessica said.

'We do not. But I believe I can point you in the right direction.'

'That would be great.'

'If you will excuse me for a moment.'

The woman rose, seemingly without effort. She stepped into the back room. She returned a few minutes later with pages from a color printer.

'I believe this is what you are looking for.'

She handed a page to Jessica. On it was an exact replica of the lion transfer tattoo.

'Wow,' Jessica said. 'That's it.'

Dalaja handed her a second sheet. 'At the top is the website from which I downloaded the image. There are ten others here on the page, but the first company, called World Ink, is the largest. I did not find that exact image on any of the others, but that is not to say it is not sold elsewhere.'

Jessica and Byrne got to their feet.

'The chai was delicious,' Byrne said. 'Thanks very much.'

'You are most welcome,' the woman replied. 'Is there anything else I can do for you?'

'I believe that is it for now,' Jessica said.

'Then, for now, *alvida.*' She spun on her heels and walked toward the back room without making a sound.

BACK AT THE ROUNDHOUSE, Jessica got on the Internet and visited World Ink. In addition to transfer tattoos, the company sold a lot of specialty items, such as pocket calendars, paint sheets, and customized scratch-and-win cards.

But it was the stock tattoos in which Jessica was interested. And they had hundreds, maybe thousands of designs. Angels, cars, flags, flowers, sports, holiday-themed, myth and fairy-tale, as well as religious and tribal symbols.

Six pages deep into the online catalog she found the lion design. It was in a collection called TinyToos, and was a perfect match. She took out her cellphone, clicked over to the photograph of Kenneth Beckman's body. There could be no doubt. Unless the victim had put this tattoo on himself – and Jessica had a problem seeing Beckman doing this, it seemed inconsistent with his personality – someone had done it for him. Quite possibly the person who'd strangled and mutilated him.

Byrne already had three calls in to Sharon Beckman to ask if her husband had a tattoo on his finger.

Jessica got on the phone to World Ink, and after a few minutes of *press one, press five, press two*, she pressed *0* until a human being picked up the phone. She identified herself and in short order was passed over to the website-catalog sales manager.

Jessica explained the bare minimum. After a little hemming and hawing, the man told her that they would be happy to help, but he was going to have to get clearance and they would need some kind of request on paper. Jessica asked the man if a fax on a PPD letterhead would suffice, and he said it would. Jessica scratched a few more notes, hung up the phone. She caught Byrne's attention, gave him the highlights. She held up the photo of the lion tattoo.

'This design is exclusive to this company,' she said. 'It's an original design. That's not to say that our guy bought it from them, or didn't duplicate it himself – the guy at World Ink said it was fairly easy to do with a scanner, PhotoShop, and the right supplies – but considering the way these tattoos are applied, I think it's a safe bet that Kenneth Beckman did not apply the tattoo himself. Even if it has nothing to do with the case, we can be pretty sure someone did it for him.'

'Like, for instance, our bad boy.'

'Could be. Now, if it *was* him, he might have placed an order online with this company. I'm going to fax them a request for a customer list, people who purchased this tattoo.'

'Do you think we'll need the DA's office on this?' Byrne asked.

'Maybe.'

'Let me call Mike Drummond and give him a heads-up.'

While Byrne made the call, Jessica printed off the tattoo of the lion. She heard laughter coming down the hall. She looked up to see Nicci Malone – a love-struck, schoolgirl-in-distress Nicci Malone – enter the duty room with Detective Russell Diaz.

Russell Diaz was the head of a newly formed tactical squad, part of the PPD's Special Investigations Unit, a job originally offered to Kevin Byrne, who had turned it down. The tactical unit was a sort of rapid-response team for high-profile cases involving special circumstances. Diaz had spent ten years with the FBI's Philadelphia field office, but had been traveling too much, he said, and joined the PPD to stay closer to his family. While in the FBI he had worked with Behavioral Science and had consulted with the homicide unit a number of times in the past few years.

Beyond that, Russell Diaz was a specimen. About six feet tall, cut from stone, close-cropped brunette hair, dreamy eyes. He was given to wearing those tight navy blue PPD T-shirts that showed off his biceps. Oddly enough, he seemed not to notice his impact on members of both the same and opposite sexes, along with everything in between. This made him even more appealing.

Tomorrow was his first tour in the new unit.

Diaz noticed Jessica, crossed the room, smiled. 'Hello, detective. Been a while.'

'Too long,' Jessica said. They shook hands. Jessica had worked with Diaz on a joint task force when she'd been in the auto-theft unit.

They had taken down an international ring, a gang shipping high-end cars to South America. 'Glad to have you on the team. How is Marta?'

Marta was Diaz's daughter. To Jessica's understanding she was some sort of musical prodigy. The fact that Diaz, long divorced, was raising her alone vaulted him from appealing to unbelievably adorable.

'She's great, thanks. Fourteen going on thirty.'

Jessica glanced down at the stack of papers and books in Diaz's grasp.

'What is this?' Jessica pointed at the book. Diaz handed it to her. It was a copy of *Dante's Inferno*.

'Just a little light reading,' Diaz said, with a smile.

Jessica thumbed through the book. It was anything but light reading. 'You read Italian?'

'Working on it. Marta is going to do her sophomore year in Italy, and I want to be able to sound hip to her friends.'

'Impressive.'

'*Che c'è di nuovo?*' Diaz asked.

Jessica smiled. '*Non molto.*'

As far as she could tell, Diaz had asked her what was new and she'd told him 'not much.' Outside of swear words, that was about the extent of Jessica's Italian.

Byrne walked into the duty room. Jessica gestured him over. She introduced the two men.

'Kevin Byrne, Russell Diaz,' she said.

'Good to meet you,' Diaz said. 'I've heard a lot about you.'

'Likewise.'

They batted shoptalk around for a while until Diaz glanced at his watch. 'I'm due back at Arch Street to wrap a few things.' The Philadelphia FBI field office was at 6000 Arch. Diaz gathered his things, including the copy of *Dante's Inferno*. He put it all in his duffel, slung it over his broad shoulder. 'Drinks later?'

Standing behind Diaz, Nicci Malone nodded like a bobble-head doll.

*

JESSICA AND BYRNE SPENT the next hour typing up the witness statements collected from the Federal Street scene, which amounted to
little more than *I don't know anything, I didn't hear anything, I didn't see
anything.*

'I think you should stay on that tattoo company,' Byrne said. 'I'll
see if I can red-light the lab on the brand of paper used to gift-wrap
Beckman's head.'

'Sounds like a plan,' Jessica said.

In the background the duty-room phone rang. Out of habit, Jessica
and Byrne both looked at the assignment desk, which was positioned
more or less in the middle of the cluttered room. Nick Palladino was
up on the wheel. They saw him reach into the desk for a notification
form, which could only mean one thing.

The homicide unit was contacted every time there was a suspicious death. Some turned out to be accidents, some turned out to be
suicides. But every time a non-hospital, non-hospice death occurred,
anywhere in the county of Philadelphia, only one phone rang.

Jessica and Byrne turned their attention back to the case, to each
other. Or tried to.

A few minutes later, out of the corner of her eye, Jessica noticed
someone crossing the duty room. It was Nick Palladino. He was
heading straight for Jessica and Byrne, a dour look on his face. For
the most part, Dino was a pretty affable guy, even-tempered, at least
for a South Philly Italian. Except when he was on a job. Then he was
all business.

This was one of those times.

'Please don't tell me we have another body on this case,' Jessica
said. 'We don't have another body on this case, do we, Dino?'

'No,' Nick Palladino said, slipping on his coat. 'We don't.' He
grabbed a set of keys off the rack, along with a two-way handset. 'We
have two.'

Lucy Doucette made the six blocks in just under four minutes. It might have been a record. On the way she outpaced two SEPTA buses and just barely dodged an SUV that ran the light on Eighteenth Street. She'd been dodging traffic since she was three. It didn't slow her down a bit.

The address was a three-story brick building off Cherry Street. A small plaque next to the door identified it as Tillman Towers. It was hardly a tower. A rusted air conditioner hung precariously overhead; the steps leading up to the door looked to be leaning at a ten-degree angle to the right. She looked at the bottom of the plaque. It said ENTRANCE TO 106 AROUND BACK. She walked down an alley, turned the corner and saw a small door, painted red. On it was a symbol that matched the symbol on the card, a highly stylized golden key.

She looked for a buzzer or doorbell and, seeing none, pushed on the door. It opened. Ahead was a long dimly lit hallway.

Lucy started down the corridor, surrounded by the smells of old buildings – bacon fat, wet dog, fruity room deodorizers, with top notes of soiled diaper. She had long ago developed a keen sense of smell – it was something that really helped in her business: sometimes some really funky things lurked in the craziest places in hotel rooms, and being able to root them out and dispose of them, by any means necessary, was a real plus.

When she got to number 106 at the end of the hallway the door was slightly ajar. She knocked on the door jamb and, out of long-ingrained habit, almost called out 'Housekeeping.' She stopped herself at the last second.

She knocked again. 'Hello?'

No response.

She took a deep breath and stepped into the room.

The space was small and cramped, with stacks of old leather-bound books in the corners reaching nearly to the ceiling. In the center were two upholstered chairs of differing style and vintage. In here she tasted long-boiled coffee on the back of her tongue.

'Hello.' The voice came from behind her.

Lucy spun around, her heart leaping. Behind her stood a compact man somewhere in his forties or fifties. He was of average height, but lean and wiry. His white shirt, which had yellowed around the collar and cuffs, appeared to be a few sizes too large. His navy blue suit coat was shiny and worn, his shoes dusty. But what struck Lucy most were his eyes. He had the dark, shiny eyes of a fierce terrier.

'Hello,' she replied, the word coming out squeaky. She hated it when her voice did this. 'I'm Lucy Doucette.'

'I know.'

In contrast to her own, his voice was soft and assured. Lucy had the feeling that he had never shouted in his life.

He took her hand in his but didn't shake it, not like an ordinary handshake. Instead, he just held it for a moment, not taking his eyes from hers. For a moment the rest of the room dissolved away, like something glimpsed through a shower curtain. His lack of physical size belied this powerful touch.

He let go of her hand, eased his own hands back down to his sides.

'What should I call you?' Lucy asked as everything now shimmered back into focus.

The man smiled a thin smile, a light that didn't fully reach his eyes. 'My name is Adrian Costa,' he said. 'You may call me Adrian or Mr. Costa, whichever makes you more comfortable.'

He gestured to the large upholstered avocado chair. Lucy saw the dust on the arms. She wanted to vacuum it.

'I'm of a mind to call you *Mr. Costa* for now,' she said. 'If that's okay.'

'As you wish.'

Lucy sat down. The chair was a lot more comfortable than it looked. It looked a little spring-busted, if the truth were to be told. Lucy had grown up with third-hand furniture, living in drafty rental houses and second-floor apartments situated above everything from bowling alleys to taverns to Chinese restaurants, places where none of the furniture matched, where nothing ever sat level on the floor. Lucy never knew whether it was the floors that were out of whack or that the tables and chairs were short-legged, but she recalled always having to put a matchbook or two under the table legs so her pencils didn't roll off when she was doing her homework. She also remembered many nights when she and her mother would walk the streets of her hometown on the night before trash day, looking for usable items with which her mother could furnish their house, or try to turn around and sell or trade for drugs. They used to call it shopping at Lawn Mart.

'What do you know about hypnotism?' Mr. Costa asked.

Lucy didn't have to think too long about this one. She didn't know much, just the things she'd seen in spooky movies, or the comedies where people got hypnotized and walked around like chickens. Lucy truly hoped she wasn't going to walk around like a chicken. She told Mr. Costa just that.

'Don't worry,' Mr. Costa said. He steepled his fingers. Lucy noticed that there were indentations on six of his fingers, as though he had recently taken off six rings. 'What I do is give you the skills you need to achieve your goal,' he added. 'Do you have a goal, Lucy Doucette? A purpose in coming to see me?'

If you only knew, mister. She tried to answer with a calm, measured response. 'Oh yes.'

'Good. Here we focus on subconscious behaviors and see how they influence your conscious life. The methods I use are tried and true. They go back to Victorian times.'

'So, the acting-like-a-chicken business is definitely out?'

Mr. Costa nodded. 'The stage hypnotist wants to give the impression that the subject is out of control,' he said. 'What I do is just the opposite. I want to give you *back* control. Control of your life. The way I do that is to help you to relax as deeply as possible so you can enter a suggestible state, a state where your memories – things you may have forgotten – can be recalled with ease, and therefore be understood and dealt with.'

'Okay,' Lucy said. She hoped she sounded more confident than she felt. 'But there is something I need to know before we go any further. If that's okay.'

'Of course.'

'How much is all this going to cost?'

There. She'd just blurted it out. By the time she was five or six years old she had already learned to shop at the grocery store and drug store, to talk to the people from the phone and electric companies, usually wielding her little-girl charms to forestall a shut-off of services.

Mr. Costa smiled his nick of a smile again. 'You won't owe me anything for now. Let's see where the road takes us. Then we'll talk about the toll.'

Lucy was more than a little surprised. 'Well, Mr. Costa, I appreciate this, I truly do. But I'm a girl who doesn't like surprises. Never have. I'd hate to get to the end of all this and find that I owe you thousands and thousands of dollars or something. It wouldn't be fair to either of us. I couldn't pay you and you'd be really mad.'

Another pause. 'Firstly, I never get angry. I've never found it to be productive. Have you?'

The truth was, she never *had* found it to be productive. Of course, that had never stopped her. 'No. I suppose not.'

'Secondly, when we have completed our third and last session, if you find then that you are satisfied with my services, that you have received true value, I want you to pay me whatever you feel is right.' He gestured to the room around them. 'As you can see, I live a modest existence.'

Lucy looked closely at the walls for the first time, at the cobwebs near the ceiling, at the thin layer of dust everywhere, at the crosshatched lines in the plaster. Once again, her desire to start cleaning was nearly physical. Then she looked closely at the photographs mounted haphazardly on the walls, dozens and dozens of them, many in chipped enamel frames, some staggered behind cracked and spider-webbed glass. They all seemed to be snapshots of similar subjects – travel-type pictures of pavilions and gazebos and gingerbread exhibition halls, places that appeared to be small-town centers, ringed by vendors with brightly colored carts, public benches sporting ads for local concerns. One frame featured a band shell in the shape of a large pumpkin. Another showed what might have been a Civil War re-enactment in progress. A number of the photographs were pictures of a younger Mr. Costa, holding a violin.

'Have you been to all these places?' Lucy asked.

'I have indeed.'

Mr. Costa crossed the room to the far wall, the wall opposite the window. There was a velvet curtain there that took up most of the width of the room. He reached behind the right side of the curtain, took hold of a frayed golden rope and pulled it gently.

Behind the curtain was a large booth, perhaps six feet wide and just as tall. It had no window, like a typical booth you might see at a carnival or in front of a theater, but rather a single door crudely cut into the front, a door with a red crystal doorknob. Above the door was a carved scroll, painted to resemble a dark purple sky with billowy clouds. Peering out from behind one of the clouds was a silvery autumn moon, with just the hint of glitter. Down each side of the booth, next to the doorway, were the words *The Dreamweaver.* Across the door, over what looked to be a round portal which showed only darkness, was another legend, this one in a gilded script:

What do you dream?

'That's pretty cool,' Lucy said. And it was true. Lucy Doucette was a small-town girl, one who'd grown up terribly poor. Her entertainment, when her mother was sober enough to take her places, and many times when she was not, had been small-town entertainment – county fairs, local home days, carnivals, parades, festivals, sometimes even wakes if they were held in the park. If there was no cover charge, and it was bright, loud, and festive, Lucy's mother would park her daughter on a bench, returning every so often a little drunker, or a little more stoned, with a corn dog, elephant ear, or funnel cake in her hand. Many times these treats were cold, half-eaten, and it wasn't until years later that Lucy figured out that these were probably items of discarded food. Somehow that knowledge did not make them taste bad, even in retrospect. When you're four years old, cotton candy, even someone else's cotton candy, was the best thing in the world.

Mr. Costa closed the curtain, crossed the room, sat down across from Lucy. 'Shall we begin?'

'Sure,' Lucy said. She took a deep breath, tried to relax her shoulders. It wasn't easy. There was a tension that had settled upon her when she was small and, although there were days when she felt it was easing, it had never gone away completely. She looked up at the Dreamweaver, at his bright little-dog eyes. 'Let's begin.'

'Today, in our first session, we are going to go back to a specific time in your life. The time you can't seem to remember. Okay?'

Lucy felt her hands begin to shake. She knit them together in her lap. 'Okay.'

'But you are not going to re-experience this event. There is no need to be concerned with that. Instead, it will be more like you are observing it.'

'Observing? Like, watching it?'

'Yes,' Mr. Costa said. 'Exactly. Like watching it from above.'

'Like I'm flying?'

'Like you're flying.'

'*Very* cool,' she said. 'What do I do?'

'You needn't do anything except close your eyes and listen to the sound of my voice.'

'You know, I have to tell you something,' Lucy began. 'In fact, I was going to tell you this when I first walked in.'

'What is that?'

'I don't really think I'm the kind of person who can be hypnotized.'

'Why do you say that?'

Lucy shrugged. 'I don't know. I think I'm too intense, you know? I hardly ever sleep, I'm always nervous. Do other people ever say that?'

'Of course.'

'I'm sure that there are some people who just can't seem to—'

Mr. Costa held up a finger, stopping her. The finger had a ring on it. In fact, all of his rings seemed to be back. All six of them.

When had he done that?

'I hate to interrupt you, but I'm afraid our session is complete for today.'

Lucy wasn't sure she understood. 'What are you saying? Are you saying—'

'Yes.'

Lucy took a few moments, letting the news sink in. She had actually been hypnotized for a while.

She stood up, grabbed her purse, walked toward the door, feeling a little dizzy. She held onto the doorjamb to steady herself. Suddenly Mr. Costa was next to her again. He was light on his feet.

'Are you all right?' he asked.

'Yes,' Lucy said. 'Kinda.'

Mr. Costa nodded. 'Shall we say tomorrow, then? Just at midday?'

'Sure,' Lucy said, suddenly realizing she felt pretty good after all. As in *really* good. Like she'd taken a brief nap.

'I believe you made some progress today,' Mr. Costa said.

Pipe smoke.

'I did?'

'Yes,' he replied. He took off his bifocals, slipped them into an inside pocket of his suit coat. 'I don't believe it was anything like a breakthrough – that may never happen, I'm afraid – but you may have opened a door. Just the slightest bit.'

Pipe smoke and apples.

'A door?' Lucy asked.

'A door to your subconscious. A portal to what happened to you nine years ago.'

Had she told him it was nine years? She didn't remember doing that.

Mr. Costa put his hand on the doorknob. 'One last thing for today,' he said. 'Does the hotel in which you work have notepads in the rooms?'

'Notepads?'

'Notepads with the hotel logo. For the guests.'

'Yes,' Lucy said. She'd only placed a million of these pads – two inches from the left edge of the desk, pen at a forty-five-degree angle across the center.

'Excellent. Please bring one of these pads with you next time,' Mr. Costa said. 'Can you do that?'

'Sure,' Lucy said. 'I'll bring one.'

Mr. Costa opened the door. 'Until tomorrow, my dear Lucinda.'

On the way through the door Lucy glanced at the small picture on the wall next to the casing, just above the grimy light switch. She only saw it for a fleeting moment but that was long enough to see that it was a photograph of another gazebo, this one a rather dilapidated pergola overgrown with ivy. It was only after she'd stepped through the doorway and the door had closed behind her that she realized she knew the house in the background of that photograph, the wreck of a bungalow with its slanted porch and rusted gutters and broken brick walk.

It was the house she had grown up in.

EIGHTEEN

IT IS SAID OF MOZART THAT HE COULD NEVER SIT STILL FOR HIS BARBER *running instead to his clavier every time he had an idea, forcing the man tasked with tonsorial duties to chase after him, ribbons in hand.*

I understand. Sometimes, when the music of the dead is loud, I cannot sit still, I must go out and begin the hunt anew.

For now I watch and wait, idling, my killing instruments at the ready.

I survey the ground before me. The cemetery looks so different in the daytime. No glowering ghouls, no hovering apparitions. Just the dead. Just a chorus of plaintive voices asking for justice, for answers, for truth.

I watch the people scramble callously about, the decaying dead underfoot, souls trampled beneath the weight of duty. We all know why we are here.

There. From the other side.

Can you hear it?

It is the rooster, a fresh voice in the choir.

The carnivale *has come to town.*

NINETEEN

M OUNT OLIVE WAS AN OLD CEMETERY IN WEST PHILADELPHIA, THE final resting place of hundreds of Civil War dead as well as of some of Philadelphia's most famous and infamous citizens.

As with other areas of the City of Brotherly Love, including the design and layout of Benjamin Franklin Parkway with its similarity to the Champs Elysées, the concept of the pastoral graveyard was based on a Parisian model.

Framed on three sides by residential neighborhoods, Mount Olive was bordered to the northwest by Fairmount Park. Incorporated in the mid-1800s, it was a non-sectarian graveyard that at one time had been nearly four hundred acres in area. It was established at a time when older, smaller urban graveyards, located in city blocks and alongside churches, had stood in the way of Philadelphia's booming development, and over the course of many years a number of the interred had been moved to Mount Olive. But even though the cemetery was a National Historic Landmark and on the Philadelphia Register of Historic Places, over the years it had become the victim of vandalism, dumping, and theft. And now, with many of the families of the dead having moved away, some areas of the graveyard had fallen into a state of disrepair.

Jessica and Byrne stood on Kingsessing Avenue. Two sector cars were already on the scene, as well as a departmental sedan and a van from the Crime Scene Unit.

A second team had already been dispatched to the other crime scene. The location of the second body was a parking lot in Northern Liberties. Nicci Malone would be the lead investigator on that case. Jessica and Byrne would be briefed by phone by Dana Westbrook.

David Albrecht appeared from behind a grove of trees at the northern end of the graveyard. He shouldered his camera, took shots of the mausoleum, the grounds, the arriving personnel. After a few minutes he approached Jessica and Byrne.

'I should have asked about this before,' he said. 'Is it okay to shoot here?'

'I don't see why not,' Jessica said. 'As long as you hang back until CSU has done its job.'

'I don't want to disrespect the dead.'

'I think it's okay.'

Albrecht looked out over the grounds. He pointed to a small monument. It was a single headstone, carved in Georgia gray granite. 'That's my father's grave,' he said. He shrugged, perhaps a bit apologetically. 'I haven't been here in a while. I guess I should probably pay a visit.'

The three of them fell silent for a moment. Finally Byrne broke the calm. 'We're going to be here for a while, David. Take your time.'

'Okay,' Albrecht said. 'Thanks.'

He put the camera at his side, traversed the grounds, stopped at the monument. He crossed himself, bowed his head.

Jessica scanned the area. On the corner, talking to a man Jessica assumed worked for the cemetery, was Josh Bontrager. When the other man left, Bontrager noticed Jessica and Byrne, waved them over.

'What do you have?' Byrne asked.

'Female DOA,' Bontrager said, pointing over his shoulder. Jessica could see a sheet-covered form about twenty yards away. Next to the body stood a CSU officer. Because the potential crime scene was so large, a wide area had been taped off around the body, the sheet that covered it secured with stakes driven into the ground.

'Do we know how long the body has been here?' Byrne asked.

'Not too long.' Bontrager took out his notepad. 'There's a service here later today, and the guy who does the digging found the body about six this morning. He said he was here late yesterday afternoon and he went by the plot, didn't see anything. So the dump occurred sometime between four yesterday afternoon and six this morning.'

Byrne looked at the fences. 'How secure is this place?'

'Not very secure at all,' Bontrager said. He gestured toward the area bordering the two main streets. 'I walked two sides of it when I got here. Lots of places where you can get in and not be seen. Lots of tree cover.'

'Did the man who works here move or touch anything?'

'He says no. As you might imagine, he's not particularly disturbed by the sight of dead bodies. But a homicide victim is another story. He said he saw the body, lit a cigarette, hit the flask of tequila he's not supposed to have, and called his boss.'

'Did he leave the area after the call?'

'Again, he says no. I'm inclined to believe him.'

'Is the body near a plot?' Jessica asked.

'Right on top of one,' Bontrager said.

'Any ID on the victim?'

'No,' Bontrager said. 'Not yet, anyway. I haven't done a full search of the area.'

Byrne took another look around. 'Is this our bad guy, Josh?'

'Oh yeah. This is our bad guy,' Bontrager replied. 'No doubt about it.'

'All right,' Byrne said. 'Let's go look at a dead body in a cemetery.'

The three of them walked onto the grounds, down a narrow weed-grown path between headstones that dated from the mid-1800s. Every tenth site or so had been tended to some degree, with the grass trimmed around the stone, plastic flowers placed. Most of the grave sites were criminally unkempt.

When they reached the top of the rise Jessica glanced over her shoulder. The place was beginning to teem. She noticed that there were now a half-dozen more people, including representatives from the DA's office. The fact that the DA had a presence let the detectives know what priority these killings were being given.

*

THE THREE DETECTIVES GATHERED around the site. Josh Bontrager looked at Jessica, then at Byrne. He crouched down next to the body. Jessica nodded. Bontrager drew back the sheet.

'Ah, Christ,' Byrne said. He spoke for everyone.

As with the previous victim, the middle-aged female's body was nude, shaved clean of all hair, as was her head. Jessica immediately noticed the bruises around her ankles. She had been shackled.

Wrapped around the victim's head was a white paper band, identical to the one that they had found wrapped around Kenneth Beckman's head. There was a red wax seal. Also identical were the blood patterns. One lateral slash to the forehead. Beneath it and to the left was another splotch, in a circular pattern. The area near the right ear was marked with blood in a figure eight.

If these were the similarities to the condition in which Kenneth Beckman had been found, there was a difference. This victim was lying on her side, behind the grave marker. One foot was resting on top of the marker. The other leg, the left leg, was bent completely back at an impossible angle. Jessica saw the bone protruding from the victim's thigh.

'ME's been here?' Byrne asked.

'Not yet.'

'Pictures taken?'

Bontrager nodded, pointed to the CSU officer who was leaning against a nearby tree and smoking a cigarette. 'Video, too.'

Jessica looked at the headstone. The victim's right leg extended toward the grave marker, which was half covered in debris and dead grass. The foot rested directly over the center.

'Kevin. Give me a hand here.'

Both detectives snapped on latex gloves. They knelt on either side of the body and gently lifted the victim's right leg, moving it just a few inches, being careful not to disturb any of the area next to the grave. They lowered the victim's leg gently. Jessica looked at the grave marker. It was not nearly as old as the ones that surrounded it, looking as though it had been positioned no more than a few years earlier. A shift in the ground had lowered it a few inches so that the marker's engraving was now covered in dirt.

Byrne motioned to the CSU officer standing nearby, who tossed away his cigarette, walked over and took a number of additional pictures. When he was finished, Byrne took out a pocket knife and began to scrape away the mud. The first thing to be revealed was a carving, one with which Jessica was not familiar. It did not appear to be a Catholic or Christian symbol – praying hands, an angel, a crucifix. As they cleared away more dirt, Jessica thought the symbol was beginning to look like a flower, a red flower with narrow petals.

Byrne brushed away the last of the mud and revealed that it wasn't a flower at all but rather a Chinese character. Beneath it, running vertically, were three other characters, all red.

A few minutes later they had the bottom of the headstone cleared of dirt, and saw what they were looking for. The person interred in this space had died on March 21, 2002.

Her name was Antoinette Chan.

Jessica looked at Byrne, a bolt of electricity passing between them.

Across town, a man had been found murdered, his head wrapped in a band of white paper. A man named Kenneth Beckman. Here in West Philadelphia, a second body is found, its head too wrapped in white paper. This victim, still unidentified, is found on the grave of a young woman who was also murdered.

Murdered, it is believed, by Kenneth Beckman.

'Let's check her hands,' Byrne said.

Byrne lifted the victim's right hand, checked it. Nothing. He circled the body, gently lifted her left hand. There, on the index finger, was a small tattoo. Instead of a lion, this time it was a rooster.

Jessica took a few photographs, her heart starting to race. She glanced over at Byrne. He wore an expression she had come to know well over the years, one that barely contained a cold rage.

Byrne squatted next to the body and began to undo the paper that wrapped the victim's head.

'Kevin, the ME's office is on the way,' Jessica said. 'You should wait.'

'Yeah, well, I should be living in Cazumel with the Corr sisters, too,' Byrne said. 'I don't see either of these things happening.'

Byrne gently unwrapped the victim's head, carefully removing the wax seal first and dropping it into a small evidence bag. The first thing that Jessica noticed when the paper was removed was that the laceration across the forehead, and the puncture wound, were in almost the same places as they'd been with the first victim.

The second thing Jessica noticed was that the dead woman was Sharon Beckman.

TWENTY

THE FEELINGS COURSED THROUGH BYRNE, SENSATIONS THAT GREW exponentially. He paced like an animal.

He stepped behind a tree as the feeling surged, filling his head like an onrush of water from a broken dam. It was followed by a moment of vertigo. He steadied himself, tried to wait it out, trying not to notice as . . .

. . . *the man walks across the cemetery in darkness . . . he is strong . . . the dead weight of Sharon Beckman's body is nothing to him . . . he does not search for the grave site, he knows where it is. He is familiar with this cemetery, all cemeteries. He places her on the ground, steels himself. He is not quite finished. He leaps into the air, and bears down with great force, breaking the dead woman's leg, positioning it back because it means some-thing to him and . . .*

Byrne opened his eyes, got his bearings. He had forgotten where he was, what he was doing.

This was getting bad.

THE CRIME SCENE SWARMED with people. Byrne glanced at his watch. It had only been ten seconds. It felt like an hour.

He walked back to the grave site. Information had trickled in about the second body. This had been found in a Dumpster behind a building at Second and Poplar. According to the initial report the victim, a middle-aged male, had been found nude, his forehead wrapped in white paper, his body clean of all hair.

Three bodies in two days. This case was about to break wide open. Wall-to-wall TV and print news, perhaps even national attention. There was a ghoul on the streets of Philadelphia, a monster who was strangling people, shaving their bodies and marking their flesh. When they had found Kenneth Beckman's body they had all hoped that it was an isolated incident, that it was some sort of personal vendetta. It was not. It was bigger than that. There were now three corpses, and everyone had the nasty feeling that there would be more.

Byrne approached Jessica. 'I have that MRI. I have to go.'

'We've got this covered,' Jessica said. 'Don't worry.'

Byrne did not want to leave. The first two hours were the most critical time of a homicide investigation. After that, memories faded, people thought better of getting involved, forensic evidence had a way of giving itself back to nature. Although neither he nor Jessica were the lead investigator on this case, every warm body was critical.

'Kevin,' Jessica said. 'Go to your appointment.'

'I want to stop by the other scene first. This is out of control.'

'I'll go,' Jessica said. 'You don't have to—'

But Byrne was already on his way. He held his cellphone up as he walked back to the car. 'Call me,' he said.

Leaving the cemetery, Byrne saw the names of the dead carved in time-weathered stone, dates marking fleeting lives, parentheses of birth and death. Out of respect, out of the disquieting knowledge that one day someone would be walking on his final resting place, he did his best to avoid stepping on the graves.

TWENTY-ONE

*A*T FIRST IT IS A MUFFLED SOUND, LIKE THAT OF A WOUNDED ANIMAL. *I hear it the moment I step inside the room. It soon becomes crystal clear.*

I will not be here long. I have much to do. I may be a poor cartwright, but my marchioness awaits.

I AM NOT ALONE *in this room. There are others here. We are all part of something, fractions of a whole. They talk to me, to each other, but I don't hear them. I hear what happened here years ago.*

I stand in the corner, close my eyes. The scene unfolds, like a stage play viewed through frosted glass, two figures forever mired in a dark and terrible vignette.

*S*HE IS A SHY GIRL, *no more than eleven. She has long blonde hair, woven into a braid.*

'*Who are you? Are you a friend of my mom's?*'

'*Yes. We are old friends.*'

'*You shouldn't be here.*'

'*It's okay. I like your dress. It is very pretty.*'

'*Thank you.*'

'*I have a prettier dress. One made especially for you.*'

'For me?'

'Oh yes. It is your favorite color.'

'Blue?'

'A very pretty *blue.'*

'Can I see it?'

'In time.'

'Where do you know my mom from?'

'We work together.'

'My mom doesn't work anymore.'

'This was from before. From a long time ago.'

'Okay.'

'Do you know the story of Eve?'

'Eve?'

'Yes. Eve in the Garden of Eden. Eve who was tempted by an apple.'

The blade removed from its sheath the creak of worn leather the sound of a little heart beating in fear—

'I don't want you here anymore.'

'I won't hurt you.'

'I want you to leave, mister.'

'Don't you want your pretty new dress?'

'No.'

The blade shimmers in the bright afternoon sunlight—

'I'm going to get my sister. I want you to leave now.'

The blade flutters and darts soaring high into the air—

'Eve.'

THE NEIGHBORS SAY THEY heard one scream that day, an unearthly wail that cooled the blood in their veins.

I hear it, too.

It is a sound that began a thousand millennia ago, a red wind that has blown through the ages, finding cracks in the world, a breeze that became a howling sirocco here, in the soul of a killer, in the festering heart of Room 1208.

TWENTY-TWO

LUCY WALKED DOWN EIGHTEENTH STREET IN WHAT SHE HAD ONCE heard, from one therapist or another, was a fugue state.

She couldn't get that photograph out of her mind.

That *couldn't* have been her house on Melbourne Road. It wasn't possible. It was just a picture of one of a million bungalows. They all looked alike, didn't they? Especially the crappy ones.

But what about that flag, Luce? Did they all have that raggedy flag hanging off the porch by a rusted nail, that stupid pennant that was supposed to mean Spring? The one you were supposed to change every three months but no one ever did, not once in all the time they lived there? They had all of them – Spring, Summer, Fall, Winter, all four seasons, each looking more tattered than the other – but they never changed Spring.

What about *that*, Luce?

What about the Spring flag?

She didn't have an answer, just as she had no idea what had happened during those twenty minutes she couldn't recall. Somehow she must have talked about the day she disappeared. What did she say? And why didn't Mr. Costa *tell* her what she'd said? Wasn't that why she went to see him?

It was all part of the process, she guessed. And she had two more visits to go.

*

FROM THE TIME SHE was six or seven years old, Lucy had been an ace mechanic. Not with cars, necessarily, although she could now do basic maintenance on most cars – changing oil, replacing plugs and belts, the occasional brake job if it didn't involve turning the drums or rotors. No, her forte was small appliances. Bring her a stopped tape player, a cold toaster oven, a dimmed lamp – and a lot of the staff of Le Jardin often did – and she would have it up and running by the end of lunchtime.

She had not gone to a vocational training school, or taken any classes, correspondence or otherwise. It was a natural ability, combined with a necessity of life.

When she was small, on the night forays during which she and her mother picked through trash they would often find all kinds of discarded items – toaster ovens, blenders, tape players. Lucy's mother would haul them back to their apartment, giddy with swag, then pretty much forget about them. Weeks later she would throw them out, and Lucy would rescue them a second time. She started with the easy ones, but eventually got better at repair.

Although she didn't know it, she was practicing reverse engineering.

By the time she was ten, Lucy would go out to dumps, finding her own things to repair. She knew every second-hand dealer in their small towns. Where most kids were reading *Dick and Jane*, Lucy pored over *Sam's Photofact*.

In addition, on her jaunts into the stores Lucy always stole the same color clothes – sweaters, sweatshirts, skirts. She even replaced some of her mother's clothes. Her mother was always falling down, ripping her clothes. Lucy got it down to a science. She could steal a brand new dress and worry the material just enough so that her mother never knew she was wearing a different garment. Her mother was a proud woman in many ways, and it broke Lucy's heart to see her going around in ratty clothes.

On this day, Lucy found herself in the Macy's near City Hall. She made her way over to the children's section, found a sweater that looked to be the right size. She picked up two of them, carried them around for a while. When she got to the women's section she selected a dress, brought it into the dressing room.

Inside she got out her small toolkit and, with her back to the mirrors – she knew all the tricks – removed the electronic tags from one sweater and the dress, affixing them to the second sweater. She slipped the first sweater and the dress into her bag, left the dressing room, replaced the other sweater on the display rack, tarried a bit to make sure that she wasn't being watched, then walked out of the store.

WHEN SHE ARRIVED BACK at Le Jardin, with just a few minutes to spare, Lucy could see that the convention guests – the members of *Société Poursuite* – were milling about the lobby. They weren't all guests, of course. It was a convention that attracted a lot of locals, as well as people from all over the tri-state area who drove in for the three days of seminars, lectures and dinners.

In all, over the next few hours there would be ninety-two new guests, and all of them had to be quickly and efficiently processed, greeted with smiles and pleasant repartee, their concerns listened to with rapt attention, their every need anticipated and met, their next three days in the city of Philadelphia – and specifically in Le Jardin – a promised and delivered haven.

Lucy stopped by the Loss Prevention office, picked up her room key.

A door to your subconscious, Mr. Costa had called it. *A portal to what happened to you nine years ago.*

LUCY FINISHED HER LAST room, room 1214, at 3:45.

She stepped into the closet, closed the door, sat down. In moments, the darkness embraced her. When she closed her eyes she saw the town of Shanksville, Pennsylvania from above, saw the school on Cornerstone Road, Lake Stonycreek, and the church on Main Street.

THE DREAMWEAVER HAD ASKED her questions, his silken voice floating above her, behind her, around her, like a warm breeze. Her own voice belonged to a little girl.

What day is it, Lucy?

Tuesday.

Is it morning, afternoon, evening?

It's morning. Tuesday morning.

What time?

Around ten. I didn't go to school.

Why not?

Mama was out the night before, and she didn't get up in time.

Where are you?

I am across the street from the church.

Are you alone?

No. Mama's with me. She is wearing her long leather coat. The one with the rip in the right pocket. She is wearing sunglasses. She asked a lady for a cigarette and the lady gave her one.

What happened then?

There was a big bang. It was loud. Even the ground shook.

What did you do?

I don't remember exactly.

Try to remember. Do you smell anything? Taste anything?

I taste milkshake.

What flavor is it?

Chocolate. But it's warm milkshake. I don't like warm milkshake.

What about smell?

I smell smoke, but not like regular smoke. Not like burning leaves, or logs in a fireplace. More like when people burn their plastic garbage bags.

What happens next?

I stand here for a long time, watching the fire and smoke rise up into the sky.

Where is your mother?

Right beside me. Or maybe not.

What do you mean?

Someone is beside me, but I'm not looking at that person. I can't take my eyes off the smoke over the trees. It is making pretty patterns in the sky.

What kind of patterns?

At first it looks like the face of Jesus. Then it looks likes birds.
What happens next?

I reach up my hand for my mother to take me somewhere. Anywhere but here. I'm scared.

Does she take your hand?

I take the person's hand, but as we walk away I realize it can't be my mom.

Why not?

The hand is too big. And rough. It is a man's hand.

Is there anything else you remember?

Yes. We get into a car. And there is a new smell. *Two* new smells.

What are the new smells?

A different kind of smoke. Different from the burning plastic smell. Like from a pipe, I think. A pipe that people smoke. Like *men* smoke.

And what else?

Apples. Empire apples. We have lots of apples in Western Pennsylvania. Especially near the fall.

Do you remember what else happened that day?

The fire. The ground shaking. Being scared.

What about the man? What happened with him?

I don't know.

What about his face? Do you see his face?

When I look at his face it isn't there.

What about the fire? Do you remember what that was? Do you remember what caused the fire?

Yes. I remember, but only because I found out later.

What was it?

It was Flight 93. It was September 11, 2001, and Flight 93 crashed right near Shanksville, Pennsylvania.

LUCY LOOKED DOWN AT her hands. She had been clenching her fists so tightly that she had eight little red crescents on the palms of her hands. She eased her fists open, stepped out of the closet, looked around. For a few crazy moments she did not know what room she was in. Most people, even people who worked at Le Jardin, would be hard pressed to tell the standard guest rooms apart, their only clues being, perhaps, the view from any given window. But Lucy knew every room on the twelfth floor. It was her floor.

She smoothed out her uniform, stepped into the bathroom, went through the mental checklist in her mind, then checked the entire room.

Done.

She opened the door, stepped into the hall. Two older men were approaching from the elevator. They were probably with the convention. Everyone on the floor this week was with the convention. They nodded to her, smiled. She smiled back, although she didn't feel it inside.

When she reached the business center on the twelfth floor – really just a small niche with computer, fax machine and printer – she sensed another guest coming down the hall. The unwritten rule was that in the hallways, elevators and most public spaces, guests, along with all front-of-the-house personnel, had the right of way. You didn't hide or sidestep from anyone, but if you were any good at your job you knew how to defer with style.

Lucy stepped into the alcove just as the man passed the door of the business center. She did not get a good look at him, just a glimpse of his dark coat.

But she didn't have to see him. It was not her sense of sight that took the floor from beneath her. It was her sense of smell.

There, beneath the hotel smells of cleaning products and filtered, heated air, was another smell, a scent that closed a cold hand over her heart, a smell that unquestionably trailed behind the man who had just passed her in the hallway.

The smell of apples.

She looked down the hall, and knew that he had come out of one of the rooms. Was it 1208? It had to be. She had just cleaned the other two rooms at that end, and they were empty.

Lucy pushed her cart madly down the hall, caught the service elevator to the basement. She left her cart in the basement, ran up the steps toward the service entrance to the first floor. She tried to calm herself as she walked toward the lobby. She didn't know what she would do if she confronted the man, or even who she was looking for.

She stepped into the northern end of the lobby. There were three men in the lobby, none of them wearing or carrying a dark overcoat. Everyone else was staff.

She went out the side door, onto Sansom Street. The sidewalk was crowded. Men, women, children, people making deliveries, cab drivers. She rounded the corner, looked in front of the hotel. Two bellmen were taking bags out of a limo for an elderly couple.

Lucy's heartbeat began to slow. She took a moment, then walked up the drive on the east side of the hotel.

The smell of apples.

It had to be her imagination. Brought on by going to see that crazy old man. She was never going to find out what had happened on those three days. Not really.

She rounded the wall at the back of the hotel, turned the corner.

'Hello, Lucy.'

She stopped, her heart in her throat, her legs all but giving out. She knew the man standing before her. She knew his *face*.

'It's you,' she said.

'Yes, Lucy,' he replied. 'It's Detective Byrne.'

JESSICA SPENT THE EARLY AFTERNOON RUNNING DATA THROUGH ViCAP, the Violent Criminal Apprehension Program. Started by the FBI in 1985, ViCAP was a national registry of violent crimes – homicides, sexual assaults, missing persons, and unidentified remains. Case information submitted to ViCAP was available to authorized law-enforcement agencies around the world, and the system allowed investigators to compare their evidence with all other cases in the database and to identify similarities.

Jessica searched the database with the most salient points of the case, those being the signature marks of the shaving of the victims, as well as the use of paper to blindfold them.

She found a similar case from 2006 in Kentucky, where a man had shaved off the hair of three prostitutes before stabbing them to death and dumping their bodies along the banks of the Cumberland River. In this case the man had shaved only the hair on the victims' heads, including their eyebrows – not their entire bodies. There was another 1988 case in Eureka, California of a man who had shaved a strange pattern into the scalps of four victims. The pattern was later identified, through the man's confession, as what he thought were the first four letters of an alien alphabet.

There were many cases of blindfolded victims, most being execution-style homicides. There were also numerous examples of pre- and post-mortem mutilations. None matched Jessica and Byrne's case.

There were no incidents where all three signatures were present.

Jessica was just about to print off what she needed when all hell broke loose in the duty room. She stood aside as a half-dozen members of the Fugitive Squad ran down the hallway, then through the door to the stairs. They were soon followed by three men wearing US Marshals windbreakers.

Why were the US Marshals there? The purview of the marshal's office, among other things, was the apprehending of fugitives, the transport and managing of prisoners, as well as the protection of witnesses.

Jessica looked across the room to see Dana Westbrook walking toward her. 'What happened?' she asked.

'We had a break.'

Unfortunately, what Westbrook clearly meant was there had been a *prison* break, not a break in Jessica's case.

'From downstairs?' The sub-basement of the Roundhouse was where the PPD holding cells were located. The holding cells were staffed by the county sheriff's office, not the police.

Westbrook shook her head. 'From CF.'

Curran-Fromhold Correctional Facility, on State Road, was a prison in Northeast Philly. In Jessica's entire time on the job she had never heard of a break from CF. 'What happened?'

'It's sketchy right now, but it looks like the prisoner got his hands on a visitor's pass and some street clothes. They've got video of him just waltzing out of the visitor's area.'

The security at CF was tight, which probably meant that the escapee had an accomplice of some sort. Jessica knew the drill. Members of the PPD Fugitive Squad would team up both with US Marshals and with officers from the Pennsylvania State Police. They would scour motels, bus stations, train stations, and of course establish surveillance of the prisoner's residence and those of his known associates. She also knew there was a pretty good chance that a head or two would roll at Curran-Fromhold.

'Fugitive Squad is all over it, and as you can see the marshals are in,' Westbrook said. 'Only a matter of time. Captain wanted me to give you a heads-up, anyway.'

This got Jessica's attention. 'Me? Why?'

'The prisoner? The guy who escaped?'

'What about him?'

'He's your AA Killer suspect. Lucas Anthony Thompson.'

BYRNE RETURNED TO THE Roundhouse at just after three p.m. Jessica had tried to call him twice, got his voicemail both times.

'How did the doctor's appointment go?' she asked.

'Good.'

Jessica just stared. Byrne knew better than to give her the bum's rush on something like this, yet still he tried. Her icy look firmly in place, the moment drew out. Byrne caved in.

'They took the MRI, now they have to read the results. They said they'd call me.'

'When?'

Byrne took a deep breath, realizing he had to play this game or he'd never hear the end of it. 'Maybe tomorrow.'

'You'll let me know the second you hear from them, right?'

'Yes, Mom.'

'Don't make me ground you.'

Jessica told Byrne about Thompson, as well as the scant information she had harvested on ViCAP. Then she gathered her notes, filled him in on the rest of the details regarding the second victim found that day. Black male, mid-fifties, no ID. Initial canvass turned up nothing.

'Has he been printed?' Byrne asked.

'The body's on the way to the morgue now. Boss is going to put Russ Diaz and his team on this. Russ did four years in Behavioral Science, you know. I have a sneaking suspicion we're going to need him.'

'What about the signature?'

'Identical,' Jessica said.

They turned back to the case files on the desk. Three bodies. Three identical MOs. Kenneth and Sharon Beckman were tied to the murder of Antoinette Chan. In the case of serial murder, the first order of business was to try and establish a link between the victims, a commonality that might lead to a denominator they all shared – job, family, circle of friends – and ultimately to the killer. Connecting Kenneth and Sharon Beckman was, of course, easy. They'd see about this new victim.

'I ordered you some garlic prawns, by the way,' Jessica said. 'But it got eaten. You know how Chinese food goes in this place. Like pork in a kennel.'

'I ate at the hospital,' Byrne said. 'But I did bring dessert.' He held up a white bag.

Jessica sat up straight in her chair. *Dessert at lunch!* She beckoned forth the bag. Byrne handed it to her.

Jessica opened the bag and saw that it was an apple fritter from that bakery on Seventeenth she liked.

'What took you to Seventeenth?' she asked.

'I had to pick up a pre-amp from a guy.'

'And a pre-amp would be . . .'

'I'm converting all my old vinyl records to digital. Some of them are old 78s, and I'm trying to clean up the sound.'

Jessica took out the apple fritter, thinking that she couldn't wait for that moment in her life – a moment she fully expected, a moment she fully intended to savor – when she just didn't care about her weight anymore, a moment when she could fully embrace the slide into middle age and obesity.

Or when she got pregnant again. Pregnant would be better.

She bit into the apple fritter. Heaven. 'You can get MRIs as often as you want.'

'We're going to have to give statements, you know.'

Jessica nodded, wiped her lips. She and Byrne had met with Sharon Beckman the day before, and now the woman was the victim of a homicide. Jessica and Byrne had become part of the timeline.

THE CALL CAME AT just after four. Nicci Malone and Nick Palladino were at the morgue with the third victim. Jessica put them on speaker.

'We're at the ME's,' Nicci said. 'You wanted me to call?'

'Yeah,' Jessica said. 'Have you checked the victim's hands for tattoos?'

'No. We bagged them at the scene. You want us to check here?'

'Yeah,' Jessica said.

The next minute took somewhere around an hour for Jessica and Byrne. They both paced, neither of them having anything to say. They heard more rustling, then Nicci put the phone back up to her ear.

'Jess?'

'Yeah, Nicci,' Jessica said. 'Is there a tattoo?'

'There is,' Nicci said. 'It's a tattoo of a swan. A tiny blue swan. It's on the index finger of his left hand.'

Someone was on a rampage in the city of Philadelphia and every resource had to be summoned to stop him. The fact that the body of Kenneth Beckman had been found a half-block from an elementary school put two other agencies on alert. Personnel had already been dispatched to Washington Elementary.

Over the next few hours the apparatus of an investigation handling multiple murders would gear up around them. Off-duty detectives would be called in, various sections of the forensic lab would be put on alert.

'Can you take a picture of the tattoo and send it to me?' Jessica asked.

'Sure,' Nicci said.

A few minutes later, Jessica received the image on her cellphone. She put it next to photos of Kenneth and Sharon Beckman that had been taken. The tattoo was in the same style. She got online to the World Ink site, put the word 'swan' in the search box, hit *Enter*. Soon a page came up with six different images of stylized swan tattoos. The third tattoo was a perfect match.

MICHAEL DRUMMOND ARRIVED AT five-thirty. The ADA had news for them.

'Before I left the office I heard from World Ink's legal department, which, for all I know, might have been a lawyer working out of his car,' Drummond said. He pulled out a fax, handed a copy to Jessica.

'It turns out that you can buy these tattoos à la carte, with a minimum of six tattoos in the order. They searched their database and discovered that, in the past year, they had sold only one package that contained the first two tattoos we found on the victims – the lion and the rooster.'

Drummond pulled out another fax.

'They mailed the package to a post-office box in Jersey City, New Jersey, which turned out to be a remailer. From there it went to a USPS box in Allentown.'

This meant that, for the moment, their most promising avenue of the investigation was blocked. Getting information on who rented a PO Box presented a whole new set of challenges. Anytime you dealt with a federal agency the red tape was massive. On this they would have to bring in the postal inspectors.

Drummond glanced at the notes in Jessica's notebook.

'So there's been a third murder,' he said. It was a statement, not a question.

Jessica picked up her iPhone, showed Drummond the photo of the victim, as well as the close-up of the tattoo. Drummond scanned the pictures, then looked at his watch. 'All right. I know where the judges will be drinking in about an hour. I'll catch them between their second and third martinis.' He gathered his papers. 'Speaking of martinis, are you coming to my party, Jess?'

Jessica had forgotten all about it. She hoped it didn't show on her face. 'Of course. Looking forward to it.'

'I'll get on the feds.' Drummond smiled, held up his phone. 'I'll call you later.'

Ten minutes later, with everything printed off, Jessica and Byrne stood in front of the material. There was no question that the tattoos purchased from World Ink were the same tattoos found on the victims.

The bad news was that, according to the material they had just received from Drummond, in the packet of tattoos mailed to their killer there were five other tattoos. Turtle, donkey, elephant, kangaroo, and fish.

Eight tattoos in all. The thought was chilling.

Would there be eight murders?

TWENTY-FOUR

THE HOUSE IN LEXINGTON PARK WAS NEARLY EMPTY, SAVE FOR THE hundred or so boxes stacked in the attic, upper hallway, living room and kitchen. The furniture was gone. The dining-room chandelier, an heirloom passed down from Jessica's grandmother, had been carefully packed and spirited away, as had all her mother's cut-crystal goblets.

Three dozen people crowded the first floor, eating wings and crab fries from Chickie's and Pete's. Among them were a who's who from the police department, crime lab and district attorney's office. Chits cashed, favors recalled, Jessica had been batting her eyelashes for weeks; Vincent had been twisting arms, sometimes literally, for months.

Also downstairs were Jessica's father Peter Giovanni, most of her cousins, Colleen Byrne and her friend Laurent, Byrne's father Paddy. Just about everyone who could be roped in was in attendance.

Byrne arrived a little late.

JESSICA AND BYRNE STOOD at the top of the stairs, at the entrance to the attic. Before them was arrayed a roomful of boxes.

'Wow,' Byrne said.

'I'm a total pack rat, aren't I?'

Byrne looked around, shrugged. 'It's not that bad. I've seen worse. Remember the old lady on Osage, the one with two hundred cats?'

'Thanks.'

Jessica noticed some hair on Byrne's shoulder. She reached over, brushed it off.

'Did you get a haircut?'

'Yeah,' he said. 'I popped in and got a trim.'

'You *popped in*?'

'Yeah. No good?'

'No, it looks fine. It's just that I've never "popped in" for a haircut. It takes me four to six weeks to make the decision, then it's another month of doubt, steering committees, estimates, near misses, appointments cancelled at the last second. It's a life-changing event for me.'

'Well, it's pretty much a haircut for me.'

'You have it *so* easy.'

'Oh yeah,' Byrne said. 'My life's a Happy Meal.'

Jessica lifted a few boxes that were, mercifully, light. At least she had taken to labeling things in the past few years. This one read ST. PATRICK'S DAY ORNAMENTS. She did not remember ever buying or displaying St. Patrick's Day ornaments. It looked like she was going to keep them nonetheless, so she could not use them in the future. She put the box by the top of the stairs, turned back.

'Let me ask you something,' she said.

'Shoot.'

'How many times have you moved in the last ten years?'

Byrne thought for a few moments. 'Four times,' he said. 'Why?'

'I don't know. I guess I was just wondering if you're still hanging onto a bunch of completely pointless, useless crap.'

'No,' Byrne said. 'Everything I have is absolutely necessary. I'm a Spartan.'

'Right. You should know that I once talked to Donna about this very thing.'

'Uh-oh.'

In the past few years Jessica and Byrne's ex-wife Donna had become good friends.

'Oh yeah. And she said that when you guys were married, and you moved from the apartment into your house, the first thing you packed was your Roger Ramjet nightlight.'

'Hey! That was a safety issue, okay?'

'Uh-huh. Still have it?'

'I do not,' Byrne said. 'I have a Steve Canyon nightlight now. Roger Ramjet is for kids.'

'Tell you what,' Jessica said. 'I will if you will.'

It was a game they sometimes played – like Truth or Dare, but without the dare. Ninety-nine percent of the time is was light-hearted. Once in a while it was serious. This was not one of those times. Still, there were rules.

'Sure,' Byrne said. 'You're on.'

'Okay. What is the most ludicrous piece of clothing you still own? I mean, something you know you will never wear again, not in a million years, but you just can't bring yourself to part with it?'

'That's an easy one.'

'Really?'

'Oh yeah,' Byrne said. 'A pair of 33-inch waist green velvet pants. Real plum-smugglers.'

Jessica almost laughed. She cleared her throat instead. No laughing was one of the big rules of the game. 'Wow.' It was all she could muster.

'Is that *wow* I once had a 33-inch waist, or *wow* green velvet?'

This was a no-win question. She opted for the velvet.

'Well,' Byrne said. 'I bought them in New York in my Thin Lizzy days. I really wanted to be Phil Lynott. You should have seen me.'

'I would pay good money for that,' Jessica said. 'A lot of women in the department would chip in, too.'

'What about you?'

Jessica glanced at her watch. 'My God. Look at the time.'

'Jess.'

'Okay. When I was nineteen, going to Temple, I had a date with this guy – Richie Randazzo. He invited me to his cousin's wedding in Cheltenham and I saved for three months for the cutest little red dress from Strawbridge's. It's a size four. I still have it.'

'What, you're not a size four?'

'You are the greatest man who has ever lived.'

'As if this were in doubt,' Byrne said. 'One question, though.'

'What?'

'You went out with a guy named Richie Randazzo?'

'If you didn't factor in the mullet, the rusted-out Toronado with the fur-trimmed rearview mirror, and the fact that he drank Southern Comfort and Vernor's, he was kind of cute.'

'At least *I* never had a mullet,' Byrne said. 'Ever.'

'I could always check with Donna, you know.'

Byrne looked at his watch. 'Look at the time.'

Jessica laughed, letting him off the hook. She fell silent for a few moments, looking around the attic. It occurred to her that she would never be back in this room. 'Man.'

'What?'

'My whole life is in these boxes.' She opened a box, took out some photos. On top were pictures of her parents' wedding.

Out of the corner of her eye Jessica saw Byrne turn away for a second, giving her the moment with her memories. Jessica put the photos back.

'So, let me ask you one more thing,' she said.

'Sure.'

Jessica took a few seconds. She hoped that her voice was going to be steady. She put her hand on one of the boxes, the one with the piece of green yarn around it. 'If you have something, some memento that is a part of your life, and you know that the next time you see it, it's going to break your heart, do you keep it? Do you hold onto it anyway? Even though you know it is going to cause you pain the next time you look at it?'

Byrne knew that she was talking about her mother.

'Do you remember her well?' he asked.

Jessica had been five years old when her mother died. Her father had never remarried, had never loved another woman. 'Yeah. Sometimes. Not her face, though. I remember how she smelled. Her shampoo, her perfume. I remember how in summer, when we went to Wildwood, she smelled like Coppertone and cherry Life Savers. And I remember her voice. She always sang with the radio.'

Heaven Must Have Sent You. It was one of her mother's favorites. Jessica hadn't thought of that song in years.

'How about you?' she asked. 'Do you think about your mom a lot?'

'Enough to keep her alive,' Byrne said and leaned against the wall. It was his storytelling pose.

'When I was a kid, and my father used to chew me out, my mother would always run interference, you know? I mean *physically*. She would physically get in between us. She wouldn't make excuses for me, and I always ended up getting punished, but while my father was upbraiding me she would stand with her hands clasped behind her back. I'd look at her hands, and she always had a fifty cent piece for me. My father never knew. I'd have to do my time, but afterwards I always had fifty-cents to blow on a water ice or a comic book when I got paroled.'

Jessica smiled, thinking about anyone – especially Paddy Byrne – intimidating her partner.

'She died on my birthday, you know,' Byrne said.

Jessica *didn't* know. Byrne had never told her this. At that moment she tried to think of something sadder than this, and found herself at a loss. 'I didn't know.'

Byrne nodded. 'You know how you always notice your birthday when you see it printed somewhere, or hear it mentioned in a movie or on television?'

'Yeah,' Jessica said. 'You always turn to the people around you and say *hey . . . that's my birthday.*'

Byrne smiled. 'It's like that for me when I go to the cemetery. I always do a double take when I see the headstone, even though I *know*.' He put his hands in his pockets. 'It will never be my birthday again. It will always be the day she died, no matter how long I live.'

Jessica couldn't think of anything to say. It mattered little, because she had never met a more perceptive person than Kevin Byrne. He always knew when to move things along.

'So, your question?' he asked. 'The one about whether or not to save something, even though you know it will break your heart?'

'What about it?'

Byrne reached into his pocket, pulled something out. It was a fifty-cent piece. Jessica looked at the coin, at her partner. At this moment, his eyes were the deepest emerald she had ever seen.

'It's a strange thing about heartbreak,' Byrne said. 'Sometimes it's the best thing for you. Sometimes it reminds you that your heart is still beating.'

They stood, saying nothing, cosseted in this drafty room full of memory and loss. The silence was shattered by the sound of a breaking dish downstairs. Irish and Italians and booze always led to broken ceramics. Jessica and Byrne smiled at each other, and the moment dissolved.

'Ready for the big bad city?' he asked.

'No.'

Byrne picked up a box, headed for the stairs. He stopped, turned. 'You know, for a South Philly chick, you turned into kind of a wimp.'

'I have a gun in one of these boxes,' Jessica said.

Byrne ran down the steps.

TWENTY-FIVE

B Y TEN O'CLOCK THEY HAD EVERYTHING IN THE NEW HOUSE. WHAT had seemed like a reasonable amount of goods in the Lexington Park house now filled up every room, every corner, every cabinet. If they put the sofa and two of the dining-room chairs on the roof, they could just about make everything fit.

Byrne stood across the street from the row house. A pair of older teenage girls walked by, reminding him of Lucy Doucette.

When he had first met Lucy at the group regression-therapy sessions she had seemed so lost. He did not know much about her life, but she had told him enough for him to know that she was troubled by a traumatic event in her childhood. He recalled her efforts at the regression-therapy group, her inability to recall anything about the incident. He didn't know if she had been molested or not. Running into her accidentally in the city reminded him how he had promised to look in on her from time to time. He had not.

'Kevin?'

It was a tiny voice. Byrne turned around and saw that it was Jessica's daughter Sophie, bundled up, standing on the sidewalk in front of the porch. The front door was open, and through it Byrne could see Peter Giovanni inside, leaning against the handrail, keeping one eye on his granddaughter. Once a father, always a cop.

Byrne crossed the street. For a long time Jessica had insisted that

Sophie should call him Mr. Byrne. It had taken a while for Byrne to change that, and it looked like it had finally taken hold. Byrne got down to Sophie's level, noticing that she wasn't as small as she had been even last year at this time. 'Hey, sweetie.'

'Thanks for helping out.'

'Oh, you're welcome,' Byrne said. 'Do you like your new house?'

'It's small.'

Byrne looked over her shoulder. 'It's not that small. I think it's pretty cool.'

Sophie shrugged. 'It's all right, I guess.'

'Plus your school is only a block away. You can sleep late.'

Sophie giggled. 'You don't know my mom.'

The truth was, he did. He soon realized the folly of his statement.

Sophie glanced up the street. The looming structure of Sacred Heart Parochial School was silhouetted against the carbon-blue night sky. She looked back at Byrne. 'Did you go to Catholic school?'

'Oh yeah,' Byrne said. He wanted to tell her that he still had ruler marks on his knuckles to prove it, but decided against it.

'Did you like it?'

How to answer *this*? 'Well, do you have a kid in your school who is always goofing off, always getting into trouble?'

'Yeah,' Sophie said. 'In my school it's Bobby Tomasello.'

'Well, in *my* school that kid was me.'

'You got into trouble?'

'All the time,' Byrne said.

'Did they make you sit in the corner?'

Byrne smiled at the memory. 'Let me put it this way. Sister Mary Alice ended up putting my desk in the corner. It saved everyone a trip. In fact, I had a corner office in every one of my classrooms.'

Sophie's face softened into an expression that Byrne had seen a thousand times on Jessica's face, a look of compassion and under-standing. 'It's all right, Kevin,' she said. 'You turned out okay.'

The jury was still out on that one, Byrne thought. Still, it was nice to hear, even if it was coming from a seven-year-old. Maybe *especially* from a seven-year-old. 'Thanks.'

They fell silent for a moment, listening to the sounds of the party coming from inside the house.

'I like Colleen,' Sophie said.

'Yeah,' Byrne said. 'She's pretty special.'

'She taught me something.'

'Oh yeah?'

Sophie nodded. She thought for a moment, wrinkling her brow, then balled her fists, extended a finger, stopped, thought a bit more, started over. This time she extended her hands, rubbed one palm across the other, lifted the index finger on each hand, bumped fists, and pointed at Byrne.

It was American Sign Language for 'Nice to meet you.'

'*Very* good,' Byrne said. 'Did you just learn that?'

Sophie nodded. 'It took me a few times.'

Byrne smiled. 'It took me *way* more than a few times.'

A few minutes later he kissed Sophie on top of her head, watched her walk back inside. After she was inside, Byrne stood and observed Jessica's family through the window for a while. It had been a long time since he'd been part of something like this.

He thought about Sophie's sign language, how determined she was, how she stayed with it until she got it right. He considered how the oldest sayings were the truest, like that one about the apple not falling far from the tree.

BYRNE WALKED DOWN THIRD Street, got into the van. He had grown up not far from here. He remembered a variety store on the corner. He used to get his water pistols and comic books there, cadging the occasional Baby Ruth and Butterfinger. He remembered a kid who got beat up once in the alley behind the store, a kid who was thought to have molested a little girl from the neighborhood. Byrne had been sitting on the corner with his cousin Patrick when it happened. He remembered the kid screaming. It was the first time he had ever encountered violence like that, the first time he had ever heard someone in so much pain. He believed that all those sounds, all the dark echoes of violence, in many ways remained.

Byrne sat there for a long time, not moving, just rolling the fifty-cent piece over his fingers, the memories of his old neighborhood misting across his mind.

Someone emerged from the shadows just outside the driver's side window of the van. Byrne sat upright. It was Jessica. He rolled down the window.

'What's up?' he asked. 'Ready to move back already?'

'You know the paper that was wrapped around the victims' heads?'

'What about it?'

'We have a make.'

TWENTY-SIX

THE CRIME LAB – OFFICIALLY KNOWN AS THE FORENSIC SCIENCE Center, but never called that – was a massive building that had once been a schoolhouse, located just a few blocks from the Roundhouse at Eighth and Poplar Streets.

The reigning sovereign of the documents section was Sergeant Helmut Rohmer. Hell Rohmer was thirty-five, and a giant, measuring six-four, weighing two-fifty. Besides his strange and eclectic taste in music, which ran from Iron Maiden to Kitty Wells, he was known for his T-shirts – always black, never bearing the same saying twice. He must have had hundreds. He was starting to receive them in the mail, even from people he had helped put away in prison. Today his shirt read:

PADDLE FASTER.
I HEAR BANJOS.

His considerable arms were ringed with rose tattoos, or some variation, which now finished with ivy circling his wrists and ending on the backs of his hands. He was always well-groomed – right down to his oddly manicured fingers. Jessica figured that his manicures had something to do with his sense of the tactile. Hell Rohmer didn't want anything interfering with his sense of touch. He was almost metaphysical in his approach to document forensics. It was one of the reasons why he and Byrne spoke the same language.

'Good evening, sleuths,' Hell said.

'Good evening, alchemist,' Byrne replied.

Hell smiled. 'I have your paper,' he said. 'You can only hide from the Weavemeister for so long.'

On the wall were six enlarged photographs of the paper found on the victims, front and back. The photographs showed the blood that had leached from the lacerations on each of the victim's foreheads, as well as the small dot of blood from the shallow puncture wound. A line, a dot, and the rough figure eight where the ears were mutilated.

'What do we have?' Jessica asked.

Hell picked up a small square of the paper sample, cut from the end of one of the bands. 'This is pricey stuff,' he said, running a finger across the slightly pebbled surface. 'It's beautiful, really. Our boy has exquisite taste.' Hell zoned for a moment, his eyes going a bit unfocused. Hell Rohmer was definitely a touchy-feely sort of guy.

'Hell?'

'Okay. Sorry. The paper is handmade, a hundred percent cotton, acid-free. Which puts it into the same category as about ten thousand brands. I'm not equipped to do a comparison test to determine the make, and I was just about to send it off to the FBI – which, as you know, can take a month or two to get back – when I saw something.' Helmut held up a sample. 'This was cut from the paper we took from the female victim. If you look here, you can see a small segment of a watermark.' Hell held the paper up to a strong light, but not too close. Jessica saw what looked like the portion of a shoulder.

'Is that a cherub of some sort?' Jessica asked.

Hell shook his head. 'The watermark is Venus de Milo. It's not on the other sample, so I'm thinking these were cut from a larger sheet.'

Hell displayed another printout. It was an extreme close-up of the edge of the paper, photographed through a microscope. 'This was cut with a large blade, which is indicated by the slight tearing of the fiber. I think he used a paper cutter, instead of an X-acto blade, scissors, or razor blade. The shearing is consistent front to back, with the fibers pushed downward. Too uniform to have been done by hand.'

Hell pointed to the sample.

'And while this might look white, it is really Felt Light Grey. Deckled on two sides, which leads me to believe it's deckled on four. The band is twenty-four inches long, which leads me to believe it was cut from a sheet that was twenty-four by twenty-six, which is fairly standard in printmaking.'

'This is printmaking paper?'

'Among other things.'

Hell put the sample down, picked up a few pages of computer printouts.

'It's the watermark that jumped out. Without it, we would have had to wait for Washington on this.' He pointed to one of the lines on the printout, highlighted in lime green. 'The manufacturer of this paper is headquartered in Milan, Italy, and the line is called *Atriana*. Really high-end stuff. Printmaking, mostly, but they make all kinds of multi-use paper – stationery, canvas, vellum, linen. But this stuff is top of the line. One sheet of this paper retails for about seventy dollars.'

'Wow.'

'Yeah,' Hell said. 'And dig this. This company also supplies the paper for the Euro.'

'The currency?'

'The one.'

'They have two distributors in the US,' Hell said. 'As far as I can tell this paper is available at only twenty retail stores across the country. Mostly art supplies and specialty paper shops. Unfortunately – for us, not our bad boy – the paper can be ordered from a dozen online retailers.'

'Are there any stores in Philly that carry it?' Jessica asked.

'No,' Hell said. He smiled, held up a 3 x 5 card with an address on it. 'But there is a store in Doylestown.'

Jessica took the address.

'No applause?'

Jessica clapped.

'Thank you. And now to the wax.' On the table sat a small covered glass dish. The wax seal was inside. 'This is standard candle wax, not sealing wax, which is why it has begun to disintegrate.'

'What's the difference?'

'Well, about five hundred years ago, sealing wax was made primarily of beeswax and something called Venice turpentine, which is an extract of the larch tree. The wax was uncolored in those days, but when the Renaissance hit, folks started to color it with vermilion, and do you really want to know any of this?'

'Maybe one of these days,' Jessica said. 'Right now I'd love to know where our boy bought this. I would like a clear video of him leaving the store, and a copy of his driver's license. Do you have that?'

'No. And what's worse, this candle wax is available at every Rite-Aid, Wal-Mart and Target in the country. But not in this color.'

'What do you mean?'

'Well, what I was getting to, before I was so brusquely interrupted, was that this particular sample was not colored with any old vermilion.'

It took Jessica a second to realize what Hell Rohmer was saying. One look at Byrne told her he'd gotten it as well. She turned back to Hell.

'No.'

'I'm afraid so. The coloring is blood. This is a bad, bad pony, this guy.'

Jessica looked at Byrne just as someone entered the lab and stopped by the door. Hell crossed the room, disappeared from Jessica's line of sight. In the reflection from one of the glass cabinets she saw that the new arrival was Irina Kohl. Irina had with her a few folders, one of which she placed in Hell's hands. Then Jessica saw the diminutive Irina get on her tiptoes and kiss Hell Rohmer flush on the mouth. Hell turned and saw that Jessica could see them in the cabinet's reflection.

The two of them, now red as raspberries, walked back to join Jessica and Byrne.

'Um, you didn't see that,' Hell whispered to Jessica.

'See what?'

Hell winked.

'I'm glad you're here,' Irina said, plowing forward. 'I think we may have something on the murder weapon.'

Irina Kohl worked in the lab's firearms ID unit, which also handled tool marks, and was in her late twenties, a prototypical lab dweller – neat in appearance, precise in manner and speech, probably a little too smart for Mensa. Beneath her lab coat she wore a suit coat, white button-down shirt, and lavender knit tie.

Irina opened a folder, removed some enlargements.

'The wire used as the ligature was made of woven multi-strand titanium.' She pointed to an extreme close-up of the ligature marks on the first two victims. Even to the naked eye the woven characteristics were visible. The flesh bore an imprint of the three-strand weave. 'We found traces of the metal in the wound.'

'What is something like this used for?' Jessica asked.

'There are a lot of uses for it. In general, titanium wire is specified for medical devices, bone screws, orthodontic appliances. In different gauges it is all over the aerospace, medical and marine manufacturing map. It is low-density and has a high resistance to corrosion.'

Irina then picked up a blown-up photograph, as well as a pair of slides.

'I also found hair samples in the ligature wound on the first two victims. We haven't gotten a crack at the third victim yet.' She pointed to the two slides. 'These are from Sharon Beckman and Kenneth Beckman.'

'Do you think this is our killer's hair?' Jessica asked.

'No,' Irina said. 'I'm afraid not. These samples are definitely not human.'

Jessica looked at Byrne, back. 'Not human as in . . .'

'Well, animal.' Irina pushed up her thick glasses. She scrunched her face, as if smelling something unpleasant. Jessica supposed this was her way of waiting for the conversation to regenerate. She also noted that the woman was wearing two different lipsticks. One shade on her upper lip, one on the lower.

'Well, *duh*, Jess,' Jessica said, berating herself. 'I mean, what else, alien?'

Irina continued, undaunted. 'Domestic animal specifically.'

'We're talking dog or cat?' Jessica asked.

'Not domesti*cated*, necessarily. What I mean is domestic as in cow, sheep, horse.' Irina got a little more animated. 'See, if we're talking the hair of domestic animals there are a number of variations in color and length. However, a lot of these identifiers are pretty general. In order to tell the difference between, say, a dog and a cat, or between a cow and a moose, you really need the root to be present. Which, unfortunately, in this case, we do not have.'

She slipped a slide onto the stage of a microscope, clipped it in.

'But we're just getting started.' Irina smiled at Hell. Hell beamed.

Irina then peered into the microscope eyepiece, did a little fine focusing. 'If you take a look here, you can see it.' She stepped back.

Jessica stepped forward, looked through the microscope.

'You see it is quite coarse. The medulla is unbroken,' Irina said. 'The pigment is fine and evenly distributed.'

'Yeah,' Jessica said. 'I was just going to say that about the medulla.' The image she saw looked like a long dark brown tube. She might just as well have been looking at a Tootsie Roll. Hell Rohmer watched Irina, sunny with admiration, seething with forensic lust. Jessica and Byrne had worked with the two of them many times. Hell and Irina liked to have scientifically clueless detectives and other investigators look though microscopes. It validated them as criminalists.

'What tipped me was the ovoid structures,' Irina added.

'Every time,' Jessica said, stepping away from the microscope. 'So what are you saying? I mean, *I* understand it. Tell us for Kevin's benefit.'

Byrne smiled.

'Well, this is not exactly my field,' Irina said. 'So I'm going to send this out. We should know something by tomorrow at the latest.'

Jessica handed Irina a card with her cellphone number on it. 'Call me the second you have it.'

'Will do,' Irina said. 'And our freaky killer better get some game.'

'Why's that?'

Irina smiled. Jessica saw her hand covertly brush up against Hell Rohmer's hand. 'We're about to make his life awfully uncomfortable.'

*

ON THE WAY OUT to the car Jessica thought about the lab and the curious creatures who toiled within. Physical evidence was, as they say, a silent witness to every misdeed, always present at crime scenes due to the simple phenomenon of transference. No individual can enter or leave any enclosed area without picking up or leaving behind innumerable items of physical evidence. But the evidence alone has little value. Only after it has been detected, collected, analyzed, interpreted and presented will it yield meaning and context.

As a rule, criminals have no idea who the people are who plug away in forensic labs all over the world and how dedicated they are to rooting out the truth. If they did know, they wouldn't be so cavalier about leaving at their crime scenes any one of the million skin cells or hundreds of hairs we shed every day, not to mention saliva, footprints, blood, or fibers from clothing.

As Jessica got into the car she also thought about how her job sometimes resembled an episode of *The X-Files*.

These samples are definitely not human.

TWENTY-SEVEN

BYRNE PARKED ACROSS THE STREET FROM THE MOUNT OLIVE Cemetery. He had stopped by the main office, spoken to the night security officer. Considering what had happened there that day, he didn't need a trigger happy ex-PPD freaking out about the man standing in the middle of the graveyard.

He thought about the vision he had gotten when he had been here before. What did it all mean?

He tried to add up the hours of sleep he had missed in the past week, but couldn't. The weight of his exhaustion prevented him from making an accurate accounting.

Byrne laid his head back on the seat. Just for a moment. Just a moment of peace.

Sleep came quickly. In the dream he was in a vast concert hall, the only person sitting in the audience. Onstage was a full philharmonic orchestra. He looked around the elegant surroundings. The floor was slicked with blood. On each seat was a severed finger.

He jumped to his feet as the music swelled, ran up the aisle to the lobby. On one wall of the lobby were two words written in bright red blood:

you know

Byrne ran from the hall, down the sidewalks, where everyone had the face of a victim he knew, a case he had investigated. He found his van in an otherwise empty parking lot. He jumped in, his heart racing fit to burst. He noticed the smell immediately. He turned around to find a decomposing body posed in the back, shaved and hairless, its eyes open, familiar eyes—

Byrne sat upright in the driver's seat, the perspiration slicking his body despite the chill in the air. Outside, the city of Philadelphia was pitch black and silent, the only sounds the occasional car trolling by. Around him the dead were still dead.

He got out of the van, breathing in deeply the cold night air.

You know.

He looked at his watch.

It was 2:52.

TWENTY-EIGHT

LUCY SPENT THE MORNING ON AUTOPILOT, HER EMOTIONS RACING between approach and avoidance. Neither of these were terms that she had ever used in relationship to her state of mind until she had started seeing psychologists. They had a different way of speaking, those people, a wholly separate dictionary. For instance, you didn't just recall something, you had *declarative memory*. Or when you applied simple logic to problems, and solved them, it was called *fluid intelligence*. And then there was her favorite. If you were the kind of person who defined yourself by your own thoughts or actions, you weren't just confident, or happy in your own skin. No, no, no. You had *independent construals of self*.

Lucy almost laughed. Her inside joke – on those rare occasions when she felt good enough to appreciate a joke, inside or out – was that she was just going through her construal cycle.

Regardless, on this day, in this place, Lucy was all but overcome by her new feelings. The craziest thing had been running into Detective Byrne the day before. She had been so hyper when she saw him that, even though she knew that she knew him, she didn't realize who he was. Until he smiled.

They had met at her regression-therapy sessions. He was the man in the group who had been dead for a whole minute. They'd gone for coffee once, shared their experiences. Well, Lucy had listened mostly, because she didn't really know what had happened to her. Yesterday he had given her his card and told her to call if she ever wanted to talk. She wondered if he could help her. She wondered if he would laugh at her suspicions of the man she thought she'd seen come out of Room 1208. No, he wouldn't laugh, but he *would* probably tell her she was imagining things.

As she worked she looked at her watch every five minutes, for the first time in a long while not really gauging her day by how many rooms she had completed, mentally recording the time she entered and left.

Each room attendant had their own section key, an electronic card similar to a guest key, that allowed them access to their rooms but not to other parts of the hotel. If an attendant said they entered a room at 9:08 and it was really 9:21, management could find it out in a second. A lot of dismissed attendants found out the hard way that computers never lie. The lock didn't say when you left, only when you entered.

Today all the rooms blended together, and Lucy had no idea how long it was taking her to finish each one.

He smelled like apples.

That could have been anything, though. There were a million plausible explanations for this. Lots of people wear dark overcoats. For gosh sake, even Detective Byrne wore a dark overcoat.

Lucy stood at the end of the hallway, near the elevators. She looked down the corridor, at the east wing. In this direction there were eight rooms. Rooms 1201 through 1208. Today she was able to swap this wing with a girl who worked on the seventh floor, promising to fix the girl's portable CD player in exchange for the favor. But it would only be for today. Lucy would have to enter Room 1208 tomorrow. She wasn't looking forward to it.

ALL ROOM ATTENDANTS GOT a fifteen-minute break in the morning. Lucy usually spent her time reading in the cafeteria or, if it was a nice day, she would run over to Rittenhouse Square for a full five minutes in the sun. It was amazing what even five minutes in sunlight could do for her mood. Today, she stepped into the small courtyard behind the hotel. She almost got lost in the cloud of cigarette smoke. You weren't supposed to smoke within fifty yards of the building, but no one ever listened and the rule had never been enforced.

When she rounded the corner at the back to the hotel she saw her friend Amanda sitting on a delivery pallet, eating a tangerine.

'Hey, girl,' Amanda said.

'Hi.' Lucy sat down next to Amanda. Amanda Cuaron was everything Lucy was not. Exotic, dark-eyed, a true Latin beauty, always flirting. Whenever Amanda was around Lucy felt like a rubber tulip.

'Hey, I forgot to ask, did you see that guy yesterday?' Amanda asked.

That guy was the Dreamweaver. Mr. Costa. Lucy wasn't sure how much she wanted to tell Amanda. Amanda was her friend and all, but Lucy had never shared secrets with her. She'd never shared her secrets with anyone. 'Yeah,' she said. 'I saw him.'

'How did it go?'

'It went okay.'

Amanda just stared at her – she was not going to get off the hook with such a brief explanation. 'Well? Was he weird? Did he wear a pointy hat and carry a wand?'

'Oh yeah,' Lucy said. 'And he had a long white beard. Didn't I mention the beard?'

Amanda smiled. 'Is he cute?'

Lucy snorted. 'Shut *up*. He's like a hundred years old.'

'Is he cute?'

Lucy just rolled her eyes. 'I'm going to see him again today.' Lucy hadn't realized that she'd made the decision to do this until this second.

Amanda smiled her lascivious smile. 'Mala *chica*.'

They both checked their watches at the same moment. They had another six minutes.

Amanda pointed to the wall next to the delivery bay. There was something carved into the stone. *RL loves TJ*.

'I wonder if they're still in love,' Amanda said.

Lucy doubted it. She didn't believe in true love. 'Well, it *is* written in stone.'

Amanda laughed. 'I think that was probably done back when this place was apartments.'

'When was this an apartment building?'

'I think up until maybe 1999. Something like that,' she said. 'I think it was kind of a famous place, too.'

'How so?'

'Well, mostly because of that little girl. You know about that, don't you?'

'What are you talking about?'

'I'm not a hundred percent sure what happened – you could ask Sergio. He'd definitely know.'

Sergio was an older guy who worked in maintenance. He had been with the building for a long time.

'But, from what I understand, a little girl got killed here,' Amanda added.

Lucy shuddered. 'What do you mean, killed? Like an accident or something?'

'No. Like *killed* killed.'

'What are you saying? She was *murdered*?'

'Yeah.' Amanda wiggled her fingers at Lucy, made spooky Halloween noises. 'They say her ghost walks these very halls.'

'Stop it.'

Amanda giggled. 'You're so easy.'

'How old was the girl?'

Amanda shrugged, peeled off another section of tangerine, offered it to Lucy. Lucy declined. 'Not sure. But not too old, though. Ten or eleven, maybe.'

'How did she . . . you know.'

'How did she die?' Amanda shrugged. 'No idea. But I don't think they ever caught the guy that did it.'

As creepy as Lucy already felt today, the feeling had just doubled.

'I think it's one of the cases this bunch of nut jobs who are staying here this week are investigating,' Amanda said. 'Or talking about investigating. God only knows what they do.'

Lucy was speechless for the moment. Amanda stood up, threw her tangerine peels in the nearby Dumpster.

'So, are we on?' Amanda asked.

At first Lucy didn't know what Amanda was talking about. Then she remembered. She had told Amanda that she would go out with her for a drink at Fluid, a dance club on Fourth Street, on Halloween Eve Night – always a crazy time in Philly, to say the least – and, according to Amanda, a ton of cute college guys always showed up. This year they were probably all going to be dressed up like Robert Pattinson.

'Yeah,' Lucy said. 'Why not?'

'Awesome. And you are definitely going to let me do something with your hair. We've got to babe you up, *chica*. Maybe get you laid.'

'*Amanda.*'

Amanda giggled. 'I'll be by your mansion around eight.'

'Cool beans.'

Amanda walked back into the hotel but Lucy stayed put. She couldn't stop thinking about the little girl Amanda had mentioned. *Murdered.* At the place Lucy *worked.* She had to find out more about it, although she wasn't sure why. Maybe because there was a dead zone in her own life. Maybe it was because for the past nine years she had felt a dark kinship with all young girls who had been touched by evil. They were her sisters.

They say her ghost walks these very halls.

Thanks, Amanda, Lucy thought. *Thanks a lot.*

TWENTY-NINE

DOYLESTOWN WAS A QUAINT TOWNSHIP OF ABOUT EIGHT THOUSAND
in Bucks County. The Ulrich Art Supply store was a standalone
building, a converted ivy-veined coach house on North Main Street,
across the road from the Mercer Square Shopping Center. The front
windows held a display of paints, canvases, brushes, easels. Halloween
decorations ringed the window and door.

On the way to Doylestown Jessica and Byrne decided not to
approach the store in any official capacity. Because this was the only
store within reach of the city that carried the paper used in these homicides, there was a chance that they might tip their hand by approaching
the store as law-enforcement officers looking for information. If
someone in the store was acquainted with the killer they might get
on the phone the minute they left. If Plan A failed, they could always
come in with guns and badges blazing.

They watched the store for a few minutes. There was a woman
behind the counter, working on a small display rack. No one entered
the store and they did not see anyone else working.

'Looks like you're up,' Jessica said.

'I thought *you* were the undercover queen.'

'I am,' Jessica said. 'But I think metrosexual is out of my range.'

'What did we say about that word?'

'Sorry.'

Byrne took a moment, scoping the terrain. 'Who am I again?'

Jessica gave it some thought. 'I'm thinking Bennett Strong.'

Byrne nodded. It was a good choice. Tough but suitably fey, given the venue. 'Where was the show?'

Jessica turned her iPhone so that Byrne could see it. She had searched the web on the way into Doylestown and found a recent print show in Philadelphia. She had also looked up the art supply store's website. There she found the owner's name. Alicia Webster.

Byrne pulled his badge from his belt, along with his weapon and his holster, put it all in the back seat. He took off his jacket.

'Want some hair gel?' Jessica asked.

Byrne just gave her a look.

ALICIA WEBSTER WAS IN her mid to late thirties. She wore a beige knit cardigan and black corduroy slacks. Her eyeglasses hung around her neck on a rawhide lace.

She glanced up as Byrne entered the store accompanied by a ring of a bell. 'May I help you?' she asked. Pleasant smile, bright eyes.

Byrne proffered a business card. On it was simply a name – no phone number, no address, no email, no website. He had a stack of them in his briefcase. Ten different names. You never knew.

'My name is Bennett Strong,' he said. 'I am the owner of Strong Galleries, New York City.'

The woman's face lit up.

'You are Miss Webster?'

The woman looked surprised that he knew her name.

'I am.' She held up her left hand, wiggled her ring finger. 'But it's Mrs.'

Byrne put a hand to his heart. 'Mea culpa.' He smiled at her. 'Mrs. Of course.'

A blush. 'How can I help you, Mr. Strong?'

'I love your store, by the way. Did I see Kolinsky sables on the way in?' It was something Byrne had seen on the store's website. He knew that the woman carried the brushes.

'Yes,' she said. 'You know your brushes.'

'And now to the point. I recently attended the PortPhilio show in Philadelphia. Did you manage to make it to the affair?'

Say no, Byrne thought. *Please say no.*

'No. I wanted to, but I'm all alone here since my son went back to school. I couldn't get away.'

'It was fabulous.'

The door opened behind them, ringing the bell again. A woman entered the store. Alicia's eyes flicked over to the new customer, then back.

'Anyway, I met a man there, a printmaker, who recommended your shop. He showed me some of his work and it was fantastic.'

'How nice.'

'I would really like to contact him, but I'm afraid I lost his card and I don't remember his name.'

'And he said he purchased supplies here?'

'Yes.'

'He was from Doylestown?'

'I don't know.'

'What did the man look like?'

Shit, Byrne thought. He had no idea what to say. He didn't even know if it *was* a man. He aimed for the middle, culling from a standard profile. 'I'm terrible at these things. But I'd say he was thirty to forty. Medium height and weight. I'm not sure of his hair because he was wearing a ball cap.' This was as vague as Byrne could get. He smiled at Alicia. 'I'm a lot better with remembering women.'

Another blush. 'Well, that's not too much for me to go on.'

'Maybe this will help. During the course of our conversation he mentioned his printmaking technique, and said he was enamored of a certain brand of paper. An Italian paper. Quite expensive.'

'Do you remember the line?'

'I do not. But he showed me a sample and the watermark was Venus de Milo.'

'Atriana.'

Byrne snapped his fingers. 'That's it.'

The woman frowned. 'That's not an item we generally keep in stock. I've only sold a few dozen sheets in the past year or so.'

Alicia turned to her computer, tapped a few keys. In a moment a screen came up. Byrne could see the reflection in her glasses. It was a database program and she had found an entry. She nodded, perhaps remembering the man.

'I'm afraid I can't give you anyone's name. Our mailing list is confidential, of course.'

'Of course.'

'If you'd like, I could take your information and have them get in touch with you.'

'That would be great.'

Just then there was a loud crash at the back of the store. Alicia spun around to see a woman at the rear, next to a toppled display rack of oil paints.

'Shoot!' the woman at the back exclaimed.

'Oh my,' Byrne said. 'Look, why don't you tend to this terribly clumsy woman and I'll stop back in a few minutes. I have to hit the ATM, anyway.'

'That would be fine.'

As Alicia walked to the rear of the store to help Jessica pick up the spilled merchandise, Byrne spun the LCD monitor to face him. His eyes scanned the screen. The problem was that he was not wearing his glasses. The customer's name was a little larger than the rest of the entry. He got that with no problem. It was a company called Marcato LLC.

Beneath that: *Attention JP Novak.* Byrne looked at the bottom. Philadelphia. In between, it was mostly a blur.

He spun the monitor back, turned on his heels, and left the store.

THEY PULLED OUT OF the parking lot and headed back to route 611.

'Did we get it?'

'I got the name,' Byrne said. 'And a partial address.'

'A *partial* address?'

Byrne fell silent.

'You weren't wearing your glasses.'

Byrne plowed forward. He checked the notes that he'd scribbled after leaving the store. 'The paper was purchased by a company called Marcato LLC. Contact name is JP Novak. The address is in Philly. Something something something something Ashingdale Road. Or Arlington. I think the number was 8180 or 5150. Maybe 6160.'

Jessica shook her head. 'You know, those glasses do serve a purpose.'

'I don't see you wearing yours all the time.'

'Mind your own business, Mr. Strong. Now, drive the car and let me start sleuthing.'

ON THE WAY BACK to Philadelphia Jessica called in the name. There was no phone listing for a JP Novak, nor anyone with that name in PCIC with a criminal record. They found more than three dozen listings for Novaks with J as an initial: John, Joseph, Jerry, Jerszy, Jacob, Joshua.

She also looked up Marcato and did not find any company with that name, LLC or otherwise. She did find a definition of the word and found that it was Italian for *marked*, and when it was applied to music it meant performing the note with an 'attack' and a sustain of two-thirds of the original written length, followed by an audible counted rest.

According to one source the *marcato* sound was 'a rhythmic thrust followed by a decay of the sound.'

Who would name their company this? Jessica wondered.

WHEN THEY RETURNED TO the Roundhouse they searched every database for a JP Novak, as well as for Philadelphia streets named Ashingdon or dozens of possible permutations. They asked everyone on the floor if they knew of any Philly streets or courts or lanes by that name or similar names. There were a few close matches but nothing exact.

After twenty minutes of strikeouts Jessica stood, began to peruse the large paper map on the wall. You could only look at a computer screen for so long before going six-eyed with fatigue. Somehow she put her finger on two possibilities.

'Look at this,' she said. 'There's a street in West Philly called Abingdon.'

Byrne shot to his feet. 'That's it.'

'There's also one called Ashingdale.'

'Shit.'

Josh Bontrager grabbed his coat. 'I'll take Ashingdale.'

Jessica and Byrne headed to the door. 'Kevin?'

'What?'

'Bring your glasses.'

THE ADDRESSES ON ABINGDON ROAD STOPPED AT 7000, SO THIS eliminated the chance of the address being 8180. Jessica and Byrne drove to the far end of the street, worked back from 5150. This was a body shop called D & K Motor Cars. No one inside knew anyone named Novak, nor a company called Marcato LLC.

The address at 6160 was a gentrified apartment building called the Beau Rive, perhaps at one time a warehouse. The front had recently been stuccoed, and all four apartments in the front had leaded-glass bay windows.

Byrne pulled over, cut the engine.

'Hang on,' Jessica said.

She got out of the car, walked up the steps to the apartment building. She walked into the small lobby and looked at the mailboxes. There were six suites. She scanned the names. The second to last name, in apartment 204, was Joseph Paul Novak.

Bingo.

She tried the buzzer twice. No response.

Jessica walked out of the building, across the street. She got back in the car. 'There's a Joseph Novak in apartment 204. I buzzed. Nothing.'

Byrne checked his side mirror, then did a U-turn, pulling up on the opposite side of the street in front of a Thai takeout. They had not stopped for lunch and the aromas were enticing. He put the Taurus in park, cut the engine. 'Want to stake it out for a little while?'

'Sure,' Jessica said.

They watched the pedestrian traffic up and down Abingdon Road. After ten minutes or so Jessica got restless. She got out of the car, crossed the street, leaned against a light pole, took out her cell. She pretended to have a conversation. Cellphones were, hands down, the best surveillance prop ever invented.

Finally the door to the Beau Rive opened. The first person to walk out the building was a woman in her sixties, well-dressed and accessorized. When she reached the sidewalk she stopped, rummaged through her purse, then turned around in disgust, stormed back inside. She'd obviously forgotten something.

The second person to emerge was a man. He was black, in his late twenties, in a real hurry. He came out of the door buttoning a white chef's jacket. Jessica leaned back against the lamppost, called out:

'Joseph?'

No reaction. He didn't even acknowledge her. A few minutes later the woman reemerged and walked the other way down the street, a little more urgency to her stride. As a woman who forgot something at home every day, Jessica sympathized.

Jessica then crossed the street, leaned against the car next to Byrne's open window, went back to pretending to be on the phone. Ten long minutes later another man came out of the building.

'This is him,' Jessica said.

'How do you know?'

'I know.'

Jessica walked across the sidewalk, gave her hair a quick fluff. 'Is that *Joseph*?' The man turned around. He was tall, broad-shouldered, in his mid-thirties. He had brown hair nearly to his shoulders, a fashionable one-day growth of beard. He wore a dark overcoat. His skin was alabaster pale.

'Do I know you?' he asked. His posture betrayed neither aggression nor retreat. Instead, he looked pleasantly curious.

Jessica continued toward him. 'We met last year. You're Joseph Novak, right?'

The man offered a half-smile but not one that fully committed himself to this conversation. 'I am. But I must confess I don't remember your name.'

'My name is Jessica Balzano.' She produced her ID, held it up. 'I just need to talk to you for a few moments.'

Joseph Novak looked at her badge, then back into her eyes. In this light his eyes were a pale blue, almost colorless. 'We've never met, have we?'

'No,' Jessica said. 'That was just a bold subterfuge on my part.'

The man smiled. 'Well played. But I can't imagine what it is I could tell you.' He looked over her shoulder. 'Or your partner.'

It was Jessica's turn to smile. She always had to remind herself that she and Byrne were not that hard to make as cops. 'It won't take a minute.'

Novak held up a #10 envelope. 'I just need to post this.' He pointed a half-block away, at a mailbox on the corner. He turned back to Jessica. 'I promise not to run.'

Jessica glanced at the envelope. It did not look like the paper found at the crime scenes. 'In that case, I promise not to chase you.'

Another smile. 'If you'll excuse me.'

'Of course.'

Novak threw one more glance at Byrne, then turned on his heels and walked toward the mailbox. Byrne got out of the car, crossed the street.

'That was good,' he said.

'I know.'

Novak mailed the letter and, as promised, began to walk back up the block. His size and bearing made for a striking silhouette in the afternoon light.

'Why don't you call Josh, tell him where we are?' Byrne said.

Jessica got on her cell, filled Bontrager in. She closed her phone just as Novak returned to the steps in front of his apartment building. Novak turned his attention to Byrne.

'I am Joseph Novak.'

'Kevin Byrne,' Byrne said.

'How can I help?' Novak asked.

Jessica pointed at the door to Beau Rive. 'Do you think we could chat inside? As I said, we won't take up too much of your time.'

Novak did not answer right away. When he saw that these two police officers were not about to leave, he relented. He gestured to the door. 'Please.'

THIRTY-ONE

A T THE REAR OF THE BUILDING, JOSEPH NOVAK'S APARTMENT WAS A large two-bedroom flat with ten-foot ceilings and an open floor plan. The furniture was modern, mostly brushed aluminum and leather. Against one wall, nearly floor-to-ceiling, were CDs in custom-made birch shelves. There had to be a thousand of them. Jessica noticed that they were sectioned off by category: Classical, Electronica, New Age, Jazz. There were also subcategories by composer, artist, era. Brahms, Beethoven, Bach, Enya, Parker, Mingus, Tyner, Mulligan, Chemical Brothers. The effect of sunlight streaming through the windows, playing off the crystal cases in rainbow hues, was dizzying.

Upon entering the apartment Novak immediately crossed the room to the large desk at the other side and lowered the screen on his laptop, clicked it shut.

'We won't take up too much of your time,' Byrne said.

'Not at all,' Novak replied. 'Whatever I can do to help.'

'Do you know why we're here, Mr. Novak?' Byrne asked.

Novak sat at the desk, crossed his long legs. 'I'm afraid I do not.'

Byrne placed a sheet with six photographs on the desk in front of Novak. Kenneth Beckman's picture was in the upper right-hand corner. They decided to start this way, inquiring about Beckman as if they were looking for a witness.

Jessica watched Novak closely as his gaze fell on the photo lineup. If the man instantly recognized Beckman there was no indication.

'Do you recognize any of these people?' Byrne asked.

Novak gave the process a few seconds. 'No,' he said. 'Sorry.'

'No problem.' Byrne left the photo array on the desk. He leaned against the wall near the large window, looking around the room, especially at the rack of complicated-looking electronic equipment and what might have been a sound mixing board.

'May I ask what it is that you do for a living?' Byrne asked.

'I am a recording engineer by trade,' Novak said. 'But I keep my hand in with all aspects of the music world. I review for jazz and classical publications.'

'Interesting,' Byrne said. 'I'm a fan of classic blues, myself.'

Novak smiled. 'I have a small but rather interesting collection of old blues. My treasure is the box set of 78s with early recordings of Mary Johnson, Scrapper Blackwell and Kokomo Arnold.'

'Sweet. Any Roosevelt Sykes?'

'Not yet.'

Jessica stepped forward. In a situation like this, she and her partner liked to tag-team the person they were interviewing. If you split the person's attention it gave your partner the opportunity to look around, checking the small details of the room. One wall had a series of shelves with *objets d'art* on it. Small sculptures, Maori carvings, as well as a unique stainless steel bracelet with a single garnet stone inlaid.

Jessica turned her attention back to the CDs. 'This *is* quite an impressive collection of music you have here,' Jessica said.

'Thank you,' Novak said. 'I've been at it for quite a while. But I did not purchase most of them. Receiving free and promotional CDs for review is one of the perks of being a music critic.'

'What's the downside?'

'Listening to terrible music.'

Jessica scanned the wall. 'So, from all of this music, do you have a favorite composer?'

Novak smiled again. 'I imagine that is like asking an Eskimo if he has a favorite snowflake. If pressed, for me there is Johann Sebastian Bach, and then there is everyone else.'

'I'm sorry to impose, but do you think I might use your restroom?' Jessica asked.

This was another old ploy for investigators. It gave you the opportunity to see a little more of a person's dwelling while they were talking with your partner. Not to mention the opportunity to check out their medicine cabinet and perhaps discover what meds they were taking. Someone's medications could tell you a lot about them. Plus, it was a hard thing for people to say no to.

Novak hesitated. His stare shifted to the hallway, then back. The question hung in the air.

'Yes, of course,' he said finally. 'The second door on your right.'

'Thanks.'

Jessica walked down the hallway. The kitchen was on the left, the bathroom on the right. At the end of the hall was the bedroom, its door slightly ajar.

Jessica stepped into the bathroom. It was spotless. On one wall was a large print, a black and white photograph of a man conducting an orchestra. The man was dark-haired, darkly handsome. He wore white tie and tails. Jessica looked at the caption: RICCARDO MUTI, 1986. Muti was the Italian conductor who had replaced Eugene Ormandy as the musical director of the Philadelphia Orchestra in 1980.

Jessica peeked into the bamboo wastebasket to the right of the toilet. Empty. She opened the medicine cabinet gently. Gently, because she had once opened a medicine cabinet in a similar situation, without thinking, only to have a few bottles crash loudly into the sink.

In the cabinet were an array of skincare products. No meds. If Joseph Novak took any medications, he did not keep them in his bathroom.

When she had exhausted her search, Jessica flushed the toilet. She washed her hands anyway, to keep up the illusion, and because it was a deeply ingrained habit.

She stepped out of the bathroom, listened. Byrne and Novak were still talking. She stepped to her right, inched open the bedroom door. The bedroom continued the rather industrial look of the apartment. There was a king-size platform bed, a pair of night stands bearing stainless steel lamps with rectangular linen shades.

But it wasn't the furnishings that nearly took Jessica's breath away. The entire room was covered in paper. She had to look closely to believe what she was seeing. At first she thought it might have been some kind of creative wallpaper. It was not. What she'd at first thought was wall-covering was really hundreds and hundreds of photographs, articles, magazine covers, newspaper clippings, drawings. All of them seemed to be about one subject. Murder.

Her eyes were drawn to a large corkboard. To it were pinned a number of tabloid pages. The page on top stopped her cold. It was a tear sheet from the sleazy local newspaper *The Report*. The headline read:

Pummeled in Pennsport!

The article was about a brutal murder in 2002. March 21, 2002 to be exact.

The photograph was of a smiling Antoinette Chan.

Jessica looked back down the hall, saw no one coming. She took her iPhone out of her pocket, stepped fully into the bedroom, and began to photograph the walls, hoping there was enough light. Then she walked back down the hall. She stepped into the living room, held up her phone.

'Detective?'

Both Byrne and Novak turned to look at her.

'I'm sorry to interrupt, but there's a call for you.'

Byrne got up, walked across the living room, took a few steps down the hall. Jessica gestured to the opened bedroom door. Byrne stepped to the opening, took in the room. He stepped back.

Their gazes met in silent understanding. Byrne flicked a glance toward the front door. She would take the door. He would take Novak.

They were out of the living room for just a few seconds, but it was long enough. They heard a loud noise. When they returned, the chair in front of the desk was on its back. Novak was gone.

'*Fuck*,' Byrne yelled.

He went for the window and the fire escape beyond. Jessica ran to the door.

She peeked out into the hallway. It was not that long – there were only four apartments on this floor – and there were stairs at only one end. She hurried over to the elevator. Silence. Novak would not have had time to call the elevator, and make it even one floor. She ran down to the stairs, eased open the door, her hand on the butt of her weapon.

The stairwell was empty.

Jessica moved silently down the stairs, her weapon held out front, low. She turned a corner, carried on circling downward, her ears tuned to the sounds around her. Traffic outside, television noise coming from an apartment on the first floor. No footsteps.

She had to make a decision when she came to the first-floor landing. Continue on to the basement or check the first floor? She opted for the first floor. She eased open the door. It led to a short hallway. The lobby was straight ahead. She still-hunted down the hall. When she came to the lobby she saw Joseph Novak sitting uneasily on one of the chairs. His right foot was tapping nervously.

Jessica stepped fully into the lobby and was just about to raise her weapon when she sensed another presence. She looked over. It was Josh Bontrager. He was leaning against the front door, a hoagie in one hand, his weapon in the other. He smiled, winked at Jessica just as Byrne came barreling into view in front of the building.

Byrne entered the lobby, caught his breath. Josh Bontrager ate his sandwich. Jessica stepped forward, holstered her weapon, and took Joseph Novak into custody.

THIRTY-TWO

LUCY FOUND HERSELF STANDING IN FRONT OF THE DOOR, THE SMALL red door with the tarnished golden key on it. She didn't even remember walking to Cherry Street. All she remembered was clocking out for lunch and then, magically, there she was.

LUCY WALKED DOWN THE hallway. It was a lot quieter than it had been the day before, or maybe that was because it was so noisy inside her head.

In a few moments she was in front of the Dreamweaver's door. This time it was closed. She knocked, waited. She heard music coming from inside, some kind of classical music. She didn't know anything about classical music. She knocked again. The music stopped. Then she heard some light footsteps. The door opened.

'Lucinda.'

She was instantly taken aback by his appearance. She might have even made some kind of involuntary noise. Mr. Costa seemed younger. Not younger as in he looked like a younger man, but more animated, quicker in his movements. His hair was combed, parted in a perfectly straight line on the right side. He wore what looked like a fresh white shirt. His shoes were newly polished. He smelled of good soap.

Lucy found herself trembling as she walked into his room. She turned slightly as she passed through the doorway, but found that the photograph – the one she was certain was the one of her house when she'd been growing up, the picture that was hanging just above the light switch – had been replaced with a different photograph, this one of a valley full of flowers and a small cabin with smoke curling out of the chimney.

Had she imagined it?

Mr. Costa closed the door behind her. They walked together into the front room.

If the man looked more youthful, his place also looked improved. He had straightened it up a little. He had even *dusted*.

Mr. Costa gestured to the green chair. Lucy took off her coat, sat down.

'I trust you slept well?' he asked.

'Not really,' Lucy said. 'I'm not sure I slept at all.'

'Understandable.'

'I think maybe you were right.'

'In what way?'

Lucy put down her purse, arranged herself in the chair. It too seemed different. Larger, somehow. She felt like a little kid sitting in it, or maybe Alice through the looking glass. 'When you said I may have opened a door yesterday. I think maybe I did.'

Mr. Costa smiled. 'This is wonderful news. What leads you to think this?'

On the way over, Lucy had debated whether or not to tell Mr. Costa about the man in the hotel. She decided to wait until after this session, to wait and see what, if anything, she got out of it. 'I'm not sure,' she said. 'It's just a feeling.'

The look on Mr. Costa's face indicated that he might not have believed her completely, but that it was okay. Lucy had the feeling that a lot of people said things like this to him – half-truths about their lives, their feelings.

'Are you comfortable?' he asked.

As comfortable as I have ever been, Lucy thought. *For some reason.*

'Yes,' she said. 'I'm fine.'

'Did you bring the notepad with you? The hotel notepad?'

Lucy reached into her bag, took out the notepad. She handed it to Mr. Costa but he put out his hands, palms toward her. 'No, this is for you to write on. Do you have a pen?'

'No,' Lucy said. 'Sorry.'

Mr. Costa reached into his coat pocket, took out a beautiful old fountain pen, uncapped it, handed it to Lucy. 'You will write something on the pad a little later.'

'Okay.'

'Are you ready to begin our session?'

'I am.'

'Now, I want you to close your eyes, and listen to the sound of my voice.'

LUCY WAS NOT FLOATING above the town this time. This time she was sitting. No, she was kneeling, sort of. She was on her knees but leaning back on her heels. And she was afraid.

Where are you?

I'm in the dark. I have a blindfold on.

Do you know where you are?

No.

Are you inside or outside?

I'm inside. Inside a building.

Is the room large or small?

Small. It feels like a closet or something.

Where is the man?

I don't know.

Has he hurt you in any way?

I don't think so.

Are you alone?

Yes. But I met someone else. A girl.

How old is she?

She's my age.

What can you see?

When I take off the blindfold I see a keyhole in the door. I can see out of the keyhole. There's a table next to the sofa. There's something on it.

What is on the table?

It's shiny. It's kind of oval-shaped.

What is it? What is the shiny object?

It's a badge. A policeman's badge.

What are you wearing?

A dress. He put a dress on me.

What kind of dress?

A spangly dress. A grown-up dress. And he calls me Eve.

Eve? Who is Eve? Someone you know?

No. He means Eve in the Garden of Eden. Eve who was tempted by the apple.

Can you see his face?

No. Not yet. But I can see his hand. He wears a big ring.

What kind of ring?

It looks like a snake. It looks like a ring in the shape of a snake.

Suddenly, in her dream world, Lucy Doucette felt herself falling. She sensed that someone was trying to save her. Someone or something.

No. It was the darkness itself. She reached out—

– a ring in the shape of a snake . . . the snake in the Garden of Eden –

—and let the darkness take her.

THIRTY-THREE

JOSEPH NOVAK SAT IN INTERVIEW A, ONE OF THE TWO CRAMPED AND oppressive interrogation rooms at the homicide unit.

They did not have much, and they probably wouldn't have been able to bring him in without his consent, but he'd run. People don't realize that once you run from the police it opens a big can of possibilities. It immediately establishes a hostile relationship. What might once have been a conversation that moved gently from casual to mild inquisitiveness now began with doubt and suspicion.

Even if you had to cut people loose, sometimes you got lucky. A lot of it had to do with the nature of the case itself, the heat generated not only within the department and the district attorney's office but also with the public. If a case broke open in the public consciousness, pressure was brought to bear on law enforcement to produce results, therefore detectives put the pressure on DAs, who worked a little harder on judges, and as a result search warrants and body warrants were granted with a little more leeway. When you searched a house or car you never knew what the search would produce. Warrants were the handmaidens of criminal charges, even when you had no idea what you were looking for.

THEY LET NOVAK SIMMER in Interview A for a few minutes. Interview A at the unit didn't look anything like the interrogation rooms on TV.

On TV the rooms had soft gray walls, dramatic lighting, clean carpeting, expensive furnishings, and were usually the size of an average living room. In reality, at least in Philly homicide, the real room was about six by eight, not much bigger than your average jail cell – which was not an accident of design.

There were no windows, just the two-way mirror, which was not much bigger than a magazine. Then there were the bright fluorescent lights overhead, the bolted-down chairs, and the short-legged table. No matter how often the room was cleaned, or even painted, it held onto the faint odors of urine and bleach. All in all, it was the Philadelphia equivalent of a visit to George Orwell's Room 101. Or so the Homicide Unit hoped.

If you had claustrophobia issues and you heard that door close, the bolt slide on the other side, you started to come apart. More than one tough guy had blurted a confession after an hour or two inside Hotel Homicide.

JESSICA SAT ACROSS FROM Novak. Byrne stood, leaning against the wall next to the observation window. Novak sat dispassionately in the bolted-down chair, his face void of all expression.

Byrne put the large file box on the table. It was almost empty but Novak didn't need to know that. Novak glanced at the box, then turned his attention back to Byrne.

'Now, where were we?' Byrne said.

Novak said nothing.

'We were having such a nice conversation. Why did you run?'

Novak still said nothing.

'Where were you heading?'

Silence.

Byrne let the questions float for a few moments, then reached out his hand. Jessica handed him her iPhone. Byrne turned the screen toward Novak and began to scroll through the series of pictures Jessica had taken of Novak's bedroom.

Novak scanned the photos, remained impassive.

'This is quite an interesting collage,' Byrne said.

Novak took a moment. 'Is it common practice for the police to be invited into someone's home, then to take covert photographs?'

'Common?' Byrne asked. 'No, I don't suppose it is.'

'I'm sure there are a number of privacy laws that have been violated here. My attorneys will have a lot of fun with this. Search and seizure, for one.'

'It's my recollection that you invited us into your home, Mr. Novak.' Byrne turned to Jessica. 'Is that how you remember it, detective?'

'It is.'

'There were no jackbooted thugs kicking in your door, no one rappelling down the side of your building and smashing in your windows. Just three people talking, two of whom were invited in.' Byrne tapped the photos on the cellphone screen. 'All of this was in plain view.'

Novak didn't react.

'Anything you'd like to share with us?' Byrne asked.

'Such as?'

'Such as why you have a room dedicated to the history of homicide in the City of Brotherly Love?'

Novak hesitated. 'It's research. I am a fan of true crime stories.'

'As you might imagine, so am I,' Byrne said. He indicated one of the photos. 'I remember many of these. In fact, I worked some of the cases.'

Novak said nothing.

Byrne tapped the iPhone screen, selecting another photograph. This one displayed a section of the room devoted to the Antoinette Chan case. It was a collage of clippings from the original stories in the *Inquirer*, *Daily News* and the tabloid *Report*, as well as from follow-up stories when Kenneth Beckman had been brought in for questioning.

'I see you are following the Antoinette Chan case,' Byrne said.

Novak crossed his hands in his lap, began to rub a finger over his left fist. A classic self-touch gesture. They were getting into a discomfort zone. 'It is an interesting case. One of many. I have research going back one hundred years. I'm sure you'll agree, this city has no shortage of crimes against persons.'

Byrne held up his hands, surrendering the point. 'You'll get no argument here,' he said. 'But let's talk about current cases first, okay?'

Nothing.

'What did you find interesting about the Chan case?' Byrne asked.

Novak leaned back in his chair, looked down, breaking eye contact with Byrne. A disconnect. 'It was particularly brutal, I thought. The weapon used was a claw hammer, if I remember correctly.'

'That's correct.'

'It seems an intimate act, using such a weapon,' Novak said, looking up briefly, then quickly away. 'A lot of passion.'

'Do you know a man named Kenneth Beckman?' Byrne asked.

'No.'

The answer came way too fast. As soon as it left his lips, Jessica saw that Novak knew it was the wrong move.

'But you went to grade school with him,' Byrne said. 'Little Kenny was in your class from second through sixth grades.'

'He was?'

'No,' Byrne said. 'At least, I don't think he was. The point is, based on your quick answer he *might* have been someone you knew, yet you said no without even giving it a moment's thought. Why was that?'

Novak shifted in his seat. 'This man you're asking me about – I take it he was in the photo lineup you showed me at my apartment?'

'Yes.'

'I don't know anyone by that name.'

Byrne reached into the box, slid the photo lineup across the table. Novak looked at it, his eyes carefully roaming across the six faces. This was clearly for show. He shook his head.

Byrne jabbed the photo on the iPhone screen, enlarging it. It was a news clipping of the Antoinette Chan case. 'You said you were doing research. What kind of research?'

'I'm writing an opera.'

'An opera?'

'Yes,' Novak said. He shifted his weight again in what Jessica knew to be an uncomfortable steel chair. 'It is an epic story of crime and punishment in this city. It covers more than a hundred years. What you are looking at here is my research.'

'Some of your research into the Antoinette Chan case named Kenneth Beckman as a suspect.'

Novak hesitated. 'I can't remember every person's name. Real names are not important to the theme of my work.'

'What is the theme of your work?'

'Crime, punishment, guilt, redemption.'

'Kenneth Beckman is dead.'

Nothing. No reaction.

'He was murdered,' Byrne continued. 'His body was found at the same crime scene where Antoinette Chan was found.'

Novak remained silent.

'Hell of a twist, no?' Byrne said. 'I'm seeing that as the end of the first act.'

Novak looked up, a smug look on his face. It was not the look of someone with nothing to hide but rather of one who has very carefully hidden everything.

'If he was involved in the murder of Antoinette Chan, I might make reference to karma, fate, all that. None of it has anything to do with me.'

'So the name Kenneth Beckman means nothing to you?'

'Nothing.'

'What about the name Sharon Beckman?'

'Is that his wife?'

Byrne just stared.

Novak fashioned a thin smile, shook his head. 'Is this the part where you say "Did I say *wife*? I didn't say *wife*. How did you know it wasn't his daughter or sister?" Is this where you say these things, detective?' Novak clasped his hands in his lap. 'I saw *Sleuth*. The original film, that is. The one with—'

'Laurence Olivier and Michael Caine.'

This time Novak's look said touché.

'You still haven't answered my question,' Byrne said.

Novak stared at the floor.

'Mr. Novak? Does the name Sharon Beckman mean anything to you?'

Novak looked up. 'No.'

Byrne let the exchange settle for a few moments. Then he removed the clear plastic evidence bag containing the sample of Atriana paper.

'Do you recognize this?' Byrne asked.

Novak took the evidence bag from Byrne, held it up to the fluorescent light. The edge of the distinctive watermark was clear.

'I do.'

'Where do you recognize it from?'

'I'm familiar with the line. It's called Atriana.'

'What is Marcato LLC?'

Pause. 'It's a publishing company.'

'Books? Magazines?'

'Music.'

Byrne nodded. 'And you use this paper?'

'Yes,' Novak said. 'I use the paper to bind special editions.'

'Where would I find a copy of one of these editions?'

'They are all over the world.'

'When was the last time you purchased this paper?' Byrne asked.

'I don't recall.'

'If we search your apartment will we find this paper? Maybe cut into five-inch-wide strips?'

'No,' Novak said. 'All the paper I had was stolen. Someone broke into my house.'

'Oh yeah? When was this?'

'Six months ago.'

'Did you report it to the police?'

'Yes.'

Novak was certainly smart enough to know that they would look this up. He probably would not have said this if it weren't true. 'What else was taken?'

'A watch, an MP3 player.'

'And paper,' Byrne added.

No reply.

Byrne stared at the man for a few moments, as if commiserating with him over the strange state of the world. 'Well, I was at your place this morning, and I have to say that if I had broken in I would've found a few more items of value than just a wristwatch, a Nano, and some paper. Some of your audio equipment would go for more than a few bucks on the corner, don't you think? Pioneer Elite, McIntosh. This is serious jelly.'

'I didn't have all that equipment then.'

'Ah, okay,' Byrne said. 'I'm sure you still have the receipts from when you purchased the equipment, yes? We may want to look at them.'

Novak remained stone-faced. 'I could probably find them.'

'Great,' Byrne said. 'That would help a lot.'

Jessica excused herself, stepped out of the interview room. She got on the phone to West Division detectives, made her request. A few minutes later she got a fax of the incident report. Novak was telling the truth. At least about the break-in. She stepped back into the interview room, handed the fax to Byrne. He read it, looked at Novak.

'It appears you were telling the truth,' Byrne said.

'Imagine that.'

Byrne put the fax into the binder, closed it. 'Yet you know what I find odd?'

'What is that?'

'With all your meticulous research into the Antoinette Chan case, you do not remember the name Kenneth Beckman. His name was in the papers – on television, too.'

Novak shrugged. 'I must have missed it.'

'Imagine that.'

'You can see why we might be interested here, Mr. Novak.' Byrne held up the bag with the paper sample. 'Here is an item belonging to you, and it was found at the scene of a homicide.'

'It was an item *stolen* from me,' Novak said. 'And while the injustice that was done to me pales in comparison to what was done to Mr. Beckman I am just as much a victim in this as he.'

Byrne took it all in, waited a few moments. 'Sounds positively operatic.'

For a few moments Novak said nothing. Then, almost on cue: 'I believe we have reached the point where I should contact my attorney.

Among other things, I'm sure he will be interested in the photographs you have of my personal and private property, and how they were obtained.'

Byrne looked at Jessica. She held up her iPhone so that Novak could see the screen. She tapped a few icons and a moment later they all watched the progress bar move left to right. The images had been deleted. Byrne looked back at Novak.

'What photographs?' Byrne asked.

The two men stared at each other for a few seconds.

'We're almost done here,' Byrne finally said. 'If you'll excuse us for a moment.'

Byrne stepped out of the room, closed the door, slid home the bolt. He bumped a fist with Jessica. They had, of course, printed the images from her iPhone before starting the interview. In addition, while holding up her iPhone in the interview room, she had also taken Joseph Novak's picture.

They met with Dana Westbrook in the coffee room. They watched Novak on the monitor.

'Unfortunately, this is not enough to hold him or get a search warrant,' Westbrook said.

'We have to consider his collage of murder stories, boss.'

'Not against the law last time I checked. If it was, I might be in jail myself. Last night I watched a double feature of *Manhunter* and *The Silence of the Lambs*.' Westbrook checked her watch. They had to be careful about how long they kept Novak. They would soon have to charge him or let him go. They'd all had a refresher course in this recently with the Eduardo Robles fiasco. 'Plus, none of the snapshots would be admissible. No probable cause, and how they were obtained would certainly be explored by any defense attorney.'

Jessica looked back into the room. Novak had not moved a muscle. He sat with his eyes closed, his long legs crossed in front of him.

'Can we put him under surveillance?' Jessica asked.

Westbrook walked back to her office, returned. She had looked at the duty roster. 'I don't have a single warm body available. There may be someone on last-out tonight. I'll talk to the watch commander and see what I can do.'

Anything could happen between now and then, Jessica thought. Still, it was what it was.

'Cut him loose,' Westbrook said.

A FEW MINUTES LATER Jessica and Byrne stood in the duty room, watching Novak saunter toward the hallway that led to the elevators.

Before Novak rounded the corner he stopped, as if he'd forgotten something. A few seconds later he spun on his heels, walked briskly back, heading directly for Jessica and Byrne.

What the hell is this? Jessica wondered.

THIRTY-FOUR

A S NOVAK APPROACHED, BYRNE WATCHED THE MAN'S HANDS. IT WAS a habit he'd acquired as a rookie and he'd never forgotten it. Watch the hands, watch the man.

Novak stopped in front of them. He did not look at Jessica, just at Byrne.

'I just wanted to say I harbor no hard feelings,' Novak said.

This isn't over, Byrne thought. *You might change your mind about that.*

Novak extended his hand.

Byrne had learned a lesson from his father many years earlier, and that was never to refuse to shake a man's hand, even if you think he is the most despicable person on earth. The reason, Paddy Byrne explained to his young son, was that if at some point in the future you needed to take that man down, he would never see you coming.

Byrne reached out.

The two men touched, and Byrne saw . . .

. . . the house bathed in darkness, light coming in the high windows, milk of an autumn moon painting everything in a sulfurous blue.

Four people here. Music plays in the background. Lilting, familiar music, soon buoyed by screams of terror and agony. Now the smell of blood in the air. Blood and jasmine.

At midnight three people stand over a dead body, blood spreading on the white tile, glossy crimson clouds reflecting faces that . . .

. . . Byrne could not see. Not yet. He held Joseph Novak's hand for an uncomfortable second too long. The gesture was not lost on Novak, who turned quickly and walked out of the duty room.

Byrne had one question circling the disturbing vision in his mind, one question to which he did not really want the answer.

Was this Joseph Novak's memory, or my own?

THIRTY-FIVE

THEY MET IN THE BOSS'S OFFICE. IN THE ROOM, BESIDES DANA Westbrook, were Russell Diaz, Nicci Malone, Nick Palladino, Josh Bontrager and Dennis Stansfield.

Byrne drew two triangles on the white board. On the first triangle he wrote a name at the top. Antoinette Chan. At the bottom left he wrote Kenneth Beckman. Bottom right, Sharon Beckman.

'Let's start with Antoinette Chan,' Byrne said. 'Let's say for the sake of argument that Beckman killed her. And let's say that Sharon Beckman was his accomplice, in that she set fire to their house to destroy any evidence. Kenneth Beckman's body was found at the original Chan crime scene. Sharon Beckman's was found on Antoinette Chan's grave. Killer, accomplice and victim, all joined in this triangle, each point completed.'

Byrne moved over to the second triangle. At the top he put a question mark. At the lower left he wrote John Doe. At the lower right, another question mark.

'Now, if our bad boy is some kind of vigilante, righting old wrongs, and his MO is to take out the lead suspect in an unsolved homicide and leave the body at the original crime scene, then move on to an accomplice and dump *that* body on the grave of the original victim, I think we can extrapolate a bit here.'

Byrne pointed at the bottom left of the second triangle.

'Because our John Doe was found on the street, we can assume that he was someone who our guy believes was responsible for a homicide that took place at that location. Who the victim was, and who the accomplice was, we won't know until we track down the original crime. We have to start here. Unless we can turn up a witness, it's the only move.'

Byrne turned to Nicci. 'Nothing on the John Doe's prints yet?'

Nicci shook her head. 'The guy was a crackhead. His fingers are so burned we couldn't get a good print. Still working on it, though.'

Byrne nodded. 'Okay, then we'll have to find a homicide committed at the corner of Second and Poplar.'

There were audible moans around the room. This was going to be a paper chase.

Six detectives pored over homicide binders for cases from the past thirty years. Unfortunately, there was no way to search the electronic databases based on where a homicide had been committed, or by status. It all had to be done by hand. It was tedious work, having to read each file. Not all of them had been filled out properly or even legibly. It was almost a peer review of the detectives who had worked in the unit over the past three decades.

Jessica flipped through the books covering 2003 to 2007. Case after case her eyes jumped from the name of the victim to the date, to the crime-scene location. Case after case took her on a grotesque tour of her city, its crimes of violence, its victims and perpetrators. It occurred to her more than once that she had been to virtually all these places, many times, often with her family as a child, or with Sophie and Vincent, blissfully unaware that someone in her city's past had been murdered there.

Every so often Jessica got up and fetched herself a fresh cup of coffee, hoping to keep on mission. The names and addresses all started to blend together, and the danger of finding herself daydreaming carried with it the hazard that she would have no idea how long she had been drifting and therefore no idea how far she needed to go back.

Fresh cup, a quick stretch, and back at it. Mid-2004. The page on which she had stopped told a charming little tale of a man who had shot his wife eleven times for having an affair with the UPS man. Jessica wondered if the guy delivered.

You're getting loopy, Jess.

She flipped a page.

'Here it is!' she shouted, almost before she knew it.

The other five detectives got up, all but ran over to her.

'June 21, 2004. DOA found in a Dumpster near Second and Poplar. Victim's name was Marcellus Palmer.'

A quick scan of the page told them the basics. Marcellus Palmer had been indigent, forty-one years old. He was found bludgeoned to death, his pockets turned inside out, his shoes missing. Jessica made a mental note, as she assumed Byrne did as well, that the COD was the same as for Antoinette Chan. Bludgeoned. Perhaps the connection was there.

They would have to go to Record Storage to get the full file, but they had made a start.

Jessica looked at the photo clipped to the summary. The new crime scene was literally a few feet from where Palmer's body had been found. It was one of Kevin Byrne's old stomping grounds as a patrolman.

'What's the status?' Bontrager asked.

'Open case,' Jessica said.

'Suspects?'

'The main suspect, also homeless, was a man named Preston Braswell, thirty-one at the time. Never charged.'

Nicci Malone sat down at a computer terminal, typed in the name. A few seconds later she had a hit. And a picture. 'That's him. Preston Braswell is our John Doe.'

The other detectives crowded around the terminal. The photograph on the screen was that of a younger, cleaner version of the John Doe. A positive match.

They now had two separate cases where the original suspect in a homicide case was found murdered and had been dumped in the precise same spot as the original homicide. One of the cases had the accomplice dumped on the grave site of the original victim. They had every reason to believe it was about to happen again. If it hadn't happened already.

Nicci sprang to her feet. Dino helped her with her coat, put on his own. 'We're off to Record Storage,' Dino said. 'Stand by.'

As Nicci and Dino left, Jessica and Byrne returned to the white board. Byrne erased the question mark at the top of the triangle on the right, then replaced it with the name Marcellus Palmer. He then erased the question mark at the lower left, replaced it with the name Preston Braswell.

Jessica took a step back, looked at the growing mountain of evidence connected with these three cases. There were three binders on the desk, each with a thickening group of folders within. She glanced at Byrne.

He was staring at something else.

He was staring at the final question mark on the board.

TWENTY MINUTES LATER THEY got a call from Nicci Malone. She had the box of files on the 2004 murder of Marcellus Palmer. She was just about to fax over the suspect and witness list. Jessica put the phone on speaker.

'How bad is it?' Jessica asked.

'Put on your Nikes. The initial list has seventy-one names.'

'*Seventy-one?*'

'Yeah. The homeless are a social group,' Nicci said. 'But it looks like there were four men besides Preston Braswell who we liked more than the others. They were all questioned and released. I think we should try to track them down first.'

Before our killer does, Jessica thought.

A few minutes later they received the fax with the four names. Jessica found them all in the system and printed off what information they had on the men, including the most recent photographs.

Because there was no information on where Marcellus Palmer was buried they would have to start on the street.

For years, and with no small sense of irony, many homeless had huddled in the park directly across from the police administration building, in what is known as Franklin Square. In general, the home-less congregate where they are fed. Not much had changed in the past twenty-five years.

The detectives divvied up the names and photographs of the four men, as well as the locations of the shelters. They would work these interviews solo, as there were too many places to visit in teams, and time was short.

Jessica would take Old City.

THIRTY-SIX

THE AREA BENEATH THE BEN FRANKLIN BRIDGE, AT THE INTERCHANGE
with I-95, had long been a refuge for Philadelphia's homeless. For
years the police referred to it as The Condos. Jessica parked, found a
break in the chain-link fence, made her way beneath the overpass.
There were a few dozen people congregated there. Stacked against the
fence were stuffed cardboard boxes, bursting plastic bags. Nearby was
a stroller with only three wheels. Cups, bottles, milk cartons, fast-food
trash. No aluminum cans, of course. Cans were currency.

There were ten or twelve people on the north side of the
encampment, mostly men. They glanced up at Jessica, not reacting in
any way. Two reasons. One, she was a woman. Two, even though she
was clearly a police officer, or at least a representative of the system,
she was not coming in all guns blazing, with the obvious intention of
uprooting them.

There were three distinct camps, with a few men off on their own.
Jessica approached the first group, showed them the photographs. No
one admitted recognizing anyone. The same with the second and third
groups of men.

As Jessica walked away from the third group, one of the men called
out to her. Jessica turned around. It was one of the older guys. He
was lying on a thick bed of cardboard.

'Say, darling, you ever been with a homeless man?' He smiled his keyboard grin, broke into a phlegmy cough. The other two men in his posse chuckled. 'Guaranteed to change your *life*. You interested?'

'Sure,' Jessica said. 'All you have to do is take a shower and get a job.'

The man looked shocked. He got back under his blanket, turned on his side. 'You ain't all *that*.'

Jessica smiled, made her way back around the camp, asking the same questions, receiving nothing. The last man pointed to a man on the other side of the embankment, someone Jessica hadn't noticed before. As she approached she saw that the man – who was surrounded by carefully placed trash bags – had his legs covered with what appeared to be a new blanket. As Jessica got closer she saw that it still had its price tag.

THE MAN WAS PROPPED against the fence, reading a paperback. Its cover was missing but Jessica could read the spine. *Great Expectations*.

'Excuse me. Sir?'

He looked up. He was black, somewhere between fifty and seventy. He wore a tattered brown corduroy blazer and a yellowed shirt. His tie, like the blanket, looked new. Jessica wondered if there was a price tag on that, too. His eyes were bright and intelligent.

'Madam.'

'May I ask your name?'

'Abraham Coltrane.'

Jessica believed the Abraham part. 'Do you mind if I ask you a few questions?' Jessica held up her badge. The man scanned it.

'Not at all.'

Jessica held up three of the photographs. 'Do you know any of these men?'

Coltrane scanned the pictures. 'I do not. Are they men of leisure, such as myself?'

'They are.'

Abraham Coltrane nodded. Jessica held up the final picture, a photograph of the fourth man believed to have been involved with the

2004 murder of Marcellus Palmer. The man's name was Tyvander Alice. 'What about this man?'

Coltrane looked again. This time Jessica saw the slightest flicker of recognition. 'Again,' he said. 'My regrets.'

'This picture was taken a few years ago.'

'I remember everyone I have ever met, madam.'

She believed he did, which was why she didn't believe the part about him not knowing Tyvander Alice. She took out a five-dollar bill, making sure that the man saw it.

'Nice blanket,' she said.

'It provides.'

Jessica lifted the price tag. 'You have a receipt for this, Mr. Coltrane?'

'It was a gift from one of my many admirers.'

'They gave you a gift with the price tag still on it?'

Coltrane shrugged. 'The young have but a nodding acquaintance with custom, I fear.'

'Thank God the court system still does,' Jessica said. 'They're really big on it. Indictment, prosecution, conviction, incarceration. You might say they are sticklers for tradition.'

Coltrane stared at her for a moment. Jessica saw the man's will begin to fade. 'May I see that photograph again?'

'Of course.' Jessica showed him. He studied it for a moment, rubbing his stubbled chin.

'Now that I've had a moment to reflect, I believe I have made the acquaintance of this gentleman.'

'Is this Tyvander Alice?'

'*Tyvander*?' he asked. 'No. I knew him by another name. I know him as Hoochie.'

'Hoochie?'

'Yes. An unfortunate and undignified sobriquet based on his love of the lesser vintages, I believe.'

Jessica handed Coltrane the five. The man touched it to his forehead, sniffed it, then spirited it away under his blanket.

Before Jessica could ask another question she saw the blanket move. A few seconds later a Jack Russell terrier poked his snout out.

His *gray* snout. The dog blinked a few times, adjusting its eyes to the light.

'And who is this?' Jessica asked.

'This is the irascible Biscuit. He is my oldest friend.' Coltrane patted the dog's head. Jessica saw the blanket bounce up and down with the movement of the pooch's tail. 'Is there anything in the world better than a warm biscuit?'

Jessica tried to think of something. She could not. There was as good, but not better. She returned to the business at hand. 'Do you know where I might find Hoochie?'

Coltrane shrugged. '"I wander'd lonely as a cloud that floats on high o'er vales and hills."'

Jessica raised an eyebrow, expecting more. There was no more. 'Bon Jovi?'

Coltrane smiled. 'Wordsworth.'

In other words, the answer was no. Homeless were just that. Jessica took out the photograph of Marcellus Palmer, the original victim found at Second and Poplar in 2004. 'Did you know this gentleman?'

'Oh yes,' Coltrane said. 'Marcellus. We shared many a tankard of kill-devil. But that was a long time ago.'

'Do you know what happened to him?'

Coltrane nodded sadly. 'I heard he came to an unfortunate end. City buried him.'

'Do you know where?'

Coltrane looked up at the concrete embankment. For a moment there was only the sound of the cars passing overhead. 'Now, I *did* know at one time. The recollection seems to be pirouetting just at the edge of my memory.'

Jessica produced another five, held it back. 'Think we could coax it back onto the dance floor?'

'I believe we can.'

The money was gone in an instant.

'Up around Parkwood, I believe.'

Jessica's phone rang. She looked at the screen. It was Byrne.

'Thank you for your time, Mr. Coltrane.'

'Always willing to do my part,' he said.

Jessica took a few steps away, answered her phone.

'Where are you?' she asked.

'Still in West Philly.'

Jessica told him what she had learned from Abraham Coltrane. Byrne filled her in on what she had missed. Two of the other homeless men who had been questioned in the murder of Marcellus Palmer were dead. The third man was long gone. Someone told someone that someone's friend had told someone that he was in Florida. Two *someones* was about the extent of any network worth exploring.

When they met back at the Roundhouse, Jessica checked a roster of the city's graveyards.

There was no cemetery in Parkwood.

THIRTY-SEVEN

Finnigan's Wake, the popular Irish pub at Third and Spring Garden Streets, in the Northern Liberties section of the city, was packed with a who's who from the department and the DA's office, as well as defense attorneys, paralegals, FBI agents, commissioners, medical examiner's investigators. As always, everyone clustered with their tribe. David Albrecht was there, shooting from the sidelines. Russ Diaz was with his new team. Tom Weyrich was there, looking a little better than Jessica had seen him look in a long time. Maybe it was the Guinness. Dennis Stansfield stood in the corner with two of his old squad mates.

The jampacked party was held on the second floor, also known as the Lincoln Level. After Abraham Lincoln was assassinated, his body was transported to Philadelphia to lie in state at Independence Hall. That night his body had been kept in a Northern Liberties funeral parlor, and the doors from that establishment became part of the second floor at Finnigan's Wake. More than one pint had been lifted to Honest Abe in this room.

As the evening wore on a number of people got up and told their Michael Drummond stories. Like all leaving parties, the first hour's worth of stories were mild, only somewhat ribald recounts of incidents that happened around the office. The second hour, seeing as Michael Drummond was about to become part of the opposition to most of the people in the room, became a little more adventurous, if not downright drunkenly libelous.

At eleven p.m. Michael Drummond himself took the microphone. Although Drummond was not yet forty, there was a lot of fresh blood in the DA's office and he was referred to as the old man.

'Yes, it's true that I joined the office after an unfortunate incident with a Model A Ford,' he said, drawing polite laughter.

He went on to thank just about everyone he'd ever worked with, on both sides of the aisle, taking particular care to heap praise upon all the judges – men and women in front of whom he would shortly be arguing for the defense – regardless of whether they were at the party or not.

Soon it became time for him to spill the beans. With a clank of a spoon on a crystal glass, he got everyone's undivided attention.

'Folks, I have an announcement to make,' Drummond said.

Everyone quieted down. This was, more or less, the reason they had gathered.

'In two weeks I will start work as a junior partner at Paulson Derry Chambers. Until then, I'm on the job. So watch yourselves.'

A rumble went through the room. Paulson Derry Chambers was one of the most prominent firms in the city. Everyone expected Mike Drummond to go for the dollar, but a junior partnership at Paulson Derry was like stepping into Valhalla. Applause followed.

'Although I didn't know him personally, I'd like to leave you with the wise words of Pericles,' Drummond added. 'He said: *"What you leave behind is not what is engraved in stone monuments, but what is woven into the lives of others."*'

'Hear, hear,' someone said.

Everyone raised a glass.

'Here's to old dogs,' a slightly inebriated Nick Palladino added.

Drummond laughed. 'And soft bones.'

Everyone returned to their small groups. The detectives gathered near the tall windows overlooking Spring Garden Street and the view of the Ben Franklin Bridge.

'Ah, *shit*,' Dino said after everyone sat down.

'What?' Jessica asked.

Dino stood up, looked in his pockets, patted himself down like a suspect. 'I can't believe this.'

'What's wrong?'

Deadpan: 'I think I left my lip gloss at home.'

Someone snorted.

Dino pointed at Byrne's man bag, hanging off the back of his chair. 'Hey, Kev. You wouldn't happen to have any in there, would you?'

Muffled laughs around the table. Byrne shook his head. 'I'm a lot bigger than you are, you know that, right?'

'I know,' Dino said. 'But you're also older.'

'By what, five or six months?'

'Still.'

'That just means it will take me a few seconds longer to get across the room.'

Dino held up both hands. 'Just don't hit me with your man bag.'

Byrne shot to his feet.

Nick Palladino ran to the bar.

By MIDNIGHT MOST OF the younger players had moved on or gone home. It was a work night. There were young families waiting. After the midnight hour the floor was left to the serious drinkers.

Jessica, who was just about out the door, stood with Byrne near the elevator. Michael Drummond found them, crossed the room. He'd had his share of cheer, and more.

'Thanks for coming, guys.'

Drummond gave Jessica a brotherly hug, shook Byrne's hand, clapped him on the shoulder.

'You do realize we'll probably go up against each other one of these days,' Byrne said.

Drummond nodded. 'Yeah. I feel like I've gone over to the dark side.'

'The money should help ease your pain.'

Drummond smiled. He glanced at his watch. 'I've got to be up in about three hours,' he said. 'We're moving my mother into an assisted-living facility.'

'Do you need another pair of hands?' Byrne asked.

'No, we're good. Thanks.' Drummond slipped on his overcoat. 'I just have to be in Parkwood around six-thirty.'

Jessica looked at Byrne, then back. 'Parkwood?'

'What about it?'

'Well, it's just come up twice in one day.'

'What do you mean?' Drummond asked.

Jessica explained what they had done that afternoon, about Abraham Coltrane's claim that Marcellus Palmer, the 2004 victim found in the Dumpster just a few blocks from where they now stood, was buried in or around Parkwood. Drummond thought for a few moments.

'Well, I'm pretty sure there *used* to be a potter's field in Parkwood,' he said. 'It closed a while back.'

'Closed?'

'Yeah. I think the bodies were disinterred and either moved to other cemeteries or cremated. I think there was supposed to be some kind of development that went in that spot, but nothing ever happened.' Drummond drained his glass, put it on the bar. 'Can you imagine living on top of a former cemetery?'

Jessica felt a chill at the idea. 'Do you know where the cemetery was located?'

Drummond shrugged. 'No idea. Sorry. I might even be wrong about this.'

'Counselor!' someone shouted drunkenly from across the room. 'You're needed for a *voir dire*.'

It was two old-timers from the DA's office. The *voir dire* was a process of jury selection, generally involving the judge and attorneys asking potential jurors about their experiences and beliefs. On the table in front of the two ADAs was one of every different kind of drink in the bar. There had to be fifty full glasses. Drummond looked back at Jessica and Byrne. 'Looks like the night isn't over for me yet. Thanks again for coming.'

Drummond slipped off his coat and staggered across the room.

*

DOWNSTAIRS, A FEW MINUTES later, Byrne held the door for Jessica. They stepped out onto Spring Garden Street.

'So, what time do you want to meet me at L & I?' Byrne asked. The License & Inspections division had city-zoning archives going back more than two hundred years. If there had once been a cemetery in or around Parkwood it would be recorded there.

'As soon as they open, detective,' Jessica said.

THIRTY-EIGHT

Thursday, October 28

THE CITY'S LAST OFFICIAL POTTER'S FIELD HAD OPENED IN 1956 IN Philadelphia's Northeast. Prior to its opening, the most active potter's field had been in a section now used as a police parking lot at Luzerne Street and Whitaker Avenue, adjoining Philadelphia Municipal Hospital, where it became the final resting place for thousands who died in the 1918 flu epidemic. At various times in the city's history, indigent or unclaimed deceased were buried in a number of places, including Logan Square, Franklin Field, Reyburn Park, even at the corner of 15th and Catharine, just a few blocks from where Jessica had grown up.

These days, in the interest of logistics and expense, many of the unidentified and indigent were being cremated, with remains stored in a room off the morgue at the medical examiner's office.

Jessica and Byrne visited the zoning-archives department of Licenses and Inspections at just after eight a.m. The L & I office was located in the Municipal Services Building at 15th and JFK. What they learned was that there had once been a potter's field located in the Parkwood section of Northeast Philadelphia, a field that had since closed.

They stopped for coffee and got onto I-95 at just after nine a.m.

*

THE FIELD WAS LOCATED near the intersection of Mechanicsville Road and Dunks Ferry Road at the southern end of Poquessing Valley Park.

On the south side of Dunks Ferry Road were blocks of two-story twin row homes, their fasciae festooned with Halloween decorations ranging from the elaborate (one had a skeleton about to climb down the chimney) to the ordinary (an already dented plastic pumpkin stuck on a gas light).

Jessica and Byrne got out of the car, crossed the road. They walked through the trees into a large open field. Here the ground was rippled – the uneven remnants of graves that had been there a long time.

There were no headstones, no crypts, no vaults, no mausoleum. The field had indeed been closed, the bodies moved or cremated, the area planted over.

Jessica looked at the rutted sod. She considered the generations of kids to come, flying kites, playing kickball, unaware that at one time the ground beneath their feet had held the remnants of the city's homeless, its indigent, its lost.

They walked slowly across the undulating earth, looking for any sign of what had once been there – a buried headstone, a grave marker of any kind, a stake in the ground indicating the boundaries of the cemetery. There was nothing. The earth had long ago begun to reclaim the area with life.

'Was this the only city field in this area?' Jessica asked.

'Yeah,' Byrne said. 'This was it.'

Jessica looked around. Nothing looked promising, at least as it might concern the cases. 'We're wasting our time up here, aren't we?'

Byrne didn't reply. Instead he crouched down, ran his hand over a bare patch of ground. A few moments later he stood, dusted off his hands.

Jessica heard a rustling in the nearby trees. She looked up to see a half-dozen crows perched tenuously on a low branch of a nearby maple. A *murder* of crows, she had once learned, and had ever since thought how odd a term that was. A flock of geese, a herd of cattle, a murder of crows. Soon another black bird landed, rustling the others, who responded with a series of loud caws and flapping wings. One of them took off and swooped toward the low shrubs at the other side of the field. Jessica followed the pattern of flight.

'Kevin,' she said, pointing to the bird before it landed out of sight. They looked at each other, started across the open field.

Before they got halfway they saw it – the unnatural gleam through the greenery, the bright white surface glinting in the sunlight.

They sprinted the last hundred feet or so and found the body lying in a shallow depression.

The victim was black, male, in his forties or fifties. He was nude, his body shaven head to toe. The ground beneath the corpse was not yet overgrown with grass. It was a former grave.

'Mother*fucker*,' Byrne yelled.

He stepped through the scene, taking care not to disturb the surrounding area. He put two fingers to the man's neck. 'Jesus Christ,' he said. 'His body's still *warm*. Let's get everyone and his mother down here. Let's get a K-9 unit.'

Then Byrne gently opened the dead man's hand. There, on the ring finger of his left hand, was the tattoo of a fish.

They both called it in – Byrne contacted the crime-scene unit, Jessica contacted the homicide unit who would then alert the MEO. They spread out to either side of the open field, weapons out. They checked the immediate area, combing the bushes, the scrub, the culverts and ditches, finding nothing.

Later they regrouped at the corner, each lost in their own thoughts. Although they had not immediately located any ID, there was no doubt in either Jessica's or Byrne's mind that the body they'd found – the dead man lying atop a former grave – was that of Tyvander 'Hoochie' Alice.

THE TACTICAL TEAM HIT the block in six cars, a combination of special-investigation detectives and members of the fugitive squad.

Russ Diaz and his squad fanned out north and east, toward the woods. A K-9 unit showed up a few minutes later. The next car brought Dana Westbrook. For the moment, this relatively quiet corner of Northeast Philadelphia – a place that had one time been a place of repose and solitude – was crawling with law-enforcement personnel.

Ten minutes later the dog and his officer came full circle, back to the parking area near the ball diamonds. It probably meant that the killer had parked there, returned after dumping the body, and then left. If that was so, the trail was cold.

WHILE CSU PROCESSED THE crime scene, Jessica and Byrne stood at the top of the hill, watching the choreography unfold below.

Detectives would soon canvass the immediate area. There was a condo development at Mechanicsville and Eddington Roads, a pair of apartments next to it. Maybe someone had seen something. But Jessica doubted it. Their killer was a ghost.

Kenneth Beckman, Sharon Beckman, Preston Braswell, Tyvander Alice.

Four bodies, eight tattoos.

Four to go.

And they didn't have a single solid lead.

THE TEAM SPENT THE entire afternoon canvassing. The residences in this part of the city were not as tightly packed as they were in the inner city, so the act of interviewing and asking the same questions over and over was a much slower, even more enervating process.

THEY RETURNED TO THE Roundhouse, followed up on a few weak leads. Nothing. By the end of the tour, the entire unit was exhausted and frustrated. Someone was solving the unsolved crimes in Philadelphia, but they were killing the killers and their accomplices. Someone was shaving these bodies clean, mutilating their faces, and wrapping them in paper. Someone who floated through the city like a phantom.

Jessica sat on the edge of a desk, a cup of cold coffee in her hand. She glanced over at the walk-in closet. Inside were the books of homicide cases dating back more than a hundred years. Inside the books were summaries of hundreds of unsolved cases, cases wherein there were suspects who were never charged with the crime, suspects who never became defendants, defendants who were acquitted for any number of reasons. The books were essentially a list of potential victims for their ghoul.

THE DUTY ROOM WAS mostly empty. The second tour had already begun, and those detectives were on the street, pursuing leads, tracking down witnesses. Jessica was envious.

'Don't you have a family to go home to?' Byrne asked.

'Nah,' Jessica said. 'Although, funny you should mention it, I *have* seen a man and a little girl hanging around my house. I should call the police.'

Byrne laughed. 'Speaking of which, how are you adjusting to the new house?'

'Well, besides tripping over the furniture and spinning in place for five minutes because there's nowhere to put a cup of coffee down, it's great.'

'Is it that much smaller?'

Jessica nodded. 'It's a lot like the house I grew up in. Same layout. The only problem is, *I* was a lot smaller then.'

'What, like a size four?'

'Smartass.'

Byrne's phone beeped in his hand. He looked at the screen, read for a moment, smiled.

'It's a text from Colleen,' he said. 'She wanted me to know she got back from D.C. okay.'

Jessica nodded. 'Wow,' she said. 'Colleen in college.'

'Don't remind me.'

Byrne picked up a tall stack of mail that was rubber-banded together on the desk. It looked like two weeks' worth of correspondence, mostly junk. Jessica wanted to mention to her partner that it was probably a good idea to check the inbox once in a while, but she figured he knew this.

As Byrne went through the pile, throwing most of the mail in the trash can, Jessica smelled the perfumed letter before she saw it. The scent was jasmine. Byrne held up the envelope, eyed it, sniffed it. It was the size of a personal note card, maybe four by six inches. Expensive-looking paper.

'A note from an admirer?' Jessica asked.

'As if,' Byrne replied.

'It's the charcoal gray suit, Kevin. I'm telling you.'

Byrne pulled a letter opener off the desk, slit the envelope, extracted the card.

As much as Jessica wanted to pry, she stepped a few feet away, giving her partner a little privacy, shoving everything she needed to take with her into her tote bag. When she looked again at Byrne, he was bone pale. Something was wrong.

'What is it?' Jessica asked.

Byrne remained silent.

'Kevin.'

Byrne waited a few moments, then took Jessica by the arm, led her to the small coffee room, closed the door. He handed her the card. It was printed on a luxurious paper, ivory in color. The scent of jasmine was now much stronger. Jessica put on her glasses, read the note, a brief message written in an elegant hand. The ink was lavender.

My dearest Detective Byrne,

It has been a long time, n'est-ce pas? I wonder how you have fared. Do you think of me? I think of you often. In fact I dreamed of you the other night. It was the first time in years. You looked quite dashing in your dark overcoat and black fedora. You carried an umbrella with a carved ivory handle. Do you carry an umbrella as a rule? No, I would think not.

So tell me. Have you found them yet? The lion and the rooster and the swan? Are there others? You might think they do not play together, but they do. I hope you are well, and that the future brings you every happiness. I am no longer scared.

– C

Jessica was stunned. She read the note a second time, the rich scent filling her head.

'Are you fucking *kidding* me?' she finally said in a loud whisper. 'The lion and the rooster and the swan?'

Byrne remained silent.

'Who the hell sent this, Kevin? Who is *C*?'

Byrne turned the envelope over and over in his hands, searching for words. Words were usually his strong suit. He always chose them carefully. He was good at it.

He told her the story.

THIRTY-NINE

J ESSICA LOOKED AT HER PARTNER. SHE WASN'T SURE HOW LONG SHE had been staring at him without saying anything, her mouth open, eyebrows raised. Then all she could muster was one word. 'Wow.'

Byrne said nothing.

'I remember her,' Jessica said. 'I mean, I remember the story. I think my father talked about it. Plus, it was all over the news for a while.' Although she'd been in high school at the time she and her friends had discussed the case, mainly because it involved sex, violence and celebrity.

In November 1990 a woman named Christa-Marie Schönburg, a cellist with the Philadelphia Orchestra, was arrested and charged in the murder of a man named Gabriel Thorne. According to the news reports, Thorne was Christa-Marie's psychiatrist, but there was a great deal of speculation at the time as to whether or not they were romantically involved, even though Thorne had been Christa-Marie's caregiver since she was a child and was three decades her senior. If Jessica remembered correctly, Christa-Marie confessed to second-degree murder, diminished capacity, and was sentenced to twenty-to-life in the women's facility at the State Correctional Institution at Muncy.

'That was your first case?' Jessica asked.

Byrne nodded. 'My first as a lead detective, yeah. I was partnered with Jimmy.'

Jimmy Purify, his rabbi in the homicide unit, had been Byrne's partner before Jessica.

'I don't understand,' Jessica said. 'Is Christa-Marie still in Muncy?'

'No,' Byrne said. 'She was released a few years ago. The last I heard she's still living in the Chestnut Hill house.'

Jessica decided not to ask her partner why he knew all this. It was not all that uncommon for detectives to keep track of people they had arrested and convicted of crimes. What surprised Jessica was that she had known none of this.

'Have you spoken to her since her release?'

'No.'

'Has she tried to contact you before this?'

'Not that I know of.'

Jessica took a few beats. She looked again at the handwriting on the note. It did not look like the penmanship of someone deranged. 'Is she, how do I put this . . . *better* now?'

Byrne shrugged. 'I don't know. The murder was pretty brutal, and she went through a battery of psychological tests at the time of the hearings. I saw some of the reports. Chronic depression. Borderline bipolar. It never came to anything because she pled out. There never was a trial.'

'Were you called at the hearing?'

'I was.'

'Did you testify?'

Byrne hesitated before answering. Jessica sensed a feeling of regret. 'Yes.'

Jessica tried to arrange the timeline in her mind. 'When was that card postmarked?'

Byrne looked at the envelope. 'Last Thursday.'

Jessica did the math. 'So she sent it—'

'Before the murders.'

Jessica felt her breath catch. She tried to process all this. It wasn't often that she was thrown such a curve. 'Is she capable of something like this? I mean, physically capable?'

Jessica knew that at least part of her question was rhetorical. The woman was a convicted murderer, after all. Obviously she was capable of violence. But violence committed in the throes of rage or passion didn't necessarily lead to cold blooded, well-calculated murder. And then there were the physical elements.

'She's capable,' Byrne said. 'The logistics? She's not a big woman, Jess, and she's obviously a lot older now. I don't think she could have done all this without some help.'

Jessica was silent for a moment. 'Okay. Maybe it's just a coincidence. The lion and the rooster and the swan.'

Byrne just glared.

'Okay, it was worth a shot.' Jessica glanced at her watch. 'Do you want to go now or in the morning?'

'Go where?'

'Kevin. We need to talk to her.'

Byrne took the note card from her, slipped it back into the envelope. 'I should probably talk to her alone.'

Byrne was probably right, but that didn't make Jessica want to go along any less. 'You have to tell the boss, Kevin. You have to share it with the team.'

Byrne glanced around the small, cramped room. There wasn't really anything to look at besides a beaten-up coffee maker and the two-way mirror looking into one of the interview rooms. He looked back at his partner.

'Tomorrow,' he said.

Jessica started to object, but Byrne continued.

'Look, this is connected with the Kenneth Beckman case, and I'm working that case. How it's connected, I have no idea. But if it turns out to be something, I'll post it. If it doesn't, then there's no need to drag all this into the mix.'

'How could it *not* be connected, Kevin? It's not as if Christa-Marie could have just now learned any of this from anyone here. She wrote the note *before* the murders happened.'

'If I tell Dana right now, what is she going to do? Send a couple of detectives to interrogate Christa-Marie? I *know* Christa-Marie. I'm the one Dana would send, anyway. There's no reason to turn this woman's life upside down until we know what this is all about.'

'So you're going to talk to her off the record?'

Byrne said nothing.

Jessica wanted to remind her partner that Christa-Marie Schönburg was a confessed murderer, a woman who had spent more than fifteen years in prison. If he didn't have some sort of as-yet-unidentified emotional attachment to the woman and her case, and he'd heard that a confessed murderer had information on fresh homicides, he'd be charging that way with the cavalry and more.

'Besides,' Byrne began, moving on to his closing argument, 'who's to say I didn't read this note tomorrow? Everyone knows I never open my mail.'

Kevin Byrne's secrets were safe with Jessica, as were hers with him. She trusted his judgment more than anyone else she knew.

'Okay,' Jessica said. 'Where do you want me on this?'

'I'll drive up to Chestnut Hill first thing in the morning. I'll call you after.'

Jessica nodded. They both went silent for a long time.

Finally Jessica asked, 'Are you okay, Kevin?'

Byrne opened the door of the coffee room, glanced out. The duty room was a ghost town. He turned back to his partner and said softly: 'I really don't know.'

TWENTY MINUTES LATER JESSICA watched Byrne gather his things, close his briefcase, retrieve his weapon from the file cabinet, grab his coat and keys. He stopped at the door, turned, gave her a sad smile and a wave. As he disappeared around the corner Jessica knew there was something else going on with him, something other than the job, something other than the horror of the four bodies dumped ceremoniously around their city.

Something he wasn't telling her.

FORTY

HE SITS ACROSS THE TABLE FROM ME, A TREMBLING WRECK OF A MAN. *In his hands is an old photograph, its colors long faded, its edges folded and creased.*

We have had our coffee, shared our pleasantries. I am not one seduced by nostalgia. It means nothing to me.

'I didn't think you were coming back,' he says.

'But you know why I am here,' I say. 'Don't you?'

He nods.

'Everything has changed now,' I say. 'We can never go back.'

He nods again, this time with a tear in his eye.

I glance at my watch. It is time, and time is short. I stand, bring my coffee cup to the sink, rinse it in scalding water. I dry the cup, return it to the cupboard. I am wearing gloves, but one can never be too careful. I return to the table. We fall silent. There is always a calm before the truth.

'Will it hurt?' he asks.

I listen to the voices of the dead swirling around me. I would love to ask them this question. Alas, I cannot. 'I don't know.'

'It's all so Cho Cho San, is it not?'

'Without the baby,' I say.

'Without the baby.'

A few moments pass. Clouds shade his eyes. 'Remember how it was?' he asks.

'I do. *All things were possible then,* n'est-ce pas? *All futures.*'

When I think of those times, I am saddened. I realize how much of it is gone forever, lost in the ductwork of memory. I stand. 'Do you want me to wait?'

He looks at the table for a moment, then at his hands. 'No,' *he says softly.*

I take the photograph from him, put it into my pocket. At the door I stop, turn. I see myself in the mirror at the end of the hall. It reminds me of the shiny crimson mirror of blood on the floor.

Before leaving I turn up the music. It is not Chopin this time, but rather Holst's Planets Suite, *a movement called* 'Venus, The Bringer of Peace'.

Peace.

Sometimes, I think, as I step through the door for the last time, the music exalts the moment.

Sometimes it is the other way around.

FORTY-ONE

THE PENN SLEEP CENTER, PART OF THE UNIVERSITY OF PENNSYLVANIA Hospital system, was located in a modern steel and glass building on Market Street near 36th.

Byrne crossed the river about six, found a parking space, checked in at the desk, presented his insurance card, sat down, speed-skimmed a copy of *Neurology Today*, one of his all-time favorite magazines. He covertly checked the handful of people scattered around the waiting room. Not surprisingly, everyone looked exhausted, beat-up, dragged-out. He hoped everyone there was a new patient. He didn't want to think they were on their twentieth appointment and still looked this bad.

'Mr. Byrne?'

Byrne looked up. Standing at the end of the long desk was a blonde woman, no more than five feet tall. She was in her early forties and wore pink-rimmed glasses. She was perky and full of energy. Insomniacs hate perky.

Byrne got up, walked over to the bubbly gal in white rayon.

'Hi!' she chirruped. 'How are *you* today?'

'Never better, thanks,' Byrne said. Of course, if that was the case, what the hell was he doing at the hospital? 'How about yourself?'

'Super!' she replied.

Her name tag read Viv. Probably short for Vivacious.

'We're just going to check your height and weight.' She led him over to the digital scale, instructed him to take off his shoes. He stepped on the scale.

'I don't want to know how much I weigh, okay?' Byrne said. 'Lately I've just been . . . I don't know. It's hormonal, I think.'

Viv smiled, zipped her lips in a dramatic gesture, recorded Byrne's weight without a word. 'Now, if you could turn around, we'll check your height.'

Byrne spun around. Viv stepped on a footstool, raised the bar of the stadiometer, then lowered it gently, touching the top of Byrne's head. 'What about height?' she asked. 'Would you like to know how tall you are?'

'I think I can handle my height. Emotionally speaking.'

'You're still six foot, three inches.'

'Good,' Byrne said. 'So I haven't shrunk.'

'Nope. You must be washing in cold water.'

Byrne smiled. He liked Viv, despite her vim.

'Come this way,' she said.

IN THE SMALL, WINDOWLESS examining room Byrne cruised the two battered magazines, picking up a dozen new 30-minute chicken recipes, along with some tips on how to get puppy stains out of the upholstery.

A few minutes later the doctor came in. She was Asian, about thirty, quite attractive. Pinned to her lab coat was a photo ID. Her name was Michelle Chu.

They got the pleasantries about the weather and the insanity of the people in the indoor parking garage out of the way. Dr. Chu ran through Byrne's history on the computer's LCD monitor. When she had him sufficiently pegged, she turned in her chair, crossed her legs.

'So, how long have you had insomnia?'

'Let me put it this way,' Byrne said. 'It's been so long that I can't remember.'

'Do you have trouble falling asleep or staying asleep?'

'Both.'

'How long, on average, does it take you to fall asleep?'

All night, Byrne thought. But he knew what she meant. 'Maybe an hour.'

'Do you wake up during the night?'

'Yeah. At least a couple of times.'

The doctor made a few more notes, her fingers racing across the keyboard. 'Do you snore?'

Byrne knew the answer to this. He just didn't want to tell her *how* he knew. 'Well, these days I don't really have a steady . . .'

'Bed partner?'

'Yeah,' Byrne said. 'That. Do you think you could write me a prescription for one of those?'

She laughed. 'I could, but I don't think your insurance provider would cover it.'

'You're probably right,' Byrne said. 'I can barely get them to pay for the Ambien.'

Ambien. The magic drug, the magic word. At least around neurologists. He had her attention now.

'How long have you been taking Ambien?'

'On and off for as long as I can remember.'

'Do you think you've developed a dependence?'

'Without question.'

Dr. Chu handed him a pre-printed sheet. 'These are some of the sleep-hygiene suggestions we have—'

Byrne held up a hand. 'May I?'

'Absolutely.'

'No alcohol, caffeine, or high-fat foods late at night. No nicotine. Exercise regularly, but not within four hours of bedtime. Go to bed and get out of bed at the same times every day. Turn your alarm clock around so you can't see the time. Keep your bedroom cool, not cold. If you can't fall asleep in ten minutes or so, get out of bed until you feel tired again. Although, if you can't see your clock, I don't know how you're supposed to know it's been ten minutes.'

Dr. Chu stared at him for a few moments. She had stopped typing altogether. 'You seem to know quite a bit about this.'

Byrne shrugged. 'You do something long enough.'

She then typed for a full minute. Byrne just watched. When she was done she said, 'Okay. Hop up on the table, please.'

Byrne stood up, walked over to the paper-lined examining table, slid onto it. He hadn't hopped anywhere in years, if ever. Dr. Chu looked into his eyes, ears, nose, throat. She listened to his heart, lungs. Then she took out a tape measure, measured his neck.

'Hmm,' she said.

Never a good sign. 'I prefer a spread collar,' Byrne said. 'French cuffs.'

'Your neck's circumference is greater than seventeen inches.'

'I work out.'

She sat down, put her stethoscope around her neck. Her face took on a concerned look. Not the *you are in deep shit* look, but concerned. 'You have a few markers for sleep apnea.'

Byrne had heard of it, but he really didn't know anything about it. The doctor explained that apnea was a condition wherein a person stops breathing during the night.

'I stop breathing?'

'Well, we don't know that for sure yet.'

'I'm kind of in the stop-breathing business, you know.'

The doctor smiled. 'This is a little different. I think I should schedule you for a sleep study.' She handed him a brochure. Color pics of smiling, healthy people who looked like they got a lot of sleep.

'Okay.'

'You're willing to give it a shot?'

Anything was better than what he was going through. Except maybe the business about not breathing. 'Sure. I'm in.'

In the waiting room, three of the five people were asleep.

BYRNE STOPPED AT THE American Pub in the Center Square Building on Market Street. The place was lively, and lively was just what was needed. He staked a place at the end of the bar, nursed a Bushmills. At just after ten o'clock his phone rang. He checked the ID, fully prepared to blow it off. It was a 215 exchange, with a familiar prefix. A PPD number. He had to answer.

'This is Kevin.'

'Detective Byrne?'

It was a woman's voice. A young woman's voice. He did not recognize it. 'Yes?'

'It's Lucy.'

It took Byrne a little while to realize who it was. Then he remembered. 'Hi, Lucy. Is something wrong?'

'I need to talk to you.'

'Where are you? I'll come get you.'

A long pause.

'Lucy?'

'I'm in jail.'

THE MINI-STATION WAS LOCATED on South Street between Ninth and Tenth. Originally activated in 1985 to provide weekend coverage from spring to autumn, addressing the issues generated by crowds gravitating to South Street for its clubs, shopping and restaurants, it had since become a seven days a week, twenty-four hours a day, year-round commitment, expanded to cover the entire corridor, which included more than 400 retail premises and nearly eighty establishments with liquor licenses.

When Byrne walked in, he immediately spotted an old comrade, P/O Denny Dorgan. Short and brick-solid, Dorgan, who was now in his early forties, still worked the bike patrol.

'Alert the hounds,' Dorgan said. 'We got royalty in the building.'

They shook hands. 'You getting shorter and uglier?' Byrne asked.

'Yeah. It's the supplements my wife is making me take. She thinks it will keep me from straying. Shows you what *she* knows.'

Byrne glanced over at Dorgan's bike, leaning near the front door. 'Good thing you can get heavy-duty shocks on the thing.'

Dorgan laughed, turned and looked at the waif-like girl sitting on the bench behind him. He turned back. 'Friend of yours?'

Byrne looked over at Lucy Doucette. She looked like a lost little kid.

'Yeah,' Byrne said. 'Thanks.'

Byrne wondered what *Dorgan* wondered, whether he thought that Byrne was dallying with a nineteen-year-old. Byrne had long ago stopped being concerned with what people thought. What had happened here was clear. Dorgan had stepped in between a misdemeanor and the law, on Byrne's behalf, and had done it as a favor to a fellow cop. The gesture would go into the books as a small act of kindness, and would one day be repaid. No more, no less. Everything else was squad-car scandal.

BYRNE AND LUCY HAD coffee at a small restaurant on South Street. Lucy told him the story. Or, it seemed to Byrne, the part she could bring herself to tell. She had been detained by security personnel at a kids'-clothing boutique on South. They said she'd attempted to walk out of the store with a pair of children's sweaters. The electronic security tags had been removed and were found underneath one of the sale racks, but Lucy had been observed walking around with the items, items which had not been returned to the racks. She had no sales receipts on her. Lucy had not resisted in the least.

'Did you mean to walk out with these items?'

Lucy buried her face in her hands for a moment. 'Yes. I was stealing them.'

From most people Byrne would have expected vehement denials, tales of mistaken identity and dastardly set-ups. Not Lucy Doucette. He remembered her as a blunt and honest person. Well, she was not *that* honest, apparently.

'I don't understand,' Byrne said. 'Do you have a child? A niece or a nephew that these sweaters were for?'

'No.'

'A friend's child?'

Lucy shrugged. 'Not exactly.'

Byrne watched her, waiting for more.

'It's complicated,' she finally said.

'Do you want to tell me about it?'

Lucy took another second. 'Do I have to tell you now?'

Byrne smiled. 'No.'

The waitress refilled their cups. Byrne considered the young woman in front of him. He remembered how she had appeared in their therapy group. Shy, reluctant, scared. Not much had changed.

'Have you been back to any kind of treatment?' Byrne asked.

'Sort of.'

'What do you mean?'

Lucy told him a story, a story about a man called the Dreamweaver.

'How did you find this . . . Dreamweaver guy?'

Lucy rolled her eyes, tapped her fingers on her coffee cup for a few seconds, embarrassed. 'I found his card in the trash bin on my cart. It was right there, staring at me. It was like the card *wanted* me to find it. Like I was *supposed* to find it.'

Byrne gave Lucy a look, a look he hoped wasn't too scolding or paternal.

'I know, I know,' Lucy said. 'But I've tried everything else. I mean *everything*. And I think it might actually be doing me some good. I think it might be helping.'

'Well, that's what counts,' Byrne said. 'Are you going to see this guy again?'

Lucy nodded. 'One last time. Tomorrow.'

'You'll let me know what happens?'

'Okay.'

THEY STOOD ON THE corner of South and Third. The evening had grown cold.

'Do you have a car?' Byrne asked.

Lucy shook her head. 'I don't drive.'

Byrne glanced at his van, then back. 'I'm afraid I'm going the other way.' He took out his cellphone, called for a cab. Then he reached into his pocket pulled out a pair of twenties.

'I can't take that,' Lucy said.

'Pay me back someday, then.'

Lucy hesitated, then took the money.

Byrne put a hand on each of her slight shoulders. 'Look. You made a mistake today. That's all. You did the right thing calling me. We'll work it out. I want you to call me tomorrow. Will you promise to do that?'

Lucy nodded. Byrne saw her eyes glisten, but no tears followed. Tough kid. He knew that she had been on her own for a while, although she hadn't brought up her mother this time. Byrne didn't ask. She would tell him what she wanted to tell him. He was the same way.

'Am I going to prison?' she asked.

Byrne smiled. 'No, Lucy. You're not going to prison.' The cab arrived, idled. 'As long as you don't carjack this guy on the way home you should be fine.'

Lucy hugged him, got into the cab.

Byrne watched the cab drive away. Lucy's face was small and pale and frightened in the back window. He couldn't imagine the burden she carried. He'd had the same experience of not knowing what had happened to him or where he had gone for that short period of time when they had declared him dead. But he had been an adult, not a child.

The truth was, Lucy Doucette had a bogeyman. A bogeyman who had kidnapped her and held her for three long days. Three days of dead zone in her life. A bogeyman who lived in every shadow, stood waiting around every corner.

Byrne had gotten a vision when he hugged her, a sparkling clear image that told him about a man who—

—*dates women with young daughters and comes back years later for the girls . . . something about red magnetic numbers on a refrigerator door . . . four numbers . . .*

1 . . . 2 . . . 0 . . . 8.

Byrne made a mental note to call Lucy the next day.

FORTY-TWO

JESSICA LOOKED AROUND THE BEDROOM. AT LEAST THEY HADN'T broken any lamps. They had, however, knocked everything off one of the night stands. She hoped her mother's Hummels were okay.

Jessica rolled over, gathered the sheets around her. Vincent looked as if he had been hit by a car.

'Hey, sailor.'

'No,' Vincent said. 'No, no, no.'

Jessica ran a finger over his lips. 'What?'

'You are a devil temptress.'

'I told you not to marry me.' She snuggled closer. 'What, are you worn out?'

Vincent caught his breath. Or tried to. He was coated with sweat. He pushed the covers off, remained silent.

'Boy, you macho Italian cops sure talk a good game,' Jessica said. 'Try to get you into round two? *Fuggetaboutit.*'

'Do we have any cigarettes?'

'You don't smoke.'

'I want to start.'

Jessica laughed, got out of bed, went down to the kitchen. She returned with two glasses of wine. If her calculations were correct – and they usually were at times like these, she had managed to get new appliances over the past two years by playing these moments just right – she would start her maneuvers in ten minutes.

On the other hand, this was not about a new washer or dryer. This was about a life. Their life. Sophie's life. And the life of a little boy.

When she slipped back into bed, Vincent was checking his messages on his cellphone. He put the phone down, grabbed his glass of wine. They clinked, sipped, kissed. The moment was right. Jessica said:

'I want to talk to you about something.'

FORTY-THREE

THE MAN WAS STABBED TWENTY TIMES BY HIS LOVER. THE KILLER, WHOSE name was Antony – a bit of Shakespearean irony – then proceeded to cut open his own stomach, finally bleeding out on the parkway, not two hundred feet from the steps leading to the art museum. The papers ran stories for nearly a week, the high drama too much for them to resist.

I know what really happened.

The murder victim had simply made a meat dish on Good Friday and Antony, being the devout Vatican I Catholic he was, and this being 1939, could not take the shame and guilt. I know this because I can hear their final argument. It is still in the air.

The voices of the dead are a shrill chorus indeed.

Consider the man stabbed over his Social Security check, his final pleas lingering at Fifth and Jefferson Streets.

Or the teenager shot for his bicycle, forever crying at Kensington and Allegheny, right in front of the check-cashing emporium where the regular customers pass by with smug indifference.

Or the grandmother bludgeoned for her purse at Reese and West Dauphin, her voice to this day howling her husband's name, a man dead for more than thirty-five years.

It is becoming harder to keep them out. When I bring one to the other side, it quiets for a while. But not for long.

*

I PUSH THROUGH THE huge rusted gate, drive along the overgrown lane. I park in the pooled darkness, remove my shovels. The voices calm for a moment. All I can hear, as I begin to dig, is the slow, inexorable descent of leaves falling from the trees.

FORTY-FOUR

BYRNE COULDN'T SLEEP. THE IMAGES OF THE FOUR CORPSES RODE A slow carousel in his mind. He got up, poured himself an inch of bourbon, flipped on the computer, logged onto the Net, launched a web browser. He cruised the headlines on philly.com, visited a few other sites, not really reading or comprehending.

Have you found them yet? The lion and the rooster and the swan? Are there others? You might think they do not play together, but they do.

He got onto YouTube. Once there, he typed in Christa-Marie Schönburg's name. Even before he was done typing, a drop-down window opened, listing a number of possibilities.

CHRISTA-MARIE SCHÖNBURG BACH
CHRISTA-MARIE SCHÖNBURG HAYDN
CHRISTA-MARIE SCHÖNBURG ELGAR
CHRISTA-MARIE SCHÖNBURG BRAHMS

Byrne had no idea where to begin. In fact, he really had no idea what he was doing, or exactly what he was looking for. On the surface he imagined he was looking for a portal, admittedly obscure, to the case. Something that might trigger something else. Something that might begin to explain Christa-Marie's impenetrable note to him.

Or maybe he was looking for a young detective who had walked into a house in Chestnut Hill in 1990 and there began a long, dark odyssey of bloodshed and tears and misery. Maybe he was really looking for the man he used to be.

The final entry on the list was:

CHRISTA-MARIE SCHÖNBURG INTERVIEW

Byrne selected it. It was three minutes long, recorded on a PBS show in 1988. Christa-Marie was at the height of her fame and talent. She looked beautiful in a simple white dress, drop earrings. As she answered questions about her playing, her celebrity at such a young age, and what it was like to play for Riccardo Muti, she vacillated between confident career woman, shy schoolgirl, enigmatic artiste. More than once she blushed, and put her hair behind one ear. Byrne had always thought her an attractive woman, but here she was stunning.

When the interview was complete Byrne clicked on the Bach entry. The browser took him to a page that linked to a number of other Christa-Marie Schönburg videos. Her entire public life was shown in freeze-frames down the right-hand side of the page – bright gowns and brighter lights.

He clicked on *Bach Cello Suite No. 1*. It was a montage video, all still photographs. The photographs in the montage, one slowly dissolving into the next, showed Christa-Marie at a number of ages, a variety of poses and settings: in a studio, smiling at the camera, a side view on stage, a low-angle photograph of her at nineteen, a look of intense concentration on her face. The last photograph was Christa-Marie at nine years old, a cello leaning against the wall next to her, almost twice her size.

Byrne spent most of the next hour watching the YouTube offerings. Many were collage-type videos, assembled by fans, but there were also live performances. The last video was Christa-Marie and a pianist in a studio, playing Beethoven's *Sonata No. 3 in A*. At the halfway point, in close-up, Christa-Marie looked up, straight at the lens, straight at Byrne.

When the piece finished, Byrne went to the kitchen, took two Vicodin, chased it with a swig of Wild Turkey. Probably not the prescribed way, but you had to go with what worked, right?

He looked out the window at the empty street below. In the distance was the glow of Center City. There was another body out there, another body waiting to be discovered, a raw, abraded corpse with a strip of blood-streaked paper around its head.

He glanced at the kitchen clock, although he didn't need to.

It was 2:52.

Byrne grabbed his coat, his keys, and went back out into the night.

FORTY-FIVE

LUCY SAT ON THE FIRE ESCAPE, WRAPPED IN HER DARK BLUE AFGHAN, one of the few things that had survived her childhood, one of the few things that she could stuff into a nylon duffel bag and take with her when she moved on, which she had done so many times in the past two years that she had nearly lost count.

She looked in the window. She had rented this room, a third-floor room in a trinity on Fourth Street, about two months earlier. The family was very nice. An elderly couple with no children, they had welcomed her like a granddaughter, and for the first two weeks had invited her to dinner every night.

Lucy, having had no experience with real family life, had begged off with a variety of excuses until the couple – Tilly and Oscar Walters – had gotten the hint.

The night was calm, the sky was clear, and for the first time in a long while she could see a few stars. Maybe they had been there all the time and she had forgotten to look. Perhaps the darkness was inside her, had made its nest in her soul, and refused to leave, refused to let up.

She wrapped the afghan more tightly around her, but she wasn't really all that cold. Maybe it was all those years in drafty apartments, all those years when the heat was turned off, all those years huddling around an electric stove in winter until the electricity too was turned off.

Since the day the plane came out of the sky, she had tried every-thing to make the feeling go away. Drugs, alcohol, men, religion, yoga, all manner of self-destruction and abuse. *Men*. Quite often the men she chose – boys, really – filled in any small gaps in the abuse, making her hell complete.

And now she was in trouble. She always knew she would eventu-ally get caught shoplifting, even though she was good at it. Her mother had sent her into stores from the time she was only three years old. In the first few years she was only the diversion, doing the little-cutie bit to distract store owners while her mother boosted cigarettes or alcohol or, once in a great while, a treat for Lucy.

But today she had gotten caught, and she was going to go to jail. Even though Detective Byrne said that wasn't going to happen, she wasn't so sure. She had wanted to tell him about the man in 1208, but for some reason she couldn't bring herself to do it.

And now, sitting on this rusting fire escape, she began to cry. It was the first time for years. She tasted the salt on her lips. She felt pathetic.

It was worse for the little girl who'd been killed. Little Stacy Pennell. Sergio had told her the story.

In 1999 a ten-year-old girl, whose family had lived in Le Jardin when it had been an apartment building, had been down in the laundry room with her older sister Cyndy. Cyndy, whose job it was to watch her runt of a sister, couldn't be bothered, it seemed. When Cyndy wasn't looking, Stacy had grabbed the keys from on top of the dryer and snuck out of the laundry room.

Sergio said that when Stacy got off the elevator she probably did not notice the man standing in the stairwell at the end of the hall, just a few feet from the entrance to the Pennell apartment.

When they found Stacy later she had been brutally murdered, her throat cut from ear to ear. Sergio said her body had bite marks on it.

It had happened in Room 1208.

It couldn't have been coincidence, Lucy thought. It just couldn't. The man in 1208 had been there for a reason. Some other little girl was going to be hurt.

Was the man who killed Stacy Pennell the same man who had kidnapped *her*?

Lucy was suddenly cold. She slipped back inside, shut the window. She walked over to the closet, opened the door, sat down, and waited for the night to embrace her.

Fifteen feet below, in the gloom of the stairwell beneath the fire escape, a man stepped into the shadows and joined Lucinda Doucette in darkness.

FORTY-SIX

FRIDAY, OCTOBER 29

IN THE SHOWER JESSICA THOUGHT ABOUT THE PREVIOUS NIGHT. VINCENT
had listened to her entire well-planned speech. He had been surprisingly receptive to the idea of adopting Carlos, considering that he was
not the most open-minded person she had ever met.

They made love a second time, this time sweet, married love, and
halfway through she saw something in Vincent's dark eyes that told
her they might actually do this. Later Vincent told her, in the twilight
before sleep, that he wanted to meet Carlos first before even thinking
about making any decision, of course. Maybe he wanted to do a little
male bonding, Jessica thought. Take the kid to a Flyers game, do a
few Jager Bombs, leaf through a copy of the new *Maxim*.

As she was getting dressed, she realized that Vincent had made
the bed – a first. She also noticed a flower on her pillow. Granted, it
was a silk flower, and Vincent had taken it from the arrangement on
the dining-room table. But it was the thought that counted.

MARCEL'S COSTUME COMPANY WAS a storefront on Market Street near
Third. Established in 1940, Marcel's carried a full line of Halloween
outfits, professional make-up, wigs, and accessories. Marcel's also

created costumes for local television shows and was quite often hired for supplemental wardrobe for Philadelphia's booming film-production industry.

But today it was all about Halloween. Marcel's was open twenty-four hours a day this week, and even at 7:30 a.m. the store was half full.

When Jessica and Sophie walked in, Jessica saw Rory behind the counter. Rory Bianchi was a kid from the old neighborhood who had always had a crush on Jessica, and ever since ninth grade they'd had the sort of relationship where the flirting went on but never went anywhere.

'The two prettiest girls in Philly,' Rory said. 'In my shop!'

'Hi, Rory!' Sophie said.

'Hey little darlin',' he said. 'Ready for the big night?'

Sophie nodded. A kid in a costume shop. Outside of a candy story, there was nothing cooler. Jessica remembered coming into Marcel's when she was a girl and Wonder Woman had been the rage.

'I have it for you right here,' Rory said.

Of all the costumes available – including Disney characters like Ariel from *The Little Mermaid*, which was Sophie's favorite movie – Sophie had picked something called the Snowflake Fairy. Jessica had tried to explain that Halloween was a fall holiday, but her words had fallen on deaf ears. Unlike her mother, Sophie loved the winter, especially snowflakes. Come December Sophie was endlessly cutting them out of construction paper and dotting the house with them.

'Do you want the wings and the wand, too?' Rory asked.

It was a dumb question, but Jessica looked at Sophie anyway. Sophie seemed to be in a fairy trance, the reflection of white satin in her big brown eyes.

'Sure,' Jessica said.

'I take it you'll want the tiara as well.'

Jessica took out her credit card as fast as she could, in case there was anything else.

SOPHIE FLOATED OUT TO the parking lot, still in a daze, the dress clutched tightly in her hands, as if Monica Quagliata might be lurking behind the next SUV – Monica with designs on the Snowflake Fairy costume.

When they got to the car, Sophie supervised the hanging of the costume on the hook in the back, pronounced it safely stowed for the few-mile journey. She slipped into the seat next to it, buckled in.

Before Jessica could start the car, a family crossed the street in front of them – mom, dad, two boys, two girls. Jessica looked over at Sophie.

'Do most of your friends have brothers and sisters?' Jessica asked. It was a rhetorical question, but one that Jessica needed to ask to get the conversation started.

Sophie didn't give this too much thought. She just nodded.

'Do you ever wish *you* had brothers and sisters?'

A shrug. 'Sometimes.'

'What would you think about having a brother?'

'A brother?'

'Yeah.'

'A *boy*?'

Jessica laughed. 'Yeah. A boy, sweetie.'

Sophie thought for a moment. 'Boys are okay. A little bossy, but okay, I guess.'

JESSICA DROPPED SOPHIE OFF at school, stopped at Old City Coffee on Church Street. Outside, she picked up an *Inquirer* and a free copy of *The Report*, Philly's sleaziest tabloid – and that was saying something. As expected, the current spate of murders was splashed across the cover.

Philly Noir, the Geometry of Vengeance, screamed the headline.

Jessica tossed the *Report* in the trash, tucked the *Inquirer* under her arm. She got into her car, wondering how Byrne was faring.

Have you found them yet? The lion and the rooster and the swan? Are there others?

What did Christa-Marie Schönburg have to do with all this?

She checked her cellphone. No calls from Byrne.

*

THE PRIMARY ROLE OF THE Department of Human Services was to intervene and protect neglected, abused or abandoned children, as well as to guarantee their well-being when there were immediate threats or impending dangers in their lives.

The Children and Youth Division provided youth and family-centered services to more than 20,000 children and their families each year.

Although the main offices were located at 1515 Arch Street there were various facilities throughout the city – temporary shelters and foster-care centers.

Jessica arrived at Hosanna House, a stand-alone brick building on Second Street. She signed in and walked to the day room at the back. She was immediately assaulted by the sound of a dozen toddlers in full morning mania. The place smelled like orange juice and crayons.

Carlos sat at a table with two little girls and a young woman of about twenty. He wore a red cardigan. He looked adorable.

Jessica watched him for a few minutes. Kids were unbelievably resilient, she thought. Just two weeks earlier this little boy's life had been hell on Earth.

But Jessica knew enough, had seen enough cases of abused and neglected children to know that many times there was residual grief and anger and fear. Most of the people she had arrested in the past five years were, almost to a man or woman, products of broken homes.

Carlos looked up and saw her. He got out of his chair, rocketed across the room, and threw his arms around her. He ran back, got a piece of paper from the table, ran back to Jessica, handed it to her.

It was a crayon drawing of a room, possibly the living room where Carlos had lived with his mother. There was something that looked like a chair and a table, and a woman in the corner with wild dark hair, eyes the size of her whole head. Patricia Lentz, Carlos's biological mother, had blonde hair, almost white.

It didn't take Jessica long to realize the figure in the drawing just might be her. Right behind her was a bright sun. Jessica's heart felt ready to beat its way out of her chest.

She looked at the table in Carlos's drawing. On the table was something that Jessica had no trouble recognizing. It was a two-year-old boy's rendition of a gun.

Jessica suddenly felt a paralyzing wave of sadness. She fought it.

'Can I have this?' she asked Carlos.

Carlos nodded.

'Stand up tall – let me look at you.'

Carlos stood at attention. His hair was combed, his face scrubbed. His sweater and pants looked new.

'This is a beautiful sweater,' Jessica said.

Carlos giggled, looked down, toyed with a button, perhaps thought better of messing with it. He was two. He knew his limitations.

'Where did you get your new clothes?'

Carlos turned toward the table, held out his tiny hand. Jessica walked over, hand in hand with Carlos. He sat down and tucked into a new drawing.

'Hi,' Jessica said.

The young woman at the plastic picnic table looked up. 'Hi.'

Jessica pointed to the drawing in her hand. 'This is pretty good for a two-year-old. I couldn't draw a straight line then. Still can't.'

The young woman laughed. 'Join the club.' She looked over at Carlos, smoothed his hair. 'He's *such* a beautiful boy.'

'Yes, he is,' Jessica said.

'I'd kill for those eyelashes.'

'Are you a counselor here?'

'No, no,' the young woman said. 'I just help out. I volunteer one day a week.'

Jessica nodded. The young woman had about her an air of competence, but also an air of sadness. Jessica felt the same way about herself sometimes. It was hard to see the things she saw every day and not be affected. Especially the kids. Jessica glanced at her watch. Her tour was starting.

'It was nice talking to you,' Jessica said.

'Same here.'

Jessica extended her hand. 'My name is Jessica, by the way.'

The young woman stood, shook her hand. 'Lucy,' she replied. 'Lucy Doucette.'

FORTY-SEVEN

WHEN JESSICA GOT TO HER CAR SHE FELT ANOTHER WAVE OF melancholy. The drawing that Carlos had given her hit home. It would probably be a long time until those memories passed from his life. Was it too much for her and Vincent to be taking on?

As she unlocked the car door she turned to see someone approaching. It was Martha Reed, the director of Hosanna House. Martha was in her early fifties, plump but energetic, with clever blue eyes that missed nothing.

'Carlos looks well,' Jessica said. 'He looks . . . happy.' It was a stretch, but Jessica couldn't think of anything else to say.

'He's adjusting,' Martha replied. Martha Reed had seen a lot of children in her time.

The woman then rummaged in her bag, took out her BlackBerry. She tapped around, got to her calendar. 'Can you and your husband be here today at around eleven?'

Jessica's heart thundered. They were getting their adoption interview. She'd known this moment was coming, but now that it was here she wondered how she was going to handle it. 'Oh yeah. We'll be here.'

Martha looked around conspiratorially. She lowered her voice. 'Between you and me, it looks really good. I'm not supposed to say that, but it looks good.'

Jessica drove out of the Hosanna House parking lot on a cloud. Before she could turn onto Second Street her cellphone rang in her hand. It was Dana Westbrook.

'Morning, boss. What's going on?'

'I just got the report on the Joseph Novak surveillance.'

'Okay.'

'We had a detective from West on him all night. Experienced guy, used to be in anti-gang, and did some task-force work with DEA. He sat on the apartment his whole tour. He said that from the time he came on until six this morning, there were no lights on in the place, no activity. About eight o'clock this morning he put on a Philadelphia Water Department jacket, grabbed a clipboard, got the super to let him in, and knocked on Novak's door. He got no answer, so he went around back, climbed the fire escape, looked in the window.'

'Was Novak home?'

'He was,' Westbrook said. 'He was sitting at his desk. It looks like, after he left the Roundhouse yesterday, he went home, shredded all of his sheet music and news clippings, and somewhere between six o'clock last night and eight o'clock this morning put a gun in his mouth and pulled the trigger.'

FORTY-EIGHT

THE AMOUNT OF BLOOD WAS STAGGERING.

Jessica stood next to the stacks of crystal CD cases. The clear boxes were sprayed with blood and brain matter. Bits of shattered skull stuck to the valance over the curtains.

Joseph Novak's body was in the desk chair at an unnatural angle – the force of the blast had twisted his body in two directions. The upper third of his head was missing. *Not missing, exactly*, Jessica thought. It was dispersed around the wall and drapes behind him. The bullet had blasted out the window. There were two CSU officers across the street at that moment searching for the slug.

Was Joseph Novak their killer? He'd seemed unshakeable when he had been in for questioning, but why had he run the previous day? What did he have to hide?

The body was removed at ten a.m.

JESSICA WATCHED THE CSU officers go through the motions. Now that the body was gone, the apartment-management company would soon contact one of the cleaning crews that specialized in crime-scene cleanup, a mini-growth industry during the past ten years. The world would move on.

The death had all the earmarks of a suicide, so there was probably not going to be a full-blown investigation. The weapon, a Colt Commander, had still been in Joseph Novak's hand when he was found, his finger curled inside the trigger guard.

Jessica would present her report to her boss, who would pass it along to the DA's office, who would then make a ruling. Unless there was any compelling evidence of foul play, this would be ruled a suicide and the homicide division of the PPD would not be involved any further.

But that didn't mean there was not a connection to the serial murders going on in the city.

Jessica got the attention of the two CSU officers who were dusting the doors and table for fingerprints.

'Can you guys give me a few minutes?'

The officers, always ready for a break, set aside what they were doing, walked through the door into the hallway, closed it.

Jessica slipped on gloves, turned the laptop to face the other side of the desk. The screen displayed a default screen saver. She touched the space bar, and in a second the screen came back to life. It was a Word document, with three short sentences.

> *Zig, zig, zig.*
> *What a saraband!*
> *They all hold hands and dance in circles . . .*

Jessica was not familiar with the passage. Was this a suicide note? she wondered. She scrolled down on the trackpad but there was nothing else. The document was just the three lines. She glanced at the corner of the window. It had not been saved.

Was this a work in progress? Was this some sort of message from Joseph Novak, some riddle left behind for friends and family by which they might make some sense of his final, violent act?

Jessica had no idea. As much as she would have liked to take the laptop with her, she had no jurisdiction over it. Not yet, anyway. She would lobby the DA's office to establish a material-witness status for the late Joseph Novak, and perhaps she would get a chance to go through it.

She looked around the place. The silence was thick and oppressive.

Jessica had to be careful about looking through the contents of the computer. The homicide unit had recently received directives from the DA's office about needing court approval for doing anything with a computer that involved clicking a mouse or touching a keyboard. If there was something on the screen to be seen, in plain view, that was one thing. If it involved maximizing a minimized window, launching a program, or visiting a web page located in a history on a browser, that was something else.

A case against a man trafficking in child pornography had recently been tossed because the detective, knowing there were thousands of images on the man's hard drive, had opened a graphics program. It turned out that every time a program was launched, there was a log of the event and a record of the precise time it happened. If the suspect was in custody at that moment, the detective could not claim that the program was already open.

Jessica clicked over to the side bar. There was no harm in looking, as long as she didn't open any files or programs. She glanced at the contents of the drive. There was one file. SARABAND.DOC. That was it. Other than that, there was nothing on the drive. No documents, no spreadsheets, no databases, no photos, music or audio files. It had all the earmarks of a drive that had been recently erased.

Any good computer-forensic lab would be able to tell when a drive had been formatted, and could usually find evidence of the files that were originally on the drive. Jessica was already formulating the case she would make to the DA's office to allow them to do just that.

In the meantime she would get a couple of warm bodies down here to canvass the building, just to see if Joseph Novak had had any visitors earlier in the day. If he had, maybe it could lead to a full-scale investigation of his death as something other than a suicide.

She took out her phone, checked her voicemail. Two messages.

When did she get two messages? Why hadn't it rung? She checked the side of the phone. With an iPhone, the switch to toggle from *silent* to *ring tone* was on the upper left, and was easily activated when you put the phone in your pocket. Too easily. The ringer had been off.

Jessica switched it back on, tapped the first voicemail message. It was from the man who was hoping to install the awnings on the new house. He wanted two grand. *Dream on.*

The second call was from an unknown caller. She played it.

'*Detective Balzano, this is Joseph Novak.*'

Jessica jumped to her feet. Her skin broke out in gooseflesh. She glanced behind her, at the dark sienna stains on the carpet and walls. She could still smell the cordite in the air, could taste the coppery airborne blood at the back of her throat. Joseph Novak's blood. She was listening to a message from the grave.

'*I want to apologize for my behavior. I can't go on like this. There is more to this than you know. Much more. You don't know him. I cannot live with myself anymore.*'

Jessica paused the message for a moment, paced the living room. Everything she looked at – the books, the CDs, the furniture itself – took on a new meaning.

She stopped pacing, tapped the button, continued the message.

'*I hear him coming down the hall. Look in the cabinet above the range in the kitchen.*'

The message ended.

Jessica put her phone in her pocket, crossed the living room into the compact Pullman kitchen. She opened the cabinets above the range hood. There she found a dozen or so cookbooks – Mexican, Italian, Cajun. She pulled a few of them out, riffled the pages. Nothing. The second-to-last cookbook was labeled *Home Recipes*. She pulled it out. When she did, something fell on the floor. It was a slim leather-bound journal. The cover was worn and creased. She picked it up. Stuck in the front was an old photograph. It was Joseph Novak at fifteen or so, standing next to a beautiful cello. Jessica slipped the picture back in the book, opened it.

It was a diary.

JUNE 22. The competition is this Saturday. But it is more than just a competition for first chair. We both know that. It is a competition for her. It will always be thus.

Jessica flipped ahead to the back of the journal. She read the final entry.

NOVEMBER 1. *All Saints Day. It is done. I know now that I will be forever beholden to him. I will never be out of his shadow. For the rest of my life I will do his bidding. My heart is forever broken, forever in his hands.*
  Zig, zig, zig.
  He is death in cadence.

Jessica closed the journal. She needed a warrant to search every square inch of this apartment, and she needed one fast. She put in a call to the DA's office, told them what she had, what she needed. She took the journal, intending to say it had been in plain sight, therefore not covered by the warrant. She stepped outside, locked the door. She told the two CSU officers they could return to the lab. She would call them when and if she needed them.

She walked across the street, grabbed a coffee-to-go at the diner, stepped into the parking lot behind. She called Byrne, got his voice-mail. She called Dana Westbrook, gave her a status report. Westbrook said she would send two other detectives from the Special Investigations Unit to aid in the search.

Jessica opened the journal. There was something under the back cover. She peeled it back gently. There was a second photograph there, an old Polaroid, a long shot of a window in a huge stone building. In the window was a figure. It was impossible to see who it was, but it looked like a slender woman. On the back of the photograph was one word scrawled in red pencil.

Hell.

Before Jessica could get the photograph back into the journal she heard someone approaching, footfalls on hard gravel. She turned.

The fist came from nowhere, connecting with the right side of her face in a dull thud. She staggered back, saw stars. The journal flew out of her hands. The second blow was more glancing, but it carried enough force to knock her to the ground. She had enough presence to roll onto the side where she had her weapon holstered.

Through the haze she saw her assailant. White-blond hair, filthy jeans, laceless sneakers. She didn't recognize him. Not by sight, not at first. When he spoke again, she knew. And there was no mistaking those eyes.

'I think we have some unfinished business, Detective Balzano,' Lucas Anthony Thompson said. 'Or should I say Detective *Cunt* Balzano.'

Jessica rolled to her right, worked the Glock from her holster, but she was too slow. Thompson stepped forward, kicked the weapon from her hand.

'You shoulda shot me when you had the fucking chance, bitch. Ain't gonna happen today.'

When Thompson took another step toward her, Jessica saw movement at the back of the parking lot. A shadow slithered along the pavement.

Someone was standing behind Thompson.

And then everything went gray.

FORTY-NINE

THE PHILADELPHIA ORCHESTRA BEGAN LIFE IN 1900. OVER THE NEXT century it held many distinctions, not the least of which was the 'Philadelphia Sound', a legacy that, under conductor Eugene Ormandy, became known for its clarity and skilled execution, its warm tonality and precise timing.

The orchestra also had a unity of artistic leadership virtually unknown in the world of great orchestras, with only seven musical directors in its entire history. Two men, Leopold Stokowski and Eugene Ormandy, held the reins from 1912 to 1980.

It was on the occasion of Ormandy's leaving that the Philadelphia Orchestra found itself at a crossroads and, perhaps in an attempt to modernize its somewhat staid image, turned to a young firebrand, Neapolitan Riccardo Muti, as its new musical director. Darkly hand-some, intensely serious to the point of almost never smiling on stage, Muti ushered in a new era, an era dominated by a man whose insist-ence on the letter of the musical law earned him the nickname – at least around the opera houses of Italy – of *lo scerif*, the sheriff.

In 1981, in a move still discussed in some circles, the orchestra rattled the classical musical world by hiring as its principal cellist a nineteen-year-old named Christa-Marie Schönburg – a tempestuous wunderkind who was taking the world of strings by storm. Within a year her name became as synonymous with the Philadelphia Orchestra's as Muti's, and when the chamber orchestra toured Eastern Europe that summer Christa-Marie Schönburg was the talk of the classical-music universe.

By the time she was twenty-two there was no doubt in the minds of the *cognoscenti* that she would surpass, in technical skill, pure artistry and, indeed, world-wide recognition, the only other woman to capture international fame on the cello, the tragic Jacqueline du Pré, the brilliant cellist whose career was cut short at the age of twenty-eight by multiple sclerosis.

And while Jacqueline du Pré made her most memorable recording with Elgar's *Cello Concerto in E Minor*, Christa-Marie put her imprimatur on the Bach suites.

For nearly a decade, from Vienna's Konzerthaus to Rotterdam's Grote Zaal, from the Royal Festival Hall in London to Avery Fisher Hall in New York City, Christa-Marie Schönburg, with her tensile, passionate music, brought audiences to their feet.

On a cold autumn night in 1990 all of that changed.

Something tragic happened on that night when Christa-Marie returned home after a triumphant performance at the Academy of Music – a benefit attended by many of Philadelphia's elite society, a fund-raiser for Philadelphia's homeless children.

Although details of the last two hours remain unknown, it was believed that Christa-Marie returned to her Chestnut Hill house at approximately 11:45 p.m., delivered there by a car service. A few hours later, according to her housekeeper, there were sounds of an argument in the kitchen, a struggle, then a scream. The housekeeper called the police.

Police arrived at around two-thirty. They found a man named Gabriel Thorne – a psychiatrist who had treated Christa-Marie for many years – sprawled on the kitchen floor, bleeding heavily from wounds to his abdomen and chest, the bloodied knife at his side. He was still alive. They called EMS, who tried to save him at the scene but failed. He was pronounced dead minutes after their arrival. The ME's office would eventually rule that Thorne bled out as a result of multiple stab wounds.

Christa-Marie Schönburg never played another public concert.

Because she confessed to the crime there was no show trial, much to the disappointment of the burgeoning cable-TV court shows. Christa-Marie Schönburg was as enigmatic as she was strikingly beautiful, and her relationship with Thorne was, for many years, cause for gossip and speculation.

The last time Byrne saw Christa-Marie Schönburg was at her allocution, when she stood before a judge and admitted her guilt regarding the murder of Dr. Gabriel Thorne.

As BYRNE DROVE NORTH he thought of the Chestnut Hill house, how when people heard what had happened they began to gather across the street early the next morning, bringing with them flowers and stuffed animals, even sheet music. It was as if Christa-Marie had been the victim, not the perpetrator.

Byrne had thought of Christa-Marie often. It wasn't just that Christa-Marie Schönburg had been his first case as the lead detective in a homicide. Something else about the woman haunted him. What drew him to her had never been entirely clear to him.

Maybe he would discover what that was today.

FIFTY

'**I**'M FINE,' JESSICA SAID.

It was a lie, but she was sticking to it.

The paramedic shone his light into her eyes for the third time, took her blood pressure for the third time, took her pulse for the fifth time.

She had been punched on many occasions in the past – when you box in the ring, it kind of goes with the territory – and this had been a glancing blow, not really that hard. But it had caught her off guard. In the ring, you brace yourself for incoming blows, and the adrenalin that flows naturally at a moment like that works as a sort of neural shock absorber. No one on Earth can be prepared for a sucker punch, which, by definition, comes out of the blue. Her head throbbed a little but her vision was clear, and her energy level was high. She wanted back in the game but they were going to make her sit there like an invalid. She had seen it many times in her years on the job, had even been the purveyor of the unwelcome news to victims of assault.

Just sit there for a moment.

Not so for Vincent Balzano. When the sector cars showed up, she made the call, found Vincent only a dozen blocks away, working an investigation of his own. He broke every speed record getting to the scene. That was the easy part. Calming him down was another matter. At the moment he was pacing like a caged animal. Unfortunately for

Vincent Balzano and his Italian temper, he was lacking a convenient punching bag. For now, at least.

Jessica's weapon had been recovered. It had not been fired.

ALL JESSICA REMEMBERED WAS hearing other footsteps but she did not know whose they were. She did not mention the journal, which had not been recovered from the scene

'No one said anything?' Westbrook asked.

Jessica shook her head. It hurt. She stopped doing it. 'No. I heard footsteps approaching. I got clocked twice. There was a scuffle. Then I faded out.'

'What kind of scuffle?'

'Not sure. I heard at least two people grunting. Then the ringing in my ears took over.'

'And you did not see the other person?'

'No, but I—'

Jessica suddenly looked at her watch, sprang to her feet. She felt dizzy for a moment, then it passed. Her anger did not.

'What is it?' Vincent asked.

'We missed it. We fucking *missed* it.'

'What?'

'The appointment at the Department of Human Services.'

'Jess.'

'Don't *Jess* me.'

'We'll work it out,' Vincent said. 'Don't worry.'

'Don't *worry*? This is why they turn you down, Vincent. This is the first big test. You don't show, you don't call, it's over.'

Vincent held her close. 'I think you have a pretty good excuse, babe. I think they'll understand.'

'They won't,' Jessica said, wiggling loose. 'Plus, they're not going to place Carlos in a home where his mother is in danger every day.'

'They know we're both cops. They know what we do.'

It all came out. The anger of this brutal case. The inability to conceive for two years. The indignity of being assaulted. All of it.

'You weren't *there*, Vincent. I was there. I saw how Carlos was living. I saw the dog shit and the fucking hypodermic needles all over the place. I saw the cockroaches and rats in the sink, the rotting food. I saw him hiding under a fucking *garbage bag*. You don't know what a hell hole it was, how bad his life was. They are *not* going to hand him over to us so we can make it worse.'

She tried to walk it off. The rage was a breathing thing within her.

Soon Jessica calmed down and let the investigation begin. It was going to be a long day – and it was just getting started.

FIFTY-ONE

CHESTNUT HILL WAS AN AFFLUENT NEIGHBORHOOD IN THE Northwest section of Philadelphia, originally part of the German Township laid out by Francis Daniel Pastorius. One of the original 'railroad suburbs,' the area contained a wide variety of nineteenth- and early-twentieth-century residences designed by many of the most prominent Philadelphia architects.

Before leaving Center City, Byrne had called ahead to schedule a time to meet with Christa-Marie. He was directed to Christa-Marie's attorney, a man named Benjamin Curtin. Reluctant at first, Curtin arranged to meet Byrne at the estate at one p.m.

As Byrne turned down St. Andrews Road he saw the house for the second time in his life. He had not been back since the night of the murder.

It was a massive, sprawling Tudor building with a circular driveway accented with cobblestones, a large gabled entrance. To the right, partially hidden by trees, was a stable, next to a pair of tennis courts. A high wrought-iron fence encircled the property.

Byrne parked his van and, even though he was wearing his best suit, suddenly felt underdressed. He also realized that he had been holding his breath. He got out of the vehicle, straightened his tie, smoothed the front of his overcoat, and rang the bell. A few moments later the door was opened by a woman in her sixties. Byrne announced himself, and the woman led him through the high, arched doorway. Ahead was a carved mahogany winding staircase; to the right were thick fluted pillars leading to a formal dining room. To the left was the great room, with a view of the pool and the manicured grounds beyond. Byrne's heels echoed in the massive space. The woman took his coat and led him into a study off the enormous foyer.

The room was darkly paneled, clubby, with a pair of large bookcases built in and a vaulted open-trussed ceiling. A fire burned in the fireplace. The mantel was arrayed with pine cones and other autumn decorations. Above the mantel was a large portrait of Christa-Marie. In the painting she sat in a velvet chair. It had to have been painted right around the time Byrne met her, that dark night in 1990.

A few moments later the door opened and a man entered.

Benjamin Curtin was in his early fifties. He had thick gray hair, swept straight back, a strong jaw. His suit was tailored to perfection and might well have cost what Byrne made in a month. Curtin was probably twenty pounds heavier than he looked.

Byrne introduced himself. He did not produce his identification. He was not there in any official capacity. Not yet.

'It's a pleasure to meet you, detective,' Curtin said, perhaps to remind Byrne what he did for a living. Curtin had a Southern accent. Byrne pegged him as Mississippi money.

'And you, counselor.'

There, Byrne thought. *Everyone knows their jobs.*

'Is Liam still keeping the peace down there?'

Down there, Byrne thought. Curtin made it sound like the boondocks. He was referring to Judge Liam McManus, who everyone knew was going to run for the Philadelphia Supreme Court in a year.

'We're lucky to have him,' Byrne said. 'Rumor is he won't be there for much longer. Next thing you know he'll be living in Chestnut Hill.'

Curtin smiled. But Byrne knew it was his professional smile, not one that held any warmth. The attorney gestured to a chair on the other side of the desk. Both men sat down.

'Can Charlotta get you anything? Coffee? Tea?'

'I'm fine, thanks.'

Curtin nodded. The door behind Byrne was closed.

'So, what brings you here to visit Ms. Schönburg, detective?'

'I'm afraid I can't really get into anything too specific, but I will say that she may have information about an open investigation being conducted by the Philadelphia Police Department.'

Curtin looked slightly amused. 'I'm intrigued.'

'How so?'

'Well, as I'm sure you're aware, Ms. Schönburg no longer lives a public life. She is by no means a recluse, but, as I'm sure you can appreciate, she does not circulate in any of the social circles to which she once belonged.'

'I understand.'

'She has almost constant companionship here, so I'm afraid I don't see how she could possibly be involved in anything that has taken place recently in Philadelphia.'

'That's what I'm here to determine, Mr. Curtin. But I have a few questions before I meet with her.'

'Is she suspected of a crime?'

'No,' Byrne said. 'Absolutely not.'

Curtin stood, walked to the window, looked out. He continued to speak without turning around. 'I must tell you that in the few years she has been out of prison there have been no fewer than a hundred requests for interviews with her. She is still very much the object of fascination not only with people in the world of classical music but also with the basest denizens of the tabloid world.'

'I'm not here to write something for the *Enquirer*,' Byrne said.

Curtin smiled again. Practiced, mirthless, mechanical. 'I understand. What I'm saying is, all these requests have been presented to Christa-Marie and she has categorically turned them all down.'

'She contacted *me*, Mr. Curtin.'

Byrne saw Curtin's shoulders tense. It appeared that he had not known this. 'Of course.'

'I need to ask her a few questions, and I want to know what her general mental state is. Is she lucid?'

'Most of the time, yes.'

'I'm not sure what that means.'

'It means that much of the time she is rational and fully functional. She really would not have any problem living on her own, but she chooses to have a full-time psychiatric nurse on the premises.'

Byrne nodded, remained silent.

Curtin walked slowly back to the desk, eased himself into the sumptuous leather chair. He placed his forearms on the desk, leaned forward.

'Christa-Marie has had a hard life, detective. From the outside, one might think she led a life of glamour and privilege and, up until the incident, she *did* enjoy the many rewards of her talent and success. But after that night, from the interrogations and subsequent allocution, to her eighteen months at Convent Hill, to her incarceration at Muncy, she—'

The words dropped like a Scud missile. 'Excuse me?'

Curtin stopped, looked at Byrne.

'You said Convent Hill?' Byrne asked.

'Yes.'

Convent Hill Mental Health Facility was a massive state-run mental hospital in central Pennsylvania. It had been closed under a cloud of suspicion in the early 1990s after nearly one hundred years of operation.

'When was Christa-Marie at Convent Hill?'

'She was there from the time she was sentenced until it closed in 1992.'

'Why was she sent there?'

'She insisted on it.'

Byrne's mind reeled. 'You're telling me that Christa-Marie insisted on being sent to Convent Hill? It was her *choice*?'

'Yes. As her attorney I fought against it, of course. But she hired another firm and made it happen.'

'And you say she was there for eighteen months?'

'Yes. From there she went to Muncy.'

Byrne had had no idea that Christa-Marie had spent time at the most notoriously brutal mental-health facility east of Chicago.

While Byrne was absorbing this news a woman walked into the room. She was about forty and wore a smart navy blue suit, white blouse.

'Detective, this is Adele Hancock,' Curtin said. 'She is Christa-Marie's nurse.'

Byrne rose. They shook hands.

Adele Hancock was trim and athletic, had a runner's body, close-cropped gray hair.

'Miss Schönburg will see you now,' the woman said.

Curtin stood, grabbed his coat, his briefcase. He rounded the desk, handed Byrne a linen business card. 'If there is anything else I can do for you, please do not hesitate to call me.'

'I appreciate your time, sir.'

'And give Liam my best.'

Sure, Byrne thought. *At the next curling match.*

Benjamin Curtin nodded to Adele Hancock and took his leave.

BYRNE WAS LED DOWN a long dark-paneled hallway past a room that held a grand piano. On that night twenty years ago he had not visited this wing of the house.

'Is there anything I should know before I meet with her?' Byrne asked.

'No,' Hancock said. 'But I can tell you that she has not spoken of anything else since your call.'

When they reached the end of the hallway, the woman stopped, gestured to the room at the end. Byrne stepped inside. It was a solarium of sorts, an octagonal room walled by misted glass. There were scores of huge tropical plants. Music lilted from unseen speakers.

Have you found them? The lion and the rooster and the swan?

'Hello, detective.'

Byrne turned to the sound of the voice. And saw Christa-Marie Schönburg for the first time in twenty years.

FIFTY-TWO

J ESSICA LOOKED OUT AT THE THRONG OF POLICE GATHERED IN THE parking lot across from Joseph Novak's apartment. There were now two scenes to process – the murder scene, and the scene where a police detective had been assaulted. Out of the crowd walked Nick Palladino, notebook in hand. He spoke to Dana Westbrook for a few moments. Every so often they glanced over at Jessica. Dino did most of the talking. Westbrook did most of the nodding.

Dino came over when they were done, asked after Jessica's well-being. Jessica told him that she was all right. But she could see by the look on his face that things had just gotten worse.

'What's up?' Jessica asked.

Dino told her.

Jessica discovered that she was mistaken about there being two scenes to process. There were three.

LUCAS ANTHONY THOMPSON'S BODY had been found dumped in another parking lot, three blocks away. His body was nude, roughly shaved clean, and there was a band of paper around his head. It appeared that he had been strangled. On one of the fingers of his right hand was a small tattoo of an elephant.

It didn't take long to determine the significance of the crime scene.

Lucas Anthony Thompson's body was found in the parking lot where Marcia Kimmelman's body had been found. It fitted the killer's pattern. Another murderer dumped at the scene of his crime.

There were already two teams watching Thompson's family members. If one of them was an accomplice they would be targeted.

Jessica looked across the lot to see someone trying to get through the police cordon. It was David Albrecht. He wanted to talk to Jessica. The uniformed officer held him back, glanced over.

'Let him through,' Westbrook said.

Albrecht came running up, out of breath.

'What did you want to say?' Westbrook asked.

'I was across the street, getting exterior shots of the building when I saw Detective Balzano come out of the front door.'

Albrecht gasped for breath. He held up a finger.

'Take your time,' Westbrook said. 'Would you like some water?'

Albrecht shook his head, gathered his wind, continued. 'Okay, okay. So I saw Detective Balzano go into the diner, and a few minutes later she came out with a coffee, and walked over here.' He indicated the parking lot, which was now teeming with crime-scene personnel. 'At first, I didn't think there was a shot, you know? I mean, a parking lot is a parking lot, right? Not the most exciting backdrop. We're not talking Robert Flaherty here.'

Albrecht looked at Jessica and Dana Westbrook, perhaps expecting a reply or a reaction. None was forthcoming. He continued.

'So anyway, I'm looking at the way the trees back here sort of frame the lot, the way that half-wall sort of provides a horizon, and I saw Detective Balzano pacing back and forth, and I thought it looked pretty good.'

He turned, pointed to his van across the street. 'I set the camera on my tripod, framed the shot, locked it down, then went into the back of the van for a filter. I wanted to use a Circular Polarizer because I wasn't getting much contrast. It took me a few minutes to find it, and when I came back around she was gone. Just papers blowing around in the wind. I looked and saw that her car was still down the block, so I knew she didn't leave. I figured she either went back into the diner or back into the apartment building. I figured I just missed her. Then I looked next to the building and . . . and I saw her lying there.' There was a slight hitch in Albrecht's voice.

'And you didn't see the assailant?' Westbrook asked.

'No, ma'am,' Albrecht said. 'I didn't. Not at first.'

'What do you mean, not at first?'

'I mean I didn't see him *live*.'

Westbrook looked at Jessica, then back at Albrecht. 'I don't know what you mean.'

'I didn't realize I was rolling.'

'Rolling?' Westbrook asked, clearly getting a little agitated.

'Yeah. When I put the camera on the tripod I started shooting. I have to admit, I'm just getting used to this camera. It's brand new. I hit the button by accident. It's a little embarrassing, but that's what happened.'

'What are you saying?' Jessica asked.

'What I'm saying is, I just watched the replay, and I think we have it.'

'Have what?'

David Albrecht held up the camera. 'I think we have footage of the killer.'

CHRISTA-MARIE SCHÖNBURG SAT IN A LARGE BURGUNDY LEATHER chair, her pale white hands folded in her lap. Even from across the room, the first thing Byrne noticed were her eyes. Not only were they a strikingly deep amber – he had noticed the same thing twenty years earlier – but they had not changed. Two decades, two *difficult* decades of incarceration, psychiatric treatment and dealing with whatever demons had possessed her to begin with had not hardened her eyes in the least. They were a young woman's eyes, still as arresting as they'd been when she was the brightest star in the classical-music firmament.

Her hair had turned a soft, shimmering silver.

She was wearing a black silk pantsuit.

On the table next to her was a pair of reading glasses and an open book.

Byrne crossed the room and found that he was at a loss for words. What power did she have over him?

Christa-Marie stood, still as slender as ever, but standing this close Byrne saw the faint lines that etched her face, her forehead, the papery skin on her hands. Still, with her cascade of silken hair, she was a beautiful woman. Perhaps even more elegant than before.

He had not stood this close to her since the night he had put her in handcuffs.

He took her hand. His first instinct was to lean forward and kiss her on the cheek. He realized at the last instant that this would have been inappropriate, to say the least. Still, the urge was present. She made the decision for him. On tiptoes, she leaned in and grazed his cheek with her lips.

She had been twenty-eight the last time he had seen her. She was now almost fifty. She had escaped, or postponed, so many of the things that can happen to a man or woman in those years. Byrne found himself wondering what he looked like to her, what the land-scaping of his face and body by his job and habits and life had done to the image she might have retained from that day in 1990.

Without a word she gestured to the other chair by the windows, perhaps five feet away. Byrne sat down, but for some reason did not sit back. He leaned forward, the way one might do at a job inter-view. Music played softly in the background. It was a cello piece, with piano.

After a few long minutes Christa-Marie spoke.

'It was her last studio recording, you know.'

'Who?'

'Jackie du Pré,' she said. 'She toured in 1973, and they savaged her. I wonder what they would have said of me.'

After she was sentenced in 1990, Byrne read a few books that had been written about Christa-Marie. The comparisons to Jacqueline du Pré were as specious as they were expected. It was said of Jacqueline du Pré that on her final concert tour, due to her illness, she could no longer feel the strings and had to play by sight. Byrne, having never played an instrument, having never been considered great at anything – he was only world-class at screwing up romantic relationships – could only imagine the horror and heartbreak of something like this happening to someone so gifted.

In Christa-Marie Schönburg's case, her skills had not eroded in the least when she was sent to prison. She was still, at the moment of her incarceration, one of the most celebrated and revered cellists in the world. Here, looking at the woman so many years later, he wondered which fate was worse.

'We came from the conservatories in those days,' she said. 'I went to Prentiss. My teacher was a childhood friend of Ormandy. They might never have found me if not for him.'

Christa-Marie arranged herself on the chair, continued.

'You know, there really weren't all that many women back then. It wasn't until much later that playing in a major orchestra, at least one of the Big Five – Boston, New York, Cleveland, Chicago, Philadelphia – was seen as a job, a full-time job that a woman could do. Gainful employment, as they used to say.'

Byrne remained silent. While he was sitting there he felt his cell-phone vibrate three separate times. He couldn't answer. Finally he just said it:

'Christa-Marie, I need to ask you something.'

She sat forward in her chair, expectant. In that instant she looked like a schoolgirl. Byrne held up the note card.

'Why did you write me?'

Instead of answering she looked out the window for a few moments. She looked back. 'Do you know those scrolls on the bottom front of the cello? The holes cut there?'

Byrne glanced at the cello in the corner. He saw what she was talking about. He nodded.

'Do you know what they call those?' she asked.

'No.'

'They're called the F-holes. Can you imagine a group of young students hearing this for the first time?'

Christa-Marie's expression soon changed from one of joyful remembrance to one of longing.

'My happiest years were at Prentiss, you know. There was no pres-sure. There was just the music. Bernstein once told me that the only thing that mattered was to love the music. It's true.'

She smoothed her hair, ran a hand across her cheek. 'I was just nineteen that first night at the Academy. *Nineteen*. Can you imagine?'

Byrne could not. He told her so.

'It has been so many years since then,' she said.

She fell silent again. Byrne had the feeling that if he did not move forward with his questions he would never again have the opportunity.

'Christa-Marie, I need to talk to you about your letter.'

She glanced at him. 'After all this time, you want to get to business.' She sighed dramatically. 'If we must.'

Byrne held up the note card again. 'I need to know what you were talking about when you wrote me, and asked if I'd "found them." If I'd found the lion and the rooster and the swan.'

She stared at him for a long second, then rose from her chair. She walked the short distance between them, knelt before him.

'I can help you,' she said.

Byrne did not answer immediately, hoping she would continue. She did not. 'Help me do what?'

Christa-Marie looked out the window again. In this light, at this short distance, her skin was translucent, the result of a lifetime spent hiding from the sun.

'Do you know the Suzuki method?' she asked.

Byrne had heard of it, but he knew nothing about it. He told her so.

'He focused on song-playing over technique. He allowed students to make music on the first day. It's no different from learning a language.' She leaned in. 'We two speak the language of death, do we not?'

Christa-Marie leaned even closer, as if to share a secret.

'I can help you stop the killings,' she said softly.

The words echoed off the misted glass walls of the solarium.

'The killings?'

'Yes. There will be more, you know. Many more. Before Halloween night at midnight.'

Her tone was flat, emotionless. She talked about murder in the same manner in which she had talked about music earlier.

'Why Halloween midnight?'

Before she answered, Byrne saw the fingers on her left hand move. At first he thought it might have just been some sort of twitch, an involuntary movement brought about by being in one position for an extended period of time. But out of the corner of his eye he saw her fingers curl around an imaginary thing and he realized she was recreating some passage she had once played on the cello. Then, just as suddenly as the movement began, it stopped. She dropped her hands to her lap.

'It is not over until the coda, detective.'

Byrne knew the word. A coda was a final section to a piece of music, generally played with some dramatic urgency – a flourish at the end of a symphony, perhaps. 'I'm not sure what you mean.'

'George Szell would often stand in his office window and see which of his players took their instruments home with them.'

Byrne said nothing, hoping she would return to the moment on her own.

'Easy for the oboist, *n'est-ce pas?*' she added. 'Not so for the bassist.' She sat up on her heels. 'Did you know that the cellist and bassist must each purchase an extra airline ticket for their instruments?'

Byrne hadn't known that.

'The Cavani String Quartet always books for five.'

'Christa-Marie,' Byrne said, hoping that his voice did not sound as if he were pleading. 'I need—'

'Will you come back on Halloween?' she asked, interrupting him. 'I want to show you a special place in the country. We'll make a day of it. We'll have such fun.'

Byrne had to find out what she meant in her note, the references to the animals. But he now knew that getting the information was not going to be easy. Before he could stop himself he said: 'Yes. I'll come back.'

She looked at him as if seeing him for the first time, her expression darkening. 'I can help you stop the killings, Kevin. But first you must do something for me.'

'What is it, Christa-Marie?' he asked. 'What can I do for you?'

Of all the things he expected her to say, what she did say nearly took his breath away. They were probably the last two words he would have expected to hear, two words that would carry his thoughts well into the dark hours of the night.

Christa-Marie Schönburg took his hand in hers, looked deep into his eyes, and said: 'Love me.'

L UCY STOOD IN FRONT OF THE DOOR TO ROOM 1208, HER HEART pounding. She wanted to go in, but she was afraid, as frightened as she had ever been in her life. She had done a little sleuthing on her own. She knew that everyone on this floor was a member of *Société Poursuite.* The group had a seminar in the Crystal Room that day, a seminar that was scheduled to run from 10:00 a.m. to 3:00 p.m., when they would break for lunch. Lucy figured that the floor would be empty from about 9:30 a.m. until perhaps 2:00 p.m.

Earlier in the day she had stood on the mezzanine and watched everyone file into the Crystal Room. Ever since she had been kidnapped, with everyone she met she was always looking for something, some gesture, some familiar posture, a word, an inflection, an accent that would draw her back to those three lost days and what had happened to her.

Once, in Carlisle, she had heard a woman's high-pitched laughter, and it had drawn her memory to a room – not necessarily a room in which she had been held, but a room that had served as a stop along the way. When she had turned to look at the woman – a doughy redhead of forty with cigarette-stained lips – the feeling had gone. She understood then that the feeling would come and go. She only needed it to stay for a moment, during which she could take a snapshot. And remember.

Right now she had a job to do.

Lucy lifted her hand to knock but found she couldn't do it. Her arms felt weak and a little too light all of a sudden. She tried again.

'Housekeeping,' she said, knocking. She soon realized it had come out in a mousy whisper.

A louder knock. *'Housekeeping.'*

Nothing.

Now or never.

She took out her section card, swiped the lock, and stepped into Room 1208.

THE ROOM WAS EMPTY.

She wasn't supposed to close the door, but sometimes they closed on their own and her supervisor was well aware of this. This was one of those times. Except that Lucy closed it herself.

She had lugged everything she needed into the room and had piled it on the bed. She breezed through her checklist. She had never worked so fast in her life.

This was crazy. What was she doing? This was all in her head. She had created a fantasy here – from the moment she'd heard about the Dreamweaver it had all been some crazy dream. The fact that a girl had been killed in this room was just a sick and tragic and horrible coincidence.

Mr. Adrian Costa had no special abilities, no special powers. The man was a charlatan, and he was lying to her. Just another long con.

Lucy flew through the rest of her duties, clocking the room at something superhuman, like fifteen minutes. When she was finished she felt a little better. A clean fresh room had that effect on her. Now she could leave.

On the way out she saw that the bottom drawer in the dresser was slightly open. She looked at the door, then back.

Before she could stop herself she eased open the drawer. Inside were three folded dress shirts. There was something glossy beneath them. She pushed the shirts aside, and saw it.

At the bottom of the drawer was a picture of her mother.

FIFTY-FIVE

BYRNE SAT IN HIS VAN. ON THE WAY TO CHESTNUT HILL HE HAD planned it all out: how he would present himself, how he would talk to Christa-Marie, how he would get the information he needed from her. He would walk in, the veteran investigator, Mr. Cool, Master of the Universe, and walk out with what he needed.

He had failed miserably.

He was leaving without one shred of information. He wondered what his next move would be. He could talk to Michael Drummond or Paul DiCarlo in the DA's office. They, in turn, would get in touch with Benjamin Curtin, and the request would be made to have Christa-Marie come into the city for a formal statement.

Byrne could all but see the attendant circus.

As soon as he started the van he saw Adele Hancock crossing the wide driveway. Byrne lowered his window as she approached.

'She wanted you to have this.'

Adele Hancock handed him a sealed CD. The cover photo was a picture of Christa-Marie at a café in Italy. Behind her was the Basilica di Santa Maria del Fiore.

'She told me to tell you that if you want to know her, you should listen to this.'

'What do you think she means by that?'

Hancock offered a thin smile. 'If you have a few years to spare, I could probably scratch the surface of that question for you.'

Fifteen minutes later Byrne found himself on the expressway. He couldn't head back to the city. Not yet. He had another stop to make.

INSIDE HIS HEAD THE urges combusted. One urge told him what he had to do, what he should do. The other told him what he ultimately *would* do.

Heading west, he opened the CD and pushed it into the player. In moments his world was filled with the soaring majesty of Christa-Marie Schönburg's cello.

FIFTY-SIX

Tommy Archer had never gotten used to the smell. Probably never would. This did not bode well for someone with a dream of one day owning his own beauty salon.

Today's offending odor – there were so many from which to choose in this line of work – was the cloying aftermath of the perm he had just finished doing on old Mrs. Smith. The perm smell was mostly ammonia, which, if he remembered correctly from his chemistry classes, came from ammonium thioglycolate.

Tommy just called it skunk.

He always told his customers that, seeing as the perm solution was very alkaline, the best way to get rid of the smell was with an acid-based product like tomato juice. He told them to apply it to their hair, leave it on for ten to twenty minutes, then shampoo and rinse.

His customers all thought he was some kind of genius when he explained this to them, but it was pretty basic science. Still, he let them believe what they wanted to believe. In his twenty-six years there hadn't been too many people who considered Tommy Archer a genius. Especially his father. On the other hand, considering what he had once done for his father, he had earned the man's undying gratitude, if not his respect. Not that the man would ever show it.

While getting the perm smell out of hair was one thing, getting the smell out of the tiny shop, the sum total of six hundred square feet that made up Country Cutz (inarguably the worst salon name in the history of the business), was something else.

Even though the temperature was around forty-five degrees, Tommy opened the two windows overlooking the street. Mrs. Smith had been his last customer for the day.

Tommy popped a tape into the player behind the register and began to sweep up. He felt a chill cross the salon. It was getting near the holiday season, which meant more work, more money, but it also meant that the loneliness would begin to descend again. He was the poster boy for Seasonal Affective Disorder.

HE WAS NOT ALLOWED to smoke in the shop. After the floor was swept and the sinks rinsed, with combs and brushes cleaned, he stepped outside and lit a cigarette. Dark already. The main street of the town was all but deserted. The lights from Patsy's Diner two blocks away and the Aamco shop across the street were all that were on.

'Are you still open?'

Tommy nearly jumped a foot. He turned to locate the source of the voice. There was a man standing right next to him. As in *right* next to him. He hadn't heard him walk up the sidewalk.

The man wore a dark overcoat.

Tommy glanced at his watch. 'Actually, we close in about five minutes.'

The man ran a hand over the back of his hair. 'I was hoping to get a quick trim. You see, I have a wedding reception tonight – I'm the cool uncle, the one with the big wallet – and, while I could probably show up in a rainbow wig, I do like to make an entrance.'

Tommy looked again at his watch, as if the answer was going to be there. He liked the man's style, though, and the *big wallet* reference was clearly meant to imply some sort of huge tip. Plus, it wasn't like he had anywhere to go. His little hamlet didn't exactly have a thriving gay community, or even a seedy part of town. All he had to look forward to was a bottle of cheap Orvieto and the DVD box set of the second season of *Jericho*. *Thank God for Netflix.*

He glanced at the man. *Nice eyes. Nice smile.*

'Just a trim?'

'Yes,' the man said. 'And I'm willing to pay double the going rate.'

'That won't be necessary,' Tommy said. 'Besides, what would I do with all that money in a dump like this town?'

THE MAN DIDN'T REALLY need too much work, but if Tommy understood anything – about both himself and most of the people he had ever styled – it was that personal grooming was just that. Personal. Everyone had a right to look exactly the way he or she wanted.

'Nice little town you have here,' the man offered.

Tommy snorted. 'Yeah, well, it is if you don't mind living in a place where you call the wrong number and end up talking to that person for an hour anyway.'

The man laughed. 'I'll bet it's not *that* bad.'

Tommy took out his hair dryer, blew the hair from the man's shoulders. When he was done he dusted the man's neck with powder.

'So, you're going to a wedding reception?' Tommy asked.

'Yes,' the man said.

'Whereabouts? Over at the Legion Hall?' Tommy took off the cape. He picked up his brush, brushed off the last stray hairs from the man's shoulders and neck.

'No,' the man said. 'This is at the Crystal Room.'

Tommy had never heard of the Crystal Room. 'Is that around here somewhere?'

'It's in Philadelphia.'

Tommy shrugged. He figured that the man was on his way across the state. They got a lot of travelers here, being so close to the Flight 93 memorial. Tommy wondered how the man had managed to find the shop.

The man stood up, straightened the crease in his trousers. 'I really appreciate this. I feel like a new man.'

A new man, Tommy thought. *I wish.*

'It was my pleasure.'

The man slipped on his coat. 'How much do I owe you?'

Tommy told him. The man doubled the price, as promised.

*

AT JUST AFTER EIGHT Tommy locked the shop. As per his explicit instructions, he left the register open, drawer out, under a solitary spotlight.

He walked quickly to the parking lot. The temperature had dropped in the past hour or so.

'Thomas?'

He spun around. He saw no one, just the long-shadowed street.

Thomas? Who the hell called him Thomas? The last person to call him Thomas had been his ex, Jeremy. But that had been in York, and that was three years ago.

'Hello?'

Silence.

Tommy stepped back around the corner. A car trundled past, one person inside, never glancing his way. He looked both ways down the street. And saw him. The man he had just given the trim to. Except now the man was wearing a dark jumpsuit, zipped to the throat.

'Benvenuto al carnevale.'

The man lifted something into the air, an object about the size and shape of a large old-school garage-door opener. Tommy heard a loud crackling sound, smelled something burning. Then his legs went south.

IN A VAN. MOVING.

Tommy blanked out. Came back.

He could not move his head.

THE VAN WAS STOPPED. The man climbed into the back, put on a pair of thin latex gloves, shut the doors. Classical music was playing on the car stereo. Violins or something.

Tommy heard something else. It sounded like a drill.

Tommy screamed.

FIFTY-SEVEN

BYRNE STOPPED FOR COFFEE IN NORTH PHILLY. HE WASHED HIS FACE and hands in the bathroom. Fatigue was a shambling monster within. When he slipped back into the van he turned on his cellphone and saw that he had five messages. All from Jessica. He called her.

'Where are you?' Byrne asked.

'I'm at Jefferson Hospital,' Jessica said.

'*Jefferson?* Why?'

'I ran into an old friend of mine today.'

'What are you talking about? Who?'

'Lucas Anthony Thompson.'

'*What?* How?'

Jessica gave him a brief recap, starting with the suicide of Joseph Novak, the voicemail from the dead, the existence of Novak's journal, and the assault by Lucas Thompson on her. Byrne took a moment to absorb it all.

'Man, I leave the city for one minute,' he said.

'Tell me about it.'

'Is Thompson in custody?'

'No,' Jessica said. 'He's dead. And Novak's journal is gone.' She filled him in on the rest of the details.

'Where did it happen?'

Jessica told him.

'That was the Kimmelman crime scene, wasn't it?'

'Yeah.'

'Have they moved him yet?'

'Yeah. CSU is all over the place.'

'I'm going to stop there,' Byrne said. 'When did they say you could get out of there?'

'About an hour or so. Vincent is with Sophie. Can you pick me up?'

'I'll be there.'

FIFTY-EIGHT

Byrne arrived in front of the hospital at about nine-thirty. Jessica was waiting, forced to sit in a wheelchair – which made everything seem so much worse than it was. Spotting his van, she got out of the chair, crossed the driveway, and slid into the passenger seat.

'You *look* okay,' Byrne said.

'I *am* okay. You know how it is. You break a fingernail and they want to do exploratory surgery. Keeps the premiums up.'

'What did they say?'

'I'm fine. No concussion. They said I'll have a headache for a day or so. They want to see me again in two weeks.'

Byrne drove slowly before pulling into the small temporary parking lot. He put the van in park. 'Tell me more about this.'

Jessica tried to organize her thoughts. It was a little difficult after getting her brain scrambled. She told Byrne what she remembered about Joseph Novak's diary.

'He wrote that he was beholden to someone,' she said.

'His word? Beholden?'

Jessica nodded. 'He wrote: *All Saints Day. It is done. I know now that I will be forever beholden to him.*'

'All Saints Day. November 1st.'

'Yeah.'

Jessica also told him about the photograph in the back of the journal.

'Any idea who the woman was or where it was taken?' Byrne asked.

'None. I didn't recognize the place.'

'And the word *hell* was on the back?'

'Yeah. Just that. Hell.'

They fell silent.

'Now it's your turn,' Jessica said. 'What happened up in Chestnut Hill?'

Byrne told her about his conversation with Christa-Marie. Jessica had the feeling that her partner was not telling her everything, but that was his way. He would tell her only what she needed to know at this moment.

'She said there are going to be more killings,' Byrne said. 'She said that she could help us.'

'And that was it? No details?'

'No details.'

'Did she sound . . . how do I put this . . .'

'Nuts?'

'Yeah. That.'

'I'm not sure,' Byrne said. 'Yeah, I suppose she did. A little. But I'd like to talk to her one more time before all hell breaks loose with her. You know as well as I do that the second I put this on the record they're going to send a half-dozen shrinks up there. She'll shut down completely.'

The rain picked up again. For a few moments there was only the sound of the music from the stereo and the staccato impact of raindrops on the roof of the van.

Byrne turned in his seat, put his hand on hers. 'You sure you're okay?'

'Good to go,' Jessica said. 'Never better.'

Byrne just stared.

'Okay, I may have been better once. I think it was the summer my cousin Angela had that Thai stick.'

Byrne smiled. He squeezed her hand, put the van in reverse. Jessica leaned forward, turned up the stereo. 'This is beautiful. Is this who I think it is?'

Byrne reached behind her seat, picked up the CD case, handed it to her.

'This is what we're listening to?'

Byrne nodded. 'Yeah. Christa-Marie's nurse gave me that. She said Christa-Marie wanted me to hear it.'

Jessica looked at the CD player, saw it was track two. She looked at the case. Track two was *Nocturne in G Major* by Chopin.

'It's incredible,' she said.

When the track was over she played it a second time.

As THEY PULLED OUT of the parking lot, Jessica read the liner notes.

'This was recorded here in Philly, you know,' she said. 'At the Prentiss Institute.'

'That's the music school, right? The conservatory over on Locust?'

'I think so.'

Jessica looked at the back of the CD. At the bottom was a brief list of credits.

'Kevin.'

Byrne looked over. Jessica handed him the CD, pointed to the last line of the liner notes.

RECORDING ENGINEER: JOSEPH P. NOVAK.

FIFTY-NINE

ONCE A STATELY MANSION, THE PRENTISS INSTITUTE OF MUSIC WAS an impressive early-1900s Georgian sandstone building, across from Rittenhouse Square on Locust Street. In the world of classical music it was considered by many to be Philadelphia's version of the Juilliard. Many members of the Philadelphia Orchestra had studied at Prentiss. While most of the courses of study were at the college level, they also maintained a prep school. A number of principal players of major orchestras around the world had gotten their training at Prentiss.

Because of the prestige of the school, and the late hour, Byrne had put in a call to the DA's office. The office had then placed a call to the school and gotten Jessica and Byrne an appointment to speak with someone.

THE DEAN OF THE Prentiss Institute of Music was Frederic Duchesne. In his forties, Duchesne was tall and sharp-featured, had thinning blond hair, hazel eyes, and an air of rumpled elegance. He met them at the front door of the institute, locking it behind them, and escorted them to his office, a large white-paneled room off the reception area. The room was cluttered with sheet music on stands, stacks of CDs, as well as a variety of musical instruments in their velvet-lined cases.

On the wall was a large framed copy of the school's charter. Duchesne offered coffee, which Jessica and Byrne declined. They sat.

'We appreciate you taking the time to talk to us,' Byrne said. 'I hope we're not keeping you too late.'

'Not at all. I sometimes don't leave here until midnight. Always something to do.' He absently straightened some papers on his desk, then stopped, perhaps realizing it was hopeless. He turned back. 'It's not often we get a visit from the police.'

'We just have a few questions,' Byrne said.

'I assume this has something to do with Joseph Novak.'

'It does,' Byrne said.

Duchesne nodded. 'I saw it on the news.'

'What can you tell us about Novak?'

'Well, as I understand it, Mr. Novak was loosely associated with Prentiss for ten years or so.'

'He was an employee?'

'No, no. He freelanced as an engineer for various recordings. The institute hires a number of different technicians based on the project.'

Byrne held up the CD he had gotten from Christa-Marie. 'He worked on this project?'

Duchesne put on his glasses. When he saw the CD he smiled fondly. 'That was recorded more than twenty years ago. Novak didn't record the original. He worked on the remastering.'

'Were you acquainted with Joseph Novak?'

'We met once or twice. I never worked with him personally, no.' Duchesne shook his head. 'Terrible tragedy what happened.'

'When was the last time you saw him?'

Duchesne thought for a moment. 'It must be two years now.'

'You've had no contact since?'

'None.'

'Do you know how many recordings he worked on here?'

'Not off hand,' Duchesne said. 'I can get that information for you.'

Byrne glanced at his notes. 'I have just a few more questions. I'm afraid some of them are probably going to seem pretty basic.'

Duchesne held up a hand. 'Please. This is a place of learning.'

'Can you tell us a little bit about the institute?'

'You want the tourist version or the potential-donor version?'

'Tourist,' Byrne said. 'For now.'

Duchesne smiled, nodded. 'The institute was founded in 1924 by a woman named Eugenie Prentiss Holzman, and is known worldwide as one of the leading conservatories. It's difficult to get into, but the tuition is free. A number of the current members of the Philadelphia Orchestra are faculty here, as well.'

'How many students do you have?'

'Right now, around one hundred sixty.'

'And this is all free?'

'Well, not the private lessons.'

'Expensive?'

'Very,' Duchesne said. 'The hourly fee can be quite high.'

Duchesne continued, relating how Prentiss recruited its students, what the general curriculum was. He also name-dropped some of the more famous alumni. It was an impressive list. When he finished he reached into his desk, produced a pair of large full-color booklets, handed one to Byrne, one to Jessica. The publication was called *Grace Notes*.

'Prentiss publishes this quarterly,' Duchesne said. 'Inside you'll find all the background you need.'

Jessica and Byrne thumbed through the booklets. Byrne held up his copy. 'Thanks.'

Duchesne nodded.

'I do have one last question, if I may,' Byrne added.

'Of course.'

'When it comes to orchestral music – symphonies – is there always a book?'

'A book?'

'Like in musical theater. Someone writes the book, someone writes the music, someone else writes the lyrics.'

'I think I may know what you're asking. You want to know if symphonies have a *story* behind them. A narrative.'

'Yes.'

'It's a difficult question,' Duchesne said. 'And one that's been a topic for discussion and debate for a long time. I believe what you're talking about, insofar as instrumental music is concerned, is called program music.'

'Program music has a story?'

'Yes and no. In its purest form, program music can be a mere suggestion of a narrative.'

'So a piece of music that follows a narrative approach might not be particularly coherent?'

Duchesne smiled. 'Tell me, detective. Where did you study music?'

'A little honky-tonk at the crossroads.'

'With the esteemed Mr. Johnson.'

'Yeah, well,' Byrne said. 'I made a different deal with the devil.'

Duchesne took a moment, thinking. 'To answer your astute question, yes. For the most part. There are a few exceptions, one being Vivaldi's *Four Seasons*.'

Jessica tried to listen closely but the only sound she could hear was the conversation flying over her head. She knew that Byrne took cryptic but detailed notes. She hoped he was getting all this. She was completely lost when it came to classical music. Whenever someone mentioned *The Barber of Seville* she thought of Bugs Bunny.

'Are there any symphonic poems, program music, that involve the use of animal imagery?'

'My goodness. Many.'

'Specifically a lion, a rooster, a swan, or a fish?'

'Perhaps the most famous of all. *Carnival of the Animals*,' Duchesne said without a moment's hesitation. 'It is a musical suite of fourteen movements. Much beloved.'

'The movements are all about animals?'

'Not all,' Duchesne said.

'Who was the composer?' Byrne asked.

'*Carnival of the Animals* was written by a great proponent of the tone poem. A French Romantic composer named Camille Saint-Saëns.'

'Do you have information on this that you might let us borrow?' Byrne asked.

'Of course,' Duchesne said. 'It will take me a little while to collate all of it. Do you want to wait?'

'Can you fax it to us as soon as you have it all together?'

'Sure,' Duchesne said. 'I'll get right on it.'

Jessica and Byrne rose. 'We really appreciate this,' Byrne said, handing the man a business card.

'Not at all,' Duchesne replied. He walked them to the door of his office, through the reception area, to the front doors.

'Were you here when Christa-Marie Schönburg studied here?' Byrne asked.

'No,' Duchesne said. 'I've been here for almost twenty years, but she had left by then.'

'Did she teach here?'

'She did. It was only for two years or so, but she was quite something, as I understand. The students were madly in love with her.'

They descended the steps, reached the side door of Prentiss.

'Perhaps this is something you are not at liberty to discuss, but does any of this have something to do with Ms. Schönburg?' Duchesne asked.

'No,' Byrne said, the consummate liar. 'I'm just a fan.'

Duchesne glanced over at the wall. Jessica followed his gaze. There, next to the door, mixed into a precise grouping of portraits of young musicians – violinists, pianists, flutists, oboists – was an expensively framed photograph of a young Christa-Marie Schönburg sitting in a practice room at Prentiss.

On the way to the van – parked just off Locust Street on a narrow lane called Mozart Place – they walked in silence.

'You saw it, didn't you?' Jessica finally asked.

'Oh yeah.'

'Same one?'

'Same one.'

In the decades-old photograph of Christa-Marie next to the door she wore a stainless steel bracelet with a large garnet stone inlaid.

They had seen the same bracelet on the shelf at Joseph Novak's apartment.

SIXTY

THE AUDIO-VISUAL UNIT OF THE PPD WAS LOCATED IN THE Roundhouse basement. The purview of the unit was to provide A/V support to all of the city's agencies – cameras, TVs, recording devices, audio and video equipment. The unit was also responsible for recording every public event in which the mayor or police department was involved, providing an official record. The detective divisions relied upon the unit to analyze surveillance footage as it related to their cases.

In this regard there was no one better than Mateo Fuentes. In his mid-thirties, Fuentes was a denizen of the gloomy confines of the basement studios and editing bays, a fussy and geometrically precise investigator who seemed to take every foray by detectives into his world as an unwelcome invasion.

Recently promoted to sergeant, Mateo was now commander of the unit. What had passed for punctiliousness when he was Officer Fuentes now bordered on the obsessive.

When Jessica and Byrne arrived in the basement, Mateo Fuentes was holding court in one of the bays off the main studio, chatting with David Albrecht.

'So, you prefer the L-series lens, then?' Mateo asked.

'Oh yeah,' Albrecht said. 'No comparison.'

'No ghosting?'

'None.'

Mateo smirked. 'So, if I mortgage my house and sell all my posses-sions, I might be able to buy a rig like this?'

'You might be able to *rent* one.'

Both men looked over at Jessica and Byrne. Albrecht smiled. Mateo frowned. It appeared that the two detectives were harshing his vibe. A few minutes later the rest of the team arrived – six detectives in all, plus Sergeant Dana Westbrook.

Mateo was outnumbered.

'And so to business,' Fuentes said. 'Ready?'

The detectives gathered around David Albrecht's camera. The LCD screen was about four inches diagonally, but Mateo had hooked it up to one of the fifteen-inch monitors from the Comm Unit.

Mateo fast-forwarded through footage of the West Philly location until he came to the sequence showing the parking lot where Jessica had been assaulted.

The video showed Jessica walking out of the diner and into the parking lot. Ordinarily this would have been a moment for hoots and hollers, for a bout of good-natured ribbing. Everyone was silent. They knew what was coming.

On the screen Jessica made a call on her cellphone, then pock-eted the phone. She leaned against the wall of the building, and opened the diary. She pulled something out of the back. This went on for a full minute. Cars passed in the foreground. A mother walking with her three small children stopped in front of the lot. The woman adjusted the jacket on a two-year-old girl, who wanted nothing to do with it. They soon moved on. Jessica continued to read.

A few moments later Thompson emerged from behind the building. It showed him sucker-punching Jessica, the diary flying from her hand. Two loose pieces of paper lofted on the wind. Everyone watching winced. The second blow took Jessica down. Thompson paced for a few moments, strutting. The audio was from across the street, just the sound of traffic. His words were unintelligible, but his gestures were not.

'There,' Albrecht said. He hit a button on the small remote in his hand. The video froze. Albrecht pointed to the right side of the screen. There, just beyond the corner of the building, was a shadow on the ground, the unmistakable shadow of a person. Albrecht restarted the video. Thompson stood over Jessica's body, but all eyes were on the shadow. The shadow didn't move.

He's watching, Jessica thought. *He's just standing there watching what's happening. He's not helping me. He's part of this.*

When Thompson got close to the corner of the building a pair of arms reached out, over his head. A second later the arms descended and Thompson all but disappeared, dragged off his feet with enormous force.

Albrecht rewound the video, played it again, this time frame by frame. The arms were dark-clad. The subject wore dark gloves. When the hands were over Thompson's head Albrecht froze the video. Silhouetted against the white of the garage behind the building, it was possible to see what the man in shadows had in his hands. It was a wire. A long loop of thin wire. He slipped the wire over Thompson's head and around his neck, yanking back and pulling Thompson from the frame.

The screen went black.

'I want a copy of this sent to Technical Services,' Dana Westbrook said. 'I want this broken down frame by frame.'

'Sure.'

'I want tire impressions from that lot and the area behind the building,' Westbrook said. 'See if we have any police cameras on that street.'

Before Westbrook could say anything else, Dennis Stansfield came down the stairs in a hurry. He bulled into the center of the room.

'Detective?' Westbrook asked. 'You're late.'

Stansfield looked at the floor, the ceiling, the walls. He opened his mouth, but nothing emerged. He seemed stuck.

'*Dennis?*'

Stansfield snapped out of it. 'There's another one.'

THE SCENE WAS A Chinese takeout on York Street, in a section of Philadelphia known as Fishtown. A longtime working-class neighborhood in the northeast section of Center City, running roughly from the Delaware River to Frankford Avenue to York Street, Fishtown now boasted a number of arts and entertainment venues, mixing arty types with the cops, firefighters, and blue-collar workers.

As Byrne and Jessica threaded through the cordon to the area behind the restaurant, Jessica dreaded what she was about to see.

A PAIR OF UNIFORMED officers stood at the mouth of the alley. Jessica and Byrne signed onto the crime scene, gloved up, and walked down the narrow passageway. No one was in a hurry.

The call had come in to 911 at just after nine p.m. The victim, it appeared, had been dead for days.

Garbage bags had been piling up behind the restaurant for weeks. Apparently the restaurant owner had an ongoing feud with the private hauling company, and it had become a matter of principle. Pushed against one wall were more than a hundred bulging plastic bags, ripped and torn by all manner of vermin, their rotting contents spilling out. The foul smell of the decomposing body was masked by a dozen other acrid odors of decaying meats and produce. A trio of brave rats milled at the far end of the alley, waiting their turn.

AT FIRST, JESSICA DIDN'T see the victim. CSU had not yet set up their field lighting, and in the dim light of the sodium street lamps, combined with the meager yellow light thrown by the security light over the back door to the restaurant, the flesh of the corpse blended in with the trash and pitted asphalt. It was as if he had become part of the city itself. Stepping closer, she saw the body.

Light brown skin. Nude and hairless. Head shaved bald. The body was bloated with gases.

The entire team was present, along with Russell Diaz, Mike Drummond, and now a representative of the mayor's office.

They all waited for the ME's investigator to clear the body for investigators. Tom Weyrich was taking a day off. The new investigator was a black woman in her forties whom Jessica had never met. She examined the body for wounds, made her notes. She opened the victim's hand, shone her Maglite, and everyone saw the small tattoo on the middle finger of the left hand. It appeared to be a kangaroo. Photos were taken from every angle.

The ME's investigator rose and stepped back. Stansfield walked forward and gently removed the white paper band that was wrapped around the victim's head.

The dead man was Latino, in his late thirties. Like the other victims he had a slash across his forehead, but this time the puncture wound was over his left eye. His right ear was shredded into a scabrous tangle of blood and ruined cartilage.

Byrne saw the victim's face, turned, and took a few steps away, his hands in his pockets.

What was *this* about? Jessica wondered. Why was he stepping away?

'I know him,' Drummond said. 'That's Eduardo Robles.'

All eyes turned to Kevin Byrne. Everyone knew that Byrne had been trying to get the grand jury to indict Robles in the death of Lina Laskaris. And now Robles was a victim of their serial murderer.

'This is where she died,' Byrne said. 'She was shot on the street and she crawled back here to die. This is the Lina Laskaris crime scene.'

On York Street, the media crews swarmed. In the mix Jessica noted CNN, Fox and other national news outlets. Among them David Albrecht jockeyed for position.

Five victims.

SIXTY-ONE

BYRNE GOT IN THE VAN AND DROVE. AT FIRST HE HAD NO IDEA WHERE he was going. But soon he found himself on the expressway, and not long after that back in Chestnut Hill, looking beyond the high iron fence at the huge house.

He saw a light in a window, a shadow cross the elegant silk drapery. Christa-Marie.

Closing his eyes and leaning back in the driver's seat, he returned to that night in 1990. He and Jimmy Purify had been grabbing a bite to eat. They had just closed a double homicide, a drug murder in North Philadelphia.

Had he really been that young? He'd been one of the newer detectives in the unit then, a brash kid who carried over the nickname of his youth. Riff Raff. He wore it with the expected cocky Irish swagger. They called Jimmy 'Clutch.'

Riff Raff and Clutch.

But that was ancient history.

Byrne glanced up at the second floor, at the figure in the window. Was she looking out at him?

He picked up the file next to him on the seat, opened it, looked at the photos, at the body of Gabriel Thorne lying on the floor, the bloody white kitchen where all this had begun.

He had met earlier in the day with a man named Robert Cole, a man who ran an independent lab that sometimes took contracts from the department when rush forensic services were needed. He had seen Cole testify a number of times. He was good, he was thorough and, above all, he was discreet. Cole had promised Byrne a rush job on what he wanted.

Byrne flipped through the case file. He looked at his signature at the bottom of the form. A much younger man had wielded the pen that day. A man who had his whole career, his whole life, ahead of him.

Byrne didn't have to look at the time of arrest, the moment he had placed Christa-Marie Schönburg in custody. He knew.

It was 2:52.

SIXTY-TWO

IN THE NIGHT, WHEN HOTEL GUESTS ARE ASLEEP IN THEIR BEDS, THE DEAD *roam the halls. They ride the elevators, take the back stairs, slip into rooms and stand at the foot of your bed. They sit on the edge of the sink when you take your shower. They watch as you make love, as you stuff the free toiletries and soaps into your luggage, thinking yourself so clever. They watch as you view late-night porn.*

Stacy Pennell walks these hallways, her small feet barely making an impression on the soft carpeting. Guests come and go, but Stacy stays on, her final words circling in Room 1208 like sorrowful little birds.

Soon she will be set free.

SIXTY-THREE

SATURDAY, OCTOBER 30

JESSICA JOGGED DOWN THIRD STREET. AT THIS EARLY HOUR THE running was not as bad as she'd thought it was going to be. Traffic was sparse, and the only people on the streets were those opening their bakeries and coffee shops, city crews, other joggers and cyclists. The hard part of running through a city was the uneven sidewalks, the curbs, the occasional stray dog.

There was a light drizzle, a condition that the weather report said would end by mid-morning. Jessica wore her rain gear and an Eagles ball cap. She was wet, but not soaked. The temperature was in the high forties. Perfect jogging weather.

As she turned the corner onto Wharton she thought about her and Byrne's meeting with Frederic Duchesne. She thought about the photograph on the wall of the Prentiss Institute, the picture of Christa-Marie Schönburg wearing the bracelet they had seen in Joseph Novak's apartment.

This morning they would get the background information on *Carnival of the Animals*, and they could begin to work on what might be the killer's twisted method.

She turned the corner and saw someone standing in front of her house. Again. She slowed up.

This time it was not Dennis Stansfield. It was Kevin Byrne. As Jessica approached she got a better look at him. She had never seen him look worse. His face was drawn and pale. He hadn't shaved. He was wearing the same clothes he'd had on yesterday. And he was just standing in the rain. He didn't seem to be looking for her, didn't seem to be doing anything. He was just standing in the cold rain, holding a large envelope in his hands. Just a few feet from where he stood was an awning that would have provided him shelter.

Jessica came to a stop, then walked the last few yards.

'Hey,' she said, catching her breath.

Byrne turned to look at her. 'Hey.'

'Want to come in? You're getting soaked.'

Byrne just looked up at the sky, letting the rain fall on his face.

'Come on inside,' Jessica said. 'I'll make some coffee, get you a towel.'

'I'm okay.'

Jessica took him by the arm, led him under her neighbor's awning. She shook the rain off her ball cap, brushed some of the water from Byrne's shoulders. 'What's up?'

Byrne was silent for a few moments. He pointed across the street, at a novelty sign in the window of a row house. It read PARKING FOR ITALIANS ONLY.

Jessica offered a smile. 'South Philly. What are you going to do?'

Byrne turned the envelope over and over in his hands. The moment drew out. 'I don't think I know how to do this anymore, Jess.'

He looked down the street, remained silent. Lights flickered on in some of the windows. Another morning in Philadelphia.

Jessica turned him to face her fully. 'There are two dozen people working these cases. Every resource available is on this. We're going to shut him down. Take the day. I'll call you every hour on the hour. If something breaks I'll—'

'We heard from the lab,' Byrne said, interrupting her. 'From Irina. We have a fix on the murder weapon.'

'Well, that's good, right? That's a good thing.'

'The killer is using strings from an instrument.'

'An instrument?'

Byrne looked down the street, back. 'The wire is a string from a cello, Jess. He's strangling them with a string from a cello. That explains the animal hair on the wire. It's horsehair from the bow.'

The implications of this were deep, and Jessica knew now why her partner had been up all night. There could no longer be any excuse for not bringing Christa-Marie Schönburg in for questioning. There were too many connections.

Jessica knew she had to tread lightly. 'How do you want to handle this?'

Byrne said nothing. A city street-sweeper trolled slowly by. They took a step back, closer to the building. When it had passed Byrne turned to her.

'When I walked into that house, twenty years ago, I felt something, you know? It was my first case as a lead investigator, and I had it all in my hand. I saw the body, the weapon, the blood. I saw the suspect, I knew the motive. I saw it all in one second. One big picture, no parts.' He looked at Jessica. He was on the edge. 'I said to myself *this is what you were meant to do.*'

Jessica wanted to jump in. It wasn't the right moment.

'I don't see it like that anymore,' Byrne said. 'Now it's all in pieces, and I'm scared that I made a mistake. I'm scared I can't do it anymore.'

'You're wrong, Kevin. I have no doubt that you can do this. I don't know anybody who does this better. But you know what scares *me*?'

'What?'

'What scares me is that this killer might go underground. That he might finish this up and disappear forever.'

'He's not done.'

Byrne said this with such finality that it stopped Jessica cold. 'What do you mean? How do you know?'

Byrne held up the large envelope. It was soaked. He didn't seem to care. 'This came in at four o'clock this morning.'

'What is it?'

Byrne pulled the document out of the envelope. But he didn't look at it, didn't hand it to Jessica. He just let it get wet. 'A body was found yesterday in a town called Garrett Corners.'

'How does this concern us?'

'It looks like it's connected,' Byrne said. 'We have to go there. We're expected.'

SIXTY-FOUR

THE DREAMWEAVER WAS WAITING FOR LUCY WITH HIS DOOR OPEN. He gave her a start. Again, he looked different. Even younger than the day before. He stood a little straighter, and his clothes looked new.

'Lucy,' he said, gesturing for her to step inside.

She almost gasped. The place was all but empty. The only thing left inside was the stand. The Dreamweaver booth.

'Are you moving somewhere?' Lucy asked.

'Yes. Quite soon.'

She wanted to ask what this was all about. She had a million questions, but she decided to wait. What was most important was to go back under, to slip back to that horrible day in 2001 and see the man's face, the man who took her somewhere and at the same time took her memory, her life. The man who was staying in Room 1208. The man who knew her mother.

'Today we are going to sit inside,' he said. 'Is that all right?'

Lucy pointed to the booth. 'Inside there?'

'Yes. Today we go all the way back.'

Lucy took a deep breath. 'Okay.'

Mr. Costa opened the door. Lucy took off her coat and stepped inside. It was like a confessional. Inside was a small bench. She sat down. When Mr. Costa closed the door, it was pitch black. She heard him sit down on the other side.

He began to speak, and—

—suddenly she was back there. The darkness around her did not change. But she sensed that she was under. It was different from the first two times because this time she knew. It was like when you were dreaming and you *knew* you were dreaming, and therefore you could not be hurt. For the first time in nine years, she felt strong.

ARE YOU ALONE?

No.

Who is there with you?

Another girl. A girl my age. Her name is Peggy.

Tell me about her.

She has on a spangly dress. And make-up. She's too little for make-up.

Are you wearing make-up?

I don't know. I can't see myself. But I am wearing high heels. They are big for my feet.

What is the other girl doing?

She's crying.

Are you crying?

No. I don't cry.

What else do you see?

I see candles. Candles and moonlight.

Why do you see moonlight?

Because I am running now. I'm running through the trees. The smell of apples is everywhere.

Is it an orchard?

Yes. It's an orchard.

Is the other girl with you?

No, but I see her. I see her up by the lake.

What is she doing?

She's not moving.

Why is she not moving?

I don't know.

Can you see the man's face?

I can't. But I know who he is.

Is he the man in Room 1208?

Yes. It's him.

You are certain?

Yes.

Did you place the note in his room? The note you wrote here last time?

Yes.

Good. Now I'm going to ring a bell for you. Is that okay?

Yes.

Can you hear the bell?

I can hear it.

It's a special bell, Lucy.

A special bell.

There is no other sound like it.

No other.

When you hear this bell at the hotel, there is something you have to do. Something you have to do for me.

Okay.

You will tell no one about this.

No one.

Remember the bell, Lucy.

SIXTY-FIVE

THE DRIVE ACROSS SOUTHEASTERN PENNSYLVANIA WAS ENERGIZING. The rain had stopped and it was a bright and sunny day. A lot of people think that the best place to view fall colors in the United States is New England, and they have a point. But the rolling hills of Pennsylvania, painted in scarlet and gold and lemon yellow, might well give New Hampshire a run for its money.

For a long time neither Jessica nor Byrne said much. Both were lost in the events of the past four days and the possibility of a break in the case, a break located far out of their jurisdiction.

Before leaving Philadelphia, Jessica had gotten Byrne to stop at his apartment, shower and shave, change clothes. He looked like two-thirds of his old self again.

THEY STOPPED FOR COFFEE on the way. When Jessica got back in the car she remembered something she had been meaning to ask her partner. It was about as far removed from the case as she could imagine.

'You didn't happen to find a piece of green yarn in your van, did you?'

'No,' Byrne said. 'Are you talking about the yarn that was around the box with your mom's things in it?'

Jessica nodded. The thought of having lost the yarn made her sick. 'I looked everywhere, asked everyone. It's gone.'

'Maybe it'll turn up.'

Jessica didn't hold out much hope for this. It was only ten cents' worth of yarn, but it had belonged to her mother. And that made it priceless.

THE TOWN OF GARRETT CORNERS was a notch on the map off I-80, set among rolling farmland. If you lived here, and you wanted something that could not be obtained at the local general store, hardware store, or pair of diners, there were a few larger towns within thirty or so miles where you could find a Wal-Mart, a Lowe's, or a Bed, Bath & Beyond. Dinner on Saturday night or special occasions was at Max and Erma's or Outback.

The police department of Garrett Corners was three officers strong. In addition to the standard duties involving processing civil matters such as court orders, writs and orders of possession, there were mortgage foreclosures and township auctions. Rarely did they deal with homicide.

The town itself was an intersection, twenty buildings deep in four directions. The municipal building was a featureless block of limestone, housing the police department, courthouse and public agencies. It was every small-town city hall east of the Rockies. Jessica and Byrne were instructed to meet the chief of police, a man named Rogers Logan.

THE WOMAN AT THE desk was in her fifties and had a lacquered, highly complex hairdo, cantilevered to one side. She also had about her an air of small-town bureaucratic efficiency that told Jessica there was no doubt who ran the office, if not the lives, of the three police officers stationed there. Her name was Helen Mott. There was a plate of Halloween-themed cookies on her desk.

Jessica and Byrne announced themselves, showed ID, and took a seat on the worn oak bench across the room. Jessica scanned the walls.

Affixed to them with yellowed tape were mostly outdated posters for D.A.R.E and other community drug and outreach programs. After a few minutes the door to the back opened, and a man walked out.

Rogers Logan was a fit sixty: military flat-top, big hands and farmer's shoulders. He walked with a purposeful gait. Behind him was a young woman in full uniform and Sam Browne.

'I'm Chief Logan,' he said. 'This is Officer Sherri Grace.'

Handshakes all around.

Officer Grace was in her late twenties, stout and surly. She was maybe fifteen pounds over her prom weight, and Jessica knew why. Cop hours and cop food would do it to you if you didn't fight it hard. Jessica waged the battle every day. Still, Officer Grace wore it well.

'Can I get everyone some coffee?' Grace asked.

'Sure,' Byrne said.

'How do you take it?'

'Like it comes.'

Grace winked and left the office.

'Coffee maker's fritzed,' Logan said, hooking a thumb over his shoulder, a sheepish look on his face. He probably figured that in Philadelphia the police department issued espresso machines and milk frothers to every squad. Little did he know. The first thing Jessica noticed when she walked into the office was that they had the same make and model of fax machines.

They retired to the squad room, which amounted to two desks pushed up against each other, a pair of large corkboards on the wall, a conference table pushed into the corner, along with five or six dented file cabinets.

A minute later Officer Grace returned with three cups of coffee in chipped ceramic mugs. The outside temperature had dropped a few degrees, and the mugs billowed with steam. She put the cups down on the desk, then put a cardboard box filled with packets of non-dairy creamer, sugar, Equal, Sweet'N Low and plastic stirrers on the table.

'I'm off to patrol,' she said. 'Nice meeting you all.'

Giving Byrne a little extra wattage in her smile, she left the office. The coffee rituals came to a close. It was time to get down to business. Logan, the country gentleman, gestured to Jessica to take his chair. Jessica smiled, declined. All three of them stood as Logan described the victim.

'His name was Thomas Archer. Twenty-six years old. Lived over in Kelton, right near the county line. He worked in the beauty salon over there.'

'Where was he found?' Byrne asked.

Logan moved over to a map on the wall, a map of Garrett Corners and surrounding townships. He pointed to a small green area just a short distance from the county line. 'He was found here, in the Shadyside Cemetery. As you can see, the cemetery is on both sides of the creek. Tommy was found on the southern end, near the mausoleum.'

At the word *cemetery* Jessica and Byrne exchanged a look. All they had really known on the way up to Garrett Corners was what the telex had told them, namely that there was a homicide victim with a possible connection to the Philadelphia murders.

'Who found the body?' Jessica asked.

'Body was found by the mail carrier. He was doing his afternoon route and he noticed a pack of dogs circling something in the ceme-tery. We've had a few problems with meth labs out here in the past couple of years, and where there's meth labs there're mean dogs. Mail carrier figured they'd gotten loose, called it in, and we went out to check it out. County game warden scooped up two of the dogs, others got away. The dogs had been at Tommy, but not too bad.'

'Where is Mr. Archer now?'

'The body was taken to the coroner's office in the county seat. They do all our autopsies, what few we need done.'

'Do they know how long the body had been there?' Byrne asked.

'Hard to say until they give it a good going-over. Not that long, though.'

'Do you have photographs of the crime scene?'

'Yeah,' Logan said. 'Unfortunately, I do.'

Logan led them to a small area off the squad room, which served as storage space for fax paper, toner, and other supplies. A folded crib leaned in one corner. Logan flipped on the overhead fluorescents.

One wall was dedicated to racks of official forms. The town might have been small, but it rivaled the PPD for forms needed. In the center was a folding conference table. Most of the table's contents were bunched to one side, and a pair of large manila envelopes sat in the middle.

Logan opened the envelopes, slid out the photographs. He arrayed them side by side on the table. The longer shots showed a rural cemetery. The close-ups were of the body. It was a sight with which Jessica and Byrne were all too familiar.

Jessica looked closely at the victim. The signature was identical to the bodies found in Philadelphia. The body was nude, and shaved clean of all hair. The band of paper was wrapped around the head, just barely covering the victim's eyes. There were three bloodstains on the paper, one lateral, one circular, along with the mutilated ear. The body was sprawled on a hillside, surrounded by low headstones. The left leg was clearly broken.

'Does this dovetail with the case you're working?' Logan asked.

'It does,' Byrne said.

'We'll need copies of these photographs, if that's all right,' Jessica said.

Logan retrieved a stack of envelopes from the top of a nearby file cabinet. He picked up two of them. 'I anticipated that. There's duplicates of everything in here.'

He handed the envelopes to Jessica. 'Thanks.'

The three of them went still for a few moments, each of them taking in the horror displayed before them in full color.

'When was your last homicide?' Jessica asked.

Logan ran a hand over his chin. 'Well, even though it's been a few years I find it a little hard to talk about. And mind you, I was in Vietnam. Two tours. Saw quite a bit. This one shook me good.'

Jessica and Byrne remained silent.

'We haven't had but two murders here in all the time I've been on the job. One was a domestic that went tragically wrong. Everyone saw that one coming, I suppose. Those two were at it for years. The other was little Peggy van Tassel.'

'Would you mind telling us the details?' Byrne asked.

Logan sipped his coffee. Jessica noticed a slight shake in his hand. He put the cup down, rattling it slightly on the worn Masonite surface. 'Little girl, eleven years old. Father worked for the county in the water department, mother was a teacher at Jefferson Middle School. Only child. Peggy went to school one day, never came home. We put the word out and by that evening we must have had two hundred volunteers for the search. We found her by Iron Lake ten days later. She'd been molested, stabbed to death. Whoever did it cut her pretty bad.' Logan cleared his throat, reached for his coffee, thought better of it. 'She had on make-up, and a woman's fancy dress. Not a dress that was for a grown woman, mind you, but a small one. One that was her size. The folks at the state crime lab said it looked like it was made for her. State police took the case.'

The idea of the killer making a dress for the little girl gave Jessica a chill. 'Was the case ever closed?' she asked.

Logan shook his head. 'There was a man who was questioned in that case. That man's name was George Archer.'

'Archer?' Byrne asked.

'Yes, sir. Tommy Archer's father. George was a state trooper for a few years, but as I understand it he was shown the door,' Logan added. 'Insubordination was the official line, but there were rumors.'

'Rumors of what?' Jessica asked.

'Like yourselves, I try to deal in facts, ma'am. If it's all the same, rumors should live and die just that. Rumors.'

Jessica nodded. *Fair enough*.

'Why did the state like George Archer in this case?' Byrne asked.

'George had been seen talking to Peggy a few days before she went missing. In fact, that's where we found Tommy Archer's body. Right near Peggy's marker.'

Jessica looked at Byrne, then back. 'He was found near her plot at the cemetery?'

'Yes, ma'am.'

Logan went through the photos on the table. He picked one up. In it, the body of Thomas Archer was visible on the right side of the frame. To the left was a clearly marked headstone.

Margaret van Tassel
April 6 1990 – September 21 2001
'Our Beloved Peggy'

'Do you think any of the girl's family might be involved in this?' Byrne asked.

Logan shrugged. 'I suppose anything's possible. But as I understand it her family were travelers. I think they moved on a long time ago.' Logan sat on the edge of the table. 'A few years later the FBI came around again, questioned George in another case, up round your way. It was a cold case.'

'The case was out of Philadelphia?' Byrne asked.

Logan nodded. 'I believe it was.'

'Do you remember any details about the case?'

'No. It wasn't ours. But I do remember that they also talked to Tommy, who swore that George was with him all during the weekend in question, right up at the house on the farm. I'm not sure that George was there, but that was Tommy's story and he stuck to it.'

'I'd like to take a look at the report on that original homicide,' Byrne said. 'The van Tassel girl. Can you reach out to the state police and have them fax that to us?'

'Consider it done.' Logan glanced at his watch. 'I've got a few things on today. If there's anything else we can do for you, let Helen know and we'll take care of it.'

'We'd like to speak to George Archer,' Byrne said.

'I'll give you directions.' Logan scribbled a few things on a legal pad, tore off the sheet, handed it to Jessica.

'You can't miss the sign,' he added. 'Archer Farms.'

Jessica and Byrne thanked Logan for his time and consideration. On the way to the parking lot Jessica turned, asked the chief one last question.

'What do they grow up there at Archer Farms?'

'Apples, mostly,' Logan said. 'They have about fifty acres of orchards.'

T HE HOUSE WAS A LARGE, AGING DUTCH COLONIAL ON A HILLSIDE, not so much the archetypal farmhouse but rather a house built on a farm, remodeled many times over the years. It was surrounded on three sides by apple trees as far as the eye could see. In addition to a triple garage there were two outbuildings; one small, perhaps for lawn and maintenance equipment; one large, perhaps for mechanical harvesters, straddle trailers, and the storage of harvest totes.

The air was heavy with the sugary-tart smell of the fruit.

Jessica pulled over on the drive, stopping about fifty yards from the house. Nothing moved. There were no vehicles in sight.

'Does it get quieter than this?' Jessica asked.

Byrne just looked at the house, at the acres of trees. There was a porch light on, but no lights were visible through the windows.

Jessica had a hard time reconciling the bucolic vision in front of her with what she had seen in the past four days, or with the story she had heard from Rogers Logan. Still, there could be no denying that the murder of Thomas Archer, who at one time had lived right here, was connected to the brutal homicides in Philadelphia.

She looked at Byrne. 'Ready?'

Byrne hesitated for a few moments, then nodded.

Jessica crossed the gravel drive, looked in the grimy garage-door window. Inside she saw a pickup truck on the right-hand side. It looked to be a five-year-old F-150. The other two bays were empty. There was a thin layer of dust on the truck. There had been rain in this part of Pennsylvania in the past three days. Chances were good that the truck had not been out.

She and Byrne then walked over to the porch. The place was eerily quiet. They were about three hundred yards from Route 68, and it seemed that even the sound of the occasional car passing by did not reach them.

The right-hand side of the porch had a rick of well-seasoned fire-wood, stacked in a rusted wrought-iron rack. The door was ringed with a grapevine wreath, strung with autumn mums and small gourds.

Jessica looked through the window in the door. She saw no activity. She knocked, listened. Byrne moved across the porch, next to the window that looked into the living room. There were sheer curtains over the opening.

Jessica knocked again, put her ear near the door. Only silence.

Walking around to the back of the house, they found a tilled vegetable garden, turned for the season. A small green-water pond sat at the bottom of a gentle hill. The back porch was smaller than the front, but boasted a pair of new Adirondack chairs. They climbed the steps, looked inside. Inside was a mud room of sorts, one that led to a large kitchen. There were no cups or plates on the table, none in the sink.

Jessica knocked again, waited. The house appeared to be unoccupied.

'Let's check the garage,' Byrne said.

They walked over to the triple garage, around the side where there was a smaller door. It was unlocked.

Byrne stayed outside while Jessica pushed open the door, stepped in. The garage was dark and dusty, smelling of axle grease and the ever-pervasive sweetness of apples. The cloying smell was even stronger in here. One wall was lined with garden and farm tools – rakes, half-round shovels, hoes, mattocks, pickaxes. The other wall boasted a collage of license plates and street signs.

Jessica walked over to the truck. She placed her hand on the hood. The engine was cold. She then took a Kleenex out of her pocket, opened the driver's-side door. The rusty hinge moaned, and she stopped. It had been so quiet that the sound went through the garage like a scream. She eased the door all the way open. There were no keys in the ignition, and the cab was relatively clean. A pine-tree-shaped deodorizer dangled from the rearview mirror.

On the seat was a small pile of papers. Jessica held the Kleenex tightly, sorted through them. There were a pair of flyers for a recent Oktoberfest in Kelton, a coupon for a free car wash. There was a brochure for tours of Philadelphia. At the bottom was a postcard depicting a beach in South Carolina. *Greetings from Edisto Island.* Jessica flipped the card over, angled her Maglite.

> *Looking forward to seeing you and everyone at Société Poursuite!*
> *I'll be staying at the Hyatt Penn's Landing. Look me up and we'll*
> *have a drink.*

It was signed, simply, R.

Jessica glanced at the date on the postmark. It was from the previous Friday.

She slipped the postcard back where it had been, closed the truck door, and walked out of the garage. She told Byrne about the postcard.

'It looks like he might be at the annual meeting of the *Société Poursuite.*'

'That's the group that handles the cold cases, right?'

'And these are all—'

'Cold cases,' Byrne said. 'Melina Laskaris, Marcellus Palmer, Antoinette Chan, and Peggy van Tassel are all open investigations, just the kind of thing a group like *Société Poursuite* would look into.'

Jessica nodded, thought for a moment. 'Logan said this guy used to be a state trooper. Maybe he's a member.'

'That convention is this week.'

It occurred to both of them at the same time.

'He's in Philly,' Jessica said.

'He's in Philly.'

SIXTY-SEVEN

I N July 1998, at a small Italian restaurant in Queens, New York
– an old-school trattoria on Astoria Boulevard called Theresa's – a
man named Paul Ferrone, a retired NYPD detective, met with two of
his oldest friends.

The three men had been meeting at Theresa's every month for
the past four years, mostly for two reasons. One, Theresa Colopinti's
chicken with peppers was the best in the city of New York. More
importantly, the second reason was that these three men genuinely
enjoyed each other's company.

After their entrée plates were cleared, they began to talk about
murder, as was their custom. Cold-case murder. Paul Ferrone's two
friends – Matt Grayson, a retired forensic dentist from Newark, New
Jersey, and Eli O'Steen, a retired judge from Brooklyn – had been
thinking about forming a group that did this sort of thing with regularity, a group that would expand beyond the three of them.

On that night they created an association called *Société Poursuite,*
an homage to the Vidocq Society, a similarly themed group named
after a nineteenth-century French detective named Eugene Francois
Vidocq.

Similar in some ways to the Vidocq Society, *Société Poursuite* –
which translated as Pursuit Society – now boasted more than three
hundred and seventy members worldwide. And since its inception on

that summer night in 1998, it had contributed to the solving of more than sixty homicides around the world.

The group met every month in New York City, with their annual conclave held in a different major city on the east coast each October, rotating between New York, Philadelphia, and Washington D.C.

This year their eleventh annual conclave would meet in Philadelphia, at the Le Jardin hotel. On the final night, an evening which would include a five-course meal prepared by the hotel's Michelin-starred chef Alain Cochel, there would be a speech by the Attorney General for the Commonwealth of Pennsylvania.

WHEN JESSICA AND BYRNE arrived at Le Jardin they were met in the lobby by the hotel's director of security, John Shepherd.

Shepherd had been a homicide detective in Philadelphia for more than twenty years. When Jessica had come into the unit, it had been Kevin Byrne and John Shepherd who had showed her the ropes. While Byrne taught her – indeed, in many ways was still teaching her – how to work a crime scene, it was John Shepherd who taught her how to walk into an interrogation room, how to position her body at first so as not to intimidate, how to walk that gossamer-thin line between treating someone like a suspect and like a witness, how to coax that first lie out of their mouths, and then, an hour or two later, how to slam it back in their faces.

The PPD had lost a great one when he retired.

John Shepherd, turned out in a smart navy blue suit, opened his arms. 'Jess,' he said. 'Beautiful as ever.'

They embraced. Even though they were still on the same side, they were no longer on the same team, and shows of affection were now allowed. 'We miss you, John.'

Shepherd looked at Byrne. 'And if I wasn't head of security here, I'd have to *call* security on this shady-looking character.'

The two men did the handshake, shoulder-bump, back-slap, I-swear-to-God-I'm-not-gay thing. *Men*, Jessica thought. God forbid they should show emotion in public. Cops were the worst.

'You look good, Johnny,' Byrne said.

'Underworked and overpaid.'

Shepherd did look healthier than he ever had. Anytime you could get away from cop food and cop hours, you looked better. Tall and Denzel-handsome, now in his salt-and-pepper fifties, Shepherd looked relaxed, and in charge.

He led them to the other side of the lobby, to the other side of a tall frosted-glass panel that somehow managed to keep the noise of arriving guests out of the tastefully appointed lounge.

They stood at the far end of the bar, away from everyone. Without asking, three cups of coffee, with creamers on ice, were put in front of them.

'So what are you up to?' Shepherd asked. 'Keeping the peace?'

'Disturbing it whenever possible,' Byrne said. 'How are things here?'

'Had a door pusher last month.'

A door pusher was one of the more unsophisticated breeds of hotel criminal. He was a guy who got into the hotel, went to upper floors, and simply pushed on doors to find one that was unlocked, or improperly closed or, God help the room attendant, left open by housekeeping. These were guys who always had a record for B & E, generally non-violent types but a real nuisance in hotel security work.

'You take him down?' Byrne asked.

'Guy hit the Sheraton Society Hill in March, moved over to the Hyatt Penn's Landing in May. We had him on tape, but he was slick – ball caps, glasses, packing his waist to look heavier. Wore a suit one time, sweats and sneakers the next. We got him, though.'

They kicked the cop talk around for a while, until Shepherd moved his stool closer and lowered his voice. 'Now, I know how magnetic and incredibly charming I am, but I think y'all are here for another reason.'

Byrne took a moment. 'There's a convention here. We think we might have a connection to a case we're working.'

Shepherd nodded. 'The serial?'

'Yeah.'

'Lay it out.'

Byrne told Shepherd the details.

'And his name is George Archer?' Shepherd asked.

'Yeah.'

'Hang on.'

Shepherd left the bar, returned a few minutes later. 'No one registered here under that name. Maybe he's staying somewhere else. Do you have a description on the guy?'

'Not yet,' Byrne said. 'We have a request in to the state police. But they may not even have a picture. The guy was questioned, but he was never arrested or charged.'

Shepherd nodded. He'd been right where Jessica and Byrne were.

'Can you reach out to some of the other hotels, see if they have a George Archer?' Byrne asked.

'No problem. I'll make a few calls.' Shepherd pointed to the other side of the lobby. 'They're setting up in the Crystal Room right now. It's going to be a big deal tonight, even bigger tomorrow.'

'Do you have cameras in there?'

John Shepherd chuckled. 'Is the pope . . . what is the pope now, by the way?'

'German.'

'Doesn't sound as good as Polish, does it?'

'No.'

'We have cameras,' Shepherd said. 'Come on.'

FROM THE OUTSIDE, THE Loss Prevention office at Le Jardin looked like any other room in the hotel. Unremarkable door, heavy-duty key lock. In the center of the hallway outside, which itself was off-limits to hotel guests, was a smoked-glass dome cam.

Inside was a small outer office, which led, through another secure door, to a larger room in which two people were working.

Shepherd spoke to a young woman at one of the desks, wrote something on the pad. While he was showing Jessica and Byrne the surveillance capabilities of the hotel, she would be putting in calls to the security directors of the surrounding hotels, looking for a guest named George Archer.

*

IN FRONT OF THEM were two thirty-inch high-definition monitors, each divided into six windows. According to Shepherd, one operator kept an eye on them at all times, two people per eight-hour shift, rotating every two hours.

Jessica scanned the monitors. The one on the right had six windows up that showed the huge atrium, viewed from the mezzanine level. A dozen people or so had congregated near the center of the room. A man and a woman, middle-aged, stood at the front desk. An elderly woman chatted with the concierge. A few seconds later the view shifted to the parking lot and front entrance. A limo idled at the front door as a pair of young bellmen pulled a number of large suitcases from the trunk. Another bellman leaned into the passenger window of a waiting cab.

The software rotated the windows, floor after floor, with a view of the elevators constantly in the upper right-hand section of the screen.

Shepherd sat down, clicked a few keys, and more than sixty small windows lined up on the two monitors. 'We've got two dome cams in every hall, clock cams in all the personnel spaces, half-zone weather-proof bullet cams in the parking lot, and four state-of-the-art 360-degree pan-and-tilt domes in the atrium and lobby, watching the desk and the money room. Not too much goes on here that we don't see.'

'This is a real voyeur's delight,' Byrne said.

'Wait until you see the bathroom cams,' Shepherd said, with a wink.

Jessica and Byrne had done a lot of work with the Audio-Visual Unit of the PPD, as well as the communications unit, which monitored the PPD street cams, for which Philadelphia was getting more and more funding.

Shepherd brought up the Crystal Room on a split screen. There was a man at the lectern, clearly an employee of whatever company was providing the PA and sound systems for the event. He performed a sound check.

'So the people in this society used to be either cops or prosecutors?' Jessica asked.

'Not at all,' Shepherd said. 'Some were in forensics, some worked for medical examiners' offices, some of them were never on the job at all. There are pretty tight membership rules and dues, which are kind of steep, so they keep out the lowlifes and the thrill seekers.'

'There goes my shot at membership,' Byrne said.

'Believe it.'

'Are they any good at what they do?' Jessica asked.

Shepherd nodded. 'That's my understanding. Every case they take on has to be formally presented to them by a bona fide agency. They don't work with the FBI or the NYPD, but just about everyone else of note has presented something.'

The three of them watched the monitors for a while, the constant rotation of views from within and without the hotel. It was a relentless flow: staff, guests, visitors, deliveries.

Was one of them their killer? Jessica wondered. Would she know him if she saw him?

WHEN JESSICA AND BYRNE returned to the Roundhouse, Jessica checked her messages. Nothing case-breaking. She checked the fax basket. There was a five-page fax from Frederic Duchesne, as promised. It was a detailed description of *Carnival of the Animals*. She brought it to her desk.

Jessica got onto the *Société Poursuite* website. In addition to a brief history, its mission statement, and an explanation of what the group was about, there were lists of its members, officers, past officers, and sub-chapters around the world. It was clear that the group chose its cases carefully, perhaps with an eye on choosing only those that had a chance of resolution.

The menu at the bottom offered links to other sites and to message boards.

'Check the message boards,' Byrne said. Jessica clicked over. There were a few dozen ongoing topics. One was a discussion of current trends in forensics. Another was a discussion of the disposition of homicide cases around the world. There was a discussion of ideas for cases for the group to tackle. This board had more than four thousand entries. Jessica clicked over, and as she scrolled through the posts her skin began to crawl.

One by one the entries appeared. They were all there. All the original homicides had been suggested as cases in which the group might be interested. Melina Laskaris, Marcellus Palmer, Antoinette Chan, Margaret Van Tassel. And they were all suggested by one user. The user name was *css1835*.

Jessica got on the phone to John Shepherd, asking him to talk to someone from the group about the criteria for posting. A few minutes later, Shepherd called back.

'I talked to the president of the group,' Shepherd said. 'He says you don't have to log in or be a member to post something on that board. He says that it would discourage people from coming forward.'

'So they have no record of who this "css1835" might be?'

'No,' Shepherd said. 'Sorry.'

Jessica thanked him, hung up. She looked back at the screen. Whoever was doing this was connected to, or had an interest in, *Société Poursuite*. Was it George Archer? Was George Archer *css1835*?

Jessica looked at the material she had received from Frederic Duchesne.

Camille Saint-Saens – *css* – had been born in 1835.

AT SIX-THIRTY DANA WESTBROOK stepped out of her office, into the duty room. 'Kevin?'

Byrne turned to look at her. 'Yeah?'

'Could I see you for a minute?'

Byrne crossed the room, dropped his weapon in his file drawer, and walked into Dana Westbrook's office.

SIXTY-EIGHT

WHEN BYRNE WALKED INTO THE OFFICE HE WAS MORE THAN A LITTLE surprised to see that, in addition to Sergeant Westbrook, there were Michael Drummond from the DA's office and Inspector Ted Mostow. In the corner, arms crossed, smug look in place, was Dennis Stansfield. Russell Diaz held down the other chair.

'Inspector,' Byrne said. 'Good to see you, sir.'

'How've you been, Kevin?'

'Better days.'

'How's the baby?'

Byrne shrugged, more or less on cue. 'Ten fingers, ten toes.'

It was an old expression, one that meant all was well with whatever case you were working on. In homicide you responded that way whether the case was going well or not.

Byrne nodded at Michael Drummond. 'Mike.' Drummond smiled, but there was no warmth in it. Something was wrong.

'Please, have a seat,' Westbrook said. Byrne took a chair near the windows.

'As you know, Detective Stansfield is working the Eduardo Robles homicide,' Drummond began.

Byrne just listened. Drummond continued.

'In the course of his investigation he discovered the existence of a surveillance camera on the opposite side of the street, just across from the Chinese restaurant. After watching footage from the time frame in question, and running the plates on the six vehicles parked on the street, he contacted and interviewed the owners. All but one checked out, and had solid alibis for where they were that night at that time.'

Byrne said nothing.

'The sixth vehicle, a black Kia Sedona, belongs to a man named Patrick Connolly.' Drummond fixed him with a stare. 'Do you know a Patrick Connolly?'

Byrne knew that Drummond, along with everyone else in the room, knew the answer to that question, along with most of the questions he had not yet heard. Byrne had been on the other side of the table too many times not to know the game. 'Yes,' he said. 'He's my cousin.'

'When Detective Stansfield interviewed Mr. Connolly, Connolly told him that he had loaned the minivan out, that he had loaned the vehicle to you. Is that true?'

'Yes,' Byrne said. 'I borrowed the van six days ago.'

'Were you driving it the night in question?'

'I was.'

'Were you in Fishtown that night?'

Again, Byrne knew that everyone knew the answer to this question. No doubt they had spoken to patrons of The Well, people who had put him in the bar that night. 'Yes.'

'Do you recall seeing Mr. Robles that night?'

'Yes.'

'Did you have a conversation or interact in any way with Mr. Robles on that night?'

Byrne had begun to answer the question when Inspector Mostow interrupted. 'Kevin, do you want your PBA representative in here?'

The Police Benevolent Association provided legal advice and representation for police officers.

'Is this on the record?' Byrne knew the answer to that question – there was no court reporter, he had not been sworn in, and no one was writing anything down. He could confess to the Lindbergh kidnapping in this room, and it could not be used against him.

'No,' Drummond said.

Byrne looked over at Stansfield. He knew what the man was trying to do. This was payback. The two men locked eyes, matching wills. Stansfield looked away. 'Then let's put it on the record,' Byrne said.

Drummond took a few seconds, looked at Inspector Mostow. Mostow nodded.

Drummond gathered a few papers, spirited them into his briefcase. 'Okay, we'll meet back here in the morning,' Drummond said. 'Eight o'clock sharp.'

Stansfield piped in. 'Inspector, I really think that we should—'

Mostow shot him a look. 'In the morning, detective,' he said. 'Are we clear?'

For a moment, Stansfield didn't answer. Then, 'Yes, sir.'

Byrne was out of Westbrook's office first. Every detective in the duty room had their eyes on him.

As Byrne crossed the room to get a cup of coffee, Stansfield followed him.

'Not so much fun, is it?' Stansfield said.

Byrne stopped, spun around. 'You don't want to talk to me right now.'

'Oh, now you don't want to talk? It seems you couldn't keep your mouth shut the past few days about me.' Stansfield got a little too close. 'What were you doing in Fishtown that night, detective?'

'Step away,' Byrne said.

'Doing a little cleanup work?'

'Last time. Step away.'

Stansfield put a hand on Byrne's arm. Byrne pivoted, lashed out with a perfectly leveraged left hook, his entire body behind it. It caught Stansfield square on the chin. The impact sounded like two rams butting heads, echoing off the walls of the duty room. Detective Dennis Stansfield spun in place, went down.

And out.

'Ah, *fuck*,' Byrne said.

The whole room shut down for a moment, drawing a collective breath. Stansfield didn't move. *Nobody* moved.

After a few moments Nick Palladino and Josh Bontrager slowly crossed the room to see if Stansfield was all right. Nobody really cared all that much – no one in the room would have denied that he'd had it coming – but it didn't serve the department too well to have one of its own sprawled spread-eagle on the floor in the middle of the homicide unit duty room. Witnesses, suspects, prosecutors, and defense attorneys came through this room day and night.

Jessica glanced at Byrne. He rubbed his knuckles, picked up his coat, grabbed his keys off the desk. When he got to the door, he turned, looked at Jessica, and said: 'Call me if he's dead.'

THE ROW HOUSE ON 19TH STREET, NEAR CALLOWHILL, WAS immaculate. Beneath the front window was a pine flower-box. In the window was a candle.

Byrne rang the bell. A few seconds later the door opened. Anna Laskaris stood there, apron on, spoon in hand, a look of confusion and expectation on her face.

'Mrs. Laskaris, I don't know if you remember me. I'm—'

'God may have taken my looks and my ability to walk more than three blocks. He didn't take away my brain. Not yet, anyway. I remember you.'

Byrne nodded.

'Come, come.'

She held the door open for him. Byrne stepped inside. If the outside of the row house was immaculate, the inside was surgically precise. On every surface was some sort of knitted item: afghans, doilies, throws. The air was suffused with three different aromas, all of them tantalizing.

She sat him at a small table in the kitchen. In seconds there was a cup of strong coffee in front of him.

Byrne took a minute or so, adding sugar, stirring, stalling. He finally got to the point. 'There's no easy way to say this, ma'am. Eduardo Robles is dead.'

Anna Laskaris looked at him, unblinking. Then she made the sign of the cross. A few seconds later she got up and walked to the stove. 'We'll eat.'

Byrne wasn't all that hungry, but it wasn't a question. In an instant he had a bowl of lamb stew in front of him. A basket of fresh bread seemed to appear out of nowhere. He ate.

'This is fantastic.'

Anna Laskaris mugged, as if this was in any doubt. She sat across from him, watched him eat.

'You married?' she asked. 'You wear no ring, but these days . . .'

'No,' Byrne said. 'I'm divorced.'

'Girlfriend?'

'Not right now.'

'What size sweater you wear?'

'Ma'am?'

'Sweater. Like a cardigan, a pullover, a V-neck. *Sweater*.'

Byrne had to think about it. 'I don't really buy a lot of sweaters, to be honest with you.'

'Okay. I try another door. When you buy a suit, like this beautiful suit you wear today, what size?'

'A 46, usually,' Byrne said. 'A 46 long.'

Anna Laskaris nodded. 'So then, an extra large. Maybe extra-extra.'

'Maybe.'

'What's your favorite color?'

Byrne didn't really have a favorite color. It wasn't something that crossed his mind that much. He did, however, have *least* favorites. 'Well, anything but pink, I guess. Or yellow.'

'Purple?'

'Or purple.'

Anna Laskaris glanced at her huge knitting basket, back at Byrne. 'Green, I think. You're Irish, right?'

Byrne nodded.

'A nice green.'

Byrne ate his stew. It occurred to him that this was the first time in a long while he was not eating in a restaurant or out of a Styrofoam container. While he ate, Anna stared off in the distance, her mind perhaps returning to other times in this house, other times at this table, times before people like Byrne brought heartache to the door like UPS. After a while, she stood slowly. She nodded at Byrne's empty bowl. 'You have some more, yes?'

'Oh God, no. I'm stuffed. It was wonderful.'

She rounded the table, picked up his bowl, brought it to the sink. Byrne could see the pain in her eyes.

'The recipe was my grandmother's. Then her grandmother's. Of the many things I miss, it's teaching Lina these things.'

She sat back down.

'My Melina was beautiful, but not so smart always. Especially about the men. Like me. I never did too well in this area. Three husbands, all bums.'

She looked out the window, then back at Byrne.

'It's a sad job what you do?'

'Sometimes,' Byrne said.

'A lot of times you come to people like me, give us bad news?'

Byrne nodded.

'Sometimes good news?'

'Sometimes.'

Anna looked at the wall next to the stove. There were three pictures of Lina – at three, ten, and sixteen.

'Sometimes I am at the market, I think I see her. But not like a grown-up girl, not like a young woman. A little girl. You know how little girls sometimes go off on their own, in their minds? Like maybe when they play with their dolls? The dolls to them are like real people?'

Byrne knew this well.

'My Lina was like this. She had a friend who was not there.'

Anna drifted away for a moment, then threw her hands up. 'We have a saying in Greece. *The heart that loves is always young.* She was my only grandchild. I will never have another. I have no one left to love.'

At the door Anna Laskaris held Byrne for a moment. Today she smelled of lemons and honey. It seemed to Byrne that she was getting smaller. *Grief will do that*, he thought. *Grief needs room.*

'It does not make me happy this man is dead,' Anna Laskaris said.

'God will find a place for him, a place he deserves. This is not up to you or me.'

Byrne walked to the van, slipped inside. He looked back at the house. There was already a fresh candle in the window.

HE HAD GROWN UP in the mist of the Delaware, and always did his best thinking there. As he drove to the river Kevin Francis Byrne considered the things he had done, the good and the bad.

You know.

He thought about Christa-Marie, about the night he met her. He thought about what she had said to him. He thought about his dreams, about waking in the night at 2:52, the moment he placed Christa-Marie under arrest, the moment everything changed forever.

You know.

But it wasn't *you know*. He had played back the recording he'd made of himself sleeping, listened carefully, and it suddenly became obvious.

He was saying *blue notes*.

It was about the silences between the notes, the time it takes for the music to echo. It was Christa-Marie telling him something for the past twenty years. Byrne knew in his heart that it all began with her. It would all end with her.

He looked at his watch. It was just after midnight.

It was Halloween.

THREE

RONDO

SEVENTY

SUNDAY, OCTOBER 31

I LISTEN TO THE CITY COMING TO THE DAY, THE ROAR OF BUSES, THE HISS of coffee machines, the clang of church bells. I watch as leaves eddy from the trees, cascading to the ground, feeling an autumn chill in the air, the shy soubrette of winter.

I stand in the center of City Hall, at the nexus of Broad and Market streets, the shortest line between the two rivers, the beating heart of Philadelphia. I turn in place, look down the two great thoroughfares that cross my city. On each I will be known today.

THE DEAD ARE GETTING louder. This is their day. It has always been their day.

I put up my collar, step into the maelstrom, the killing instruments a comfortable weight at my back.

What a saraband.

Zig, zig, zag.

SEVENTY-ONE

THE MASSIVE STONE BUILDINGS SAT ATOP THE RISE LIKE ENORMOUS birds of prey. The central structure, perhaps five stories tall, one hundred feet wide, gave way at either end to a pair of great wings, each of which bore a series of towers that fingered high into the morning sky.

The grounds surrounding the complex, at one time finely mani-cured, boasting Eastern Hemlock, Red Pine, and Box Elder, had fallen fallow decades earlier. Now the trees and shrubs were tortured and diseased, ravaged by wind and lightning. A once impressive arched stone bridge over the man-made creek that ringed the property had long ago crumbled.

IN 1891 THE ARCHDIOCESE authorized and built a cloister on top of a hill, about forty miles northwest of Philadelphia, establishing a convent. The main building was completed in 1893, providing residence to more than four dozen sisters. In addition to the vegetables grown on the nearby fifteen acres of farmland, and grain for the artisan breads baked in the stone ovens, the fertile land around the facility provided food for shelters throughout Montgomery, Bucks, and Berks counties. The sisters' blackberry preserves won awards statewide.

In 1907 four of the sisters hanged themselves from a beam in the bell tower. The church, having trouble attracting novitiates to the nunnery, sold the buildings and property to the Commonwealth of Pennsylvania.

Five years later, with four new wings built onto the original building – including two tiered lecture halls, a pair of autopsy theaters, a state-of-the-art surgery, and a non-denominational chapel built into one of the apple groves – the Convent Hill Mental Health Facility opened its doors. With its two hundred beds, sprawling grounds, and expert staff, it soon gained a reputation as a thoroughly up-to-date hospital throughout the eastern United States.

In addition to its main purpose – the treatment and rehabilitation of the emotionally disturbed – the facility had a secure wing maintained and staffed by the Commonwealth of Pennsylvania Department of Corrections. In its twenty beds slept some of the most notorious criminals of the early twentieth century.

By the early 1950s the facility's funding had begun to dry up. Staff were laid off, buildings were not maintained, equipment became outdated and plagued by time and disrepair. Rumors of inhumane conditions at Convent Hill circulated. In the 1970s a documentary film was made, showing deplorable and sickening conditions. Public and political outrage followed, with a million dollars being pumped into the coffers.

By 1980 Convent Hill had once again been forgotten. More gossip of corruption circulated, as did tales of incalculable horror. But the public can only be outraged about something for so long.

Convent Hill closed for good in 1992 and its inmates and patients were moved to other state-run mental health facilities, as well as to correctional facilities throughout New York and Pennsylvania.

Over the next eighteen years the grounds were bequeathed to the elements, the vandals, the ghost-hunters and derelicts. A few attempts were made to secure the facility, but with its nearly two hundred acres and many points of entry, much of it surrounded by forest, it was impossible.

The fieldstone wall near the winding road that led up to the entrance still bore a sign. As Kevin Byrne and Christa-Marie Schönburg approached, Byrne noticed that someone had altered the sign, painting over it, rewording the message. It no longer announced entry to what had once been a state-of-the-art mental-health facility, a place of healing and rehabilitation, a place of serenity and peace.

It now announced entry to a place called Convict Hell.

As THEY DROVE THE twisting road leading to the main buildings, a thin fog descended. The surrounding woods were cocooned in a pearl-gray mist.

Byrne thought about what he was doing. He knew the clock was ticking, that he was needed back in the city, but he also believed that the answers to many of his questions – past and present – were locked inside Christa-Marie's mind.

'Will you come back on Halloween?' she had asked. 'I want to show you a special place in the country. We'll make a day of it. We'll have such fun.'

A special place.

Christa-Marie wanted him to come here for a reason.

Byrne knew he had to take the chance.

ONCE THEY CRESTED THE hill the ground leveled off, but the fronts of the buildings were still somewhat obscured by pines, evergreens, and barren maples. The walkways were crosshatched in rotting branches, matted with fallen needles. The arched entrance was flanked by two massive rows of Palladian windows. The roof boasted a main cupola, with two smaller watchtowers.

As he parked the van Byrne heard the call of larks, announcing an impending storm. The wind began to rise. It seemed to encircle the stone buildings like a frigid embrace, holding inside its many horrors.

BYRNE GOT OUT OF the vehicle, opened Christa-Marie's door. She gave him her delicate hand. They walked up the crumbling steps.

The two immense oak doors were secured by large rusted hinges.

Over the years the doors had been marked with epithets, pleas, confessions, denials. To the right of the entry was an inscription carved in the weathered stone.

Christa-Marie turned, an animated look on her face.

'Take a picture of me,' she said. She smoothed her hair, adjusted the silk scarf at her neck. She looked beautiful in the pale morning light.

Taking a photograph was the last thing Byrne had expected to do. He took out his cellphone, opened it, framed Christa-Marie in the doorway, and snapped.

A moment later he pocketed his phone, put a shoulder to one of the huge doors, pushed it open. A cold breeze rushed through the atrium, bringing with it years of mildew and decay.

Together they stepped over the threshold, into Christa-Marie Schönburg's past, into the infernal confines of Convent Hill.

SEVENTY-TWO

THE DEAD WALK HERE. THE DEAD AND THE INSANE AND THE
forgotten. If you come with me, and hear what I hear, there is much more
than the whistle of the wind.

There is the young man who came here in 1920. He had been wounded
at St. Mihiel Salient. He bleeds from both wrists. 'I am going home,' he
says to me. 'First to Pont-à-Mousson, then home.'

He never left.

There is the solicitor from Youngstown, Ohio. Twice he has tried to take
his life. His neck is deeply scarred. He cannot speak above a whisper. His
voice is a dry wind in the night desert.

There are the two sisters who tried to eat each other's flesh, found in the
basement of their Olney row house, locked in an embrace, wrapped in barbed
wire, blood dripping from their lips.

They gather around me, their voices lifted in a chorus of madness.

I walk with my lover.

I walk with the dead.

SEVENTY-THREE

THEY STROLLED ARM IN ARM THROUGH THE HALLWAYS, THEIR HEELS echoing on the old tiles. A powdery light sifted through the windows.

Overhead was a vaulted ceiling, at least thirty feet high, and on it Byrne saw three layers of paint, each a dismal attempt at cheerfulness. Lemon yellow, baby blue, sea-foam green.

Christa-Marie pointed to a room off the main entry. 'This is where they take you on arrival,' she said. 'Don't let the flowers fool you.'

Byrne peeked inside. The remains of a pair of rusted chains, bolted to the wall, lay on the ground like dead snakes. There were no flowers.

They continued on, deeper into the heart of Convent Hill, passing dozens of rooms, rooms pooled with stagnant water, rooms tiled floor to ceiling, grout stained with decades of mold and long-dried blood, drains clogged with sewage and discarded clothing.

One room held six chairs still in a semicircle, the cane seats missing, one chair curiously facing away from the others. One room had a three-tiered bunk bed bolted to the floor over a decayed Oriental rug. Byrne could see where attempts had been made to tear away the rug. Both ends were shredded. Three brown fingernails remained.

One room, at the back of the main hallway, had rusted steel buckets lined against the wall, each filled with hardened feces, white and chalky with time. One bucket had the word *happy* painted on it.

They took the winding staircase to the second floor.

In one meeting room was a slanted stage. Above the stage, on the fascia, was a large medallion made of crisscrossed black string, perhaps an occupational-therapy project of some sort.

They continued through the wing. Byrne noted that many of the individual rooms had observation windows, some as small and simple as a pair of holes drilled into the door. Nothing, it seemed, went unobserved at Convent Hill.

'This was Maristella's room,' Christa-Marie said. The room was no larger than six by six feet. Against the wall, a long-faded pink enamel, were three threadbare stretchers. 'She was my friend. A little crazy, I think.'

The massive gymnasium had a large mural, measuring more than fifty feet long. The background was the rolling hills surrounding the facility. Scattered throughout were small scenes, all drawn by different hands – hellish depictions of rape, murder, and torture.

WHEN THEY TURNED THE corner into the east wing, Byrne stopped in his tracks. Someone was standing at the end of the wide hallway. Byrne could not see much. The person was small, compact, unmoving.

It took Byrne a few moments to realize, in the dim light, that it was only a *cutout* of a person. As they drew closer, he could see that it was a plywood pattern of a child, a boy perhaps ten or twelve years old. The figure wore a yellow shirt and dark brown pants. Behind the figure, on the wall, was painted a blue stripe, perhaps meant to mimic the ocean. As they passed the figure, Byrne saw pockmarks in the plywood, along with a few holes. Behind the figure were corresponding holes. At some point the figure had been riddled with bullets. Someone had drawn blood on the shirt.

They stopped at the end of the hall. Above them the roof had rotted away. A few drops of water found them.

'You know at the first note,' Christa-Marie said.

'What do you mean?'

'Whether a child has the potential to be a virtuoso.' She looked at her hands, her long, elegant fingers. 'They draw you in. The children.

At Prentiss they asked me a hundred times to teach. I kept refusing. I finally gave in. Two boys stood out.'

Byrne took her hand. 'Who are these boys?'

Christa-Marie did not answer right away. 'They were there, you know,' she eventually said.

'Where?'

'At the concert,' she said. 'After.'

There was a sound, an echoing sound from somewhere in the darkness. Christa-Marie seemed not to notice.

'That night, Christa-Marie. Take me back to that night.'

Christa-Marie looked at him. In her eyes he saw the same look he had seen twenty years earlier, a look of fear and loneliness.

'I wore black,' she said.

'Yes,' Byrne said. 'You looked beautiful.'

Christa-Marie smiled. 'Thank you.'

'Tell me about the concert.'

Christa-Marie glided across the corridor, into the semi-darkness. 'The hall was decorated for the holidays. It smelled of fresh pine. We debated fiercely over the program. The audience was, after all, children. The director wanted yet another performance of *Peter and the Wolf.*'

Byrne expected her to continue. She did not. Her eyes suddenly misted with tears. She walked slowly back, reached into her bag, retrieved a piece of paper, handed it to Byrne. It was a letter, addressed to Christa-Marie and copied to her attorney, Benjamin Curtin. It was from the Department of Oncology at the University of Pennsylvania Hospital. Byrne read the letter.

A few moments later he took her hands in his. 'Will you play for me tonight?'

Christa-Marie moved closer. She put her arms around him, her head on his chest. They stood that way for a long time, not moving, not speaking. She broke the silence first.

'I'm dying, Kevin.'

Byrne stroked her hair. It was silken to his touch. 'I know.'

She nestled closer. 'I can hear your heart. It is steady and strong.'

Byrne looked out the window, at the fogbound forest surrounding Convent Hill. He remained silent. There was nothing to say.

SEVENTY-FOUR

JESSICA COULD NOT FIND HER PARTNER. SHE HAD STOPPED BY BYRNE'S apartment, visited all his familiar breakfast and coffee haunts, checked his favorite watering holes, hoping not to find him. She had not.

Byrne had not called into the unit nor, more importantly, shown up for his deposition, his on-the-record statement about his whereabouts on the night Eduardo Robles had been killed. Jessica knew that the inspector had smoothed it over with the DA's office, but it was unlike Byrne in any number of ways, not the least of which was his commitment to keeping his word.

Jessica spent the remainder of the morning reading through the material on *Carnival of The Animals*. There were indeed fourteen movements, not all of them devoted to animals. One was called *Fossils*; another, *Pianists*; yet another, *Finale*. For some reason the killer had chosen eight of the movements. But they were all there, and it was all making slow sense.

Beyond this, all these victims were related to cold cases. They were all suspects in homicides. Or suspected of complicity in homicides.

The connection to a group like *Société Poursuite* and a man named George Archer could not be overlooked.

All these people were in some way culpable. In the eyes of their killer, they were all guilty of something. But why *these* people? What linked them? Why the cases of Antoinette Chan, Marcellus Palmer, Marcia Kimmelman and Melina Laskaris? Why not any of the other hundreds of unsolved cases sitting in the dusty books on the shelf?

AT ONE O'CLOCK JESSICA put a call into the Department of Motor Vehicles. If George Archer had a driver's license in the Commonwealth of Pennsylvania, they would be able to get a photograph.

She skipped lunch and spent the early afternoon on the phone with the lab and the DA's office. Michael Drummond was in court, but his secretary promised Jessica that he would get back to her.

By four o'clock she learned that there was no one named George Archer registered at any hotel in the greater Philadelphia area.

She also put in a call to Chief Rogers Logan in Garrett Corners. At her request Logan paid a visit to Archer Farms.

George Archer had not returned to his house.

AS THE FIRST HALF of Jessica long day wound down, there were no new leads. The three other lead detectives – Josh Bontrager, Nicci Malone, and Dennis Stansfield – were all on the street, chasing down their leads. Josh had interviewed members of the Chan family. All had concrete alibis. Nicci Malone had taken the morning to drive to Weirton, West Virginia to speak to Marcellus Palmer's son and daughter-in-law. She learned nothing of value. God only knew what Stansfield – obsessed now more than ever with Kevin Byrne – was doing.

It seemed the Byrne/Stansfield conflict had settled for the time being. There would probably be some kind of fallout from the incident, but it wouldn't be tonight. The homicide unit had a few other things with which to be concerned.

JESSICA ARRIVED HOME AROUND five-thirty, made a quick dinner for her and Sophie. After dinner Sophie modeled her Snow Fairy costume. She looked adorable.

Outside, the wind picked up, swirling leaves in the street. Perfect

Philly Halloween weather. And there was never a shortage of atmosphere or things to do in Philly on Halloween.

There was the Ghost Tour, which took participants on a candle-light excursion to Society Hill and Independence Park. There was the tour of Eastern State Penitentiary, once voted the number one haunted house in America. Then there was the Mutter Museum, and the home of Edgar Allan Poe.

But if Philadelphia was attached to its horrific past, it was nothing if not creative. Jessica had already seen news footage of people trick-or-treating in pink body suits, with a band of paper wrapped around their heads. The new favorite costume in Philly, it seemed, was the victim of a serial murderer.

Jessica took Sophie out for trick-or-treating early. This year was different from previous years. Trick-or-treating among row houses was a frontal assault. Within an hour, they hit a hundred or so houses. Sophie returned with a pair of bulging pillowcases.

WHILE SOPHIE DIVVIED UP her swag on the living-room floor, Jessica showered and prepared for her undercover assignment at the hotel.

Before she left the house, she caught her reflection in the hallway mirror. *Not bad*, she thought. The simple black dress was okay, if a little tight. Time to ease up on the cannoli from Termini's.

The hard part, of course, was the gun. Though in many ways the perfect accessory, most designers did not allow for the bulk of a weapon when creating a line. It was never the Smith & Wesson collection for Dior, or Vivienne Westwood presents Frocks with Glocks.

Just to be on the safe side, she packed a small duffel with jeans and a hoodie, stowed it in the car. She had no idea where this night would take her.

THE TEAM MET IN Le Jardin's Loss Prevention office. There were ten detectives in all, including Josh Bontrager, Dennis Stansfield, Nicci Malone, and Nick Palladino. Most were in plain clothes, the remaining few had on PPD windbreakers.

They were briefed by John Shepherd on the layout of the floors, the location of surveillance cameras, the hotel protocol for emergencies. They went briefly over the program for the evening, which included a lavish dinner, a number of speakers, along with a keynote address by the attorney general for the Commonwealth of Pennsylvania. In addition, in the smaller meeting rooms there were various panels and demonstrations. According to Shepherd, excluding front- and back-of-the-house staff and personnel, there were close to one thousand people in the building.

Every so often Jessica glanced at the door. Byrne had not shown.

After John Shepherd had completed his briefing, Dana Westbrook addressed the task force. They had received more than seventy DMV photographs of men named George Archer. None were registered to the man at the Archer Farms. The sheriff's office, in addition to detectives from the Pennsylvania State Police, were showing the photographs to neighbors and vendors in the area, trying to match the photo with the man who ran Archer Farms.

FOR THE FIRST HOUR Jessica worked the reception table, just outside the Crystal Room. The double-length conference table was draped with white bunting, and carried a few hundred name tags, programs, and pins bearing the slogan *He escapes who is not pursued.*

As people filed by, Jessica watched their movements, their behaviors. Overall, it was a rather staid-looking group. Conservatively dressed, quiet in demeanor, polite in manner. In the course of an hour she handed out more than fifty name tags.

At eight o'clock three men approached from across the lobby, one of them quite inebriated. They were in their forties, white, casually dressed. As they got closer, the shortest one – the drunk one – did his best to focus on the table, on the name tags, and finally on Jessica.

'Whoa!' he said, reeling a little.

'Welcome,' Jessica said.

'My name is Jukka Tolonen,' the tall blond man said, introducing himself.

'Jay Bowman,' said the other. Jessica scanned the table, found the name tags she was looking for, handed them both a tag and a program.

'Thanks,' the two men said in tandem, both sounding a little embarrassed for their friend.

'You know,' the drunk one said, 'I've been coming to this convention for, I don't know, five years? Most of the women look like Mrs. Marble.'

Jessica was pretty sure the man meant Miss Marple. 'What's your name?' she asked.

The man looked at his friends. 'You hear that? She asked my *name*, dude. She's hitting on me!'

'I think she wants to give you your name tag,' Tolonen said. He had an accent. Maybe Finnish.

'Oh.'

The drunk man made a production of reaching into his pocket for his wallet. He pulled it out, made a bigger deal of extracting one of his business cards, a big smile on his face as if this were the cleverest bit ever. 'It looks like I'm somebody named Barry Swanson,' he said. 'Like the frozen dinner.'

Like the frozen adolescence, Jessica thought. She handed Barry Swanson his ID and a program. Swanson immediately dropped it all on the floor. Tolonen picked up the material, clipped the name tag on his wobbly friend.

'Sorry,' Bowman said to Jessica. 'He's a forensic chemist. He doesn't get out much.'

Jessica watched them walk away, wondering how crimes ever got solved.

WHEN JESSICA WAS RELIEVED by a member of the task force, a detective out of West Division named Deena Yeager, she walked over to the front desk, surveyed the crowded lobby. David Albrecht had not gotten permission to film inside the ballroom, but he was allowed to shoot footage in the lobby and out on the street. Jessica saw that he had snagged some talking-head interview time with some pretty heavy hitters.

Just about everyone in the room had some connection to law enforcement. There were retired detectives, prosecutors, forensic professionals of every discipline, men and women who worked in the processing of fingerprints, hair and fiber, blood, documents. There were pathologists, anthropologists, psychologists, people who worked in behavioral science and mathematics. She'd heard there was a small contingent from *Keishicho*, the Metropolitan Tokyo Police Department.

She saw Hell Rohmer and Irina Kohl, pretending to be merely colleagues. It didn't take a seasoned detective to detect the occasional brush of hands, or the more than occasional longing glance. She saw judges, lawyers, bailiffs, along with a handful of ADAs.

She did not see Kevin Byrne.

SEVENTY-FIVE

L ucy Doucette stood at the end of the hallway on the twelfth floor.

Her shift ended at six-thirty, but she asked Audrey Balcombe if there were any credits to be had and it turned out that three of the guests had requested housekeeping twice a day. She imagined these people were in some kind of lab or forensic work and had a serious germ phobia. Regardless, she was able to stay on for an extra two hours. Now she was just killing time.

Lucy knew that the moment she swiped her card in the electronic lock on the door to 1208 it would go on the record. She was scared out of her wits to go back in there, but she had been scared so long it just didn't matter anymore.

She looked over her shoulder. The hallway was deserted, but Lucy knew she was not alone, not technically. She had once been in the main security station and had seen the big monitors. All staff knew where the closed-circuit cameras were. At least, the cameras they knew about, the obvious ones on the ceiling. At the end of each hallway was a sideboard and a mirror, and Lucy always wondered if the mirrors were two-way mirrors and maybe had a camera behind them.

Before she could stop herself, Lucy knocked on the door to Room 1208.

'Housekeeping.'

Nothing. She knocked again, repeated the word. Silence from within. She leaned closer to the door. There was no sound of a TV, a radio, a conversation. The general rule was two announcements, then enter.

Lucy tried one last time, got no response, then swiped her card, eased open the door.

'Housekeeping,' she said once more, her voice barely above a whisper. She slipped inside, let the door close behind her. It shut with a loud and final click, meaning that the lock had irrevocably registered that she was in Room 1208.

THE ROOM LOOKED EXACTLY the same as it had the last time. The minibar was untouched, the bed had not been slept in, the wastebasket beneath the desk was empty. She peeked into the bathroom. Nothing had been disturbed in there, either. The toilet paper was still in a point, the soaps wrapped. Sometimes the nicer guests tried to hang the towels back the way they were, but Lucy could always tell. They never got them exactly right. She could also tell if someone had taken a shower or bath, just by the smell, the damp sweetness of body gel and shampoo that hung in the air.

She stepped back to the door, put her ear to it, listened for sounds in the hallway. It was silent. She walked to the closet, opened the door. The garment bag hung there like a body at a gallows. She reached out slowly, turned over the ID tag, her hand shaking.

THIS BAG BELONGS TO GEORGE ARCHER.

Lucy felt a chill ripple through her body. His name was George Archer. All these years she had tried to imagine her kidnapper's name. Everyone had a name. Whenever she read a newspaper or a magazine, whenever she watched a movie or a TV show, whenever she was in a place like a doctor's office or the Bureau of Motor Vehicles and someone said a name out loud she wondered: *Is that his name?* Could that person be the man in her nightmares? Now she knew. George Archer. It was, at the same moment, the most benign and the most frightening name she'd ever heard.

She closed the closet door, walked quickly over to the dresser, her heart pounding. She eased open the bottom drawer. The same shirts were inside – one blue, one white, one white with thin gray stripes. She mind-printed the way they were arrayed in the drawer so she could put them back in precisely the same manner. She bunched the three shirts together, lifted them. They seemed almost hot to her touch. But when she looked beneath the shirts, she saw that the picture was gone.

Had she imagined it?

No. It *had* been there. She had never seen that particular photograph before, but she knew where it had been taken. It had been taken at the ice-cream parlor on Wilmot Street. It was a photo of her mother, and her mother was wearing the red pullover sweater that Lucy had taken from Sears at the mall.

Lucy turned, looked at the rest of the room. It suddenly seemed foreign, as if she had never been here before. She put the shirts back in the drawer, arranging them carefully. She noticed something in the pocket of the shirt on top, the blue one. It was a piece of paper, a piece of Le Jardin notepad paper.

Lucy slipped her fingers gently into the pocket, took out the paper. It read:

Meet me here on Sunday night at 9:30. Love, Lucy.

It was her handwriting.

It was a note she had written and had left in the room for Mr. Archer to find.

She looked at her watch. It was 9:28.

The room began to spin. It felt for a moment as though the floor beneath her was about to give way. She slammed the drawer shut. It no longer mattered if she didn't get everything back the way it was supposed to be. The only thing that mattered was getting out of this room.

She recoiled from the dresser as if it were on fire, and suddenly heard—

—the bell.

Her bell. Her *special* bell.

Lucy felt calm, completely at peace. She knew what she had to do, what she *must* do. She walked to the hotel room door, propped it open. Then she entered the closet, closed the door, sat on the floor.

Once inside she smelled apples, pipe smoke, the essence of George Archer, the essence of evil. But this time she was not afraid.

As footsteps passed by the closet – two sets, a few minutes apart – the night closed in around her, and Lucy Doucette remembered it all.

'IT'S OKAY, EVE,' HE SAID. *'There's been an accident. I will take care of you.'*

He held out his hand. On it he wore a ring in the shape of a snake. The air was thick with smoke, the sky darkened from it.

'What kind of accident?' she asked.

Mr. Archer opened the door to his car. Lucy got in. 'A plane crash,' he said. 'A bad plane crash.'

'Where's my mom?'

'She wants me to watch after you. She's going to go help the people where the plane crashed.'

'My mom is?'

'Yes, Eve.'

Mr. Archer started the car.

HE LED HER DOWN *the narrow wooden steps, through a small door into a drafty room with stone walls. The room was lit only with candles. It seemed as though there were hundreds of them. The room smelled like bad perfume and fermenting apples. Even the dust and cobwebs were cold.*

When Mr. Archer left, and Lucy heard the door at the top of the stairs lock, she saw that there was another girl sitting there. She was about Lucy's age, eleven or so, but she was wearing a grown-up dress. It was spangly and short, and had straps over the shoulders. The girl's face was smeared with make-up. She had been crying for a long time. Her eyes were red and puffy.

'Who are you?' Lucy asked.

The girl shivered.

'I'm . . . I'm Peggy.'

'Why are you here?'

The girl did not answer. Lucy looked at the girl's arms and legs. There were deep purple bruises on them. Then she looked over and saw a second dress hanging from one of the pipes in the ceiling.

A LONG TIME PASSED. *Hours and hours of which Lucy had no mind, no memory. Days of darkness.*

On the third day she took a bubble bath. The bathroom was in a small room off the cellar. The walls were a pink enamel. The sink had gold-colored faucets.

When it was dark Mr. Archer came downstairs to get her. He brought her up to the dining room for the first time. The table was set for grown-ups. Wine glasses and more candles. Lucy found herself in her own grown-up dress, and wearing high heels that were too big for her. Mr. Archer was dressed up like a man in an old movie. He had on a white bow tie. He walked to the kitchen.

Lucy looked at the window. She walked across the room, edged it open, slipped through.

'Eve!' Mr. Archer yelled.

Lucy ran. She ran as far and for as long as she could, through endless apple orchards, tripping and falling, scraping her knees and elbows, mushing the rotting apples beneath her. She looked over her shoulder, watching for Mr. Archer. She didn't see him. She soon came to a large pipe that emptied into a lake, crouched down inside, waited. She didn't know how long she was there. Hours and hours. She must have cried herself to sleep, because the next thing she knew there was a light in her face.

'It's okay,' the man with the flashlight said.

But it wasn't. It wasn't okay.

THEY TALKED TO HER *for hours, but Lucy didn't say a word. What happened to her was locked away inside.*

Her mother took her home. Time passed, and the man with the ring in the shape of a snake faded from her mind but took up faceless residence in that nest of fear inside her, flying overhead in the darkness of her dreams.

At night she would hear him humming, she would hear the sound of the car door slamming, the creak of the old wooden steps, the softness of his voice, she would hear—

The bell.

The bell rang again.

It seemed to come from far away, as if it were at the end of that long drainage pipe in which she had crawled. For the briefest of moments she smelled the sewage, felt the dampness of the air. Then it was gone.

Lucy looked around. It took a while for her to realize where she was. She was in the hotel. Le Jardin. She knew every inch of this place. She looked around the dark closet, felt overhead.

How much time had passed? She didn't know. She stood, opened the closet door, stepped into the room. The air had changed, changed in a way you could only know from being in a place day after day, knowing its walls, it ceilings, its corners, its very presence.

The door to the hallway was closed. Lucy looked at her watch. She hadn't been gone long. She had to get out of this room. Mr. Archer could be back any second.

She turned to leave, but suddenly felt lightheaded. She sat on the edge of the bed for a moment. Her mind began to clear, but something was wrong. Something felt wet underneath her. She got up, looked at her hands. They were coated in bright, glossy scarlet. She turned around and saw, in the dim light, the form under the blood-soaked sheets.

Lucy felt the contents of her stomach come up inside her throat. She backed away, certain that her heart was going to explode. She could no longer hold it in. She vomited on the floor.

Then she looked at the telephone on the desk. It seemed a mile away. The smell of her own vomit reached her at the same time as the metallic smell of blood. She was going to be sick again.

She ran to the bathroom.

SEVENTY-SIX

JESSICA WATCHED THE SHOW FROM THE BACK OF THE CRYSTAL ROOM. The speaker at the lectern was a pathologist from Toledo, formerly with the Ohio Bureau of Investigation. He was talking about a cold case that took place in a suburb of Toledo in 1985, a case involving a woman and her elderly mother who were bludgeoned to death with a long piece of steel, believed to be the support beam of a single bed frame.

Behind the lecturer, photographs of the crime scene were projected on a screen.

Jessica watched the photographs come and go. She realized that the man could have been from Tucson or Toronto or Tallahassee. In some ways it was all the same. But not to the families of the victim. And not to the investigators whose task it was to root out the people responsible for the crime and bring them to justice. She had been at it long enough, and knew enough people in her line of work, to know that an unsolved crime eats away at your soul until it is either closed or replaced by a new horror, a new puzzle. And even then it does not disappear, but rather makes room.

She thought about Joseph Novak's diary.

What was his connection? All she could find on Marcato LLC was that it had been formed nearly fifteen years earlier, and listed as its primary business the publishing of music. Joseph Novak, by all accounts, had a partner. But no one at any bank had any record of anyone other than Novak.

'Detective?'

A man's voice. Close. Jessica spun around. It was Frederic Duchesne, the dean of Prentiss Institute. He had approached without a sound. Not good. She was distracted, which meant she was vulnerable. She took a deep breath, tried to fashion a smile.

'Mr. Duchesne.'

'I'm sorry if I frightened you,' Duchesne said.

Frightened wasn't the word, Jessica thought. Provoked would be a better term. 'Not a problem,' she said, meaning something else. 'What can I do for you, Mr. Duchesne?'

'Frederic. Please.'

'Frederic,' she said. She glanced around the room. All was well. For the time being.

'I was wondering if you received the material I sent.'

'Yes, we did. Thank you very much.'

'Do you have a moment to talk?'

Jessica glanced at the clock over the door. It was just slightly little less rude than looking at her watch. She had a little bit of time. 'Sure.'

They walked to a quiet corner of the room.

'Well, when you were in, your partner asked about program music. Symphonic poems.'

'Yes,' Jessica said. 'Do you have further thoughts on this?'

'I do,' Duchesne said. 'Aesthetically, the tone poem is in some ways related to opera, the difference being that the words are not sung to the audience. There are examples of absolute music that contain narrative of sorts.'

Jessica just stared.

'Okay, what I'm getting at is that, while there may be nothing in the music itself, a lot of times material has been written as an adjunct to the music – a poetic epigraph, if you will.'

'You mean, written after the fact?'

'Yes.'

Duchesne looked out over the room, then back.

'Are you a fan of classical music, detective?'

Jessica sneaked a covert glance at her watch. 'Sure,' she said. 'I can't say I know too much about it, but I know what I like when I hear it.'

'Tell me,' Duchesne began, 'do you ever go to concerts?'

'Not too often,' she said. 'My husband is not a big classical-music fan. He's more of a Southside Johnny guy.'

Duchesne shot a quick glance at Jessica's left hand. She never wore her wedding ring – or any jewelry, for that matter – when she was in the field. Too many opportunities to lose it, not to mention having it give away your position when you needed silence.

'That was terribly forward of me,' Duchesne said. 'Please forgive me.'

'No harm done,' Jessica said.

'No, I've made a fool of myself. Mea culpa.'

Jessica needed a way to wrap this up. 'Mr. Duchesne – Frederic – I really do appreciate this information. I'll pass it along to the other detectives working the case. You never know. It might lead to something.'

Duchesne seemed to be a bit flustered. He was probably not used to being shot down. He was not bad-looking in a Julian Sands kind of way, cultured and refined: probably a hell of a catch in his social circle. 'Please feel free to call me anytime if you think of something else that might be helpful,' Jessica added.

Duchesne brightened a little, although it was clear he realized what she was doing – trying to placate him. 'I certainly will.'

'By the way, what brings you here tonight?'

Duchesne pulled a visitor badge out of his pocket, clipped it to his sport coat. 'I've done some work as a forensic audiologist,' he said. 'Strictly on a contract basis. My specialty is physical characteristics and measurement of acoustic stimuli.'

You never know, Jessica thought. She extended her hand. They shook. 'Have fun.'

As she watched Duchesne walk across the room, her cellphone vibrated. She looked at the screen. It was Byrne.

'Kevin. Where are you?'

All she heard was the hiss of silence. She wasn't sure Byrne was still there. Then: 'I've got to go in for more tests.'

It didn't register. 'What are you talking about?'

Another pause. 'They read my MRI. They want me to go back for more tests.'

'Did they say what it was about?'

'They don't want you back because everything is all right, Jess.'

'Okay,' Jessica said. 'We'll deal with it. I'll go with you.'

More silence. Then Jessica heard a bell on Byrne's end. Was that the sound of an elevator? 'Where are you?'

No answer.

'Kevin?' The silence was maddening. 'When do they want you to—'

'The original homicides. The cold cases. It was right in front of us. I didn't get it until I was driving up the parkway.'

Byrne was talking about Benjamin Franklin Parkway.

'What do you mean? What's on the parkway?'

'I drove by the hotel, and it all fell into place,' he said. 'You never know what's going to make sense, or when it's going to happen. It's what ties them together.'

Jessica got an earful of loud static. Byrne said something else, but she didn't understand it. She was just about to ask him to repeat what he'd said when she heard him loud and clear.

'There's a package for you with the concierge.'

The concierge?

'Kevin, you have to—'

'It's the music,' he said. 'It's always been about the music.'

And then he was gone. Jessica looked at the screen on her phone. The call had ended. She called Byrne right back, got his voicemail. She tried again. Same result.

There's a package for you with the concierge.

She walked out of the Crystal Room, across the lobby to the concierge desk. There was indeed a package for her. It was a pair of nine-by-twelve envelopes. Her name was on them, scrawled in Byrne's handwriting. She stepped away, looked inside each envelope. Files, notes, photographs, charts. It was not the official file, but rather a second one that Byrne had been keeping.

She raised Josh Bontrager on the handset. A few minutes later they met in a small meeting room on the first floor. Jessica closed the door, told Bontrager about her phone call from Byrne. Then she opened one of the envelopes, put the material on the table.

THE FIRST FOUR PAGES on the top of the pile were photocopies of the death certificates for Lina Laskaris, Marcellus Palmer, Antoinette Chan and Marcia Jane Kimmelman.

Why had Byrne dropped off this information? She'd seen all of it before. What was in here that he wanted her to notice?

Jessica scanned the pages, taking in the relevant data: Name, date of birth, address, parents, cause of death, date of death.

Date of death.

Her gaze shifted from document to document.

'It's the dates, Josh,' Jessica said. 'Look.'

Bontrager ran his finger down each page, stopping at the entry for date of death. 'Marcellus Palmer was killed on June 21. Lina Laskaris and Margaret van Tassel were killed on September 21. Antoinette Chan was killed on March 21. Marcia Jane Kimmelman was killed on December 21.'

'Those are all the first days of the seasons,' Jessica said. 'The killer picked these cases because the original homicides took place on the first days of spring, summer, fall and winter.'

'Yes.'

'This is what Kevin meant when he said it came to him when he drove by the hotel. He was talking about the Four Seasons.'

The next documents in the file were copies of the photographs of the animal tattoos *in situ*. Jessica put the photographs side by side, six in all, spread across the table. 'These are all animals in the *Carnival of the Animals* by Saint-Saens.'

They looked at the photographs left to right. Six tattoos, six fingers. Six *different* fingers.

There was one other item in the first envelope. Jessica reached in, slid it out. And they had their answer.

Inside was a small booklet, about the size and shape of a *Playbill*. It bore a date from 1990. Jessica looked at the cover.

CHRISTA-MARIE SCHÖNBURG, CELLO
AN EVENING WITH SAINT-SAENS AND VIVALDI
SELECTIONS FROM *THE FOUR SEASONS*,
CARNIVAL OF THE ANIMALS AND *DANSE MACABRE*
ARRANGED FOR THE CELLO BY SIR OLIVER MALCOLM

Jessica opened the booklet. The program began with brief selections from each part of *The Four Seasons*. After that were selections from *Carnival of the Animals*.

Et marche royale du Lion was the lion. *Poules et Coqs* was the rooster. *Tortues* was the tortoise. *L'Éléphant* was the elephant. *Kangourous* was the kangaroo. *Le Cygne* was the swan. *Aquarium* was the fish. *Volière* was the bird.

There were eight selections in all.

'Someone is recreating her last performance,' Jessica said.

Bontrager pointed to the last part of the night's program. '*Danse Macabre*?' he asked. 'What do you know about it?'

'Nothing,' Jessica said.

Bontrager sat down at the computer, launched a web browser. In seconds he had a hit.

The wiki entry gave them the basics. *Danse Macabre* was written by Camille Saint-Saens originally as an art song for voice and piano. What had Duchesne said?

'*A lot of times material has been written as an adjunct to the music – a poetic epigraph, if you will.*'

'See if there's a narrative that goes with this,' Jessica said.

Bontrager did a search. He soon got hits. 'Yeah,' he said. 'There is. It was originally a poem by a guy named Henri Cazalis.' Bontrager hit a few more keys. In a moment the poem appeared on the screen.

The poem began:

> *Zig, zig, zig, Death in cadence,*
> *Striking a tomb with his heel,*
> *Death at midnight plays a dance-tune,*
> *Zig, zig, zag, on his violin.*

It all began to make sense. *Striking a tomb with his heel* explained the bodies found in the cemeteries, their legs broken. *Zig, zig, zig* was on Joseph Novak's computer. Jessica's gaze continued down the page, a symmetry forming.

> *Zig zig, zig, Death continues*
> *The unending scraping on his instrument.*
> *A veil has fallen! The dancer is naked.*

Jessica thought: *The dancer is naked.* The shaved bodies.

'Is there an explanation for this?' Jessica asked. 'Some sort of source material?'

Bontrager scrolled down. 'It says the poem was based on an old French superstition. Hang on.' He did another search. He soon had the synopsis of the original superstition.

'According to the superstition, Death appears at midnight every year on Halloween, and has the power to call forth the dead from their graves to dance for him while he plays his fiddle. His skeletons dance for him until the first break of dawn, when they must return to their graves until the next year.'

The two detectives looked at each other, at their watches. It was 9:50.

According to what they were reading, there were two hours and ten minutes left. And they had no idea where or whom the killer was going to strike.

Jessica opened the second envelope. Inside were six transparencies. The clear plastic sheets were 8½ by 11 inches. At first it was not clear what was printed on them. Jessica looked at the lower right-hand corner of one. There she saw a number she recognized as the homicide case file number. She soon realized that it was a transparency of the forensic photograph of the wounds to Kenneth Beckman's forehead, a photograph of the white paper band that encircled the victim's head.

Jessica took the transparency, held it up to the white wall. There was the Rorschach blot of blood on the left, which had come from the mutilated ear, a shape she had originally thought of as a rough figure eight. There was the straight line across the top, as well as the oval of blood underneath. In this format, a photographic transparency, the blood looked black.

Why had Byrne made these into transparencies?

She held up the next sample. The second transparency was from Preston Braswell's head. It was identical. She looked at the third sheet, this time the evidence photograph of Eduardo Robles. Identical. There was no doubt in her mind, or in the mind of anyone else investigating these homicides, that the signature for each of these murders was identical, and all but confirmed a single killer.

Except that they were *not* identical.

'Josh, bring that lamp closer.'

Bontrager got up and pulled the table lamp across the desk. Jessica sorted through the transparencies, her heart beating faster. She put them all in the order that made the most sense at that moment.

'Turn off the overhead light.'

Bontrager crossed the room, shut off the fluorescents. When he returned, Jessica held the stack of transparencies up to the bright lampshade.

And then they saw it.

There were five lines, but they were in slightly different places, one above the other. The puncture wounds were in different places, too. On the left side, the bloodstains left by the killer's mutilation of the victims' ears formed a stylized clef.

'My God,' Jessica said. The clarity was almost painful. 'It's a musical staff. He's writing music on the dead bodies, one note at a time.'

Bontrager sat back down. He entered the search phrase: '*Danse Macabre sheet music.*'

In seconds they had a visual representation of the sheet music. The two detectives compared the samples with the transparencies. They were identical. The killer was carving the final measure of *Danse Macabre* on his victims.

He was done with *The Four Seasons*. He wasn't *quite* done with *Carnival of the Animals*. There were two notes yet to write in the measure.

Jessica glanced back at the poem. The answer was in there. She read it all again.

Her stare fell on a phrase in the middle.

A lustful couple sits on the moss
So as to taste long-lost delights.

Is the lustful couple Christa-Marie Schönburg and Kevin Byrne? Is their
killer taking them back to the night they met?

Jessica looked at her watch. It was 10:00. They had less than two
hours to figure it all out.

And Kevin Byrne was nowhere to be found.

SEVENTY-SEVEN

L UCY HID IN A SMALL ROOM OFF THE LADIES' LOCKER ROOM IN THE basement, near the rear of the hotel. There were two other women in the room. They spoke animatedly in Spanish. Lucy did not understand the words, but she didn't have to. There was something going on in the hotel, and Lucy had to figure that they had seen the blood in the hallway.

Meet me here on Sunday night at 9:30. Love, Lucy.

She had to leave. They were going to discover what had happened, if they had not already done so. They were going to check the lock on the door to Room 1208 and think that it was her. Plus, there were all kinds of ways to know that someone was in a room, scientific things. She had wiped down everything she remembered touching, but she couldn't have gotten all of it.

She listened to the other girls in the locker room. They would soon be going on shift. When the locker room was empty, she would slip out the back door.

What had she done?

SEVENTY-EIGHT

J ESSICA AND BONTRAGER STOOD IN THE GIFT SHOP OFF THE LOBBY. Jessica had briefed Dana Westbrook on their findings and Dana in turn briefed the rest of the team.

Jessica thought about the people milling around the lobby and the lounge, drinks in their hands. Something nagged at her. She couldn't put her finger on it.

'I want to see that guest list again,' Jessica said.

'Hang on. I'll get it.'

A minute later Bontrager returned, handed her the small stack of papers. She put it down on the gift-shop counter.

Her stare moved down each of the pages. She didn't know what she was looking for. She scanned the list of cities. Pittsburgh, Los Angeles, Montreal, Sao Paulo, Zurich, Cincinnati.

She leaned against the desk, took out her iPhone.

She remembered the crime-scene photos. There was something about one of the photographs. She scrolled through the photos she had taken. Nothing jumped out. There were photos of the Federal Street scene, shots taken at the Mount Olive Cemetery. There were also photos taken of the alley where Eduardo Robles was found, as well as the paupers' graveyard in the Northeast. The last roll was pictures taken in and around Garrett Corner, Archer Farms, as well as pictures she had taken of the state police file on the murder of Peggy van Tassel.

She had three pictures of the crime-scene photos. The scene was bloody and stomach-churning. One photo was a close-up of the girl's stomach.

Jessica zoomed in on the picture, on an area where the girl's killer had bitten her. As she got closer she saw that it was not one of the bite marks, it was a bruise instead. She increased the size one more time. The image was beginning to blur, but it was still clear enough. The bruise looked to be in the shape of a snake.

A ring?

Had she seen someone tonight wearing a ring in the shape of a snake?

Yes. A man wearing a ring of that description was one of the three men who had come up to the table, one of the Three Stooges. It was not the inebriated one, Barry Swanson. Nor was it the tall Finn.

What was the other one's name?

She remembered. She saw the name tag in her mind's eye. It was Jay Bowman.

Bowman.

Archer.

Jessica walked the perimeter of the Crystal Room, her heart racing. Table after table. She didn't see him. She walked to the other side, her eyes scanning, searching. No. He was not here. She hurried out to the lobby. The man calling himself Jay Bowman was not to be found. She got on her comm. In seconds she had John Shepherd.

'There's a guest here. He's registered under the name Jay Bowman.'

'Hang on,' Shepherd said. Twenty long seconds later: 'We've got him. Room 1208.'

THE SERVICE ELEVATOR WAS agonizingly slow. For a moment Jessica considered getting off and taking the stairs, but that would probably delay her. Josh Bontrager and John Shepherd were taking the passenger elevator, which was on the other side of the hotel. On the twelfth floor they would be able to form a loose perimeter. There were now uniformed officers stationed at every exit on all the floors.

When she got out on the twelfth floor she passed a handful of guests. Two women about her age, dressed provocatively as French housemaids. A shorter man dressed as a wizard. A pair of boys about ten. None of them were George Archer.

She met up with Bontrager and Shepherd at the end of the hallway leading to the east wing. They moved down the hall, ears attuned to the sounds coming from the rooms. They reached Room 1208. Silence from within. Jessica made eye contact with the two men.

Bontrager knocked. No response. He knocked again.

Shepherd stepped forward, touched the electronic card to the top of the lock. Jessica and Bontrager drew their weapons. Jessica nodded. Shepherd swiped the card, turned the handle, and pushed open the door.

Jessica rolled into the room first, her weapon high. There were no lights on. She reached out, felt along the wall, found the switch. It turned on a single light overhead, along with an under-cabinet light on the minibar across the room.

'*Police*,' she said. No response. She stopped just short of the bathroom door. She nudged it open with her foot. Bontrager flanked her on the right. He reached around the corner, turned on the light.

The bathroom was empty.

They edged forward, deeper into the hotel room. Jessica saw it first. There was a small pool of blood drying on the carpet in front of the desk. Next to it was the unmistakable stain of vomit. She touched Bontrager's arm, nodded at the stain. Bontrager saw it too.

They counted a silent three. Jessica rolled into the main part of the room first, her weapon raised.

It was a slaughterhouse. Blood slathered the walls, the floor. A spray of crimson dotted the window overlooking Seventeenth Street.

Josh Bontrager stepped forward, opened the closet. It was empty. He looked under the bed. 'We're clear,' he said.

Jessica holstered her weapon.

The body on the bed was covered with a single sheet. There was a full body print on the sheet, painted in blood. Josh Bontrager got on the far side, Jessica the near. They each grabbed a corner of the sheet, pulled it back.

George Archer had been savaged. His throat was cut from ear to ear. His chest was crushed. There were bite marks across his stomach.

There were also bruises across his thighs, bruises in the shape of a snake ring.

The ring sat on the pillow next to his head. It was caked with skin and hair, bits of drying flesh.

Jessica stepped forward, checked the dead man's fingers. No tattoos.

John Shepherd got on his two-way, raising the head of the hotel's security detail. 'Lock the building down,' he said. 'No one goes in or out.'

THE LOBBY WAS IN chaos when Jessica entered. There were a dozen uniformed officers deployed at exits, elevators, and service hallways. The restaurant's doors were closed. Inside Jessica saw patrons at candlelit tables, elegantly dressed, sipping their wines, perhaps figuring that, if you had to be locked down, being locked down inside a Michelin-starred restaurant with one of the most extensive and lauded wine cellars in the state was not such a bad thing.

Inside the Crystal Room, in an attempt to keep the crowd at ease, a member of the protection detail made his way over to the attorney general's table, tapped his watch. The AG got up calmly, shook a few hands, but quickly walked out a door at the back of the ballroom.

Jessica had changed into her jeans and hoodie. On her way out of the ladies' room she heard from Shepherd in her earpiece.

'Jess. One of the wait staff saw something near the rear service entrance. Just east of the kitchen.'

'What did she see?'

'Blood.'

JESSICA AND BONTRAGER MET John Shepherd in the kitchen. Shepherd pointed out the handful of red dots leading to the rear entrance.

Shepherd stepped forward, swiped a card. They entered the area near the loading dock. A PPD officer was deployed behind the building. When he heard noise he spun around, his hand on his weapon. He was young, in his mid-twenties, a little spooked. Jessica showed her badge, and the kid looked quite relieved to have a detective on scene.

'How long have you been here?' Jessica asked

'A minute or so,' the officer said. 'I just got the call.'

The blood spots trailed over to a parking space, then disappeared.

'Did you see anyone leave?'

'No, ma'am.'

Jessica stepped back into the service area, looked at the door to her left.

'Where does this lead?' Jessica asked.

'Women's locker room.'

Jessica pushed through the door, her weapon low. The locker room had three benches, a row of sinks, a single shower, a pair of toilet stalls. Jessica checked them all. The room was empty. She looked at the inside of one of the toilet-stall doors. There was a smear of blood there.

Whoever they were looking for was gone.

SEVENTY-NINE

IN THE LOSS PREVENTION OFFICE JESSICA STOOD BEHIND JOHN Shepherd. He rewound the video files. The recordings shuttled between different views, so there was a six-second rotation between each of four cameras on the twelfth floor. Even in a hotel as pricey and profitable as Le Jardin, they did not have the resources to devote a hard drive to each of the scores of cameras in and around the property.

Shepherd rewound the recording to when Jessica and the other detectives came to Room 1208, then kept going. A handful of people backed up to their rooms, as well as the stairwell at the end of the hallways. Shepherd carried on until he saw one of the room attendants exit the room backward, then retreat down the hall. He stopped, played it forward.

In normal time the view showed the room attendant walking down the hall, toward Room 1208. The attendant was female, petite and slender, with her light-colored hair in a braid. Here the view began its rotation, shifting to the area near the guest elevators.

'Do you know who this is?' Jessica asked.

'Hard to tell,' Shepherd said. 'I know a lot of the room attendants – most of them, in fact. But from this angle it's difficult.'

When the view returned to the eastern hallway, they saw the attendant stop in front of 1208 for a few seconds. She didn't knock, she didn't try the door. She just stood there, perhaps listening. The camera then cut away to another view, again to the elevators, where it stayed for six seconds. No one came or went. It then cut to a view of the other end of the hallway, the western wing. Two women came out of a room there. The next cut was to the service elevators. Empty. Back to the young woman in front of 1208. The recording caught up with her as she knocked on the door. There was no audio, but Jessica could see her lips move. In the split second before the cut-away she lifted her hand, and appeared to swipe a card in the electronic lock.

The recording moved again to its other locations. No other people were visible.

They watched the rotation for the next minute and saw no activity. When they returned to the eastern hallway they saw a man heading away from the camera. He was in costume, a wizard's costume. He moved slowly, so that by the time he reached 1208 the camera had rotated. When the camera returned he was gone, and the door to the stairwell was just closing.

'Shit,' Shepherd said. He rewound the recording with the joystick, and toggled it back and forth. There were no details visible. It was impossible to tell if the man had entered the room or just passed by. With his hat, long coat and what appeared to be gloves on his hands, there were no identifiable details.

Shepherd pointed to the time code in the lower right-hand corner of the frame.

'Right around here is when we went up,' he said.

A minute later Jessica saw herself and Josh Bontrager walking down the hall. A few seconds later Shepherd joined them. They went inside the room.

'I'm going to interrogate these locks,' Shepherd said. 'I'll be right back.'

While Shepherd was gone Jessica toggled the video back and forth. She saw nothing new. She looked at the menu down the right side of the screen. She saw that one of the selections was the rear loading dock. She clicked over. It was a static shot from above one of the three docks behind the hotel, showing the loading bay, a pair of Dumpsters, and the hotel's shuttle bus parked in a space. There was no movement. In the upper right-hand corner she could see a sliver of Seventeenth Street.

She was just about to click back over – she was certain that John Shepherd didn't want her messing around with the computers – when she saw a view that she had not seen before. It was above the side door to the loading dock, the man door, not the huge corrugated steel door. The view cut away, but before it did she saw something. She ran it back.

There was no mistake. It was Kevin Byrne standing near the mouth of the alley.

Jessica checked the time code.

Was this when Byrne dropped off the package with the concierge? If so, what was he doing at the rear of the hotel?

Jessica heard the door open in the outer office. She clicked back to the paused recording at the beginning of the clip of the twelfth floor. Shepherd reentered the office.

'I interrogated all four locks along the path,' Shepherd said. 'The lock on 1208, the service elevator, the security door leading out to the loading dock, and the door on the dock itself. All four locks register the same card. It is signed out to one of the room attendants. Lucinda Doucette.'

Why is that name familiar? Jessica thought. 'Do you know her?'

'Oh yeah,' Shepherd said. 'Sweet kid. Shy.'

'Do you have a photograph of her?'

'Sure,' Shepherd said. He moved to another computer terminal, tapped a few keys. He input Lucinda's name and a few seconds later her ID page came up. He hit *print* and the color printer began to cycle. Seconds later, Jessica was looking at Lucinda Doucette's young face. Jessica knew her. She was the young woman at the Hosanna House, the one who'd been sitting at the little table with Carlos.

Jessica had no choice. She called in an all-points bulletin on the girl.

Shepherd hit a few keys, printing off one hundred copies of Lucinda Doucette's photograph. 'We need to get this to all the sector cars in the area.'

When John Shepherd grabbed the printed photos and left the office, Jessica's cellphone rang. It was Nicci Malone.

'Nicci. Why aren't you on channel with this?'

'I'm not in the hotel anymore.'

'What do you mean? Where are you?'

Nicci gave her the location. It was a few blocks away.

'What's going on?' Jessica asked.

Detective Malone hesitated. 'You better get over here right away.'

L ucy walked up Sansom Street in a fog, stepping from shadow to shadow. Everyone who passed her was a danger. They all knew what she had done. She could see it in their eyes. There was traffic, conversations, street sounds all around her, but she didn't hear the sounds. All she heard was the white noise in her head, raised to an insane volume, the static of her impending madness.

What *had* she done?

All she remembered was the bell. It had rung twice.

What did it mean?

She kept walking. Block after block passed. Walk. Don't Walk. Red light. Green light. There were people all around her, but they were ghosts. The only person who lived in her world right now was a dead man. A man lying under the sheets, soaked in blood.

All that blood.

At 22nd Street her legs felt as if she could not take another step, but she forced herself, she knew she had to keep moving.

When she reached the corner of Sansom and 23rd something jolted her out of her dark reverie. There were police cars all up and down the streets, their lights flashing on the walls of the buildings. Groups of people were gathered on the corners, chatting with each other, pointing at the church. Lucy had walked this way many times.

She was pretty sure that there was a small cemetery next to the church. What was going on?

It didn't matter. It had nothing to do with her. She knew what she had to do. She knew who she had to call. She crossed 23rd Street. There was a policeman standing in the middle of the street, directing traffic away from the church. Lucy pulled up the collar on her coat, angled her head away from him. As she passed, she chanced a glance. He was looking right at her. She quickened her pace, made it across the street. When she had gone half a block she stepped back into the shadows, glanced back. The cop was still looking in her direction.

Lucy ran. She tried to get her bearings. The river was just a few blocks to her left. Ahead was Chestnut, Market, Arch, Cherry.

Cherry.

There was only one place for her to go.

Lucy stood in front of Apartment 106, her breath coming in hot, painful waves. She had run nearly six blocks and her sides ached. She tried to calm herself, to catch her breath. She could hear the sound of a television coming from one of the other apartments on this floor. Somewhere a dog was barking. She knocked softly, but there was no response. She tried again. Nothing.

She tried the doorknob. It turned in her hand. She pushed open the door, and stepped into Mr. Costa's apartment.

The flat was completely empty. This time, even the Dreamweaver booth was gone. The floor had been swept, the walls were bare. She could smell the cleaning products – Spic 'N Span, Lemon Pledge, Windex, Scrubbing Bubbles.

Lucy moved slowly through the living room, glanced into the tiny kitchen. The old appliances remained, but that was it. There was no dinette table, no chairs, no dishes in the sink, no strainer. She turned back to the living room. On the right was a door that she figured led to a bedroom. She stepped lightly, but the old wooden floor still creaked under her weight. She stopped, waiting for the light to go on, for Mr. Costa to appear suddenly as he was likely to do. But it didn't happen. Lucy inched open the door to the bedroom. It too was empty. No furniture, no clothing, no personal items of any kind. There was a single window overlooking the street. That was it.

But it wasn't.

There was something on the wall. A small picture in a frame. Lucy reached over, flipped the light switch, but it didn't work. She crossed the bedroom, pushed the curtain to the side. A wedge of illumination from the street lights across the road spilled into the room. She took the small picture from the wall, angled it toward the borrowed light. The photograph was old, kind of blurry. It was a picture of a little girl, no more than two years old. She sat on a beach. In front of her was a bright red plastic bucket. In her hand was a small shovel. She squinted at the sunlight. She wore a floppy flowered sun hat. Chubby cheeks, chubby knees.

Lucy knew the face, the eyes. The last time she had seen those eyes they had been red with crying.

It was Peggy van Tassel.

Lucy's hands began to shake. She tried to plug it into everything that had happened in the past few days and she could not. Then she tried to put the picture in the pocket of her coat but it wouldn't fit.

She knew what she had to do. She would get to the nearest phone and call Detective Byrne. The longer she waited, the worse it was going to get for her.

Before she could take a single step, she heard the floorboards creak, felt the warm breath on her neck. Someone stood right behind her.

'Police,' the man said. 'Get down on the floor and put your hands behind your back. Do it now.'

Lucy felt her legs go soft. The photograph slipped from her grasp. It crashed to the floor.

'Now,' he repeated.

Lucy got down on the floor, next to the shattered glass, put her hands behind her back. She felt the man take her arms by the wrists, then slip a plastic band around them, tighten it.

He left her there like that for a full minute. She dared not turn to look at him. She heard him pace around the room. Then he spoke.

'Can you hear them?' he asked softly.

Lucy didn't know what he was talking about. She tried to listen hard, to figure out what he meant, but there was only the roar of terror in her head.

'The dead are all over the city,' the man continued. 'Tonight it belongs to them. It always has.'

A few moments later the man shone a flashlight on the broken photograph on the floor, spotlighting the little girl's face. He held it there for a long time.

'You could have saved her,' the man said. 'You could have saved her and you did nothing.'

Lucy's mind began to spin. This man was not the police.

She was pulled roughly to her feet. She felt the man's breath right near her ear.

'You're as guilty as George Archer.'

EIGHTY-ONE

THE ST DEMETRIOS ORTHODOX CHURCH WAS A LONG RECTANGULAR
building with a single cupola. Behind it was a graveyard, a
small neighborhood cemetery, easily a hundred years old. There
was a waist-high brick wall surrounding the courtyard, which was
accessible by a double wrought-iron gate. In the light thrown from
the headlights of the sector cars and departmental sedans, the
headstones cast long shadows over the grounds, as well as onto
the walls of the row homes on either side. The flashing lights
projected images nearly ten feet tall, giant specters overseeing the
dead.

As Jessica approached the scene, Nicci Malone came jogging up
to her side. Nicci pointed to a young couple standing near one of the
sector cars. They looked terribly frightened.

'These two were walking up the street about a half-hour ago. They
said they were not really paying attention but when they got here to
the edge of the block they saw someone walking in the shadows to
the center of the cemetery. They said it was a man carrying something heavy over his shoulders.'

'Did they get a good look at the guy?' Jessica asked.

Nicci shook her head. 'Too dark on that side. But they still watched
what he was doing. They said he dropped the parcel to the ground,
unwrapped it. When they saw that it was a body, they froze. Then

they saw the man position the leg, propping it up on one of the low headstones.'

Jessica knew what came next. She remained silent.

'Then, according to our witnesses, the man jumped high into the air and came down on the leg. The woman said she heard the sound of the breaking bone all the way on the other side of the cemetery.'

A news helicopter roared overhead. Jessica wondered what this grotesque display might look like from above.

'What about the vehicle? Did they get a look?'

Again Nicci shook her head. 'They were both pretty much over the edge at this point. We were lucky they had the wherewithal to call us.'

Jessica glanced at the street corners. She did not see any police cameras. This was not a high-crime or high-drug-traffic area. She looked at the walls of the stone church. She did not see any surveillance cameras there, either.

When she stepped into the gated graveyard, Jessica saw the corpse, the now-familiar signature. The body was nude, a white middle-aged male, shaved clean. There was a band of paper around his forehead. The left foot rested on the headstone. Jessica crossed over to the plot, aimed her Maglite at the dead body, and saw the sharp bone protruding from the skin, just above the left knee. She thought about the line from *Danse Macabre*.

> *Zig, zig, zig, each one is frisking,*
> *You can hear the cracking of the bones of the dancers.*

Then Jessica leaned in, moved the victim's left leg a few inches, directed the beam of her flashlight at the headstone. At the top she saw:

O Theos na tin anapafsi

The name of the person in the grave was Melina Laskaris.

She angled the light to the victim's right hand, which was on the ground, palm up. On the ring finger she saw a small tattoo of a donkey. It was the seventh animal, which meant there was one more to go.

Before Jessica could stop her – and she didn't really want to stop her – Nicci Malone stepped forward, knelt down, pulled off the bloodied white headband. When Jessica saw the victim's face, the triangle was complete.

The dead woman was Lina Laskaris.

Her killer was Eduardo Robles.

The accomplice, the harmony in this horror show – the broken body sprawled before them in this crumbling graveyard – was Detective Dennis Stansfield.

EIGHTY-TWO

H E STOOD IN SHADOWS, JUST A BLOCK FROM THE LE JARDIN HOTEL, the sounds of his city all around him, the flashing police lights a few blocks away. He felt the hand on his arm.

'Kevin.'

Christa-Marie looked fragile, sculpted from moonlight. She raised a hand to his cheek, a warm finger tracing the lines in his face. She slipped her hand around the back of his head, leaned forward and kissed him, gently at first, then with a growing passion.

A moment later she leaned back, looked into his eyes.

'It's time, isn't it?' she asked.

'Yes,' Byrne said. 'Are you ready?'

'Yes.' She took his hand in hers. 'Take me home.'

EIGHTY-THREE

' Jess?'

It was Russell Diaz. The city block had been taken over by law enforcement. Residents had begun to drift out of their houses. Endlessly, the helicopter flew back and forth, hovering overhead. Jessica looked around. David Albrecht was not to be found.

'You have a minute?' Diaz asked.

She did not. But she knew that this was coming, just as she knew what it was about. 'Sure.'

Diaz looked at his two men. 'Give us a second.'

The two officers walked a few feet away, leaned against Jessica's car. When Diaz felt they were out of earshot, he spoke.

'You know what I have to ask, don't you?' he said, lowering his voice.

Jessica remained silent. It was a rhetorical question. Diaz plowed ahead. Niceties were over.

'I need to talk to Kevin,' Diaz said. 'Have you heard from him?'

'Not since earlier this evening.'

'About what time was that?'

Jessica had to think about this. She had to be accurate. This was all going on the record. 'Maybe an hour ago.'

'He called you?'

'Yes.'

'Did he mention where he was going?'

Now she had to be careful. Byrne had not said anything specific. 'No.'

'Is he still driving that van?'

'I don't know.'

Diaz looked out over the gathering crowd, back.

'I want to show you something.'

They walked over to the unmarked police van. Diaz opened the sliding side door. Inside was a rack of electronic equipment, surveillance monitors, three locked gun racks. Diaz grabbed a laptop off the front seat, opened it, put it on the floor of the van. The screen instantly displayed a flow chart. On it were six different squares. Diaz clicked the first one.

Seconds later three separate documents cascaded across the screen. Jessica recognized them as PPD witness statements, presented in .pdf format.

'We have statements from three people who live on West Tioga Street,' Diaz said. 'Neighbors of Sharon and Kenneth Beckman. They all stated that they saw Detective Byrne at the Beckman house an hour before her son reported her missing.'

'She was next of kin, Russell. Both Kevin and I were there that morning. We made notification.'

'As you know, he returned a short time later. Did you accompany Detective Byrne back to the premises?'

'No,' Jessica said. 'He returned to follow up. We had received additional information.'

'What was the information?'

Diaz knew the answer to his question. He was testing her. 'That Kenneth Beckman was questioned in the murder of Antoinette Chan.'

'When did Detective Byrne return to the Roundhouse?'

'It had to be around three.'

'What did he say about the interview?'

'He said that Sharon Beckman didn't answer the door.'

Diaz took a moment, then tapped another square on the chart. This was the ME's preliminary report on Joseph Novak. 'The coroner puts the time of death for Joseph Novak at between eight p.m. and six a.m. Do you know where Detective Byrne was during those hours?'

This was getting so bad, so fast. Was Diaz making an attempt to establish some sort of conspiracy here?

'I do not.'

'Did Detective Byrne mention anything about seeing Mr. Novak again that day?'

'No.'

Diaz hit yet another button on the laptop. A grainy video began to play. It was the stationary image of a city street at night.

'This is PPD surveillance footage near the corner of Frankford and York.'

At the thirty-four-second mark on the video a man crosses the top of the frame, hesitates for a moment, walks off frame. A few seconds later, a second man walks across the frame, right to left. He continues off. Diaz rewound the recording. He pointed to the lower right of the image, at a van parked on the street. 'This tag is registered to a man named Patrick Connolly. He is Detective Byrne's cousin. Connolly stated that he lent this vehicle to Detective Byrne last week.'

Jessica looked closely. It was clearly the Sedona minivan. She looked closely at the whole image. 'I believe Kevin already acknowledged that he was there that night. This is not new information.'

Diaz hit *play*. The image scrolled by in slow motion this time. He freeze-framed it as the first man walked into the frame. 'This is Eduardo Robles.' He hit *play* again. Robles disappears off frame, walking down the alley, the alley in which his body was found. The second man enters the frame. Diaz froze the image again.

'Do you recognize this person, detective?' he asked.

Jessica noted that she had gone from *Jess* to *detective*. To another person it might have gone unnoticed. Not to anyone in law enforcement. 'No. Sorry. It could be anyone.'

'Not exactly.' Diaz hit a few keys, zoomed in. It increased the size of the pixels, but some things were obvious. Like the man's left hand. 'It can only be a white male, so it can't be "just anyone".' He pointed to something next to the figure. 'We took measurements on this standpipe. This person is over six feet tall. He is wearing a dark overcoat and a dark watch cap.' Diaz reached onto a shelf. He produced a photograph of Kevin Byrne, a picture that Jessica recognized instantly.

It had been taken a year ago at a benefit in the Poconos. It was of Kevin and her standing with a bunch of kids. Kevin wore a dark overcoat and navy blue watch cap.

Jessica said nothing.

Diaz directed her gaze to the body on the ground across the cemetery from where they stood. 'Everyone was well aware of the friction between Detective Byrne and Detective Stansfield. Add to that the incident between them at the Roundhouse and you can see what I'm faced with, right?' Diaz closed the laptop, squared himself in front of her. 'I now have a dead cop, and Kevin Byrne is missing again.'

Diaz opened a second laptop. There on the screen were two microscope photographs of hair shafts. Diaz pointed to the one on the left. 'This is a sample taken from a brush belonging to Sharon Beckman.' He pointed to the example on the right. Jessica was far from an expert, but to her eye the samples were identical. 'This was found on the driver's seat of Kevin Byrne's van. They match.'

Jessica recalled the hair on Byrne's shoulder.

'Did you get a haircut?'

'Yeah. I popped in and got a trim.'

Jessica began to feel nauseated. She remained silent, which was just as well because she had no idea what to say. Diaz closed the side door of the van, signaled to his two men. They approached, stopped a few feet away.

'Look, Jess. If you were looking at this from the outside, you would see why we need to talk to Detective Byrne.'

Jessica knew that Diaz was right. In her career she had brought people in for questioning based on far less.

'I don't know where he is, Russ. I've left five voicemails for him in the past half-hour.'

'When was the last time you called?'

'Five minutes ago.'

'Want to try again?'

Jessica took out her phone. She put it on speaker, hit Byrne's speed-dial number. It rang twice, and his voicemail greeting came on. There was no point leaving a sixth message. Jessica closed her phone.

Diaz nodded. 'Detective Byrne carries a 17?'

He was referring to a Glock 17, the standard-issue service weapon for PPD detectives. 'Yeah.'

'Does he carry a second piece?'

My God, Jessica thought, her heart in free fall. She was betraying one of the most important people in her life. She wondered how Kevin would handle the same situation if someone was asking these questions about her. 'Sometimes.'

'Today?'

Jessica told the truth. 'I don't know.'

'Does he pack anything else?'

Diaz meant knives, spray, knuckles, batons. 'No.'

Diaz processed it all. He looked out over the burgeoning mass of people, then back at Jessica. 'You know him better than anyone. I know you are close. I know this has to be hard for you.'

Jessica said nothing.

Diaz handed her a card. 'That's my cell on the back. If you talk to Kevin, have him call me.'

Jessica took the card, said nothing.

'You know this is going to move forward, right?'

'I know.'

'It's better for everyone if he walks in the front door.'

Diaz hesitated a few moments, then turned and walked away.

JESSICA LOOKED OUT OVER the cemetery. In all, there were probably thirty or forty people on scene. Jessica knew most of them by name, yet she had never felt so completely alone in her life.

A few minutes later Josh Bontrager emerged from the crowd.

'You okay, Josh?'

'No,' he said. 'I am *not*.'

'What's wrong?'

Bontrager bowed his head for moment. 'He was my partner, and now he's dead.'

'Josh, he wasn't really your partner. You were paired with him for one case.'

'Doesn't matter. Today he was my partner. Today I let him down.'

Jessica knew what he meant. She had certainly let Kevin Byrne down today.

'And I didn't even like the guy.'

Jessica left Josh to his thoughts for a few moments. She then filled him in on everything that Diaz had said.

'That's ridiculous,' Bontrager said.

'I know.'

'What are we going to do?'

'I'm going to try to find him before they do.'

'I'll go with you.'

'No, Josh. I can't ask you to do that.'

'Well, with all due respect, I don't remember you asking. It's something I'm volunteering for. Okay?'

Jessica lowered her voice as a pair of CSU officers walked by. 'Josh, there's a good chance I'm going off the reservation here. There's a *very* good chance I'm going to lose my job tonight. Maybe worse.'

Bontrager took a few steps away, looked out over the scene. The medical examiner's blue and white van came rolling up slowly. They would soon be loading Dennis Stansfield's body into the back for transport. Bontrager turned back. 'Remember my first days on the job?'

Jessica remembered them well. They'd been investigating a case that eventually took them up the Schuylkill River into Berks County. Josh Bontrager had been on temporary assignment. 'I remember.'

'Kevin wasn't too crazy about me at first, you know.'

'It just takes a little time for him to warm up to people.'

Bontrager looked at her, offered a smile. 'Bechtelsville, Pennsylvania may not be a hotbed of intellectuals, but we do know people,' he said. 'I knew right away what a closed group this is. I was the new guy, and a really inexperienced guy at that.'

Jessica just listened. She had gone through a brutal initiation period herself.

'In those first few months I made a lot of mistakes.'

'You did fine, Josh.'

'No, it only looked that way. I can't tell you how many times Kevin took me aside and showed me the ropes. How many times he covered for me.' Bontrager put his hands in his pockets. He looked across the cemetery. 'Nobody wanted me to have this job. Not really. I heard all the jokes, you know. All the stuff said behind my back. People thought I didn't, but I did.'

Jessica remembered well the hard time Josh had gotten. It was always bad enough for the new guy in the unit, but doubly so for Josh Bontrager, considering his background.

'You toughed it out, Josh,' Jessica said. 'You've earned the right to be here. You're a damned good detective.'

Bontrager shrugged. 'Well, it was you and Kevin who went to bat for me back then. I wouldn't even be here if it wasn't for you guys. If I lose it all tonight, I can live with that.'

'It might get worse than that, you know. Much worse.'

Josh Bontrager looked at her. Sometimes, with his clear eyes, open smile, and seemingly untamable cowlick, he looked like a kid, some country boy who'd got off I-95 at the wrong exit and wandered into the city. Other times, like right at this moment, he looked like a homicide detective with the Philadelphia Police Department.

'The Amish have an old saying,' Bontrager said. '"*Courage is fear that has said its prayers.*"' He drew his Glock, checked the action, holstered it, snapped it in. 'I've said my prayers, Jess.'

Jessica glanced at the crime scene, then back. 'Thanks, Josh.'

'I'm going to lock my car,' Bontrager said. 'I'll be right back.'

As Josh walked across the street, Jessica thought about what Byrne had said.

It's always been about the music.

Before she could make a mental list of their options her phone rang. It was David Albrecht. She answered.

'David, now is not really a good—'

There was static on the line. 'What's going on?' he asked.

'What do you mean?'

'I heard the call go out. Is there another victim?'

'What do you mean, you heard the call go out?'

'I heard it on the police radio.'

'You have a scanner?'

'Well, yeah,' he said. 'Of course.'

Jessica hadn't considered this. It made sense. 'Where are you, David?'

'I'm following Detective Byrne.'

Jessica's pulse spiked. She waved Bontrager over. 'You're with Kevin?'

'I'm right behind him. He was parked near the hotel. I saw a woman in the van. I thought you guys were together. I followed.'

'Where are you?'

'Hang on,' Albrecht said. 'Let me check my GPS.'

A few agonizing seconds passed.

'We're on Bells Mill Road.'

Bells Mill Road cut through the northeast section of Fairmount Park, traversing the Wissahickon Creek just west of Chestnut Hill.

'Do you know where he's going?' Jessica asked.

'Not a clue,' Albrecht said. 'But I kind of like it that way. This is so—'

'Which way are you heading?'

'We're going east. Northeast, technically. My GPS says we're coming up on something called Forbidden Drive. Is that the coolest name of all time or what? I think I'm changing the name of my movie to *Forbidden Drive*.'

'David, I want you to—'

'Hang on.' A loud blast of static. The coming storm was playing havoc with the signal. 'He's slowing down. I'll call you right back.'

'David, *wait*.'

Dead air. Jessica hit the button to call right back. She got David Albrecht's voicemail.

She told Josh what Albrecht had said.

'He's on Bells Mill?' Bontrager asked.

'Yeah.'

'Where do you think they're going?'

'I don't know.'

Jessica put the location into the Google Maps app on her phone. Seconds later she had a map of the area. She really didn't know anything about that part of the park. She fished out her keys.

'Let's get on the road,' she said. 'We'll figure it out on the way.'

EIGHTY-FOUR

BELLS MILL ROAD WAS A TWO-LANE BLACKTOP THAT SPANNED AN area between Ridge and Germantown Avenues. At its western end, where it became Spring Lane, there were houses, but as it made its way into Fairmount Park it became wooded and dark. As Jessica and Bontrager drove, the night was cut only by the headlights of their car.

On the way Josh Bontrager dialed David Albrecht's number twenty times, getting his voicemail each time. At the same time Jessica speed-dialed Byrne's cellphone with the same result.

'Maybe Kevin left his phone somewhere,' Bontrager said.

Jessica thought about this. 'No. He turns it off sometimes, but he always has it with him. He's just not answering.'

Bontrager went silent for a few moments. 'Don't all phones have some kind of GPS in them?'

Jessica didn't know about all phones. 'What are you saying, Josh?'

'If we could slip through a warrant, maybe we could get a fix on Kevin's phone.'

Jessica had thought of this. But it meant bringing someone into the loop. There was no doubt in her mind that an APB on Kevin had gone out. Police were looking for him and his vehicle. If she reached out to someone to help find him, she would be taking the chance that it would leak, and it would all end badly.

She looked at her watch. It was 10:24. Time was running out.

She had no choice. She knew who she had to bring into this. She called Michael Drummond.

'THIS IS MICHAEL.'

'Michael, it's Jessica Balzano.'

'Hey, Jessica. How are you?'

'I hope I didn't wake you.'

'Not a chance. I'm stuck at a Halloween party,' he said. 'What's up?'

'I need a warrant for a cellphone track.'

Drummond was silent for a moment. 'What do you have?'

Jessica told him the bare minimum.

'Who's the target?'

Jessica had no choice here, nor did she have a cover. 'Kevin Byrne.'

Once again, Michael Drummond fell silent for a few moments. 'This is about your serial?'

Jessica knew she was now on the record with this. If she lied, it would all come down around her.

'Yes and no.'

'Spoken like a true politician. But I'm going to need a little more if I'm going to get a warrant. You know it has to go through the chief.'

All search warrants related to a homicide case had to be approved by the chief of homicide in the district attorney's office.

Jessica had no choice. 'He might be in some trouble, Michael.'

Jessica heard Drummond take a deep breath, exhale slowly. 'I'll need his phone number and his carrier.'

Jessica gave him the information.

'I don't know if I can get this through at this time of night.'

'I understand.'

'Let me see what I can do,' Drummond said. 'Where are you?'

Jessica told him.

'Are you alone?'

'I'm with Detective Bontrager.'

'Hang tight. I'll call you back.'

Jessica clicked off her phone. She stood in the middle of the road, in the impenetrable country darkness. The road stretched into the gloom in both directions. Dark, forbidding, unknown, silent.

EIGHTY-FIVE

DARKNESS.

They were moving. There was tape over her eyes and her mouth. Her hands were still bound together behind her back with the plastic band.

Lucy tried to listen to sounds around her. She heard the sound of the road beneath her. They were on a paved road, smooth, maybe an expressway, although she did not have the sense that they were traveling at high speed. Every so often she heard the sound of something passing. It was a distinct rhythm. *Light poles?*

Underneath it all was the sound of the heater fan. There was no music coming from the radio, no conversation. Then she heard humming. She didn't know the song.

Lucy rolled to her right, then her left. The movements were small but she could feel the plastic on her wrists shift a little bit each time. If she had strength anywhere in her body it was in her arms and hands. You didn't lift as many mattresses as she had without getting stronger.

Left.

Right.

She flexed her wrists, relaxed.

Little by little she felt the plastic start to give.

EIGHTY-SIX

D RUMMOND CALLED BACK TEN MINUTES LATER.

'Michael,' Jessica said. 'What do you have for me?'

There were a few seconds of silence. At first Jessica thought the call had been dropped. She looked at the screen. They were still connected. She put the phone back to her ear. It was now quiet in the background on Drummond's end. He had either left or stepped away from his Halloween party.

'I don't know how to say this, Jess.'

This was not good, whatever it was. 'Just say it, Michael.'

Another pause. Jessica heard the rustling of paper. 'I just heard from the Hudson County prosecutor's office. They issued a search warrant yesterday to the Mailboxes USA location in Jersey City.'

Drummond was talking about the location to which the tattoos had been mailed from World Ink.

'Do we have something?' Jessica asked.

'We do. But it's not good news.'

'What did they say?'

'They got the records of where the material was forwarded to from Box 1606. The tattoos from World Ink. The package went to an address in South Philly.'

Jessica waited. And waited. 'Michael.'

'It was Kevin Byrne's address. The tattoos went to his home address.'

Jessica felt the ground shift beneath her. She wanted to speak, but her breath had not yet caught up to her words. 'It's not possible.'

'It's the only piece of mail the location ever forwarded from this box, under this registration. It was sent about a month ago.'

Another long pause. Drummond continued. 'Half the department is looking for him, Jessica. If I take this warrant request to the chief they're going to use it to locate Kevin and bring him in.'

'Okay, Michael. I understand,' Jessica said. 'But I have a favor to ask.'

'What is it?'

'I need a head start. There's an explanation for all of this. I just need to get to Kevin first.'

Silence for a moment. 'I can't break the law, Jess. You know and I know that there is now a record of us having this conversation.'

'I'm not asking you to break the law. I just need some time. Besides, who's to say what we talked about? Maybe we talked about the Phillies.'

'How about that Chase Utley, eh?'

Jessica took a moment, her mind spinning. 'All I'm asking for is a little window. Kevin is innocent. Let me bring him in.'

The next few seconds were excruciating. Finally: 'If the office brings me into this I'm going to have to drop the hammer. You know that, right?'

'I know.'

'But maybe it doesn't have to be immediately. Maybe I can't get a cellphone signal. Maybe my phone was off.'

Jessica felt a cool wave of relief. 'Thanks, Michael.'

'Good luck, detective.'

Jessica clicked off. She filled in Josh Bontrager on the parts of the conversation that he had not heard. She began to pace. The rain began to fall a little harder. She barely noticed.

'Okay,' Jessica said. 'The killer was working toward this night for a reason.'

'*Danse Macabre*,' Bontrager said. 'Midnight on Halloween.'

'Right. The killer is doing this for Christa-Marie. Why?'

Bontrager thought for a moment. 'If he is true to form he's going to kill one more person to fill in the last note.'

'If this is all coming down to Christa-Marie, there must be a connection.'

'She can't be a target, though. She was convicted of murder. She didn't get away with anything, not like the other victims.'

'Unless there's something we don't know about,' Jessica said.

'*I'm scared that I made a mistake*,' Byrne had said.

Jessica took out her phone again. She called a man named Gary Peters, a friend of hers who worked the city desk at the *Inquirer*. They got their pleasantries quickly out of the way.

'What do you need?'

'I need you to check something for me.'

'Shoot.'

'I need you to look up an obituary,' Jessica said. 'It would be in November 1990.'

'What's the name?'

'Gabriel Thorne.'

'Okay,' Peters said. 'What am I looking for?'

'I just need the notice.'

'Got it,' he said. 'Do you want me to fax it to you?'

'Can you email it to me?'

'Not a problem.'

Jessica gave him her email address. 'ASAP, okay?'

'On the case, detective.'

Two minutes later Jessica's phone dinged with the arrival of the email. She tapped it, opened it. It was a .pdf file from the *Philadelphia Inquirer.*

Prominent Psychiatrist Dead at 58.

Jessica quickly skimmed the obituary, soon finding what she was looking for.

'"Services will be held at St. Stanislaus, followed by interment at the Briarcliff Cemetery,"' she read out.

'Does it have an address?' Bontrager asked.

Jessica had to enlarge the image. Her eyes scanned the file. 'Here it is. It's at 122 Sawmill Road.'

They looked at each other. 'Any ideas where that is?' Bontrager asked.

'No,' Jessica said. 'Hang on.'

She tapped over to her Google Maps app, put in the address. Soon a map appeared with a big red push pin at the center.

'Oh *hello*.'

'Where is it?' Bontrager asked.

Briarcliff Cemetery was a small suburban graveyard that abutted a number of large estates. One of them belonged to Christa-Marie Schönburg.

THEY TURNED ONTO SAWMILL ROAD. The darkness was complete. A fine mist coated the ground; the headlights barely cut through the miasma. The road was serpentine, and more than once Jessica had to slow the car to a crawl. According to the GPS the back entrance to Briarwood Cemetery was approximately a mile ahead.

They took a slow bend to the right.

'Stop!' Bontrager yelled.

Jessica hit the brakes. 'What is it?'

'Back up.'

Jessica put the car in reverse. She backed up slowly for fifty feet or so. As she did, she saw what had caught Josh's eye. On the right side of the road were tire tracks cutting through the high grass, leading into the woods. A pair of small trees had been recently knocked over and splintered. Jessica angled the car so the headlights shone into the forest. There, about twenty feet in, was a vehicle, its motor still running. The lights were off but they could see warm exhaust spilling into the cold night air.

Jessica looked over at Bontrager. They drew their weapons, exited the car, walked down the culvert, up the other side. As they stepped closer to the vehicle Jessica saw more of it. It was a van.

A familiar van.

EIGHTY-SEVEN

LUCY DOUCETTE REMEMBERED A TIME WHEN SHE WAS ABOUT FOUR or five. Her mother had worked for a few months at a Dollar General and the money had flowed in. They were rich. That Thanksgiving they had a Jennie-O turkey breast, gravy, Hungry Jack mashed potatoes. All her favorites.

The thought of it made her stomach clench. She could not remember the last time she had eaten.

She had made slow progress on the plastic band around her wrists. She wasn't anywhere close to being able to slip her hands out. Not yet.

Ever since the van had stopped, a few minutes ago, she had lain motionless. She didn't know where they were or what was happening. It was better to be still for the moment.

At first she thought it was her imagination, but she heard footsteps. Footsteps *approaching*.

Lucy held her breath.

EIGHTY-EIGHT

THEY APPROACHED THE VAN, WEAPONS DRAWN. JESSICA TOOK THE driver's side, Josh Bontrager flanked right, a few paces behind. The immediate danger was the threat from the back doors.

At the rear bumper Jessica stopped, raised her left hand, made it into a fist. Bontrager stopped. Jessica put her ear to the back doors, listened. Silence from within.

Jessica held up five fingers. Bontrager nodded.

Jessica crept up to the driver door, counted down silently from five. There were no lights in the van, so the side mirror did not reflect the inside. She held her weapon in her left hand, trained on the door, slid her right hand along the panel.

On four she opened the door, stepped to the left in attack stance, weapon leveled. The driver's seat was empty, as was the seat on the passenger side. Keys in the ignition.

Bontrager opened the passenger door on five, pointed his flashlight inside the van. Behind the driver's seat were a pair of side racks. Strapped into them were David Albrecht's equipment – tripods, equipment cases, lights, microphone stands, a short ladder.

Jessica flipped on the van's interior light.

There was no one inside.

Near the back doors they could see the video camera on its side.

The camera was on, the blue rectangle of the flip-out LCD screen glowed. Jessica took a single latex glove out of her pocket, snapped it on. She crossed to the back of the van, opened a door. Reaching in, she tilted the camera back onto its side. There had to be two dozen buttons.

'Do you know how to operate one of these?'

'Sort of,' Bontrager said. 'I took the video of my cousin's wedding last year.'

'There's video at an Amish wedding?'

'My cousin left the church. She married English.'

Bontrager put on a glove, looked closely at the camera for a few moments. He hit a button. They heard a whirring sound, then a click. The side of the camera opened.

'There's no tape,' Bontrager said.

Jessica scanned the back of the van, looking for a tape. Then she went back to the front of the vehicle, searched through the console and the glove compartment. Empty.

'Sometimes there's a memory card,' Bontrager said. He clicked a few more buttons. Different menus flicked by on the LCD screen. 'Yeah, the card's still in there.'

Bontrager thumbed a few more buttons, the screens ticked by. He hit a button. A video copied to the memory card began to play.

There were only twenty seconds or so of video and audio, but it was chilling. The video showed someone walking up to the camera along a dark lane. The camera was shaky, showed the figure from the shoulders down.

'It's you,' a voice whispered. Was it Albrecht speaking? Impossible to tell.

Without another word, the door of Albrecht's van was yanked open. The video spun into a collage of images: trees, night sky, the side of the van.

The image then became a stationary shot along the ground, showing Sawmill Road stretching out into the darkness. This continued for a few moments before the screen went black.

Bontrager stepped a few paces away from the van, pointing his flashlight at the ground. 'Jess.'

Jessica walked over. On the trunk of a fallen tree was a small pool of blood. A few more drops on the grass led deeper into the woods, over trampled branches.

Weapons in hand, the two detectives stepped into the forest.

EIGHTY-NINE

Lucy couldn't move. She was lying on a cold stone floor. A draft was coming from somewhere. She had been yanked roughly out of the van, walked down some stairs, and deposited on the floor. Then she heard a door slam and a lock turn.

Then, nothing.

The good news was that her captor had not tightened the plastic band around her wrists. She still had a little slack. She rolled over and began to work on the band, flexing and relaxing her wrists. After a few minutes her lower arms began to feel numb. She stopped for a while, started again. After ten minutes or so it felt as if she might be able to begin to work her hand free.

When she had been dropped on the floor she'd felt a small puddle of water. She rolled over and over until she was on top of it. She angled her body so that her hands got wet. The water was freezing. She had never done well in science classes, but she figured that this might be a good thing, if it helped her hands contract and not the band.

She took a deep breath, bracing against the pain she knew was coming, and started to twist her wrists out of the plastic band. *No dice.* She wet her hands a second time. They were growing numb again, but she couldn't stop.

The third time she tried, she felt the band slip over the base of her thumbs. With great effort she pulled her right hand out of the plastic band.

Lucy stood up, a little shaky, pulled the tape from her mouth. She gulped the cold air.

There was virtually no light in the room. With her hands out front, she felt along the wall. It was a small room, a cellar of some sort. Stone walls. There was a bench, a couple of old chairs. Everything had a deep layer of dust on it. She felt her way over to the door, listened for a while. Silence. As gently as possible, she tried to turn the knob.

Locked.

NINETY

T HE TRAIL OF BLOOD STOPPED ABOUT TWENTY YARDS INTO THE WOODS, where the forest became thick and tangled before dropping into a steep gorge.

Jessica and Bontrager shone their flashlights into the ravine, but the beams were instantly swallowed by darkness.

'Albrecht is hurt pretty bad,' Bontrager said.

'If this *is* Albrecht's blood.'

Bontrager looked at Jessica, then back at the blood trail, which was quickly being washed away in the drizzling rain. 'You're right. We don't know if this is Albrecht's.'

'We have to call it in, Josh.'

Bontrager hesitated a second, no longer. He ran back to the road, called PPD dispatch, identified himself and their position. Dispatch would contact the closest emergency services agency and police K-9 units.

Jessica returned to the road. They stood on the shoulder.

'I'll stay here,' Bontrager said. 'I'll wait for the search team.'

'It's over, Josh. Even if Mike Drummond keeps his word, they're going to put all this together.'

Bontrager took a few steps away, thinking, turned back.

'Okay. Here's what happened. I was following a lead. I saw the vehicle, pulled over, discovered the blood. I called it in. Before I could get back to my car I was ambushed. This is why I'm a little unclear on the details after that.'

'No one is going to buy that.'

'Maybe yes, maybe no. We'll worry about that later.'

Jessica considered the scenario. 'Are you sure?'

'Yeah,' Bontrager said, planting his feet apart. 'Make it look good.'

Jessica took a step back. 'Josh . . .'

'I know you box, so try not to kill me.'

Jessica put on one of her wool gloves, hesitated. This was getting deeper and deeper. 'Are you *sure* sure?'

'You're talking me out of it.'

Jessica reared back and threw the punch, pulling it a little. It caught Bontrager on the right side of his jaw. Bontrager reeled back, nearly toppling over.

'Wow.'

She had bloodied his lip.

'Jesus Christ. Are you okay?'

Long pause. 'I'm fine. I may never sing with the opera again, but I'm fine.' He reached down, gathered some dirt from the side of the road, scuffed up his suit coat.

Jessica looked from the van, back to Josh, then up Sawmill Road. According to the map she was about a mile away.

She wanted to tell Josh to call or text her, keeping her in the loop, but it was not a good idea. That would put everything on the record.

'You sure you're all right?'

Bontrager rubbed his jaw, which was already starting to swell. 'Go.'

Jessica checked the action on her Glock, snapped it back into her holster, and started down the road.

NINETY-ONE

THE SMELL OF JUST-TURNED EARTH FILLS MY SENSES. EACH SHOVELFUL brings with it a plaintive voice: a plea of innocence, a shout of unrepentant pride, a wail of sorrow. I hear them all.

With the swing of his crimson hammer Kenneth Beckman took Antoinette Chan to the other side. His wife Sharon had helped. They too smell the earth now, rich with fur and blood and bone. They are joined by Preston Braswell, Tyvander Alice, Eduardo Robles, Tommy Archer, Dennis Stansfield, so many others. The earth always reclaims.

Tonight, in this place, white skeletons pass through the gloom. They are all around me.

There is one more note to play. I hear the player coming, creeping through the night. I push the sounds of murders past from my mind, listen for the footfall as it approaches.

There. Can you hear it?

I hear it.

One more note.

My instruments are ready.

NINETY-TWO

J ESSICA WALKED DOWN THE ROAD IN A DARKNESS SO PURE AND complete that she could not see her own feet. The drizzle made the going even slower. Her only guide to the road was the white stripe on either side, along with the compass app on her phone, which she was reluctant to use. It seemed to put a spotlight on her. According to the GPS, she would be coming up on the parcel in a few minutes.

She passed a drive every so often, a gravel lane that snaked back into the woods.

When she came to the rear entrance to the Briarcliff Cemetery she saw that it was unmarked. Instead there were two fieldstone pillars, connected by a chain with a padlock on it. On one of the pillars was a rusted sign warning that trespassers would be prosecuted. Jessica clicked on her Maglite, aimed it at the ground, and headed into the cemetery.

THE ONLY GOOD THING about walking through the woods was that she was now somewhat sheltered from the rain. Before long she came up to the southern end of the graveyard. She couldn't see far, but she did see lights in the distance. There appeared to be three large houses, perhaps a quarter-mile apart. She continued down the access road, passing crypts, monuments, row after row of manicured graves and expensive headstones. This was a world apart from the Mount Olive cemetery.

At eleven-thirty she reached the far end of the cemetery, the area that abutted the rear of Christa-Marie Schönburg's house.

Just as she was about to cross the field, to the rear of the property, her Maglite found a headstone bearing the legend:

DR. GABRIEL THORNE
HEALER AND FRIEND

The grave had recently been dug up.

As JESSICA GOT CLOSER she was overwhelmed by the size of the house. It was a three-story Tudor, half-timbered, with cross gables and a steeply pitched roof. Two massive chimneys rose at either end, both topped with chimney pots. A large deck jutted out over the backyard.

SHE COULD HEAR NOTHING but the rain.

Jessica studied the windows in the back of the house. There were faint lights in three of them. She watched for movement, for shadows. She saw none.

Jessica put her two-way handset on silent, crossed the backyard, and stepped onto the rear deck.

THE SLIDING GLASS DOOR was locked. Jessica walked down the steps, rounded the house to the east wing. She tried to lift the windows. All were shut tight.

She had no choice. She found a fist-sized rock in the garden, stood atop the air-conditioning unit, broke out the window in the first-floor bathroom.

*

ONCE INSIDE, SHE RAN a towel through her hair, wiped her face. She opened the bathroom door. Straight ahead was a long hallway, leading to a large foyer and the front door. She left the bathroom, walked slowly down the hallway. To the left was the entrance to a small pantry, beyond that the kitchen.

Soft music played somewhere in the house.

Jessica saw that most of the rooms were lit by candles, dozens of them casting a pallid yellow light in the cavernous spaces.

She made her way cautiously down the hallway, watched by the eyes of dead ancestors peering down from huge oil paintings overhead. In the dim candlelight, objects waxed and waned – the occasional sideboard, end table, armoire. Each held danger. Jessica drew her weapon, held it at her side.

She approached a room, its door ajar. There was only darkness within. She edged up to the room, slowly inched the door open with her foot.

In borrowed candlelight she saw shapes in the room. A pair of bookcases, a sewing machine, a chair. There were two other doors. She could not clear them. There was no time. She had to take the chance.

She moved deliberately, right shoulder to the wall, sweat trickling from her shoulders, down her back.

Before she turned the corner, into what she was certain was the main hall, she stopped, tuned her ears to every sound. The music continued: a string quartet. Beneath it she heard a woman's voice, humming the melody.

Jessica took a deep breath, rolled the corner, her weapon held low.

Someone stood at the foot of the grand staircase, not fifteen feet away from her. It took Jessica a moment to adjust her eyes.

Kevin Byrne.

He was at the base of the steps, splendid in a dark suit, white shirt and deep burgundy tie. Above him was an enormous crystal chandelier. Jessica looked at Byrne's hands. He held a single white rose.

No, Kevin.

Please, no.

Before she could speak, Jessica looked up to see Christa-Marie at the top of the stairs. She wore a long black dress and a simple strand of pearls. Her hair was soft and luminous, a brilliant silver. She was radiant. She descended slowly, her slight hand on the railing, never once taking her stare from the man at the foot of the staircase.

When she reached the final step Christa-Marie paused.

Kevin Byrne handed her the white rose.

NINETY-THREE

THERE IS BEAUTY SO RARE AND EPHEMERAL THAT IT HAS CONFOUNDED THE poets for centuries. Byron, Shakespeare, Keats, Wordsworth – all failures. This is the beauty that is Christa-Marie. From the first moment I saw her she has owned my heart, taking it around the world, then into the deepest confines of hell.

I have never asked for it back.

I've always known that we would have this one last moment together, this moment when our hearts would once again be joined.

NINETY-FOUR

CHRISTA-MARIE STOOD FACE TO FACE with Byrne. Jessica watched, mesmerized by the tableau as Byrne took Christa-Marie by the hand and led her to the center of the hall, beneath the exquisite chandelier.

A new song began, a waltz. They danced.

As the strings played, Kevin Byrne and Christa-Marie Schönburg moved in beautiful, fluid lines, as if they had danced together all their lives. When they were finished, Byrne took Christa-Marie in his arms and kissed her.

The scene was so surreal, so unexpected, that Jessica found she had been holding her breath the entire time. She snapped out of it. She had a job to do.

She opened her mouth to speak.

She didn't get the chance.

The front door burst open, the sound of the battering ram echoing through the cavernous space. A pair of SWAT officers rolled into the foyer, their AR-15 assault rifles high. They were followed by Russell Diaz and two of his men, all three of them with weapons drawn. They ran down the main hall toward Byrne and Christa-Marie.

Diaz reached the couple first, stopping a few feet away. He pointed his weapon at Kevin Byrne.

'Down on the ground!' Diaz shouted.

Byrne edged slowly away from Christa-Marie, his hands out to his sides.

'Get down . . . on the fucking . . . *ground*!' Diaz repeated.

Christa-Marie stepped back, a look of horror and confusion on her face. The house was suddenly filled with silence. Byrne eased himself to the floor, put his arms out to the side. Two uniformed officers pinned him down and pulled his hands behind his back. They handcuffed him.

Seconds later, more people streamed through the door – Michael Drummond and Dana Westbrook among them. A dozen more officers spilled into the house.

Byrne was read his Miranda rights. As they took him into custody, Jessica put her weapon on the floor. She stepped into the foyer, her hands held high.

NINETY-FIVE

Lucy felt her way back to the long bench. She had stopped a few moments earlier, having heard muffled shouts from somewhere far away. Or had she? She didn't know. But all was silent now, and she had to get on with her business.

There were two drawers. She opened them, felt around, discovered some sandpaper, an oily rag, book matches, a pair of short screwdrivers. She felt the tips. One slot head, one Phillip's.

On top of the bench were a few more rags, along with a small stack of papers, some dried-out magazines. There was also an old lantern. Lucy picked it up, gave it a shake. There was liquid inside – she immediately caught a whiff of old kerosene.

She went back to the drawer, found the matches, opened one pack. They were damp. She tried them anyway. One by one, they smeared on the flint strip. Not even a spark. She found another pack, felt the matches. The top row seemed damp, the back row less so. She peeled off the top row of matches. She picked up one of the old magazines, tore off a page, rolled it up.

She tried the first match, got a spark, but the paper didn't light. On her third try she got a flame. She held the lit match to the rolled-up paper, got a torch going. She then pushed down the lift lever on the lantern. The wick caught, and the room was suddenly bathed in a warm glow. Lucy had never been more grateful for anything in her life.

NINETY-SIX

THERE IS A MOMENT, ALMOST SEXUAL IN ITS FEELING OF RELEASE, WHEN a police detail winds down. Most of the time during this period of deceleration, in the minutes and hours after an arrest, there is a lot of handshaking and backslapping and fist-pumping in the air; never a shortage of gallows humor. But not this time. The personnel who made their way through this enormous Chestnut Hill mansion found no joy or happiness in this arrest. This was one of their own.

KEVIN BYRNE WAS IN custody and en route to the Roundhouse. Christa-Marie Schönburg had been taken to Mercyhurst Hospital as a precaution. Her private nurse, Adele Hancock, had been at the opera. She was contacted and was on her way to meet Christa-Marie.

Before long it was Jessica, Dana Westbrook, and Michael Drummond, along with a few officers, searching and securing the house. Soon it would be November 1, All Saints' Day, twenty years to the day when Christa-Marie had been arrested in this very place.

WESTBROOK TOOK JESSICA ASIDE. They stood in silence for a full minute, neither of them finding the right words to say. 'We'll sort this out,' Westbrook said. 'There's a hell of a lot about this I don't understand.'

Jessica just nodded.

'Kevin's arrest warrant came from on high,' Westbrook added. 'I had no choice but to serve it. You know that, right?'

Jessica said nothing. She could not get the image of Kevin Byrne in handcuffs out of her mind. The two of them had made so many arrests over the years, hunted down and brought to justice so many bad people, that she could not fathom Byrne being on that side of it all. The thought was beyond nauseating.

'So, I'll see you at the Roundhouse?' Westbrook asked.

Jessica looked at her watch. 'Give me an hour.'

'You got it.'

Westbrook took a few more moments, placed a hand on Jessica's shoulder and, perhaps trying and failing to find words, crossed the large atrium, stepped through the front doors and left.

Jessica glanced across the hall, at the steps which she had seen Christa-Marie descend earlier. She had to clear her mind. She had to think.

'Do you want me to drop you somewhere?'

Jessica turned around. It was Michael Drummond.

'Josh has my car,' Jessica said.

'Okay,' Drummond said. 'As soon as that scene is clear I'll send him back.'

Drummond stepped away, made a quick phone call. When he was finished he made his way over to where Jessica stood.

'I'm sorry it came down this way,' he said.

'I don't have much to say to you.'

'What are you talking about?'

'I just needed a little time, Michael. That's all. A little time.'

'I didn't make the call, Jessica.'

Jessica looked up sharply. 'You didn't? Then how did the fucking cavalry just happen to show up?'

'Police work, detective.'

'What are you talking about?'

'Russ Diaz followed up with Kevin's cousin Patrick. It turns out that Mr. Connolly's van had a LoJack installed.'

The LoJack was a recovery system that allowed police to track and recover a stolen vehicle.

'Russ called it in as a routine stolen vehicle, and got this location,' Drummond continued. 'I had nothing to do with it.'

Jessica's anger and rage did battle with her embarrassment for assuming that Drummond had dropped a dime.

'And just so you know, I talked to Detective Diaz,' Drummond said. 'Kevin is going to be handled with respect. I won't stand for any cowboy shit.'

Jessica had so much to say that nothing would come out. What she really wanted to do was scream.

'We're going to need your full statement tonight,' Drummond added.

Jessica nodded. She picked up her service weapon, slipped it into her holster.

'I know this is hard for you, detective, but the good news, for the people of Philadelphia anyway, is that this nightmare is over.'

The feelings inside Jessica began to swell. The one feeling missing from all of it was doubt. She had no doubts about her partner. Her work, the task of proving Kevin Byrne's innocence, started right now. Before she could make a move she noticed someone standing to her left.

'Ma'am?'

Jessica turned. Standing there were two patrol officers from the Fourteenth District. The one talking to her was a big kid, twenty-three or so. He was pale as a ghost, but his hands were steady. 'The house is clear, ma'am.'

Jessica looked overhead, at the high ceiling, the large rooms. 'Are you sure? It's a big house, officer.'

The kid looked a little unnerved, then turned to look behind him. Four more officers stood there, and a pair of detectives from North that Jessica recognized. The kid was saying that a total of eight police officers had searched the house and that it was empty.

'I'm sorry,' Jessica said. 'It's not a good night.'

'No, ma'am,' the kid said. 'There are two locked doors – one in the attic, one in the cellar. Other than that, the structure is clear.'

He waited a few moments, perhaps to see if there was anything else. Jessica shook her head. The officer touched the brim of his cap, and together, single file, the eight cops walked out.

As the sound of the sector cars disappeared down the driveway, Michael Drummond put on his coat. He looked at Jessica, but remained silent. He walked through the door, closed it behind him.

The house was still.

Jessica was alone.

NINETY-SEVEN

LUCY PUT THE LANTERN ON THE BENCH AND GOT HER FIRST REAL look at the room. It was smaller than she'd thought. There was no window. It had been bricked in a long time ago. Dust and cobwebs were everywhere. There were mouse droppings along the wall.

Peggy.

Lucy closed her eyes, tried to blot it all out.

She looked at the doorknob. It too was caked with dust. She picked up an old rag, cleaned it off. It was an old-fashioned white porcelain knob, set into a cast-metal plate. She felt along the neck behind the knob, and found the set screw. She angled the screwdriver behind the knob found the slot, gently turned. A few seconds later the set screw fell out. She carefully pulled off the knob, holding the spindle tightly. She didn't need the knob on the other side falling to the floor and making a racket. Then she went to work removing the plate. Four screws. Although she could not see that well, it looked like the screws in the plate were nearly stripped. She'd have one chance to get them out.

She looked at the head on the screwdriver, which was also rounded, dull with age and use. She put the screwdriver into the slot, put all of her weight behind it, doing her best to keep the tool perpendicular to the door.

She took a deep breath and tried to turn it. Nothing. She backed off, tried again. This time she felt purchase.

The screw turned. Not much, but it turned.

Yes, Lucy thought.

A lock was just a device with moving parts, right? If there were moving parts, Lucy Doucette could handle it.

She set about her task.

NINETY-EIGHT

THE HOUSE WAS SILENT IN A WAY THAT NO SMALL SPACE COULD EVER be; silent like a presence. Every so often its tranquility was broken by rain hitting the huge windows in the great room or a branch scraping a gutter.

Jessica had lived most of her life in a place too small, a place where the extra closet or tiny room was a premium. This was a fact of life in a Philadelphia row house. But this place – with its high ceilings, tall doorways and cavernous rooms – was too much. She didn't think she could ever live somewhere like this, although the likelihood of that happening was somewhere between never and *absolutely* never.

As she peered out of the front windows, anxious to get back to the Roundhouse, her phone rang. She jumped at the sound. She hoped it was going to be Josh telling her he was on the way. It was not. It was a number she did not recognize. She answered.

'Hello?'

'I'm calling for Detective Byrne.'

It was a man's voice.

'Who am I speaking to?' Jessica asked.

'My name is Robert Cole. I'm trying to reach Kevin Byrne. He gave me this number as a backup.'

'I'm his partner, Detective Balzano. Is there something I can help you with?'

'I have that report he wanted.'

'The report?'

'He had me red-ball a DNA test. Cold case.'

'I'm sorry,' Jessica said. 'What agency are you with?'

Cole went on to tell her that he ran a private, independent lab, and the work he had done for Byrne was off the record. He also told her that the job was the twenty-year-old homicide case of Gabriel Thorne.

'How much of the file do you have?' Jessica asked.

'I have copies of everything.'

'The crime-scene photos?'

'Yes.'

'Can you send me the DNA summary and the photos of the crime scene?'

'Sure,' Cole said. 'I can send the photos now, but it will take a few minutes to scan the DNA summary. It's on another computer.'

Jessica gave him her email address. Thirty seconds later the file arrived on her iPhone. Jessica tapped the file, opened it.

Cole had sent her four photographs. The first photograph was of the hallway in which she now stood. The fact that it had been taken twenty years earlier, in the precise space she now occupied, gave her a chill.

The second photo was of the kitchen. And it was a horror show. Gabriel Thorne's body was supine on the white tile floor, lying next to the kitchen island, a pool of blood beneath him, his chest butchered.

Jessica walked down the main hall, stopped at the kitchen, turned on the light. The room had not changed. Same island, same white tile, same light fixtures. She scanned the photo and the real room, item by item. They were eerily identical, right down to the color of the kitchen towels on the rack next to the sink.

The other two photos were of the floor leading into the pantry, which was just off the kitchen, and the music room just off the pantry. The music room too was identical, except that now the cello in the corner did not have blood on it.

According to the brief summary attached to the photographs, it was believed that Christa-Marie Schönburg had stabbed Gabriel

Thorne in the music room, then followed him into the kitchen. When he collapsed, she had continued to stab him in the chest.

Jessica tried to imagine the scene that night. She could not. But she knew what she had to do. If she was leaving shortly, locking the house behind her, she had better snuff out the candles in the music room. One by one she blew out the dozen or so candles, the scent of burned paraffin filling her head.

When the room was dark, lit only by the gas lamps on the deck at the rear of the house, she walked back into the hall, checked her watch. *Where the hell is Josh?* She called him, got his voicemail.

JESSICA'S PHONE RANG AGAIN. She answered, but the call began to drop out. She ran down the hall toward the front door, but was still unable to get a signal. By the time she made it across the great room, she was able to hear. It was Robert Cole.

'Did you get the photos?' he asked.

'I did.'

'I'm having some trouble scanning the DNA report. I could keep trying, or I could just read it to you. Which do you prefer?'

'Read it to me.'

Cole read her the report. As he did, Jessica felt a cold finger run up her spine. It turned out that, in addition to Gabriel Thorne's and Christa-Marie's blood on the murder weapon and the floor of the kitchen, there were two other distinct DNA profiles found.

In other words, two other people had been present on the night of the murder.

What did it mean to the case? What did it mean to Christa-Marie's guilt on that night so long ago?

Jessica felt gooseflesh break out on her arms as she listened to the rest of the report.

She thanked Cole, hung up, her mind spinning.

This changed everything.

She stepped back to the front doors, opened them, fully expecting to see a sector car from the Fourteenth District at the gate. There was none. This was strange. The house would not be searched for evidence and cleared for at least twenty-four hours, and a police presence was standard procedure.

She keyed her two-way handset, spoke into it. No response.

What is going on?

She closed the doors, walked back into the main hall.

That was when Jessica Balzano heard the music.

NINETY-NINE

As Jessica moved across the great room the music grew louder. It took her back to the first time she'd heard this piece in Byrne's van, the nocturne by Chopin.

She soon realized it *was* coming from the music room, but it sounded live, not recorded. It sounded like someone was playing the cello in that room.

'*The house is clear, ma'am.*'

From across the hall she noticed candlelight illuminating the room, candles she had just put *out*. As she approached the entrance, peering around the doorway, she saw someone sitting in a chair at the opposite side of the room. It was Christa-Marie. She held the beautiful cello between her legs and was playing the nocturne, her eyes closed.

It made no sense.

Why is she back? Who let her come back?

Jessica drew her weapon, held it at her side, rounded the doorjamb, and saw a second figure standing in the shadow of the short hallway leading to the kitchen.

It was someone she knew very well.

T HE FIGURE IN THE HALLWAY DID NOT MOVE. CHRISTA-MARIE continued to play, the notes rising and falling with the sound of the wind outside. As the piece came to a crescendo Jessica stepped fully into the music room.

'Is it now?' the figure in the hallway asked.

Jessica did not know how to answer. Too many things could go awry with the wrong answer.

The figure emerged from the shadows.

Michael Drummond had changed his clothes. He now wore a navy suit with thinner lapels. It was a style that might have been popular with fifteen-year-old boys when Drummond had been a guest, and probably a student, in this house.

There was something bulky in one of his suit-coat pockets. Jessica watched his hands.

'Teacher is mad at me,' Drummond said softly.

Jessica glanced at Christa-Marie. She was lost in the music.

'Is it now?' Drummond asked again.

'No,' Jessica replied. 'It's then, Michael. It's Halloween night, 1990.'

The notion registered on Drummond's face. His features softened in a way that told Jessica that his mind was returning to that night, when all things were possible, when love burned brightly in his heart, not yet tempered by the horror of what was to come.

'Tell me about that night, Michael,' Jessica said. She began to inch closer to him.

'We went to the concert. Joseph and I.'

'Joseph Novak.'

'Yes. When we came back, he was here.'

'Doctor Thorne?'

'Doctor Thorne!' Drummond spat the name like an epithet, glanced into the kitchen, then back. Jessica circled closer.

'What happened?' she asked.

'We argued.'

As Jessica closed the distance by another few inches, she noticed a shadow to her left, right near the entrance to the kitchen, just a few feet from where Michael Drummond stood. She looked over. So did Drummond. Someone was standing there.

'Joseph?' Drummond asked.

But it wasn't Joseph Novak, of course. Somehow, Lucinda Doucette was standing there. Lucinda Doucette from the Hosanna House and Le Jardin.

In one fluid motion Michael Drummond reached for Lucy, pulling her close to him. He now had a straight razor in his hand. He flicked it open.

Jessica leveled her weapon. 'Don't do it, Michael.'

'Zig, zig, zag.'

Everything Jessica had seen in Drummond's face, everything that told her he might be ready to give all this up, was gone. What stood before her now was a feral, calculating killer.

'Let her go.'

Drummond held Lucy even more tightly. Jessica saw the young woman's legs start to sag.

'I have a little more work to do,' Drummond said.

'Not going to happen.'

Drummond brought the razor up in a flash. The gleaming blade was now less than an inch from Lucy's throat. 'Watch.'

'Wait!'

Drummond glanced at the clock. It was 11:51.

'There's no time left,' he said.

'Just put down the razor. Let her go.'

Drummond shook his head. 'Can't do it, detective. There's one note left to play.'

'We'll get you help,' Jessica said. 'It doesn't have to end this way.'

'But it *does*, don't you see? This must be completed.'

Jessica glanced again at the grandfather clock in the hallway. 'It's not midnight yet. Let her go.'

'Look how many unfinished symphonies there are. Beethoven, Schubert. I am not going to leave a legacy like that.'

Jessica looked at Lucy. The girl was going into shock. Jessica knew she had to keep the man talking.

'Why these people, Michael? Why did you choose them?'

'They got away with murder, Jess. Surely you can understand that. They won't be missed.'

'They had families,' Jessica said. 'Sons, daughters, mothers, fathers. It's not up to us.'

Drummond laughed. 'We can't do it all, you and I. I've watched it for years. Police do their jobs, prosecutors do their jobs. Still people get away with it. Tonight all these people dance with the dead. Eddie Robles, Kenny Beckman, his sow of a wife. So many more.'

'What about George Archer?'

Drummond smiled. 'I'm not guilty on that one, your honor. But believe me, it wasn't for lack of effort. I tracked him for years. Ever since I got out of law school.'

'Who, Michael? Who killed him?'

'Do your job, detective. I did mine.'

Drummond leaned away from Lucy, the razor moving away from her throat momentarily. Jessica sighted down her weapon. She had a shot.

'Then why Lucy?' Jessica asked. 'She's innocent.'

'No, she is *not*.' On the word *not*, Drummond pulled Lucy closer. Jessica no longer had a line of sight. 'It's because of her that Peggy van Tassel is dead.'

'I don't understand.'

'Little Lucy could have told the police about George Archer. She didn't, and who knows how many other little girls Archer killed? This little piggy is part of the problem.'

Drummond stopped at the doorway to the kitchen. 'That's far enough, detective. Put your weapon down.'

Jessica did not move.

11:54.

'Do it *now*.'

'Okay, Michael,' she said. She lowered her Glock to the floor. 'It's down.'

Jessica glanced to her left. Through the doorway she could see the bare feet and rolled-up trousers of a body on the floor, a few drops of blood on the tile. She also saw the knife on the counter. It was the precise scene from that night twenty years earlier, a re-creation of the murder of Gabriel Thorne. Except that there was a new twist. There was a band of white paper and a red candle on the counter.

Jessica looked again at the kitchen floor.

Is this David Albrecht's body?

The horrors were piling up.

'Look,' Jessica began. 'Dr. Thorne is already dead.' She pointed to the kitchen.

Drummond glanced into the kitchen, at the body on the floor. He looked back at Jessica. His mind was gone, lost in some kind of vortex between the night of Thorne's murder and now.

'It really is *then*?' he asked.

'Yes.'

Drummond began to nod rapidly. 'He was going to take her away, see,' he said. 'For good. That's why he had to die.'

'I understand.'

Drummond turned slowly toward the stereo cabinet behind him, touched the *play* button.

Christa-Marie seemed to return to the moment. She began to play a new piece, plucking one of the strings – the same note, twelve times.

'What is *Danse Macabre* without the chorus?' Drummond asked. He turned up the sound.

A moment later, beneath the resonance of Christa-Marie's cello, was a mix of sounds – street sounds, sirens. Beneath it all a chorus began to sing:

> *Zig, zig, zig, Death in cadence,*
> *Striking a tomb with his heel,*
> *Death at midnight plays a dance-tune,*
> *Zig, zig, zag, on his violin.*

But somehow the loudest part of this new background was the sound of a baby cooing.

'The dead own the world tonight,' he said. 'Listen to them. I've been collecting their voices for years.'

11:56.

The voices began to grow in volume. Screams, shrieks of terror, death wails.

'Look,' Jessica said. She circled to her left. She had to get into the kitchen. 'My gun is down, Michael. I can't hurt you. The doctor is dead. Let the girl go. We'll talk.'

'It's not about me. It's never been about me.' Drummond began to sweat. He waved the razor around, bringing it perilously close to Lucy's face. The chorus of screams grew in the background. Christa-Marie's playing increased in volume.

> *The lady, it's said, is a marchioness or baroness*
> *And her green gallant, a poor cartwright.*
> *Horror! Look how she gives herself to him,*
> *Like the rustic was a baron.*

'She gave herself to him,' Drummond said, pointing at the body on the floor. 'She doesn't have long, you see. It had to be done.'

'Who doesn't have long?'

'Teacher. She's dying. That's why I had to write faster.'

Drummond took one step backward, into the kitchen, dragging Lucy with him. 'Listen to them all,' he said. 'Can you hear?'

'I hear, Michael.'

11:58.

Jessica moved forward.

'What about Gabriel Thorne?' she asked, gesturing to the body on the kitchen floor. 'Christa-Marie didn't kill him, did she? It was you, wasn't it? You and Joseph Novak?'

'Thorne was in love with her. He manipulated her.' Drummond shook his head, his eyes filling with tears. 'Joseph was weak. He was always weak.'

'But you let Christa-Marie take the fall.'

Tears ran down his cheeks. 'I've had to live with that for twenty years.'

Drummond backed to the center of the kitchen as *Danse Macabre* neared its final glorious section.

From somewhere beneath the cacophony came a man's voice: 'Michael.'

INSIDE, WHERE THE MUSIC lives, in that gilded hall, I watch and wait. Teacher knows what I must do.

There is one note left to play.

One final note.

AT THE SOUND OF the man's voice everything slowed. Drummond held Lucy even more closely. Slowly, he lifted the straight razor to his own forehead and drew it swiftly across. Bright crimson blood washed his face, spilling onto Lucy.

Again, from somewhere: 'Michael.'

Drummond hesitated for a moment, his head cocked to the sound. 'Dr. Thorne?'

One more note.

One more voice.

Drummond looked at Christa-Marie, playing furiously in the music room.

They push forward, they fly; the cock has crowed.
Oh what a beautiful night for the poor world!

Midnight.

Michael Drummond lifted the razor high into the air. He pulled back Lucy's hair, exposing the white of her throat.

'Teacher . . .' he said.

As he brought the razor down Jessica saw the body on the floor move.

It was not David Albrecht.

Detective Kevin Byrne rolled to his right, raised his Glock 17 and fired, slamming a single bullet into Drummond's head, just above the man's right eye. Thick gobbets of bone and brain tissue burst from the back of Drummond's skull, onto the white-tiled wall.

Drummond collapsed face down onto the counter, onto the band of cloud-white paper, his bloodied face painting the sheet in a grotesque parody of a musical staff. His body slumped to the floor.

Jessica looked into the kitchen, the sounds of the discharged weapon ringing in her ears. As she stepped into the corner of the music room, and embraced Lucy Doucette, she met Byrne's gaze. He was covered with blood, not his own. He had been lying in wait. He looked at her, but his eyes saw something else, perhaps something that had happened in this room a long time ago, something that had just now come to a close.

The Echo Man was dead, his symphony now complete.

FOR THE SECOND TIME THIS NIGHT, THE PHILADELPHIA POLICE Department processed a crime scene at this address. Dozens of personnel moved like silent ghosts through the now brightly illuminated spaces.

OUTSIDE, JESSICA AND BYRNE stepped into the shadows. When they were alone, out of earshot, she turned to him, her anger at being left out of the loop seething within her. 'You've got about five fucking seconds to start explaining all this.'

'I know you're upset.'

'I'm way past upset,' Jessica said. 'When did you set all this up? Yesterday?'

'No,' Byrne said.

'Bullshit.'

She paced. Byrne gave her time.

'Jess, trust me on this. The arrest was real. Diaz and his team had evidence that the tattoos were mailed to my address. They also had hair and fiber evidence from my van. They came in hard to get me. I was completely blindsided.'

'What the hell were you doing here?'

Byrne looked at the house, then back. 'I'm not sure my answer is going to be good enough for you.'

'Try me.'

Another pause. 'I knew the answer to all of this was locked inside Christa's mind. I knew time was short, but I had to work that angle.'

Jessica just listened, deciding not to tell Byrne that she already knew about the evidence Diaz had. But she now realized that it was Drummond who had planted the evidence, hoping to buy himself more time tonight, counting on the arrest of Kevin Byrne.

'When we got to the Roundhouse they patted me down,' Byrne said. 'They took my cellphone. Russ Diaz started scrolling through the calls I'd made today. He also saw the folder that holds the photographs. He saw this.' Byrne held up his phone. 'I hadn't really looked at it before. When I did, it all fell into place.'

Byrne tapped the screen, showed Jessica a picture. In it, Christa-Marie stood on the steps of a huge stone building. Next to the scarred oak doors was an inscription. Byrne tapped the screen again, enlarging the words.

What you leave behind is not what is engraved in stone monuments, but what is woven into the lives of others.

Jessica looked at Byrne. 'This is what Drummond said at his leaving party.'

Byrne nodded.

'And this picture was taken at Convent Hill,' she added.

'Yeah.'

Jessica recognized the place. It was in the photograph that she had found in Joseph Novak's journal. The photo captioned with the word *Hell*.

'Drummond had been to Convent Hill to visit Christa-Marie. That was where he got the inscription. From the Roundhouse we called the Prentiss Institute and had them look through the records. Michael Drummond studied with Christa-Marie. Both he and Novak were her students on the day when Gabriel Throne was murdered.'

Jessica took a step away, absorbing the new information. She turned back, her anger far from dissipated.

'I had my weapon out, Kevin. More than once.'

'I know.'

'Something could have gone really wrong, really fast.'

Byrne pointed to the six SWAT officers gathered on the grounds. They had a direct line of sight to the eastern side of the mansion, the side where the kitchen and the music room were located.

'At no time were you in jeopardy, Jess. They had Drummond in their sights through the windows. If he had made a move toward you they would have taken him down. We just hoped it wouldn't be before he talked. We had to get him to make the admission.'

'Why? What are you talking about?'

Byrne held up a CD in a crystal case.

'What is that?' she asked.

'It's the whole event. Christa-Marie has a very sophisticated recording studio upstairs. The music room has six microphones in it. Mateo is up in the studio now. He's like a kid in a candy store.'

'You're saying everything that happened in there was *recorded*?'

Byrne nodded. 'When Drummond got here tonight he slipped upstairs, into that room, started the whole process. It's all on here. Christa-Marie playing *Danse Macabre*, including the background of Drummond's sick recordings of death screams. He finally got his magnum opus.'

Jessica's head was spinning. 'What about Lucy?' she asked. 'I don't care how good the SWAT guys are – Drummond had that razor at her throat.'

Byrne looked away for a moment as the ME's transport van pulled into the long drive. He looked back.

'We didn't plan on Lucy,' he said. 'I had no idea she was here.'

NINETY MINUTES LATER, WITH the house sealed and guarded, Byrne was waiting for Jessica in the large circular drive. They would head back to the Roundhouse to begin the long process of piecing together the horrors of the last few weeks.

Jessica stepped through the front door, closed it behind her. She looked at her watch. It was 2:52.

It was All Saints Day.

TUESDAY, NOVEMBER 2

THERE WAS NO SHORTAGE OF MEDIA INTEREST. FOR THE STILL PHOTOG-
raphers and videographers alike, the Tudor house at Chestnut Hill
was a feast of images. It would probably be on the list of horror tours
next Halloween. The road in front of Christa-Marie Schönburg's house
was crowded with national and international media. Two days after
the horror, the numbers were still growing.

For the police, the whole story would take far longer to assemble.

The investigation revealed that Michael Drummond and Joseph
Novak had both attended Prentiss, had both taken private lessons from
Christa-Marie Schönburg. Over the years the rivalry between the boys
had grown, not for first chair in an ensemble but rather for the affections
of Christa-Marie.

On Halloween night 1990, it came to a head. Although investigators might never know exactly what had happened, they believed
that Michael Drummond and Joseph Novak killed Gabriel Thorne
that night. Drummond, being the dominant one of the pair, held this
over Novak's head for the next twenty years.

The two men formed a small, unprofitable company, through which
they published limited-edition reproductions of sheet music, penned
reproductions in the composer's hand. The paper they used was Atriana.

When Drummond, who had taken a job at Benjamin Curtin's law firm – Paulson Derry Chambers – learned of Christa-Marie's illness, his own psychosis led him down a path of destruction, a reign of terror that would be felt for a long time.

It was Michael Drummond who had supplied the forged visitor's pass and clothing to Lucas Anthony Thompson.

Real-estate tax records traced back to Drummond led to a small commercial building in South Philly. Police found his killing room full of recording equipment, as well as a cache of nearly two hundred CDs and audiocassettes – all meticulously dated – of street and human sounds, some of them of people in their death throes. It would be months, maybe years, before police forensic audiologists would be able to make sense of the recordings, if ever. Michael Drummond had been building to this dark dénouement for a long time.

At Josh Bontrager's direction K-9 officers from PPD found an unconsious David Albrecht at the bottom of the ravine on Sawmill Road. Albrecht had lost a lot of blood, but paramedics reached him in time. Investigators were certain that he had been attacked and left for dead by Michael Drummond, but Drummond would escape this charge posthumously.

None of this explained the murder of George Archer.

Lucy Doucette, in her statement, told police about the man she had met. The man who called himself Adrian Costa. The Dreamweaver. Police checked with the management of the apartment building off Cherry Street. The landlord said that a man had rented Apartment 106 for six months, paying cash in advance. He gave police a vague description.

They had showed Lucy the video recordings made on Halloween Night at the hotel, recordings of the hallway on the twelfth floor. Jessica had freeze-framed the image of the man in the wizard's costume and mask passing by the camera.

Lucy said she couldn't remember.

Jessica had also visited Garrett Corners again, researched the name Adrian Costa. No one with that name had ever been registered as a voter or resident of the area. The people knew the reclusive van Tassels to be travelers, carny people. The only photograph of the family was nearly fifteen years old. When Jessica revisited Peggy van Tassel's grave, she looked at the two plots next to it. One was the grave of a man named Ellis Adrian. The other was the last resting place of an Evangeline Costa.

Was the Dreamweaver Peggy van Tassel's father?

From what the investigators could gather, it appeared that Florian van Tassel had tracked Archer for years but had not known for sure that it was Archer who had kidnapped both Peggy van Tassel and Lucy Doucette back in September 2001. As the Dreamweaver, van Tassel enticed Lucy to submit to hypnosis sessions during which van Tassel determined that he had been right. George Archer had killed Peggy. It seemed that van Tassel also gave Lucy a post-hypnotic suggestion to leave a note for Archer in his room, drawing him up there at 9:30p.m., then instructed her to open the door to Room 1208 at the right moment.

The enhanced video taken from the twelfth-floor hallway that night showed the man dressed as a wizard – believed to be Florian van Tassel – with an old-style school bell in his hand.

While all of this was circumstantial, it wasn't until forensic results started to come in that police issued an arrest warrant for Florian van Tassel, aka The Dreamweaver. Blood belonging to George Archer was found on the old photograph left behind in the room where the Dreamweaver had met with Lucy Doucette.

The George Archer file sat in a file cabinet at the Roundhouse.

The case remains open.

MONDAY, NOVEMBER 8

BYRNE SAT IN THE SMALL LUNCH-ROOM AT THE BACK OF THE Roundhouse. The four-to-twelve shift had already come and gone and were out on the street. Byrne, who had been on administrative leave since the shooting, sat by himself, a cold cup of untouched coffee in front of him.

When Jessica entered the room and approached him she saw something else on the table. It was Byrne's fifty-cent piece.

'Hey, partner.'

'Hey,' Byrne replied. 'You finish that FAS?'

A Firearms Analysis System form was a trace request sent to the Bureau of Alcohol, Tobacco, Firearms and Explosives.

'All done.' Jessica slid into the booth across from Byrne. 'You heading home?'

'In a while.'

They sat in silence. Byrne looked tired, but not nearly as tired as he had looked recently. He'd gotten the results from all his follow-up tests. There was no tumor, nothing serious. They said it was a combination of fatigue, poor diet, insomnia, with a Bushmills chaser. Jessica glanced at the menu displayed over the counter in the corner, and thought about how eating in this place might be part of the problem.

Byrne looked up, at the scarred booths, the plastic flowers, the line of vending machines against the wall, at the place to which he had come to work for more than twenty years. 'I didn't do my job, Jess.'

She'd known this was coming, and here it was. Everything she planned to say vaporized from her mind. She decided to just speak from her heart. 'It wasn't your fault.'

'I was so young,' Byrne said. 'So arrogant.'

'Christa-Marie confessed to the crime, Kevin. I wouldn't have handled it any differently. I don't know any cop who would.'

'She confessed because she was ill,' Byrne said. 'I didn't dig any deeper. I should have, but I didn't. I turned in my report, it went to the DA. Just like always. Boss says move on, you move on.'

'Exactly.'

Byrne spun the coffee cup a few times.

'I wonder what her life would have been like,' he said. 'I wonder where she would have gone, what she would have done.'

Jessica knew there was no answer to this, none that would help. She waited awhile, then slipped out of the booth.

'How about I buy you a drink?' she said. 'It's fifty-cent Miller Lite night at Finnigan's Wake. We can get hammered, drive around, pull people over, do some traffic stops. Be like old times.'

Byrne smiled, but there was sadness in it. 'Maybe tomorrow.'

'Sure.'

Jessica put a hand on Byrne's shoulder. When she got to the door she turned, looked at the big man sitting in the last booth, surrounded by all the whispering ghosts of his past. She wondered if they would ever be silent.

H E FOUND HER BEHIND THE HOTEL. SHE WAS SITTING ALONE ON A stone bench, on her dinner break, an untouched salad next to her. When she saw Byrne she stood up, hugged him. He held on as long as she wanted.

She pulled away and turned, brushing off the bench for him. *Ever considerate*, Byrne thought. He sat down.

They were silent for a few moments. Finally Byrne asked, 'You doing okay?'

Lucy Doucette shrugged. 'Just another day in the big city.'

'Did you have any problems giving your statement?' He had put out the word that she was to be treated with kid gloves. The report back was that she had been. Byrne wanted to hear it from her.

'Yeah,' she said. 'But if I never go back to a police station for the rest of my life, that will be okay with me.'

'About that other matter,' Byrne said, referring back to Lucy's detainment for shoplifting. 'I talked to the DA's office, and to the owner of the store on South. It's all smoothed over. Just a big misunderstanding.' Because Byrne had intervened before Lucy was charged there would not be a record.

'Thanks,' she said. She looked at Byrne, at the bench, at the surrounding area. 'Where's your man bag?'

'I'm not carrying it anymore.'

Lucy smiled. 'Were you getting grief from your fellow officers?'

Byrne laughed. 'Something like that.'

A wink of silver caught Byrne's eye. It was a small heart-shaped pendant around Lucy's neck.

'Nice necklace,' he said.

Lucy lifted the heart, ran it along the chain. 'Thanks. I got it from David.'

'David?'

'David Albrecht. I went and saw him in the hospital.'

Byrne said nothing.

'We're kind of in this thing together, you know?' Lucy said, perhaps feeling the need to explain. 'I guess he's going to be okay?'

'The doctors say it looks good.'

Lucy dropped the pendant, smoothed it against her uniform. 'He's got some offers on his movie, you know.'

'I heard that,' Byrne said. 'So, are you guys an item?'

Lucy blushed. 'Oh *please*. We're just friends. We just *met*.'

'Okay, okay,' Byrne said.

'*Gosh*.'

Two young women walked by, no more than eighteen or nineteen, smartly dressed in their crisp new Le Jardin uniforms. They eyed Lucy with something akin to awe.

When they passed, Lucy looked at Byrne. 'Rookies.'

They sat in thoughtful silence. The autumn sun warmed their faces.

'What are you going to do, Lucy?'

'I don't know,' she said. 'Maybe go home for the holidays. Maybe go home for good.'

'Where's home?'

Lucy Doucette looked up at the hotel, down Sansom Street, then over at Byrne. In that moment, for the first time since he'd met her, she looked a lot more like a woman than a little girl.

She said: 'A long way from here.'

FRIDAY, NOVEMBER 12

THE WOMEN SAT AROUND THE SMALL TABLE, A GAME OF GIN RUMMY in progress in front of them. Between the ashtrays, Styrofoam cups, cans of Diet Pepsi and Diet Mountain Dew, the bags of pork rinds and barbecued chips, there was hardly room for the cards.

When the petite young woman in the oversized blue parka walked into the room, Dottie Doucette stood up. Dottie was terribly thin. She looked older than her forty years, but a light had come back to her eyes, her friends all said. It was faint, they averred, but it was there.

When Lucy hugged her mother, Dottie felt as if she might break.

Lucy wanted to ask her mother about George Archer. She had talked to some of the women who had known her mother when they were younger, and she'd learned that Dorothy Doucette had gone out with George Archer a few times. That was probably when the man had put his eye on Lucy. Lucy knew that her mother felt guilty for so many things. Dottie Doucette did not need this burden now.

Dottie let go, wiped her eyes, reached into her pocket. She showed Lucy her chip. Six months sober.

'I'm proud of you, Mama.'

Dottie turned toward the women at the table.

'This is Lucy, my baby girl.'

The women all fussed over Lucy for a while, and Lucy let them. She'd stay on for a month or so, taking a room at a boarding house in town, in exchange for housekeeping duties. From the moment she got off the bus, she knew that she would not be staying forever, just as she knew that in many ways she had never left. Not really.

Her mother slipped on the pilled sweater that was draped over the back of the folding chair. Lucy recognized it as one she had stolen from the JC Penney's a long time ago. The sweater was getting on in years. Her mother needed a new one. Lucy promised herself she would buy it this time.

'Take me for a walk?' Dottie asked.

'Sure, Mama.'

Out in the lobby, Lucy helped her mother on with her boots. As Lucy was tying the laces, she glanced up. Her mother was smiling.

'What?' Lucy asked.

'I used to do the same thing for you when you were small. Funny how life comes full circle.'

Yeah, Lucy thought. *Life's hilarious.*

They walked, arm in arm, down the path that led to the town park. The temperature was falling. Lucy bunched the sweater around her mother's neck.

Winter was coming, but that was all right. In the end, Lucy Doucette thought, the sunshine was inside. And now that she remembered everything, she could begin to forget.

THURSDAY, NOVEMBER 25

S HE HAD COOKED FOR TWENTY. LIKE MANY ITALIAN THANKSGIVING gatherings, the meal began with a full pasta course. This time, Jessica and her father made Jessica's grandmother's fresh ravioli, the filling a delicate and savory balance of beef, pork, and veal.

For the first time, Sophie helped serve.

By six o'clock the men were sprawled around the living room, snoring away. Tradition called for them to be awake by six-thirty and ready to take part in Round Two.

At ten after six, Jessica opened the front door. South Philly was alive with the holiday. She looked left and right, didn't see Byrne's car. She wanted to call him, but she stopped herself. He had a standing invitation every year, and this year he'd said maybe. With Kevin Byrne, when it concerned events like this, 'maybe' usually meant no. But still.

Jessica was just about to close the door when she looked down. There, on the front steps, was a small white package. She picked it up, closed the door, walked over to the kitchen. She slit open the Scotch tape with a knife. Inside was a ball of yarn. Green yarn. When Jessica brought it into the light she saw that the yarn was the same shade as the oddly constructed cable knit sweater that Kevin Byrne had been wearing around the Roundhouse of late, a sweater, he told her, that had been knitted for him by Lina Laskaris's grandmother, Anna.

Jessica checked on her family. The men were still in a turkey-and-Chianti-induced coma; the women were doing the dishes and sneaking cigarettes out back. Then Jessica walked upstairs into the bedroom, closed the door behind her.

She unspooled the yarn, brushed back her hair, gathered it. She took the yarn, tied her hair into a ponytail, checked herself in the dresser mirror. The autumn had long since taken back the highlights bestowed by summer. She turned to the side, and for a moment had a memory of her mother tying back her hair with green yarn on her first day of school. How much youthfulness the world had then, how full of energy it had been.

She could use some of each.

As the new mother to a rocketing little two-year-old-boy, Jessica was going to need all the vitality and vigor she could muster. The papers had come through a week earlier, and Carlos Balzano was at that moment downstairs charming the entire family.

Jessica looked one final time at the yarn in her hair. In some ways, it was just as good as the original.

No, she thought as she turned out the light and descended the steps. In some ways it was even better.

For every light there is shadow. For every sound, silence.

In this massive room the silence was complete. Considering that there were nearly twenty-five hundred people in the Verizon Center, it was all the more profound.

The last note of *Sinfonia Concertante* sifted through the hall, and the applause began.

As the conductor turned to the audience, Byrne saw people noticing Christa-Marie, heard their whispers. The story had broken wide a few weeks earlier, the account of Christa-Marie's innocence in the murder of Gabriel Thorne. Byrne could not imagine the courage it had taken for Christa-Marie to come to this place on this night.

Soon the applause turned from the stage and was offered to the woman in the tenth row. A soft spotlight found them. The conductor walked to the footlights and bowed. The orchestra rose to its feet.

Byrne didn't know how much time together they had left, but he knew that he would be with Christa-Marie until the end. More than that, he wondered how it sounded to her. He wondered if it sounded the same, if it meant what it had meant twenty years ago when she had been the brightest star in the heavens.

Kevin Byrne took Christa-Marie's hand and held it as the applause grew, the sound echoing across the deep chasms of memory, the vast and merciful landscape of time.

ACKNOWLEDGMENTS

Special thanks to:
Meg Ruley, Peggy Gordijn, Jane Berkey, Christina Hogrebe, Don Cleary, Mike McCormack, Kristen Pini, and the great team at the Jane Rotrosen Agency.

Kate Elton, Susan Sandon, Georgina Hawtrey-Woore, Jason Arthur, Rob Waddington, Emma Finnigan, Claire Round, Glenn O'Neill, and everyone at Random House UK.

Darin Brannon, Tara Klein, Francis Gross, Jane Sembric, Ray Villani, Douglas Bunker, Diana Richardson, Sandra Brancaleone, and Tacy Dooley.

Jennifer Kallend at the Curtis Institute of Music; Evan Evans at Le Meridien Philadelphia; Emily McCarthy at Ritz Carlton Philadelphia; Frank Thompson at Sheraton Society Hill.

Gino Rafaelli for his kindness and time, and the librarians at the CH-UH libraries for putting up with my many requests.

Detective Eddie Rocks, Sgt. Joe Rosowski, Lt. Edward Monaghan, and the brave men and women of the Philadelphia Police Department.

Mike Driscoll and the staff at Finnigan's Wake; Patrick Ghegan, Dom Aspite, Joe Sickman, Bob Mulgrew, Al Kurtz, John Dougherty, Vita and Adjani DeBellis, and the rest of the Philly crew.

My father, Dominic Montanari. Nine and change, Pop.

The city of Philadelphia and the Commonwealth of Pennsylvania for letting me create hotels, institutions, and townships, and for letting me move streets, buildings, and neighborhoods. I promise to put everything back where I found it.